THE THINGS WE'VE SEEN

Agustín Fernández Mallo was born in La Coruña in 1967, and is a qualified physicist. In 2000 he formulated a self-termed theory of 'post-poetry' which explores connections between art and science. His Nocilla Trilogy, published between 2006 and 2009, brought about an important shift in contemporary Spanish writing and paved the way for the birth of a new generation of authors, known as the 'Nocilla Generation'. His essay *Postpoesía: hacia un nuevo paradigma* was shortlisted for the Anagrama Essay Prize in 2009. In 2018 his long essay *Teoría general de la basura (cultura, apropiación, complejidad)* was published by Galaxia Gutenberg, and in the same year his latest novel, *The Things We've Seen*, won the Biblioteca Breve Prize.

Thomas Bunstead was born in London in 1982 and currently lives in west Wales. He has translated some of the leading Spanish-language writers working today, including Maria Gainza, Juan José Millás and Enrique Vila-Matas, and his own writing has appeared in publications such as the *Brixton Review of Books*, *LitHub* and the *Paris Review*.

Fitzcarraldo Editions

THE THINGS WE'VE SEEN

AGUSTÍN FERNÁNDEZ MALLO

Translated by

THOMAS BUNSTEAD

'It's a mistake to take the things we've seen as a given.'
—— Carlos Oroza

'Toto, I've a feeling we're not in Kansas any more.'
—— *The Wizard of Oz*

BOOK I

San Simón Island (*Fossil Fuels*)

PART ONE

Invitation and first day

There's so much we take for granted. On the morning of 15 September 2014, as I sat down to write after breakfast, the noise from the road works out in the street made me forget what I was writing about, and something I'd seen on television the previous day came to mind instead: a news item about the fact that one tenth of the earth's surface has been constantly on fire, through no fault of human beings, for more than two hundred years. A look at a dynamic map of all the fires currently raging on the planet would reveal a multitude of these expanding red zones being carried forth by surface winds, in Africa especially, the continent referred to by experts in the field as the Heart of the Inferno. I found it startling to consider that our human modernity had developed side by side with this incandescent presence.

Some years ago, a musician friend told me about a long stint he'd once spent in an African jungle. Wanting to make recordings of instances of silence in nature, he had travelled to Lake Tanganyika in Tanzania, the second largest and second deepest lake on the planet. 'So deep,' he said, 'that there's no oxygen in the waters at the very bottom. They're fossil waters.' A helicopter had dropped him off in a clearing in the surrounding jungle with nothing but a tent, a change of clothes and some survival snacks, plus the necessary gamut of recording equipment, all manner of tapes and ambient microphones. He saw no fires burning, or if he did, he didn't mention them to me, but he did say that, after a month and more of wandering those jungles, what struck him most was the utter absence of silence. The way in which the sounds of the natural world got inside his head day and night was something he recounted with genuine unease, and not because the sounds were strident or clashing in any way, but because of their unerring persistence. In the following months, during trips he sought to undertake as consecutively as possible, the same experience played out in the jungles of Brazil, the forests of Alaska and at a polar station a long way south of Patagonia, leading him to the conclusion that silence does not in fact exist in nature; rather it's a fantasy fabricated by our culture, a concept we've simply dreamed up. And this was something my friend couldn't understand. Or, he understood it, but he refused to accept it. The last I heard, his search for a piece of silence on Earth was still ongoing.

On that September morning, these and other thoughts were interrupted when I got an email containing the first mention I'd ever come across of San Simón, an island situated in the Vigo estuary in Galicia. The sender was someone who went by the name Rómulo, and I was being invited to take part in the third instalment of a programme called Net-Thinking, the aim of which, from what I understood, was to reflect on digital networks by bringing together both communications professionals and artists who, like me, sometimes use the internet as a space, and a tool, in our work. I had to read the message a couple of times before I remembered where I'd met Rómulo: at the launch of a mutual friend's book, at which we'd exchanged only a few words. The people participating in the programme, the email explained, would stay in a hotel on the island – attached images showed some fairly smart facilities – and there was mention too of another participant, Julián Hernández, whom I knew both in his capacity as a member of the punk band Siniestro Total and through his literary involvements. Rómulo wanted the two of us to take part in a panel discussion. I wasn't sure at first, but what finally won me over was mention of something that struck me as unusual: the idea was for there to be no audience present, only people watching a live stream that was due to be broadcast on various online platforms. In previous years these live streams had apparently attracted large viewerships, in Spain and Latin America especially. I was at the end of a period of intense work, during which I had barely left Mallorca; a few days on a different island, I said to myself, might do me some good.

A few hours later I realized I had in fact heard of San Simón before; it was a mystery how I'd managed to forget. In 1995, the journalists Clara María de Saá, Antonio Caeiro and Juan A. González had made a documentary called *Aillados*, which is Galician for *Isolated*, along with an accompanying book, both concerned with the years in which this collection of craggy rocks, no bigger than three football stadiums laid end to end, had served as a prison camp, with inmates drawn particularly from people in Pontevedra province who'd opposed the coup that precipitated the Spanish Civil War. I still owned the book; in fact, it had travelled with me from my native La Coruña to Mallorca, accompanying me every time I'd moved house – at least five times – since 1996. The house I now live in is organized in such a way that I can see all of my books at a glance. I keep none in boxes, none stowed away in wardrobes or back rooms, but there are so many of them now – two bookcases, each holding more than three thousand volumes – that it still took a while to lay my hands on it. Remarkably, it hadn't fallen to pieces, and there were only one or two damp stains on it. I flicked through its collection of photographs and survivor testimonies. San

Simón was described variously as a place of severe hunger, where people were routinely tortured or lined up against walls and shot, and as actually being easier on inmates than other penal institutions of the day. I went back to Rómulo's email. The island is currently run by a foundation named Island of Thought. It had a ring to it. *Island of Thought* vs. *Island of Repression*, I said to myself. With that, the idea of fifteen people getting together to talk about the opposite of isolation – social networks – struck me as more suggestive still. Fifteen people transmitting ideas across the world from a place of isolation. I went on Google Earth and took a look at the island. It has an unusual shape, like two balls, one large and one small, joined by what in the images appeared to be a bridge spanning a rocky formation covered in green algae. On further inspection, I was reminded of the ground plan of Roma-Fiumicino airport. A connection that filled me with satisfaction, since the full name of Roma-Fiumicino is the Intercontinental Leonardo da Vinci Airport, which in some way bestowed upon the island a Renaissance air. Frankly, I went to bed that night excited about the trip. As always, I fell asleep attempting to conjure four white dots behind my eyelids, four dots that were once upon a time a permanent presence, but that at some point in my life vanished and never came back.

I took a flight from Mallorca to La Coruña one morning in October, staying in my parents' house for a few days – only occupied now in summer – before the transit to San Simón. A taxi took me to the town of Redondela, whose docks are the launching point for boats going out on the Vigo estuary. On board, I looked back towards the coast, letting my thoughts drift over it, until, after nearly three hours, San Simón suddenly appeared in the water up ahead. The lush greens of the island showed silver under the midday sun. A few minutes later an old, white building with stone foundations came into view, protruding among all the vegetation. Drawing closer to the dock, we saw that a shore boat had been sent out to collect me; I was the last in the group to arrive. A young sailor with blonde hair and sunglasses was at the helm and he gestured for me to pass my suitcase across. We skipped over the waves to shore. The sun was out but the wind remained biting, and I wrapped a heavy raincoat around myself. The island grew in size as we approached, as did the looming white building, some four storeys tall and set on stone foundations, its back wall crumbling directly into the sea. 'That's it,' said the boatman, 'the hotel.' I don't think anywhere in Galicia was better connected to the world at that moment than this island, given the state-of-the-art satellite receivers that had been brought in for the occasion.

Rómulo was there at the jetty to meet me. The boatman lifted my suitcase out and set off back the way he had come. I wheeled my suitcase behind me along the stone jetty, which was covered in seaweed and still wet from high tide, and we embarked on the climb up some granite steps with restored walls and geometric brakes of shrubs on either side. This brought us out at a gravel esplanade with buildings all around it. One of them, formerly one of the prison's principal wings, they told me, was to be the location for the Net-Thinking meeting. Next to that was a dining hall with high French windows; inside, two waiters and one waitress, all quite young, were putting chairs out and laying a large table; the waitress was clearly pregnant. There was a chapel on the opposite side of the esplanade. Its door was open, giving a view of the room inside, bare save for a stone altar set into the wall, atop which stood a life-size wooden saint. Saint Roch, I was told; he was missing both hands, someone having either snapped or sawed them off, I don't know which. We were on our way to the hotel, but stopped to take in the conference room. It was quite small, and with its fifteen chairs arranged in a circle it reminded me of a room in a driving school. At the back were three professional video cameras on tripods and two large screens on which messages were going to be shown in real time from people following proceedings on Twitter. 'We've got thousands of followers,' said Rómulo, 'people sometimes tweet from the US and Australia, you'll see. Not to mention the messages on Facebook and other platforms. They come flooding in.' We returned to the esplanade and went along an avenue of eucalyptus and myrtle shrubs to the hotel, where the room keys had been placed in their respective pigeon-hole-like compartments. 'Help yourself,' said Rómulo, pointing to my key, which was for room 486. 'It isn't a hotel, then?' I said. 'It was once, but it went under. Not enough people came.' 'So, it's just us here?' 'That's right,' he nodded. 'Nobody will be coming to the island over the next three days and, barring an emergency, nobody's going to be leaving either.' A young man with blonde hair came over, and Rómulo introduced him as Javier, the director of the foundation. It was a beautiful place, I said; I'd noticed how well tended the gardens were, while at the same time they'd succeeded in leaving them wild. I asked why the place was so underused – why no residencies for artists, writers, musicians, historians or even scientists? It was the perfect place for all kinds of projects. The money wasn't there, he said. I see, I said to myself: the political will wasn't there, is what he meant.

I went up to my room with my suitcase. There was no lack of mod cons, but that did nothing to change the monastic air of the place. My room overlooked the rear of the island. In the far distance you could see Rande Bridge on the mainland, not so dissimilar to Brooklyn Bridge, though in its case steel is outweighed by concrete. A trail commenced below my window and led down to a small stone bridge across the narrow strip I'd seen on Google Earth, connecting San Simón to the other, smaller island. I saw a building on the smaller island, modernist-looking and stuccoed light blue, a single storey high and surrounded by towering eucalyptus trees. In the farther distance a security guard was checking the perimeter, picking his way between some rocks; he had a gun at his belt as well as a truncheon, a detail that always draws my eye. He moved in the direction of the chapel and disappeared down a track. I stepped back from the window and opened my suitcase, not taking my clothes out though; I've never seen the point of unpacking when I'm on a trip. From one of the side pockets I took a small chunk of black basalt rock with red mottles on it, like flecks of paint or blood. I'd found it in a ditch next to a road in the north of France years before, and kept it with me ever since as a kind of amulet. I took *Aillados* from another of the pockets and put it on the table. Knowing my tendency to get bored at conferences, I immediately came up with a way of killing time: I would seek out the locations of the photographs in the book – all of which were from around 1937 – and take my own photos of them as they now were in the present day.

Everybody was there when I went down, sharing anecdotes from previous iterations of the conference; I was the only one, it turned out, who hadn't taken part before.

17

We set off for the dining room a little before 1 p.m. I asked Javier if the island was inhabited all the year round. When he said that it wasn't, I said, 'What, not even the security guard?' 'In winter he comes during daylight hours,' he said. 'The boat comes to take him back to the mainland at night.' 'Who looks after the place at night then?' Javier, giving a lop-sided smile, said, 'It doesn't need looking after at night. It isn't the kind of place where anyone would want to spend a winter's night, I can assure you.'

It was during lunch – octopus empanadas, grilled sea bass and a choice of red or white wine – that I first saw them: a table with fourteen people sitting at it sending out tweets. Every now and then one would look up and say something, but to no reply from any of the others, and they'd instantly go back to tweeting. Next to my napkin was a map of the island split across three panels, with notable places marked along with historical explanations and descriptions of the locations in the current day. This was something that had been apparent from the moment I arrived, that everything on the island was explained by way of a before/after binary. At the first opportunity, I excused myself and got up from the table. I had nearly two hours before the panel discussions were due to start, at 4.30 p.m.

I grabbed my copy of *Aillados* and took one of the paths at random, going along with one eye on the book, trying to identify the places depicted in the photographs. It all looked very different now. It was no use trying to orientate by the trees, which had either been chopped down or grown considerably. Similarly, some of the tracks and paths had been cleared, while others were so overgrown as to have disappeared from sight. I decided to change tack: I would focus on one photo at a time, and simply walk until I came to the place in question. I passed two of the prison wings, the doors of which I tried but found locked. I hopped over a wall onto the bay, made my way between the rocks I'd seen the security guard navigating earlier on, small crabs scattering and hiding away at my approach. There were no signs of human activity recalling any culture this side of the 1960s, only the remnants of a few boats and pieces of scrap metal, all worn down by sand and sea, and which could just as easily have passed as being five or five thousand years old. I left the coastline and went back towards the interior of the island, coming past a large number of abstract, semi-anthropoid sculptures, which gave me something of a fright. Plaques detailed the names of the sculptors and the construction dates; they were all from the 1990s, when it appeared a concerted effort had been made to renovate the island. I reached the stone bridge that led to the smaller island. A bronze plaque here revealed that although it was part of San Simón Island, it had its own name – San Antón – and had served as a lazaretto in the nineteenth century; during the civil war, any prisoners who fell ill would have been held here. The hinges to the doors at either end were still there, but not the doors themselves. I hurried across, and went on, stepping over inch-high foundation blocks; it was like a to-scale plan of the former installations. I walked around the light blue-stuccoed building: a plaque by the main door informed me that it now housed historical archives. I looked in through a window. Inside, a neat draughtboard of Formica tables and chairs, with cobwebs hanging between them. Each of the tables had a computer on it, and by my calculations these would have been from around 1997, since I was able to make out 'PC Intel 486' on the sides of the machines. I turned and went down a faint track that brought me out at a seawall, which I followed as far as a clearing with a series of what were undoubtedly graves: rectangular granite slabs of different sizes, tinted green and light orange by lichens, and unmarked. I saw one that was particularly small, seemingly for an infant, though it too bore neither name nor date. Everything on the island had its corresponding information plaque, I said to myself, everything but the graves; the before/after binary didn't apply here. The wall was pocked unmistakeably with bullet holes, though whether or not from stray firing-squad bullets I didn't know. I checked my watch: not long left. I hurried back. Crossing the bridge, I leaned over the railing and looked down at the water flowing by. Silvery fish drifted slowly along, not as a unified shoal but each giving the impression of following its own course; they criss-crossed and surfaced singly, and there was no way of telling whether the laws of nature went with them; they looked like sardines to me, but I know nothing about fish so doubtless they weren't. Crossing the bridge and approaching the buildings I had walked straight past before, I saw that I had come to one of the places in the book. I opened it and found the photograph. Taking out my mobile phone, I lined the picture up and took it.

I felt like I was looking at two identical rivers, each flowing past me at a different rate.

Vellos fronte ó pavillón

21

The talks threw up nothing unexpected. The ideas proposed, most of which were to do with managing the online aspect of businesses, didn't interest me. Thousands of people did indeed send in messages via Twitter. I remember thinking that people ought to have some idea what they're talking about before deciding to tweet about it. Thinking my silence might be making the organizers uncomfortable, I decided to offer something up about times when communities, whether human or animal, are isolated for long periods – though not long in the evolutionary scale of things – and a tendency that has been observed whereby the larger animals shrink in size and, by contrast, the smaller animals, everything up to rabbit-size, grow larger. This is what had happened on Flores Island, near modern day Java: the resident humans and elephants had shrunk over time, while the various rodents had begun to grow far larger, gigantic in fact, eventually reaching sizes we in the present day would find shocking. The reason being an innate survival mechanism that's shared the world over and results in the balancing out of different species. The most disconcerting thing to the anthropologists who found the fossils on which these discoveries were based, I continued, was that though the humans' brains had shrunk, this did nothing to diminish their intellectual capacities; only their will had been affected. A point came when they began to neglect the most basic aspects of survival, coitus included, ultimately paving the way for the group's extinction. Everyone listened as I spoke, but when I finished, they sat saying nothing, as though expecting me to go on. A tweet appeared on the screens, written in unmistakably Argentinean Spanish: 'Go, *chavón*! So with you on all of that.' I said all of this, I added, with regards to the isolation that sometimes occurs in certain networks, for example in private groups on Facebook, or on networks used exclusively by the military or financial corporations. I think this was my only contribution to proceedings that afternoon. The truth is, I found it intimidating being watched on the internet in that way. Speaking in front of an invisible audience is not something I'm used to. There's a golden rule: eye speaks with eye (with screens intermediate or not), voice speaks with voice (telephone), text speaks with text (letters, other kinds of written messages), but the mixing and crossing over of different channels is not a thing to be entertained. And in that place, everything was mixed and crossed over. There was a view through the window of the estuary and the mainland beyond. The boats moored there were a single, indistinguishable mass of colour; the one that had left us on the island would have been among them, I thought – phrasing it to myself, I noticed, as though the boat were never coming back. I spent the rest of the time studying the other participants' faces; I could discern no sign of plastic surgery, either on lips, cheeks or elsewhere, or indeed any of the habitual characteristics you'd expect to find in a sample of twenty-first-century humanity chosen – as this one supposedly was – at random.

There was still a little daylight, and it wasn't yet time for dinner, so I decided to take the book on another walk round the island. This time I went in the opposite direction. Leaving the complex, I climbed a steep slope, bisected by what was referred to as the myrtle path: an avenue not more than a hundred yards long, overhung by the myrtles, the tops of which joined overhead, though the early evening sun broke in at ankle height and lit the way. I became aware of layers upon layers – dozens of layers – of matter beneath my feet. I knew there were hundreds of bones and hundreds of teeth below me, hundreds of knives and forks, items of clothing and photographs and weapons, and a great many more objects besides that I'd never set eyes on – some that anyway would be unrecognizable to me – but the sensation I had was not of each of those objects singly, but rather the sum of them, a rusty, incandescent magma, a kind of San Simónian earth's core, a generator of its forward propulsion, or something along those lines, anyway. The myrtle path brought you out at a bandstand whose circular platform led to a set of granite steps, which in turn wound down to a path that sloped away to eventually skirt the edge of the island. Descending the steps, I opened the book and found another match. I took my phone out and took the photograph. I went back to the hotel. It was almost time to join the others for dinner, but I went on my blog and uploaded the photo from the book alongside the one I'd just taken, supplying each with the same caption: 'Flesh.'

Colocados na baixada das escaleiras, ó final do paseo dos mirtos —que enlaza coa avenida de Teruel—, están: Manuel Barros, un asturiano, outro asturiano —este foi fusilado en Vigo poucos días despois de facerse a foto—, Laterre, Secundino González, Agra, Dito, Germán, coñecido como "o burro de Asorey", xa que sempre o tiña que levar ó lombo, Reisiño, Espalladoura, o Roxo, Asorey, Piruel, Agra, Paco Cautivo, outro asturiano e Ismael Caamaño.

And I don't know why I put that. What I really wanted to say was: 'The disappearance of flesh.'

The subject of the disappearance of flesh was on my mind during the dinner, most of which I spent not saying anything to anybody, while everyone else, fewer geeks among them now than at lunch, put down their smartphones from time to time and spoke to one another. I looked at the menu: vegetable tart, veal cheeks with potatoes, fruit salad, red wine, coffee – a list that led me to reflect on the special nature of eating, a process through which it was as though the food, dead when you bought it at the supermarket, came back to life in being cooked. A kind of ritual in which, by the act of eating, we made something sacred disappear forever. I went outside to smoke. I marked out a circle with my toe in the gravel. Through the high windows, I saw the

25

others drinking wine, lifting forks to mouths, gesticulating, checking Twitter, and all this that I now see, I said to myself, will also disappear in a matter of minutes, never to return again. When I went back to my seat, they had already brought dessert. Picking up my cutlery, I noticed a folded piece of paper poking out from under my plate. Opening it, I found something written inside: 'I need help.' Instinctively I glanced around: nobody seemed to have noticed. I looked behind me. One of the male waiters, quite fat, hair cropped almost to a zero and a trace of the indigenous Latin American about his features, nodded in such a way that I knew for certain it was from him. I neither smiled nor returned the nod, glancing along the table: a heated discussion was taking place about trolls on social media. I put the note in the inside pocket of my jacket and went on eating. When the waiter came over with the coffee, neither of us made any allusion to the note's existence.

After dinner, everyone went back to the hotel. Somebody, I don't remember who, had gone to the effort of bringing gin, tonic and lemons, and gin and tonics were being prepared in the former cafeteria. I was too tired to start drinking, and just had tonic water. To one side, a group was discussing the internet. I said to them that in my view the important thing about the internet was its bodilessness – the fact of it being, in a manner of speaking, one gigantic brain that drifts around the planet without ever encountering the fat, muscles and bones that would tether it to the earth, and that as it drifts it projects all manner of different shadows, which, paradoxically, don't come about through contact with any kind of body either. Hence the confusion, I continued, concerning everything to do with the net: it's a primitive organism, still only half-finished, in a phase similar to that of the microorganisms that one day clambered out of the water, millions of years before they became the amphibians that were the precursors of the humans of today. Judging by the group's silence, I don't believe my intervention convinced anyone in this case either.

I decided to go for a walk. The breeze carried hints of eucalyptus and the sea. I went in the direction of the chapel, and once I got there kept on going. I soon came in sight of a small prison building, three storeys high. I was approaching it over a rise, putting me at eye-level with the third floor, two of the windows in which had lights on. I was surprised to find myself creeping forward as quietly as I could, before stopping and squatting down. At the nearest window to me, one of the waiters and the waitress were locked in an embrace by the bed, her very large belly hindering their proximity. She closed the curtain, and a moment or two later the shadow play showed the man taking her from behind. In the next bedroom along, the waiter who had left the note for me was sitting on his bed gazing down at the floor, head bowed, elbows on his knees; his head, with the very short hair, resembled the surface of the moon – I looked up at the sky, the moon was full up there as well. I stayed put for several minutes, nothing changed. The sex proceeded so quietly it seemed like a scene from a silent movie; I got up when everything was over. Thinking to go on past the building, I started down the steep slope that led to it. Turning towards the main entrance, I found the waiter I'd seen sitting on his bed moments before, in the same posture but on a small stone bench, and still as porcelain. This stopped me in my tracks. I said hello; I could hardly just ignore him. He offered me a cigarette, which I refused. He apologized for the note, saying that I struck him as a person to be trusted, the only one on the whole island, he said, and that he had to tell someone, had to tell someone that he couldn't take it any more, it was driving him mad, and that if he were to end up doing something he regretted, I could always say he'd warned me, and the note would be my proof. I asked him to be a little clearer, what did he mean exactly, and he pointed at the building behind him, again saying he couldn't take it any more, that if they went on like this he'd end up doing something he regretted. 'She's my wife. You'd be hard-pressed to tell at the moment, but we are married. The very first chance she had, she got it on with that guy. We've been here over a week, making the place ready for you lot, and she and him have been at it constantly.' He started telling me how much he liked his job, serving the food, laying tables, checking dishes, cleaning the limescale off the glasses before putting them out, and cooking and making bread; in Uruguay he had been a first class baker, he knew how to make all different kinds of breads, he said, and at this calmed down somewhat, before coming out with certain things I found unsettling, such as: 'Life is a layer of soil no bigger than a dirty napkin,' and 'God is a dishwashing machine, the big dishwashing machine,' then adding that in Argentina he'd worked as a pastry chef, and that 'intelligence is the final barrier to be demolished,' and that he sometimes felt afraid, very afraid, and that at that particular moment he was 'on the very cliffs of fear,' and even these latter statements, though including no mention of dirty napkins or God or dishwashing machines, unsettled me all the same, and then, suddenly addressing me more formally, he said he'd seen my remarks on the Net-Thinking panel, well, he hadn't seen them directly, but in the kitchens while watching the talk on his tablet as he cooked dinner. 'It was me who sent the tweet, "Go, *chavón*! So with you on all of that." Remember, mister? I thought you really hit the nail on the head there. I never knew that about large animals in isolated communities shrinking, and smaller ones growing gigantic, and all because of survival, you could have said "getting bigger" but you said "growing gigantic" and that's just perfect, perfectly put, the exact same thing's happened to me, back in Argentina my wife and I had a very active social life, we were always going out with friends, going to dinner, family barbecues, but when the crash happened and we had to emigrate to Spain, leaving all our friends and family behind, we came to form a kind of island together, a big island, because as you know when it comes to people, the smaller an island, the harder it is to inhabit, and in the end, just as you, sir, said during that talk, the strong grow weak and the weak grow gigantic. In the same way, my wife, who was the weak one back in Argentina, is gigantic now, while me, I'm wasting away. The things you said during the talk, sir, made everything clear to me. I'm sorry, I'm crying now, I just don't know how it's come to this, would you like a cigarette?' Again I said no. 'I met my wife in Uruguay, in Cabo Polonio, which is this beautiful place by the sea, I was twenty-two and had a summer job in a hotel, the only hotel still going there, I was trying to put a little money aside. Paula – that's her name – who can't have been more than sixteen at the time, showed up one day with her parents and her younger brother, great little guy he was; I remember taking their bags up to the suite on the top floor, and then seeing Paula go straight through to the living area, picking up the remote control and flicking through till she came to the Savage Nature channel, at which point she takes out a box of felt-tip pens and a sketch pad buried at the bottom of a holdall with their swimming costumes in it and, leaving the TV on, she goes down to the pool, finds herself a lounger and puts her headphones in. I go over to her, ask if I can bring her a soft drink, and she, without a word of reply, opens the pad – a big one, A3 – shoves her little brother away, who's been tugging on her bikini bottoms non-stop to get her to go in the water with him, takes the lids off the pens and starts drawing the hotel. I ask her what she's drawing, and she doesn't answer at first, but then, taking out the right headphone, says to me she draws whatever she feels like drawing, and what she feels like drawing at this particular moment is a dream, an eternal dream, that's how she puts it, "I'm drawing an eternal dream," and I, having had express orders from the boss to look after these people because they happen to be relations of his, decide to bring her a soft drink, and then Paula goes on to spend the whole rest of the morning and afternoon not moving an inch, immersed in her drawing, and when it comes time for supper and I go up to take their orders, the mother says to me that Paula still hasn't come back, she must be down by the pool still, and that I should take her a sandwich, and on the TV in the living area I see some animals, similar to reindeer, and they mate very briefly before going their separate ways, and I take Paula her sandwich and see she hasn't touched the drink, I don't know what she drank that whole day, nothing I suppose, the pens are scattered all around the lounger with the lids off and her fingers are covered in ink, and I step on one of the pens, a red one, it splits but this doesn't faze her in the slightest, I know it was red because the ink went all over the sole of my shoe and I spent the next few days going around leaving red marks on the hotel floors, one of the cleaning ladies pointed it out to me and the boss made me go and buy new shoes, the hotel only gave you one pair of shoes with your uniform, you had to just get on with it, and so, like I was saying, I take the sandwich out to the pool, music's still blaring out of her headphones, I don't know what she's listening to, something light and very orchestral, probably one of those Sinatra knock-offs, where I come from they're everywhere, and, taking the plate and putting it on the low table next to her, she smiles at me and, taking out her headphones, says: "I'm going up to watch the birds migrating on the Savage Nature channel," and leaves her sandwich right where it is. That night the mother calls down to reception asking for a light breakfast to be brought early the next morning, at eight, and so there I am the next morning at eight sharp, and I go in, and the parents and the brother are asleep but not Paula, Paula's in the living area, sitting in the dark watching TV, the Savage Nature channel, face bathed in the metallic-blue light you get from old Uruguayan TV sets, she looks like she hasn't been to bed, and some birds, says a voice off-screen, are undertaking a transcontinental migration, they migrate without knowing why they do it, the experts don't understand it either, there are disagreements over whether climate change is to blame, in reality nobody understands anything, and Paula doesn't notice me come in, I go away again and not long after that she's out by the pool once more – see what I'm saying? – she was always out by the pool, there on that same lounger, drawing with all those different felt-tips, and she goes on drawing the outside of the hotel, an 'eternal dream', as she'd called it, and inside each of the windows she draws these intricate scenes, but when I take a closer look I see they aren't domestic scenes, and they aren't your usual kind of summer scenes either, they're set exclusively on the moon: each and every one of the rooms has the surface of the moon inside it, and an astronaut, the same one, hitting a golf ball, and that's all, and I say to myself this girl is *lo-co*, and off I go again, and come evening, when I take them their supper, they're all sitting together at the table and I witness a family fight, the mother tells Paula she doesn't want her watching the Savage Nature channel any more, there's been quite enough avian migrations for one holiday, and that the title itself says it all, that channel is for *sa-va-ges*, and Paula bursts out crying and runs out of the suite, I finish serving them, it's a few more minutes before I'm all done, and then I go out and find her on one of the landings, the one between second and first floor, she's sitting there crying, I ask if she's okay, though she obviously isn't, and she tells me she can't stand her mother any more, calls her a tyrant and says that on top of that she's had breast implants, more than anything in the world she hates these new breasts of her mother's, she had nursed at a pair of breasts that didn't exist any more, they were simply something else now, it was like those new breasts had been a way of blotting her out, the daughter, forever, like a way of blotting out her birth, her first words, her first steps, and, in short, everything that made her the person she was today, and that, truth be told, her mother had done it because she hated her daughter too, and I have no idea what to say to this, the things she's saying are hardly normal but that doesn't mean they don't make sense, eventually I get her to come down to the kitchens with me, I cook a steak for her, one of the staff steaks, not quite the same quality as the food we served guests but, you know, acceptable, and she wolfs it down before asking for a glass of milk, drinking milk with your dinner is for gringos or little children, I say, but that's what she wants, a glass of milk to wash her steak down, fine, no problem, I go get the milk, and then pull up a stool and sit next to her, behind us the frying pan is sizzling, there's smoke coming off it, I tell her it's steam dropping into the oil from the extractor hood though in fact it's cockroaches clambering up the side of the pan and then having no way to get back out again and getting fried, and when she finishes eating I say why doesn't she come down to my room in the basement, nobody'll bother us there, and she says, Okay, and the first thing she does when we get there is to turn the TV on, again hammering at the remote until she finds Savage Nature, she then asks me to turn the light off, and we sit in silence watching the birds migrate across the screen, and she says: See, these birds don't get it either. Don't get what? I say. They don't get why they migrate, she says, but they do it all the same, and then she says that what she wants to do is leave, go away, away from her family, and then we kiss; it's intense, her initiating the whole thing, and we spend the rest of the night making plans for our joint getaway, like the birds, she says, and keeps on saying, *like the birds*, and this all happened four years ago now, and look,' he gestured to the building once more, 'now here I am on this island, getting smaller all the time, shrinking while she and that other rat are growing gigantic, and,' he says, 'she's pregnant, to top it off she's pregnant, we're due to have a baby girl in just over a month's time.'

He stopped there. Neither of us said anything else.

I had noticed previously the way people, when at a loss for what to do, take their phones out and start amassing screens with their fingertips. I did this now, while he lit and made short work of another cigarette. Then, as the silence between us began to grow thin, I told him I ought to be getting back.

When I made it back to the hotel everything was in darkness. I took my key from my pigeonhole and glanced into the cafeteria before going upstairs. On the bar, balloon glasses and half-melted ice cubes. The chairs arranged in echoes of the various groupings. For some reason, one I can't now explain, it felt wrong to go on surveying this empty scene. I went up to my room, opening the shutters as soon as I went in. The swaying branches of the palm tree outside, natural megaphones, amplified the wind. Darkness had swallowed the small bridge and the light blue of the former lazaretto building. I thought about the Intel 486's on their respective desks, and about their hard disks, deep in a dream that might or might not have been eternal but certainly had no defined end: birds that could no longer migrate, or were dead. In my bed, I leafed through a book I'd brought with me, *Physics at the Residencia de Estudiantes*, produced by the publishing arm of that institution. After reading 'Stellar Universe', a talk given by Arthur Eddington in 1932, which made reference to the Belgian physicist and priest Georges Lemaître, who in 1927 had been the first to mathematically prove the existence of a Big Bang and thereby that the universe was expanding, I turned out the light. I didn't think I'd have any trouble getting to sleep, but my thoughts then began to tilt in the direction of the island's perimeter and the sea all around. And I was very nearly asleep, only for the faces of the men and women on the island with me to emerge in my thoughts with such physical presence that I only need have reached out a hand and I would have been able to touch them. I got out of bed. With the light still off, I turned on my computer and started to write:

I was in my bed a moment ago, the wind was up, the room
full of the sound of the sea, and as I tried to get to sleep I
was presented with the faces of the men and women also
here on the island; I had the sense they were all sitting
around a table, firstly in the dining hall in the former
prison but then in other places as well, and they start
talking very fast, I can't keep up with what they're saying,
can't follow their facial expressions either: images that
erupt with just as much force as if they were real. In the
group there's one man, or the face of one man, who isn't
on the island, someone I've never seen before, but everyone else in the group knows him, knows his face, and they
talk to him as though they've known him forever; within
a moment or two he's gone but no one minds, they go on
talking as though he were still there. And I feel a strong
urge to put an end to them, all of them, every single one. It
isn't about wanting to *kill* them, no, there's no ill intent,
it's both more general and abstract than that: a wish just
to stop them from existing, nothing more. It doesn't seem
to have anything to do with the island having been a
hideaway for the Knights Templar, or the pirate Francis
Drake having taken refuge here, or it being a lazaretto in
the 1900s and a prison during the civil war, or with the
firing squad executions that took place here, or the fact
that it later served as an orphanage, or with the unmarked
graves, or with the fact that the island is a prison in and
of itself. No, this desperate urge of mine for destruction
isn't about any of this, it's more general, something in the
stuff of the island, a feeling that's linked to iniquity when
it comes about for iniquity's sake: iniquity without reason.
And after that I want to put an end to the young man with
his sunglasses and sleeveless wetsuit who's supposed to be
coming to get us in the shore boat. Hold him underwater
till he literally sleeps with the fishes. So that it's just me

here, on my own. Who will dare apportion the blame...

I knew 'blame' was the last thing I should write because as soon as I did, the desire I'd been writing about, this impulse to put an end to certain things, immediately went away. I opened the control panel on my blog, pasted this text in the compose field and set it to upload at 4.10 p.m. the following day, at which time we'd all be together for the first session of the afternoon and there wouldn't be any way of retracting the post. I fell asleep once again trying to conjure the four dots behind my eyelids that had vanished all those years before. I thought I could glimpse one of them a long, long way back in the ocular sphere. It looked like a deep-sea amoeba, a spermatozon racing along, an astronaut lost in interstellar space.

Day Two

I was first down for breakfast. Rays of sunlight, not yet warm, poured in through the high windows. I served myself coffee from a thermos, and made up a plate of bread and smoked salmon. Outside, somewhere out of sight, birds were singing. I like this quality birds can have, being so forcefully present in a place and at the same time invisible. I took small sips of the coffee: the roasted flavour took me back to not being allowed it when I was a child. One way of telling whether you feel well in a place – well in the foetal sense – is if you shut your eyes and feel neither hot nor cold, and neither fearful nor fearless. I wished none of the others would join me for breakfast, that they'd somehow been eliminated. Paula, the waitress, came in and asked me if everything was alright, was there anything I needed. There were cuts on her wrists that she was trying to cover up with the sleeves of her waitressing outfit. Marta, who worked for the organization, came in and, standing with a folder to her chest, told me she'd spoken to Julián, who'd had something urgent come up in his personal life, and therefore wasn't going to be able to take part in my panel, but that they'd already found someone to stand in for him. Julián would be back at seven in the evening, by which time the day's events would be over; they'd arranged for the boat to bring him back to the island. I finished my coffee and said I'd see her in a couple of hours, when the morning sessions were due to begin. I left the dining room through the back door. On passing the Ladies', the door to which was ajar, I caught sight of Paula standing at the mirror. She had her blouse open, her bra lowered and a cone-shaped suction device on the nipple of her right breast. A see-through tube, milk flowing down it, connected the nipple to a bottle that was also see-through, and half-full of that liquid; she was squeezing a small pump in one hand. She didn't see me. I went out onto the gravel esplanade and ran into Javier, who was coming out of the chapel. He said he was thinking about renovating it, having the doors reinforced, for example. Some months earlier, somebody, they didn't know who, had defaced the chapel walls and taken a saw to Saint Roch's wrists. He said to go and have a look. Though I said I'd seen it the previous day, he wouldn't take no for an answer. We went inside. The look on Saint Roch's face was as though he was witnessing something embarrassing. His arms, bereft of the hands, were hollow tree trunks, but without any rings by which to count their age, I thought. A latent discomfort prompted me to suggest we go back out. The echo of our footsteps as we left the building sounded different to those when we'd gone in. I brought up the question of artist residencies on the island again. Again Javier said it simply wasn't possible. 'To give you an idea of the state of things here, we're going to shut indefinitely next month, so November onwards. We aren't going to be shouting it from the rooftops – to be on the safe side – but over this winter, though it could be for longer, we won't have the gardener, who usually comes once a week, or the security guard, and we'll cancel the shore boat. We'll have to hope the funding comes through in spring from the Galician government, or another body. If not, this place will be left to the plants and the rats.' 'The rats?' I said. 'Do you get a lot of them?' 'Not at the moment,' said Javier, 'but six months with no human inhabitation and the place'll be crawling with them. They swim across from the mainland.' I remembered an article I'd read once about animal rights groups setting hundreds of minks free. The minks had swum across the Vigo estuary as well, landing not far from San Simón at the Cíes Islands, where they settled, eventually laying waste to all vegetation and animal-life. If a group of minks bred in captivity, with their atrophied genetic imperative, had managed such a thing, why shouldn't the far more worldly sewer rats be able to make it across a strait that was after all a shorter distance? At that moment Mario, one of the symposium speakers, came over. Orange juice in hand, he mentioned an exhibition in the chapel a few years before, a homage to a Galician poet I would surely like, Carlos Oroza – I nodded – and said the opening had been quite something: the walls had been hung with photos from different phases of his life, original editions of his books had been placed around on lecterns, as well as manuscripts in glass cases that the author had made available for the occasion. Once Mario and Javier had gone, leaving me in front of the building,

I thought it would be a good moment to take *Aillados* on another tour. Something sent me back in the direction I'd gone the night before, to the place where I'd encountered the unhappy waiter, and after a few minutes' walk that's where I found myself. Time, and various renovations, had changed the installations almost beyond recognition, but on looking closely, I knew I'd found another match. Holding the book open in front of me, I positioned my phone to create the same frame for the shot. I took the picture.

De pé están Caeiro, Pantaleón e Dámaso. Anicados Pedro Carballo e Reisiño

I heard a voice calling me from behind. It was Nacho, a journalist from *Voz de Galicia*, shouting down from the slope that the session was about to start. I said I was just coming, and that they should begin without me.

I can't remember the rest of the morning very well, even though I took part in one of the panels, but I do remember a tweet coming up on one of the big screens that said:

We aren't always aware of the true power of social networks.

And this seemed far-fetched to me. And, shortly after that one, another that read:

Reality as refuge. You take shelter in reality to stop people hassling you on Twitter.

Which struck me as altogether true.

As soon as the afternoon sessions began, at 4.45 p.m., a look on Mario's face told me that my blog post had gone out. Mario retweeted it. It wasn't long before the others were glancing at me too, and further retweets began to appear on the screens ahead of us. It could have been hundreds or it could have been thousands of followers, all across the globe, that went on to retweet it in turn, and soon a thread of comments appeared. Within a quarter of an hour nobody was thinking about the point under discussion, the focus shifted to the thread instead, with opinions shared about my impulse to destroy the island along with all my fellow island inhabitants, who, aware of the thousands tuning in to watch, shifted uncomfortably in their seats. The discussion grew animated, people started talking over one another. Someone decided to turn the air conditioning up. Never had I felt power in its pure state, not as I did in that moment. I know it's something I ought to feel ashamed of, but I can't. None of this fallout was premeditated; my destructive impulse had been and was always abstract – and when I say abstract, I don't mean unreal, but rather that it wasn't fitted to any determined scale or time, like the formulation of an infantile desire, and that's that. I thought that the net, that great, untethered brain, had found its body at last, a receptacle in which to take bodily form, and that this body was none other than the island. It took in the rocks, the trees, the prison wings, but also the clothes, the weapons, the cutlery and plates and cups, the personal diaries, ink and pens, glasses, shoes, medication, torture instruments, bullets that had hit their mark and bullets gone astray, and bones, above all bones, piled up in geopolitical layers beneath our feet. I had not finished articulating this when Julián appeared in the doorway; as if magnetized, everyone looked his way. The shore boat had just dropped him off, several hours earlier than anticipated. He still had his suitcase with him. This I hadn't counted on. Julián's presence changed the conditions of the island so that they were once more the same as they had been the night before when I wrote my blog post, such that, naturally, the effects of the blog post were annulled and destroyed. It put an end to people shifting in their seats, and to the sweats they'd variously broken out in as well, and the online comments projected by my text across various social networks were the shadow of what had occurred. Julián, unaware of the pacifying effect he'd had, stood there in his big glasses saying nothing at all, until proceedings came to an end. Afterwards nobody brought up what had happened – whether out of embarrassment or any other feeling, I do not know.

The dinner passed without incident. It was the final night and the mood was more relaxed and the red wine flowed more freely. As usually happens when a large number of people sit at a table together, sub-groups of four or so people formed, with a fifth person who flitted between the groups and acted as an involuntary link between them. Julián was across from me and Nacho was on my right. Next to Julián was Javier, the foundation director, and next to him was Mario, the digital adviser. For once the discussion wasn't about the island's financial straits, but revolved around a story about a nun who in the 1980s had stolen newborn babies from a doctor's surgery in Madrid and given them to other families. As proof of death, the real parents had all used another baby – the same one, which had been kept in a cold storage room at the hospital. Javier went on to tell us about the island facilities being used as an orphanage in the 1950s. All of this prompted us to comment that, historically, we only ever keep a record of evil deeds. In fact, we only legislate for that which we consider to be pernicious; it never occurs to anyone to legislate for good or happiness. It was as though evil was actually held in higher regard than what's good. By this same logic, what's good, with no one keeping an account of it or checking it in any way, is a kind of echo that resounds to the ends of what is known, and its expansion, like that of the universe, will know no limits. And another consequence to this: it makes it pointless, utterly redundant, to ever discuss good, and that has the effect of making it even more invisible. Hence why, contrary to popular belief, it's revolutionary to speak of good things. So deep were we in these discussions that we didn't notice the waiter taking away the dessert and bringing the coffee. I turned my cup over, and Mario asked what on earth I was doing, to which I replied that I liked seeing where porcelain objects come from. This one had been made in Sargadelos.

More gin and tonics followed that night. Somebody had washed up the balloon glasses and straightened the chairs. In groups, people talked into the night. In an attempt, I think, to mollify or at least temporarily forget my wish to do away with everything and everyone, I was friendlier to people than usual. I was among the last to leave. Not everyone could fit inside the lift; I took the stairs. Coming to my floor, I was immediately aware of a figure in the darkness of the hallway, and turned on the light to see that it was the waiter, standing outside the door to my room. 'I was waiting for you,' he said in a low voice. He had something, or more than one thing, in his hands. 'We might not get the chance to talk in private at breakfast, so I wanted to give you this now.' He held out his hands: one held a cookie in the shape of an animal, like a big-bellied dog. 'I made it myself, earlier on,' he said, 'I thought it would be a nice gift for you, something to thank you for the understanding you showed me the other night when I was telling you about the problems I've been having. Knowing how to listen is just as important as knowing how to talk. Paula and I made up.' That was great news, I said after a few seconds' hesitation, but he really needn't have gone to all the trouble; I'd just happened to be passing by. 'There's lots of different ways to pass by,' he said, 'and the way you have of doing it is magical. I don't believe in magic, but your presence was so timely, you ought to spend your time passing by, or through, places, instead of shut in a room writing novels, just that would do it, you have the power to cure people just by going through a place.' Blushing slightly, I accepted the cookie, which smelled freshly baked. Again, the shape put me in mind of a dog with a big, or pregnant, belly. 'I also brought you this, it's from Paula, she's very grateful to you as well.' He handed me a plastic bottle. 'She wanted to do something creative.' I unscrewed the lid, the contents smelled of breast milk, still warm. I spent a few seconds looking at the two objects, not knowing how to say to him that none of it made any sense. Instead I just thanked him, before excusing myself, saying I didn't feel very well. He moved off then, not before telling me I'd always have a friend in each of them – and in their daughter-to-be as well. 'You'll always have a friend in her,' he said, before heading down the stairs.

I went into my room, putting the cookie and the milk down on the table. Getting into bed, I closed my eyes. I hesitated over turning off the light. I picked up the book, *Physics at the Residencia de Estudiantes*. I tried to read the rest of the 'Stellar Universe' chapter, the talk by Sir Arthur Eddington on the Belgian priest Lemaître who, as I've said, discovered the fact of the universe's expansion, but I found I couldn't get beyond the phrase, 'There are some stars so dense that a tonne of their matter would fit inside a matchbox.' I got up, opened the minibar, totally empty, and put both cookie and milk inside. I got back into bed. The rustling of the palm trees served to amplify the noise of the wind once again.

Day Three: Departure

Breakfast. The boat isn't due to come until 12.30 p.m. Julián and I, our heads splitting, decide to deal with the hangover by going outside for some air, taking coffee and cupcakes with us. We set out with no destination in mind. As he kicks pebbles along, I ask if he knows that Venus takes 243 Earth days to rotate about its axis, but only 224 to orbit the sun, which means a day on Venus lasts longer than a year on Venus. No, he didn't know that, says Julián. We come to the shore. 'You look like the Saint Roch inside the chapel, but with glasses,' he laughs. 'At least nobody's stolen my hands,' I say, making mine tremble, nearly spilling the coffee. We sit on the neatly sawn stump of a eucalyptus. I start counting the rings but lose count at thirteen. We drink the coffee while still eating the cupcakes. A song starts up. It's coming from some far-off place, but the acoustics mean we somehow hear it with complete clarity, as though we're sitting inside a struck note. We both look out across the water. It turns out to be a small fishing boat, low to the water, that's coming across the strait; the fisherman, I suppose, has a portable hi-fi on board. It's a rap song, but seeing as I don't like rap I have no idea which one. I watch as the boat sails past a plinth which, out in the water, stands at least a metre clear of the surface. The day is particularly clear and I'm able to make out a human figure standing on the column, whether of stone or metal I can't tell; it's the first time I've noticed it. I point it out to Julián. He tells me it's Jules Verne, a statue of Jules Verne, whose *Twenty Thousand Leagues Under the Sea* was inspired, in part, by the island. 'At high tide, the head only just pokes out,' he says, 'maybe that's why you haven't seen it yet.' I drain my coffee cup. I'd love another one but haven't got it in me to go and actually get it. Julián says he's staying put too. The boat is soon lost from sight, the beats in the rap song mixing, intermingling with the lapping of the waves. The sun is squarely ahead of us now. Julián picks a small stone up from between his feet and throws it out to sea. I do the same, with a slightly larger stone. Neither of us saying anything, we take it in turns to throw stones. Within a few minutes, we've joined forces to pick up a rock the size of suitcase; we each take an end, rolling it to the edge before hurling it out into the water. After the splash, it gives off a low, muted sound as it sinks to the depths. So it is very deep here.

'Julián', I say, 'I've a feeling we're not on the island any more.'

Solo residency

When I got back to La Coruña, rather than taking the plane I was booked on to Mallorca, I stayed in the family home which, as I've said, is uninhabited at that time of year. I spent a few days working out all the clothes, books, food items, electronics and toiletries I'd need to see me through a minimum of two months on the island. Having dealt with the question of supplies, I contacted a boat hire firm; for the date I had in mind, they only had yachts available. I knew that travelling by car to the coast near San Simón, and arranging a boat from there, would mean someone finding out about my plans before I'd even set off. So, at 7 p.m. on 5 November, the captain of a forty-foot yacht and I set sail from the city port. The Costa de la Muerte treated us kindly: the ocean like a millpond, the night sky clear. Looking back, the coastal towns and villages resembled an uninterrupted, if decaying, set of teeth. I pointed this out to the captain, who pretended to see it as well, and said he'd been thinking the same thing, though I could tell he was lying. I also mentioned the fact I've never understood the supposed luxury of pleasure boats or the social status they confer; to me they're nothing but caravans on water, and not even with the benefit of an ejector button for making a quick escape. This the captain roundly disagreed with. The sun was coming up when, as we passed the town of Ribeira, it started to rain and a west wind picked up, tossing the boat around. I went to my cabin.

I woke at 6 p.m.; the sun broke intermittently between the clouds, we passed the Ons Islands, skirted the Cíes Islands, the captain pointed them out to me, doing so with arm outstretched and forefinger very straight, as though it weren't obvious what was staring us in the face – a nautical custom, I supposed, come down from at least as far back at Columbus's discovery of what we today call the Americas. I told him about a summer when I was in my teens, likely 1982, when La Coruña was awash with hippies who had been ejected from southern Galicia's first ever communal settlement on the Cíes Islands, established a number of years earlier. All ragged and barefoot, they drifted around the cities with blankets on their backs; all they'd ask you for was cigarettes, nothing else. The hippy moment was over by then, punk was in full swing, so nobody paid them any mind. While I was telling the captain this, the occasional flicker of a smile on his face, I thought about the hundreds of old men who, according to what I'd read in *Aillados*, had been imprisoned on San Simón towards the end of the civil war with barely anything to eat and almost no provisions made for their hygiene. Their days were spent drifting around barefoot, flea-ridden blankets covering their backs, and their hair matted and shaggy since they weren't allowed a barber. On we sailed, neither of us saying much. It would have been nine in the evening when we got to San Simón; we moored at the jetty on the rear side of the island, the one facing out towards the estuary mouth. I pointed to Venus and asked if he knew that a day on Venus lasted longer than a year on Venus. No, he didn't, he said, and I added that this is why Venus belongs to another world, an inverse world, or something of that kind; the captain seemed not to be listening. I got off with my suitcase, we shook hands, and he waited for me to make it along the small jetty and onto dry land before launching. He bid me farewell with arm held high, again as though pointing to something, but this time something up above us, up in the stars.

I found my way to the hotel easily enough. The front of the building shone white under the full moon on the far side of the gardens with their scattering of eucalyptus trees. I had brought a sleeping bag with me just in case. I only had to slide my ID card in between lock and doorframe and jiggle it a little for the door to come open. Taking a torch from my suitcase, I shone it on the pigeonholes in reception: no keys. I pulled open the drawers under the counter: propaganda biros, old pads with details of guest bookings, and an old accountant's calculator, the kind with very big buttons for which I feel a special dislike. Then, in the largest drawer, I found the keys, all thrown in together. Searching through them, eventually I came up with the one for the room I'd stayed in; there was something reassuring in the known quantity of it. With this now in hand, I turned the reception computer on, its screen instantly lighting up. I knew I wanted to avoid having lights on at night – at least in any of the rooms facing towards the mainland and Redondela – but it was a relief to find the electricity on, which would make it far easier to cook and keep warm. I'd also need to be careful with cigarettes; in the dark, the lit cherry can be seen from a distance of a mile. I checked for internet. After trying a few different things, I saw that it was pointless. I checked my mobile phone, but that wasn't getting me online either. This absence seemed to me a setback, but a liberating one. I pressed the button for the lift, which travelled down from the fourth floor. Just as I stepped in, I thought better of it;

if I were somehow to get stuck inside, I'd end up dying of starvation. I walked up the stairs with my suitcase, which took some doing, heavy as it was with tins, jam jars and freeze-dried foods; I was panting by the time I got to my room. The key worked first time and I went inside. There was a damp smell. I closed the curtains and turned the torch on. The bed made, new soap, clean towels. The thought came to me that it had been readied specifically for my arrival, but that couldn't have been true. I then accidentally leaned my arm against the light switch for the briefest of seconds, before instantly returning it to the off position. It took a moment for it to dawn on me: the light hadn't actually come on. I flicked the switch again, and again, and nothing happened. I tried once more, leaving it for longer this time, but still nothing. I went back down to reception, using the torch to light my way, and took out several keys at random; the lights were not working in the corresponding rooms either. I went back to my room. The crossing had left me feeling exhausted. I took out the small chunk of red-mottled black basalt, the one I'd found in a roadside ditch in the north of France years before; I put it on the table, in exactly the same place as before. I got into bed and fell asleep looking over at it, illuminated in a rectangle of moonlight from the window. The shutters open. The palm tree.

I spent my first days there acclimatizing, organizing the food, changing the room to make it my own, and going out for walks wearing the camouflage overalls I'd bought so I wouldn't be spotted from the coast; they were so big on me that when I looked at my reflection in the pond I was presented with an image of a deep sea diver or an astronaut. I cooked my meals in the kitchens, which had no food stored in them, only what I'd brought. The bird-song at dusk was deafening. Having found none of the lights working anywhere in the hotel, I spent no small amount of time hunting for a general switch for the whole complex; undoubtedly it had been switched off by the last security guard to leave. I didn't find it. The trees had shed their leaves, which now lay thick along the footpaths. Here and there I came across palm trees with circular scatterings of dates on the ground around them, pecked at by birds or nibbled by rodents. I went inside each of the wings, and experienced the silence inside all of them as a kind of physical substance, very dense. I'd often stop on the gravel esplanade and contemplate the chapel facade. One day I went in. A small mouse ran up the saint and into the hole in one of his wrists, disappearing inside the arm. I went straight back out again. In the latter part of the day, I'd sit in the hotel foyer, which had magnificent views over the bay, and read one of the many books I'd brought, though usually opting for *Physics at the Residencia de Estudiantes*, which, I have to admit, I hadn't finished after two years of carting it from place to place. I happened to have some coins with me, and used these to extract cans of Nestea from the dispenser by the entrance. I'd cast the occasional glance down towards the estuary, almost always still and glassy, and in whose waters the statue of Jules Verne was now clearly visible to me, his head always emerged at some point during that part of the day.

I crossed the bridge to the smaller island that first week, pausing to take a look at the silvery-backed fish below. Along they streamed in a disparate mass, like the last time I'd seen them. The former lazaretto building, with its light blue stucco and grates on the windows, and only one storey high, was accessed by climbing a short set of steps. I had only to nudge the door with my shoulder and it swung open. In the main space, the morning sunlight streamed in, lighting up the cobweb that joined tables, computer and chairs into one single net. I sat down at one of the computers. I pressed the On button and, as is usual with Intel 486s, the purring of the hard disk sounded like a chugging steam engine. At that point I noticed the PC had the same number as my room, 486, and had to laugh. I looked up at the window on the rear of the building, and through it at the bridge and the hotel beyond, the window to my room, the palm tree. Looking at the screen once more, I found Velázquez's *Las Meninas* as the screensaver, program icons and folders arranged across it. I got up from the chair and turned on the rest of the computers. Within a few minutes I had twelve screens featuring Mari Bárbola, the macrocephalous dwarf in *Las Meninas*, staring back at me. I began looking through the computer files, all of which were to do with the running of the prison. One, labelled 'Origin (36)', contained scanned pages of the prisoner arrival logs between 1936 and 1939, and of material concerning logistics and housekeeping, along with arrest sheets accompanied by short notes from the respective authorities. For example:

It is my honour to inform you that, in accordance with your orders by telephone, the prisoner has been placed under strict surveillance by us, being removed to the lazaretto and there placed in isolation with a pair of guards posted.

These measures will continue as long as the prisoner remains with us here and providing no orders from V.S. to the contrary are forthcoming.

Viva España!
THE INSPECTOR
Pontevedra, San Simón Penal Establishment, 30
September 1937.

I found little else that day.

Late the next afternoon I came across a document, a
transcription of what appeared to be a prisoner testimony, that I read straight away:

I have been a prisoner here for two years. At the end of my
first year, the old men were brought in one day, and what a
sorry sight. They were brought over on the *Aurora II* in
lots, there being too many of them to fit all at once. We
were nearly eight hundred inmates then, and with the old
men we numbered over a thousand. They have been with
us a year and more than half have died. They brought no
clothes with them, save what they wore and a blanket they
were each given on arrival. They sleep in the same place
as us, but during the day keep to themselves. They do not
address us, or only on occasion to beg some tobacco to
smoke, when there is any, which is rarely. In the nights, we
all have to sleep cheek-by-jowl on the floor, where we
bunk down with neither mats nor any pillows. The damp
gets into you down to your stomach. We are so numerous
that many are forced to sleep wedged up against one
another. I was imprisoned on trumped-up charges. Even
the town notary and a priest testified on my behalf, but all
counted for nought. We do not know what this legion of
greybeards stand accused of. Their treatment serves only
to deaden the life in them. There are those who claim them
for the fathers and grandfathers of the inmates at
Pamplona prison, while others say that, on account of
their age, the Regime has deemed them good for nothing

and brought them here to see out their final days. Not long ago, less than a year, the problem of the fleas began. They have always been a feature, but now there are more. No provision is made for the old men to wash themselves and some, their minds addled, cannot look after themselves. But of course the guards do not make them wash either, to them it is all one. The liveliest among them, the most cussed, go around each day collecting the others' blankets and exterminate the fleas by boiling them in cauldrons beyond the eucalyptus plants near the bridge, down by the shore. A white foam comes up thickly in the cauldrons they use, the thickness of your hand at least, like lard to look at – it is the nits themselves. They then ditch this water in the sea and in such great amounts that more than once has it been mistaken for the foam of the waves coming in. The fish under the bridge congregate the day long in expectation of this moment, for they eat this foam – this I was told by a guard still with some humanity about him who treats us kindly. The old men are given their food apart, and a bowl to eat it from, and made to line up in all weathers at three cauldrons on the esplanade by the chapel. These old men are nothing but skin and bones, such that their feet barely make a sound as they walk over the gravel. We look out at them from the dining hall; it is a sad sight, but one of the other inmates has pointed out that the less they eat the better it is for us. The queues are so long and they shuffle forward so slowly along the myrtle path that it takes the old men who start at the back of the queue hours to reach the cauldrons. The footpath that encircles the island was made by us, with pick and spade. Keeping it to ourselves we named it Avenida de Teruel since its construction coincided with the Republicans taking Teruel. Once, Prado Castro, one of the officers here, lost his temper because the old men were taking very

long in queuing for their meal. He flew out of the officers'
wing and kicked over the cauldron, the contents of which
spilled across the gravel. A sight it was, all the old men
down on hand and knee, eating off the ground. In the
dining hall we all stood to get a better view, everyone
silent. In the main they appear absent, spittle runs down
their chins, they talk to themselves, they walk around
waving their arms or with hands deep in pockets scratching their parts, on account of the fleas; they seem bereft of
all spirit, or that is what those in charge here believe.
Hardly do they talk to one another, as though they cannot
see their companions, as though each was already dead
and buried. I had the good fortune of completing the first
two years of my medical studies at Santiago de
Compostela, that was where I was when the soldiers came
and dragged me from the lecture hall – I was nineteen
years of age – but I have enough knowledge of the human
body to tell that these old men are sure to die for want of
nutrients, that is if the fleas do not finish them off first. We
must make do without bread and milk, but there is far
more they make do without. They have no teeth, yet on
occasion they are given bones to champ on. These they
take with them down to the cove and, placing a blanket on
the rocks, crush them all to dust with stones, then drink it
down in water. Most do not have shoes. One day they
decided to sing together. They congregated in B Wing, the
largest of all, for the guards rarely go there, and, according to Gundín, one of our number and formerly a band
player in La Coruña, the sound is better in that wing on
account of the high ceilings. They sang popular songs,
most of these not Galician, since, as I have said, they come
from all over. The guards, away in their quarters, at first
believed the sound to be coming from a boat bringing
officers over from the mainland, one they had been

awaiting for several days, for they tend to sing when they are on leave and merry with wine, but they looked out to sea and saw nothing. People have told me the guards were even put in fright by these voices. We were resting after the day's work, we had been rebuilding the cemetery wall that had been knocked down by high seas, and Gundín himself, sitting eating on one of the graves, said we were hearing the angels themselves in song – rarely had he heard a song of such harmoniousness. A few minutes passed, and the guards entered B Wing and beat the old men roundly. Their ire was not that the old men should sing, but by their own having been mistaken. Apparently there was one who, though not dying there and then, succumbed to his injuries a few days later. After that incident we went on to call that wing, The Wing of the Angels. If the guards were to catch wind of this I do not know what they would do to us. The question of coitus is not resolved. We are allowed visits once every two months, but we are forbidden from physically touching our women. The visiting room is inside a lean-to, with a chicken wire grate before you, and then, two metres away, another grate, with the families on the far side. We may not even touch their hands. The guards walk up and down in the part between the two grates. There have been times when the guards have asked to lie with some of the women in exchange for treats for us, such as food or cigarettes. Everyone refuses, everyone except one whose name I will not mention out of respect for the woman, who is a good woman, but thanks to her the husband now boasts fresh tobacco in his pipe every day. Not including the old men, who only leave this place in a coffin, there is much coming and going of inmates between this prison and other ones. Those of us who remain and do not go anywhere can number no more than two hundred. One of the day visitors, the woman of an inmate from Redondela, says there are people appearing in the ditches around the town every day, and some of them are men who were taken from here. A month ago, in November, they took fifty men, the strongest – for road building, they said. That is something we have always been threatened with, very hard work it is, and with bad tools, but others say at least it is a way of getting out and having shoes on your feet and decent clothes on your back. For myself, I would rather not leave the island, there is nothing good occurring out there. In any case, the old men, in their hunger, kill rats and take them to eat among the rocks, roasting them over a fire, and on account of this the typhus is now among us too. Now they have put more than thirty of them in the lazaretto. Nobody, the guards included, may cross the bridge. Every other day they put food down for them at the far end of the bridge and lock it from this side. The old and sick stand over there banging on the gate. Only once the guards have gone may they open it and come out for the food. They hurry forward, stumbling over one another, and scuffles break out, all within the confines of the bridge. Sometimes the food falls into the estuary and again the fish, waiting below, get a bite to eat. Other guards go by in a shore boat to make sure none of the old men jump into the water. Not that they could reach the mainland swimming – no man can, the currents across the strait are too strong – but it is all one, they keep watch all the same: there is nothing else for them to do. Most of the inmates are here on account of their ideas, only their ideas. There is nothing worse than ideas and the fickle way they have of mutating. Ideas cannot be seen in the way the pages in this typewriter can be seen, ideas cannot be touched or drawn or captured in a photograph either. Once a year a photographer always used to come by my village, Vilagarcía de Arousa, and he took portraits of the families. My father used to recount the man's tales to us, of his travels far and wide, some of those tales were happy and others were sad, and later he would take our photograph and in our faces you could never tell whether we were happy or sad. A photograph is a thing with a life all its own. Photographs do not depict ideas. Ideas, at best, may be written down, recounted and written down – this is the only way ever to catch a sight of them. I am fortunate, as I say, for I can read, and, thanks to the job I have been given by the assistant to the prison secretary, I have access to this typewriter, which is dangerous, everything being put down here clearly and legibly, but for this same reason typewriters are the best invention there has ever been: whatever you type on them goes on, in ever widening circles, forever after. I prevailed upon them to allow me to bring some poems onto the island, they are the work of a young poet from Granada who goes by the name García Lorca, I do not know if this is his real name or if it is, as is the way among writers and artists, a made-up one. I copied these poems down by hand, using copies that had also been written out, which the head of the Physiology department at Santiago had in his office, naturally with his permission. He had brought them from France, where someone else had let him copy them out. The guards read them but did not understand a word, and this is only the reason they let me keep them. I have underlined them using pencils of three different colours – blue, green and red – the which initially made the guards think the whole thing a secret code, and I a spy, but a guard from Pontevedra with whom I am on good terms, whose name I will not mention so as to avoid compromising him, convinced them that this was not the case, that these poems were trifles, fanciful things I write for my own amusement, and so I am left in peace. A few days ago, here in the offices, I found the guard I am friendly with holding the poems, and he told me to come with him. I feared the worst. He led me to the far end of the myrtle path, ordered me to sit down on some rocks, he stood directly behind me so that I could not see him, and said that I, who knew how to read well, should read him one of the poems, any one, and I did. When I finished he was in tears. He said to me: 'That poet writes very well, it is a shame for your lot that wars are not won by the pen.' When I was young my mother told me terrible tales of this island, which, seen from the mainland, above all in spring-time, with the trees all decked in green, is a lovely sight, very lovely. Those tales, to a one, made mention of the typhus; the foreign soldiers brought this sickness with them and were quarantined here, I am talking of the nineteenth century or longer ago. The prison has its own photographer. Every now and then, at no fixed intervals, we are given clothes that look presentable and they take photographs of us. I saw them once, they are kept with all the files in B Wing. Any person seeing them would think we are taking part in town festivities. There we are, all smiles, good shoes on our feet, and it fills me with rage to think we will forever be like that, fixed in the photograph, our faces untroubled. I dislike it greatly, and that is what leads me to write this, to make the situation clear, to make it as clear as can be. I would like to make those photographs disappear, or for no person ever to look at them again. The old men are the only ones not included in the photographs, for they are considered as good as dead. At most, general, group photographs are taken of them, all packed together like a herd of beasts, not posed, none of their features in focus, and this has to do with no one even knowing their names, though at the same time they are not assigned numbers

– even that they are not worthy of. Just yesterday they
took a photograph of them outside B Wing, The Wing of
the Angels, where they sang together that day. The film is
taken off in the shore boat to be developed; I get to see the
photographs when they are brought back after being
developed in La Coruña, which is where the General
Headquarters are – they always want to have a look before
bringing them back here. Father Nieto is the worst of
them. He wears a gun under his cassock. He says that to
kill is not by necessity evil, that God allows for the death
of insects during harvest and of the lice on our heads.
They took a man and led him out to the wall, I do not
recall his name, they meant to kill him. They lined him up
against the cemetery wall, to avoid having to transport
him once dead. When they shot him he fell to the ground
but did not die, and, as he lay dying, Father Nieto went
over and began to tap him about the face with his stick, as
though he were an animal, and said to him: 'Die now, you
heathen red.' A ship called the *Upo Mendi* docked just a few
days ago; it is a freighter, very large, larger than four
fishing boats put together, and it is said that Basque
prisoners are being held on it, and in worse conditions
than us, but none of us know for certain where they are
from. The idea is apparently to leave it there, anchored a
few hundred yards offshore, until it turns to rust and
sinks of its own accord, taking all those on board down
with it. I do not know how those men on board will be able
to bear it on there without committing some terrible act.
Time will tell. My friend the guard has told me there are
rats on board the size of his forearm. There are those
among us who have tried to take their lives. I know of no
such cases among the old men. I am certain that these old
men do not know they are inside a prison, they think they
are in a sanctuary, or gone to heaven or hell already, the

which with every passing day I feel more convinced there is no telling the difference between. But worst of all is that which cannot be seen: the noise. A noise that comes not from the sea, that is certain, and that keeps us from sleeping. I cannot get used to the waking every two hours and hearing this noise. The guards say they do not hear a thing, but we can hear it very well. Another inmate, Benito, says it is issuing from the earth itself, others say it is the generator for the electric lighting in the officers' wing; to me it is all one where it comes from, all I know is that thanks to this noise it has been two years since I have slept for more than three hours at a stretch.

It ended there. It said further down that this testimony, the author of which was unknown, had been discovered in 1998 during renovation works; it was found in the cellars of the wing later to become the hotel, hidden behind a false wall. The account, it said, had been typewritten on unbound sheets held inside a tanned leather folder. Most significantly, when the whole thing was taken to the Forensic Institute in Santiago de Compostela, the skin was found to be that of a human, probably a male over seventy years old. I looked away from the screen. I hadn't eaten all day, but found myself gagging now. I decided to go back to the hotel. I crossed the bridge. A procession of old men crossed behind me.

I decided to spend what was left of the daylight sitting in the foyer armchairs. I drank the last two Nesteas from the dispenser, which, since I'd used up all my coins by then, I was forced to open with a kick. For the first time I felt an urge to surf the net, to just be online. Not wanting to waste my mobile data, I tried the computer in reception, but as on the first day got nothing. Only then did I try on my phone but that, unsurprisingly, gave me nothing either. I kept on trying, over and over, practically pummelling the touch screen by the end. I don't know how many fingerprints I left on that screen, but far more, surely, than the total number of megabytes I'd been promised when I took out my phone contract. Never had I hated my phone as I did in that moment. I lay down on the sofa, put my feet up and closed my eyes. As I was falling asleep, the thought came to mind: 'I saw the greatest minds of my generation destroyed by Facebook.'

It was night when I opened my eyes. Reaching around for my glasses in the dark, I remembered I'd neglected to turn the lazaretto computers off. I went out and saw the lit-up windows, a reddish glow in the distance, and undoubtedly visible in the darkness from the coast. I broke into a run, jumped the hedges, cut along an old path, and, stumbling several times along the way, made it to the bridge, a gust of wind then almost knocking me off my feet before I got up the steps and into the wing. The screens shone with the rusty reddish light that predominates in *Las Meninas*. I didn't waste time turning them off one by one, but went straight over to the plug that controlled the power for the whole building and pulled that out instead. It didn't fall dark straight away. A brief couple of seconds, a brightness falling dim, and Mari Bárbola, the macrocephalous dwarf, giving you a harder stare than ever.

One night, from the bed, I saw it was beginning to snow outside. I went over to the window, the lights on the far side of the estuary were hidden from sight, the mass of treetops appeared to me a cinema screen as empty as it was vast. In the moment of returning to bed in the darkness, the minibar caught my eye. Strange as it might seem, I hadn't given it the slightest thought since I'd been there. I opened it, thinking there might be a drinks can in there. It took me a few seconds to remember what the objects inside were: the pregnant dog cookie and the bottle of breast milk, both untouched and both exactly where I'd left them two months before. There was no way I'd be picking either of them up. It was then that I felt briefly woozy for the first time, like I was about to disappear. I shut the minibar door, and resolved to leave it that way.

Back in bed again, I watched the snowflakes falling on the palm tree, and thought how no two snowflakes are the same, but all, without exception, have six points distributed symmetrically around a single centre point. I know that in any place where symmetry is lacking, it's because, in that portion of planet Earth, the forces of nature are in conflict; eddying river water and human migration flows are such sites of conflict. Thus a snow-flake can be called an isolated point, a place in which the forces keeping the crystals from flying apart are not in competition with anything. Snowflakes are bunkers, isolation chambers, unreachable bubbles; these were my thoughts as I lay in the bed, staring blankly out at the precipitate of each and every one of those snowflakes. And this thought concerning bunkers and points of isolation brought with it another in turn: the possibil-ity of the existence of a place where, densely packed together, all the memories of a person are contained: a neighbourhood, a city, a room or street beyond which a person would relinquish their memories, and thereby all awareness, of what had gone before; they'd only need to go back across the threshold of that street for all the instability and turbulence that is memory to be activat-ed once more. This, I believe, is why I didn't open the minibar door again, so as not to re-experience that wooziness, so as not to disappear. So as not to be confronted by such a turbulent portion of the universe.

For a while after that I spent much of my time scouring the 486s. I found that, save for certain details, the contents of all the computers were the same, logically enough given that all the records on them were official. Aside from this, and due to the layer of snow that settled on the island, I tried to spend the rest of the time in my room. At one point I tried sleeping in another, bigger room, one of the suites, but went back halfway through the night. I realized that, as far as habits go, once a space has been made your own, something begins to grow in all other spaces that I can't put my finger on but very closely resembles fear. I combed all the prison buildings, lean-tos and basements in search of a mains switch; I never found it. I'd also go to the eucalyptus stump where Julián and I had sat and eaten our breakfast on the last day. This gave me the chance to count its rings; I came up with 75; perhaps the tree had been planted by some inmate or other, I said to myself. The stump was a good place to sit, but I quickly saw that where I felt truly peaceful was the chapel. I would sit, legs dangling off the stone altar set into the wall – a leftover from the days of priests giving Tridentine Mass, backs to the congregation – and Saint Roch at my side. I would light a cigarette and imagine the Galician poet Carlos Oroza's retrospective, which Mario had told me about. The walls had likely been covered in photographs, I thought, and there would have been display cabinets with first editions, showing the work of one of the godfathers of spoken word, on the same level as Ginsberg, with whom the poet had rubbed shoulders in the 1950s. Indeed, the city of

New York awarded him the International Underground Poetry Prize – the exact date escapes me. I knew Oroza's work from his collection *A Feeling of Weightlessness in the Air*, a few lines from which came back to me. Sitting on the altar, I recited them to the empty space:

Today three bridges thought to be identical collapsed
No one knows why
No hint of a sign
It's a mistake to take the things we've seen as a given.

When you are talked about
A feeling of weightlessness in the air.

I sat astounded, imagining the people at the opening of the exhibition, talking, drinking, smoking, taking photographs of one another between the Saint Roch statue and Carlos Oroza's belongings. I would have liked to photograph that event, I thought, or to film it: to have seen the looks on those people's faces. It's like when you gather a group together, saying you want a photo, but then press the button to record video instead – they're expecting a photo, but you press record. Then you watch it back and you fall over laughing, and the people you tricked also find it the funniest thing. An unimaginable number of strange contortions pass over a person's face in the moments before they're frozen in a photo. I thought I'd have liked to perform that same trick with the photos in *Aillados*, to have witnessed what the people in them were saying immediately prior to the capture of those images, the looks they gave one another and the tiny fluctuations of expression just before their portraits were taken; that surely wouldn't have been funny. It was while sitting on the chapel altar that I saw a second mouse run up Saint Roch's legs and inside one of his hollow arms. I don't know if it would have occurred to the people who stole those hands that by doing so they were letting out various cubic litres of fifteenth-century air, until then trapped inside the saint's body. Of those cubic litres, some molecules must be in our lungs. What on earth was it about those hands that moved someone to steal them, who would want a saint's hands on show in the hallway of their house. Although, it's also true, I told myself, that anyone who saw the rock I'd picked up in a roadside ditch in northern France would think me quite strange. Something I noticed from reading all those files on the 486s was the sense that they were all discussing the same person. I'm not suggesting they'd all been written by the same inmate, and far less that San Simón had never in fact been home to prisoners or the whole thing the product of some unbalanced mind; no, what I want to get across is that in conditions of isolation, there's a tendency for bodies and brains to meld together into a single consciousness, into a receptacle for identical reagents, and that, in reality, it is this great unification, to put it one way, which the repressive authority seeks to bring about: to annul all individuality, to make everyone speak as if with one and the same mouth. And so I rejected the possibility of being absorbed by the island and becoming one more inmate, and felt the saint was on my side in that, watching over me. I even went so far as to wonder if the saint's wooden fingers might have had fingerprints, and if those fingerprints might have matched my own. Peering inside the hollows of his arms again, I saw a primitive cathedral, a high-vaulted cave in the torchlight, like the Neanderthal caves with handprints or sometimes hunting scenes depicted on the walls. Yes, something very ancient resided in that wooden body and not only did it pray for me, it was also at work in stopping the island and I from merging. This I think was the definitive reason why I liked sitting on that altar with the saint at my side.

Around that time, during nights when I laid with numerous blankets over me, listening to the wind as it shook the palm tree outside my window, I envisaged a bird's eye view of all the hotel rooms with all the beds neatly made, ready for whoever might slip under their sheets, and just the one body occupying this multitude of beds, my own, a kind of doll that had been carefully deposited there. This vision comprised the most intense sensation of solitude I could ever remember having felt. After that I would fall asleep trying to conjure the four dots that used to float behind my eyelids, looking for some company before I fell asleep, but no. And so, resolving to alter my routines, which I thought must be the source of the unease I was experiencing, I decided I'd do something not about the routines themselves but, more radically, about time itself, within which those routines functioned. The idea was to create a new timetable for myself by going to bed an hour later every day, and getting up an hour later; after a month I would have turned the twenty-four-hour cycle on its head. This meant eating breakfast at 8 p.m. or dinner at 10 a.m., a loss of a sense of time I'd never experienced except for in the city of Las Vegas, where, as is well known, the casinos are bereft of natural light to stop you from knowing whether it's day or night, thereby cancelling out the circadian rhythm altogether, in order that you go on gambling. My San Simón timetable was even more radical than what happened in Las Vegas, because I was creating a Las Vegas inside my own body, all of a casino's lack of light lodged inside my own body, which prompted in me the turbulence of a physical disorder though I wasn't actually ill. At the same time, I stopped seeing rabbits, birds, rats or any of the other animals I'd become used to seeing around the island – I only saw their tracks in the snow. I didn't know if this was to do with the creatures' normal seasonal cycles, or if, being unused to the presence of humans at that time of year, they were hiding from me. I started naming the makers of these tracks – tiger, hummingbird, lemur, wolf and so on – phylogenies that gave rise to a parallel fauna, renderings of the particular island orchard that had begun to flourish inside my mind. And then, looking out from my window early in the morning one day, I saw tracks in the snow that alerted me to the presence of another person on the island. They went in a straight line across the island. After my initial shock, which was considerable, I thought they must be tracks I'd made. But some minutes later, going outside, I saw that this wasn't so: these tracks, though human footprints, weren't at all like my own, being far larger and very rectangular, and the tips not pointed. I spent the following days inside my room, shutters closed, listening out carefully for any sound or hint or sign of human presence, which never manifested. And the same thing went on happening, the footprints appearing in the early hours, then to be covered over by the falling snow. I became used to them. After a time, I followed them to see where they were coming from and where they went, finding that they sprung up between the rocks on the small western cove and, keeping to all the most pronounced paths, crossed the island and vanished again among the rocks on the eastern side, at the water's edge. Anyone would have thought that someone was emerging out of the sea, day on day, walking straight past the hotel and then re-entering the water on the far side of the island. I also went down to the lazaretto bridge at times and found these footprints mixed up with rabbits' tracks, or mixed up with those of birds or rats in the graveyard, and then thought of them as someone might think of an astronaut's footprints, but not a pioneer astronaut like Neil Armstrong, for example, but an astronaut for the end of something, an astronaut for an ending. I also thought a lot about the handless Saint Roch, and how I would have liked him to be in my room, always at my side.

On one of these days, while I was eating a 3 p.m. breakfast in my room, with the television on but the sound down, I jumped half out of my seat at a message notification on my phone. When I reached for it and looked at the words on the screen, my heart shrank to half its normal size: 'It's a mistake to take the things we've seen as a given.' I sat very still then, as though bracing for something. It was from an unknown number. I tried to send a reply message, I tried other numbers, but, as had been the case to date, there was no signal, and then my heart, already having halved in size, shrank to a quarter of its normal size, as though on the cusp of vanishing altogether. I got up from the chair and left the room. I spent half an hour pacing the hallway outside, rereading the message over and over, I don't know how many times. I went back into the room. The snowfall had slackened off in the previous hour, the laptop was in sleep mode, the news playing on the television. I remember the dimensions of the screen being such that the female presenter's face was life-size, and it occurred to me that this was the most true-to-life news programme I'd ever seen. I put the camouflage jumpsuit and my boots on, steeled myself and went outside. I made my way to the snow-covered myrtle path. In the darkness, unlike what happens with vision – all detail blending into one single, undifferentiated thing – something happens to sounds to make them more distinguishable, seemingly more distinct from one another. I was able to make out the wind zigzagging across the waters on the jetty side, and, away on the lazaretto, the eucalyptus trees rustling, and a window or door banging in one of the prison buildings, but in among these sounds there was one I couldn't identify, a constant, uninterrupted hum coming not from the high-tension power cables in the town across the estuary, from which I often saw sparks flying in the night, or from the motor of any boat, or the winter animals burrowing down to be nearer the earth's warmth. No, it was a sound I'd never heard before, on the island or anywhere else. I carried on walking, passing the chapel, leaving behind the small gravel esplanade, and the noise remained constant, growing neither quieter nor louder. I am not an idiot and neither am I crazy, and I know that a writer of the genre known as magical realism would have argued there was some gigantic magnet secreted somewhere underground, and that a Russian writer of sci-fi dystopias would claim the island as the place where one era was due to come to an end and another, the era of one kind of extraterrestrial or another, begin, and that a realist twenty-first-century Spanish writer would point to this sound as the echo of civil strife that had never properly been laid to rest, and that a French writer from the 1950s would attribute it to the self, or the psyche itself which, like a stomach, goes on endlessly auto-digesting, and an American writing at the close of the twentieth century would say the sound was issuing from a machine, because very near the island, possibly even on the lazaretto itself, a depraved multinational was working day and night to create an identical version of this island, but no, really, I am not an idiot and neither am I crazy, and it became clear to me that the ringing in my ears had nothing to do with literature, was not a mirror for anything or a representation either, it was just a thing that was happening. I stopped then, took a breath, and it felt to me that this sound could only be love in its pure state. There was no rational reason for me to think this, yet I knew that for the first time in my life I was in the presence of pure love made manifest, and when I say pure love I mean exactly that: love stripped of all embellishment, a self-propagating love that appears of its own accord. This thought had yet to fully form when I became aware that all of this love was entering my body, starting deep inside, covering every inch of me and flowing out through my feet, as though I were the earthing element for the planet, the earthing element for love in this world, and then I felt afraid, extremely afraid, because, unlike what happens in novels, there was no way for me to put this thing inside a story and thereby to exorcize it. I moved off again, leaving a trail of footsteps alongside those mystery ones, but I couldn't have been said to be following them; I wondered if everything I'd experienced during my time on the island wasn't a prologue to the arrival of this noise, which had been coming into being through a chain of infinitesimal moments finally to culminate inside me at this particular moment. I also asked myself if the footprints of that end-of-days astronaut and pioneer weren't one more manifestation of a love that, simply, I had not known how to interpret. I turned off to the right, down the path that led directly to one of the jetties, and stopped to look at the water. There are those who sing songs to keep fear at bay, which is a way of sweetening it, and others who talk to themselves, which is a way of making it rot inside, and others still who look for the scientific origin of fear as a way of making a mere object of it, and understanding the futility of these methods made me feel more afraid still: double fear. I hurried to retrace my steps, and these and other thoughts carried me back to the hotel entrance. I went inside, and the noise dropped away. It would have been 9 p.m. but according to my timetable still morning. I took a cold shower, which, as with vomiting, is unpleasant to go through but makes you feel better afterwards. I resolved to forget about the noise for now, go on with my usual round and simply see what the next day brought. I opened some sardines, which I ate directly from the tin, not putting them on a plate, and on the television saw the closing stages of a weekly review programme, images of an armed conflict, a politician in the onset of Alzheimer's, a man in a wheelchair lamenting not having stuck to the speed limit. After nearly an hour of calm, I broke out in a sweat, my mouth felt dry, I splashed water over the nape of my neck, left the room, began pacing the hallway, read the text message again: 'It's a mistake to take the things we've seen as a given.' Nothing would quell my growing agitation. Not that I was an expert, but I had in the past been a fairly assiduous reader of the Western mystical tradition – Master Eckhardt, St John of the Cross, Angelus Silesius, St Teresa of Ávila – and, according to their writings, they'd all experienced pure love, but for them the experience had been accompanied by overwhelming joy and not sensations of fear, from which I deduced that it hadn't been pure love these mystics had been presented with but something else, a love enveloped in some kind of literature – no doubt about it. I felt like going up to my room, but my legs refused to carry me there. I then realized that my agitation was due to being cut off from the noise outside. I needed that noise. I needed, no matter the cost, to experience that love again. I went and got my video camera, not having taken it out of my suitcase until then, inserted a tape, the only one I'd brought with me, a sixty-minute one, put on my boots and pressed record. I went down the stairs and out into the snow, trying to place my feet in the prints I'd made previously so that my footfall wouldn't interfere with the pure love sound, which continued to resonate in my every cavity. Keeping the camera straight ahead, at chest-height, I walked to the chapel, and past it, stopping when I got as far as the jetty. The temperature had dropped, the tide was going out and had left curved lines in the sand like the orbits of planets, or as though the waves had been leaping out to sea in stages. It was close to freezing. I looked at the sky: the stars, unlike me, shone without a hint of a tremble. I went back to the hotel the same way I'd come. I opened the door to my room, turned the camera off, sat down. I plugged the camera into the laptop; it took a few minutes to find a program to digitize the tape. The images began to transfer: me going back downstairs and out the main door, where the background noise struck up in the laptop speakers. The snow appeared dark on the screen, but the footprints were white, some of them a nuclear white, which gave the path the look of a night sky flecked with brilliant white stars. The background noise as registered by the camera had the same penetrating quality as the real thing, but was more stop-start, coming in and out. The camera passed by the chapel, went down to the jetty, and the background noise, still stop-start, kept on until the hotel door was arrived at once more, and opened; the background noise then grew quiet and the only sound became that of my footsteps climbing the stairs. The images crossed the hotel, my hand reached out to open my bedroom door, and the camera honed in on the table where the sardine tin stood empty beside the laptop. I stopped the playback, rewound the tape, put it inside the camera again and, going out of the room intending to retrace my steps, pressed record. To the chapel once more, the noise just as loud in the background but more stop-start than before, entering my body as though some data were missing, which did nothing to shake my conviction that I was resounding inside a love that was physically completely unadulterated. I was back at the room again within twenty minutes. I sat down at the table, connected the camera again, the tape began to play, and everything was exactly the same as it had been the previous time, same sky of white footprints, same chapel belfry, same curved marks at the tideline and same frozen jetty, followed by my empty chair on entering the room. Only one thing had changed: the background noise was now louder on the tape than it was outside. I disconnected the camera. I still had my waterproof jacket, boots and gloves on from before; I rewound the tape again, pressed record, and again went outside, where, indeed, the noise had grown quieter. I once more retraced my steps, came back, watched the video. I repeated the operation several times over, and progressively the background noise in the recordings became louder, while at the same time growing quieter outside. It was close to dawn when, on my twentieth time out and back, the noise had dwindled completely outside the hotel and could be heard with utmost clarity on the playback. I had to rewind and watch it over again a number of times to be completely sure this wasn't some aural hallucination. I got up, opened the shutters a little way. The sun was coming up. It should have been my dinner time, but I wasn't the slightest bit hungry. In the daylight, I could see my muddy-snowy tracks, which at certain points went down as far even as the stone below. I put the tape on again; I thought perhaps I now understood: the successive recordings had been having the effect of *erasing the sound outside*. Such that the world outside the room was being stripped back and the pure love sound, with its pure associated fear, had been distilled in the tape in the form of a love that could be understood, a love with all the normal trappings, a kind of love apt to actually being digested. I had this tape now, I could take it with me and, any time I wanted to have that feeling again, all I needed to do was watch the tape and listen; above all *listen*. I then remembered the text I'd found weeks earlier on the lazaretto computer, the inmate making reference to a noise that cut through days and seasons and whose origin he had been unable to identify. And it came to me that – *yes* – the island was now in silence. And, I don't know how to explain why, but, as though magnetized, as though I myself had become a very fridge magnet, I went over to the minibar and opened the door. Untouched, the pregnant dog cookie and the bottle of breast milk. A wooziness came over me, quickly growing intense. The last thing I remember was tottering over to the bed. From that moment on, for almost a year, all trace of me is lost. A period I have no memory of whatsoever.

PART TWO

1.

The summer of 2015 saw me living in an apartment in the East Village, on East 3rd Street, between Avenues B and C. The nearby places of note were, to the north, a bar called Sidewalk – a haunt for musicians, and a place to get something to eat – and to the south, Houston Street – one of the city's main arteries, running all the way along the West Village, Soho and the Lower East Side – and to the west a CitiBank cash machine with a Spanish-language option that I stopped by every day to take forty dollars out, a kind of daily allowance I gave myself: always forty dollars. I already knew by then that it didn't matter how much money you carried around with you in that city, come nightfall it would have turned into a group of migratory birds.

I went and sat out on the terrace at Sidewalk late in the afternoon every day, when the low sun struck newspapers, cigarette butts, crushed cartons and puddles, giving rise to a new kind of urban skin. I usually had nachos and guacamole to eat, lager to drink. On one such occasion, I heard the unmistakeable rattle of Luis's motorbike coming down the street. He parked in front of my table. He was wearing a black polo shirt and black shorts; his arms and legs showed a surprisingly deep and uniform tan. He wanted to show me a text message he'd just received. A woman he was friendly with had invited him to an opening at a gallery in Red Hook, a mixed industrial-residential neighbourhood quite a long way out in South Brooklyn. It was a collective exhibition, he said, video installations. We ordered a couple of beers. A woman came by, she and Luis exchanged hellos, and the next day's party came up; she was invited too. She

didn't look working class to me, but had blue overalls
on, the kind car mechanics wear, and a jacket at least two
sizes too big. 'That's Lucy, she's a sculptor,' Luis told me
after she'd gone. 'She hit hard times, started working
as a carpenter. She makes furniture and sells it to boutiques on the Upper East Side. She's making a killing
now.' A couple of fire engines screamed past – could it
have been my apartment that was on fire, I wondered?
A mania of mine: however far away bad events may
be, I fear I'm going to be on the receiving end all the
same. 'It was such a shock you showing up at my door
the other day,' said Luis, 'you looked terrible, like you'd
just swum the Atlantic. How many years since we last
saw each other?' 'I don't know, a few.' 'Is the apartment
I got for you okay? It wasn't easy finding one in such
a great location at that price.' 'Yes, yes, all good, thank
you.' 'And do you know now what you've come to New
York for?' So I wouldn't have to admit that I didn't, that
I didn't even know how I'd come to be in the city, I said:
'Yes, yes, it was just the jet-lag that first day, I couldn't
think straight. I haven't come for anything in particular, clear my head a bit, do some writing, that's all. I
have a routine: I go to the Instituto Cervantes Library
in the morning, on 49th Street, to get out of the apartment more than anything; I take the subway there but
walk back afterwards. I read and do a little writing. It's
got a peaceful off-street garden with a fountain in the
middle. There's a mirror at the back of the garden, and I
have no idea what a mirror's doing in a garden, I always
thought gardens were mirrors in and of themselves, or
metaphors for some other thing, but it's one pointless
addition that I like; plus when I look in it, amazingly, I
find that I look alright. The building's a former stables
and inn – the old stagecoaches used to set off from there to

76

Boston. I usually work until 1 p.m. and, on my way back, sometimes take a small detour along the East River; I like looking across at the gap-toothed Brooklyn skyline. I find a bench and sit down, it's me and these guys who go fishing there. Not many people know the East River's really good for fishing – sole and cod in particular. The fishermen sit saying nothing, and I watch the things the river carries past. You can spend hours staring into that eddying mass: empty bottles, planks of wood from boats, weeds, seaweed, bits of plastic and dead fish, all spinning past, the water swallowing them down only to spit up different things that look exactly the same. What do you think?' 'Sounds like a pretty good programme to me,' Luis said. Knowing him to be a systematic avoider of the sun, I asked about his tan, which he said had come about as a result of inhaling pure oxygen. I laughed at this, though I didn't know why. He told me he'd very nearly died some months earlier, had technically been in a coma, because of an allergic reaction to something they put in some over-the-counter pills he'd been taking, not dissimilar to aspirin. 'It's a lie,' he said, 'this thing about tunnels and lights at the end of them when you're dying. What actually happens is you smell something, a smell that takes you back in time, way back, all the way to a thing you recognize as your very deepest memory, it's the smell of the cell, the fabric, the molecule you once were – or something along those lines, anyway. That's what I remember. Afterwards they told me they'd been pumping pure oxygen into me. When, after four days, I came round, I had this crazy tan all over. I've come to the conclusion it's because of the pure oxygen I was breathing day and night.'

At 6 p.m. the next day, he pulled up on his motor-bike outside my apartment with an extra helmet. When we arrived in Red Hook, having crossed Williamsburg Bridge and taken the East River road, we found that the exhibition was going to be inside a corrugated iron shed, recently repainted red, and the videos, most of which had no sound, were going to be interpreted live by a local band called Pink Rest In Peace, who were new to me. There was a guy cooking meat and vegetarian burgers on the pavement; just then, wearing a pair of gloves that looked gigantic to me, he was heating up the coals. We were then informed that the screenings weren't going to be inside the gallery but out in the open air, on a big screen. I looked around, couldn't see any big screens. A woman, Lucy no less, the one who'd stopped by at Sidewalk the previous day, pointed over at the jetty, where a group of artists were readying for a projection on the side of a lorry trailer. 'Us spectators are going to sit on that esplanade, on the ground,' she told me, 'the musicians are going be standing up, and the films are going to be projected onto the trailer canvas.' 'What about the lorry driver?' I said. 'We talked to him,' she said. 'He's going to be asleep in the cab.' She made a motion like she was pouring alcohol down her throat; he was drunk, or a drinker. Lucy was wearing the same outfit as the previous day.

The musicians showed up late. Musicians always show up late, and they still had to plug everything in and do the sound check. We ate hamburgers and drank beer as we waited. The crew's clothes, second-hand items intentionally ripped and frayed, struck me as tremendously sophisticated. At 8.30 p.m., over eight hundred of us went and sat down on the newspapers covering the esplanade. Before the projection, each artist took the microphone and introduced their respective pieces, short pieces, none of them longer than five or six minutes.

There were some genuinely good things, but the music, a sort of primitive Noise – something akin to La Monte Young or early Velvet Underground – struck me as quite dated to be accompanying such work. One of the closing pieces threw up some images that seemed familiar, though they flashed on and off too quickly for me to work out why. The artist who'd made this video had explained that it was to do with a previously unexplored aspect of the war in Afghanistan, namely relationships between American soldiers and Afghan civilians in the occupied territories. It featured testimonies from men and women involved in that war, but was underpinned by archive images from other wars where there had been analogous relationships. A few minutes later, I realized what the familiar images had been, as further images of San Simón came up, more obvious this time; a pair of men posing in a room, sufficiently close to the camera that the bridge from San Simón to San Antón was visible through a window in the background. The presence of a palm tree just outside the window seemed to suggest the photo had been taken in the very room I'd stayed in, or one of the ones on either side. I got up, said to Luis I was leaving, claiming my stomach was hurting, that the nachos at Sidewalk hadn't agreed with me.

On my journey home, during which I had to change subway train several times, I saw almost no one. A woman standing under a streetlamp in a park talking on her phone, while her son imagined he was playing a game with somebody. A young guy dressed up for a party who had to sidestep a rat at the stop for Lexington Avenue. At another stop, a sports bag, very large and with a gold finish, was half hanging out of a rubbish bin, and the light fell on it in such a way that it looked like a gigantic golden pip; the ridiculous thought occurred to me of this bolus as the generator for all of New York City's power, the mains switch for the whole island, or something along those lines, anyway. I walked the final part of the way down Second Avenue, with the photos of San Simón still playing in my thoughts, as though instead of me holding them in my memory, they had me inside them. I didn't stop to look in the shop windows as usual, which, if by day they are rivers that have been put on pause, by night and with the businesses closed, resemble hieroglyphics which I often lost myself in deciphering. It was a little after half past midnight when I got back to the apartment.

I was very much on guard the following days, going about with a kind of cautiousness I couldn't explain. One evening I asked Luis if he could put me in touch with the woman who'd made the video piece. He said he didn't know her personally, he'd need a couple of days to look her up, though as it turned out he got hold of her number that same day. He told me her name was Skyler, and helped make sure I'd be pronouncing it correctly, given my well-known facility (or otherwise) with languages. After we finished dinner, I sent her a text message. She replied the next day, saying I was welcome to go by her studio, which was on the Lower East Side, just a couple of blocks along Houston Street from my apartment on Henry Street, and when I got there I knocked on the door of a daylight basement, the street-level windows of which were miniscule. Almost immediately I heard footsteps approaching. We shook hands; both of us had bony fingers. I followed her down a level to the basement proper. The studio was divided into her workspace and office, with just a plywood panel as a partition; we sat on the office side. A song was playing which I immediately

recognized as something by Sparklehorse. 'The singer killed himself,' I said, as a way of breaking the ice.
'Yeah,' she said drily, 'I know.' Her short, spiky hair was
bright blonde, and she was wearing cut-off jeans, a loose,
plain dark shirt and sandals with a slight heel; anyone
would have said her features looked Eastern European.
I didn't say anything about my stay on San Simón, or of
course about the fact that I was a writer, just mentioning
how much I liked the video I'd seen in Red Hook, and
that I really wanted to know more about those particular images, where she'd come across them; I claimed I
thought they had been taken somewhere in my native
lands, that my interest was merely sentimental. I think
it was this word, 'sentimental', that made her relax. She
slipped her left sandal off and began dangling it on her
toes. She got up, opened the fridge, took out a couple of
soft drinks and gave one to me. From the same fridge,
she removed a semi-transparent plastic box, quite large
and not dissimilar to a lunch box, and put it down on
the table. Inside, a film can and lots of photos. I took out
a handful of the photos, they were freezing. 'Black and
white photos keep better in the cold,' she said. 'These
are all of a place called San Simón Island. Is that near
where you come from?' I nodded, and went on looking
through the pictures. 'I was given them by Antonio the
baker,' she continued, 'he's Spanish, Spanish as in from
Spain, he's got a bakery near here on Clinton Street, it's
a cafe too and they make my favourite cookies. Ever
since I've had a studio in this neighbourhood, that's
nearly five years now, I've been going to his bakery
for breakfast.' I sipped at the drink, it tasted awful, and
while pretending to be looking distractedly through
the photos nodded for her to continue. 'When Antonio
found out that I was an artist, and how a lot of my work

deals with wars from this century and the last, he told me he was in the Spanish Civil War, in an internment camp; how exactly he came to be in the States he didn't say, but a few days later he told me he had lots of photos of the war he'd been in, and if I wanted to look at them or use them as material he'd be happy to let me borrow them. I seemed trustworthy, he said, he couldn't see me going and stealing from an old man. A few days later he invited me up to his apartment above the bakery, and I looked the material over, and saw that some of the photos had him in them, him as a young man posing alongside another man, both dressed in sort of rural outfits, though it was obvious to me which one was the guard and which was the prisoner. The emotional bond between them was also clear. Antonio didn't say anything about that, and neither of course did I, but he did tell me it was the first time he'd ever shown anyone the photos; he was in his nineties now, he said, it was time somebody else saw them. And then, as Antonio went on talking, it struck me that the reason he'd kept it all to himself for so long wasn't the emotional bond with his jailer so much as the taboo at that time, and during that war in particular, of both betraying your side and your own sex. In fratricidal disputes, betrayal of one's own is the only utterly unforgiveable thing. There's an unconscious tendency to think that betraying your country is somewhat akin to the moment of leaving home – not a happy moment, but one that people will come round to in the end – but when it comes to a civil war, if you side with the enemy, well then you're basically asking for a savage dispute, the kind families descend into when there's a contested inheritance. Do you know what I mean?' 'Yes, yes, of course.' 'Well,' continued Skyler, 'if on top of all that, you're betraying your side to go off with someone of your own sex, that's like certain death. Everything that goes into us acting either cruelly or generously has its origin in, or can at least be explained by way of, the mechanisms of sex and war, it's like sex and war are representations, to-scale drawings, of far more than the firing of bullets and physical contact with other bodies.'

Skyler fell quiet then, and I broke the silence to ask if she knew Antonio's full name. She shook her head. I tried to convince her to introduce us, saying she and I could go to the bakery together, claiming, completely falsely, that I thought he might be a relation of mine. 'No, I don't think he'd like that,' she said, 'and even less if you think you might be related; if he left your country and never went back, there must be a reason. This is America, people don't have to explain themselves here.' I looked at my watch, it had been more than an hour and Sparklehorse was still playing. It was time I got going. Seeing me to the door, she smiled and wished me luck, not without first saying I should call her if I ever felt like going for a walk together. She had a nice smile, I said to myself as we shook hands again, though her teeth were very white. I'm suspicious of people with very white teeth.

I actually didn't go looking for the bakery, worried as I was that I'd be tempted to go in and start asking questions, when what I really wanted was to forget the whole story, which was suddenly taking up far too much of my headspace. Some days later, taking a small detour on my way to the CitiBank cash machine, I saw the bakery up ahead. It had a classic, 1950s-looking neon sign – 'Antonio's' – flickering eye-catchingly on and off over a lead grey awning. Feeling like I wanted to keep my distance, I instinctively crossed the street. I stopped opposite, also on instinct, to take the place in. The establishment was narrow, reminding me of my apartment, which also had something tubular about it, with white, yellowing wall tiles. At the counter, on the left hand side, an elderly woman served customers, and on the right there was a single row of tables, all unoccupied except for one with an old man sitting at it, the table top bare except for his hands placed in front him as he gazed out into the street. I guessed this had to be Antonio. Skyler hadn't been exaggerating about the bakery's popularity: the queue stretched almost out onto the street. After a minute, in which nothing changed, I went on my way, continuing to the CitiBank cash machine. Clouds moved in and a strange rain shower followed, the raindrops fat but dispersed, bringing with them that smell of wet city. Sheltering under the small cash machine awning, I put my card in the machine. The little motor inside started up with the usual assembly line crunch and whirr. As I waited for the instructions to appear, I looked at the little console framing the keyboard. Years of people resting their hands on it before keying in their pin numbers had worn the metal surface away, eroded it almost, the result being a curious sketch, which, apart from denoting the obvious fact that in New York City more people are right-handed than left-handed, reminded me of the peak of energy you see in depictions of the so-called Compton effect.

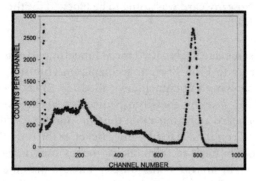

This being what happens when a stream of photons collides with any substance, which then causes another stream of photons to be released, in turn generating the energy peak on the right-hand side, this intense burst, which sometimes remains stuck inside the bombarded object. It's by no means a rare occurrence, it happens frequently, for example in each and every one of the millions of x-rays taken in hospitals around the planet, but in that moment it seemed to me something else altogether: as though every time someone took money out of the cash machine, the machine also sent a burst of light back at the person – a mechanism that would be like the passing of a very ancient baton, a pact, a fire, one that, like that endlessly burning Africa, will continue to rage on inside us. And then I saw the following exchange take place:

Person at cash machine says: 'Give me the fire.'

Cash machine ejects money and says: 'Take the fire.'

I heard someone behind me ask what the hell I was up to. A queue had formed. I'd missed the machine ejecting my dollar bills and then a security mechanism kicking in that meant it had sucked the money back up. Shit, I said. Now my card was going to be blocked for the forty-eight hours.

That same day, Luis called me at lunchtime. He suggested we go to Film Forum, a cinema on Houston. They were showing a documentary called *The Ballad of Genesis and Lady Jaye*, by the French director Marie Losier. I hadn't heard anything about the film, and far less the director. 'You'll have to buy me a ticket, is the only thing,' I said. 'I'm blocked from taking money out for the next forty-eight hours.' I was waiting outside the cinema at 9.50 p.m. The beginning of July, rain. To kill time, I looked at what was showing on the other screens. At 10 p.m. I felt my phone vibrate in my pocket. It was Luis, saying he wouldn't be able to make it, since his studio, which was on Havemeyer Street in Brooklyn, had flooded. 'At least I had all my work stacked on pallets,' he said. 'Shall I come over and help bail out?' I said. 'No need, the others here are on it already.' Straight away, and sacrificing much of my next day's food money, I bought a ticket and went in to see the film. The credits were rolling already. I was the only person in the auditorium. I took a seat in the middle, glancing all around, especially into the darkness at the back. I felt afraid. I got up and walked out again.

Rather than returning directly to my apartment, I decided to have a wander; the rain had left a fresh, cool night. With my few remaining dollars I stopped and ate at a Mexican food chain. A Tuesday, almost all the tables unoccupied. On the TV screen, images of the Wall Street Stock Exchange plummeting, followed by the then-Pope, Ratzinger, making an address: 'God doesn't fear the news. God is the News.' I had the amusing thought of seeing myself from out in the street, almost like something out of a Hopper painting. At the far end, a group of young guys were taking down some large helpings of frijoles; their night was only just beginning, I guessed, and this was them getting it off to a good start. A photo on the wall facing me, a snowy New York City scene, reminded me of my first visit to the city, January 2002, when it had been snow-covered as well. It was the first time I'd seen anyone getting a hair cut out in the street. I couldn't remember which street it had been on, but it was in the same area in which I now found myself. The barber was cutting hair whole handfuls at a time, like someone pruning a tree, though not without care. The locks of hair fell directly onto the snow. I'd gone by the same place again an hour later, and there was no sign of the two guys, only the locks of hair on the sidewalk – their contact with the snow had caused it to melt, leaving what looked like feline paw scratches from very ancient times. Hair stores information about all the things we eat and do, we carry thousands of hard disks around with us on top of our heads, I had thought at the time. I took lots of photographs of those locks. I didn't go by that place again during the rest of my first stay in New York.

I let a few days pass without having much contact with the world: no calls to Luis, not really checking email. But I went back to Antonio's, this time stopping directly outside and looking in the window. A light rain was falling. The same woman serving and Antonio at the same table, sitting in the same posture. The queue unfailingly long, people ordering watered-down coffees and half a dozen pastries or rolls to go. Then, suddenly, my nostrils flared at a familiar smell: breast milk. I looked carefully, and saw cookies in the shape of pregnant dogs arranged in a row in the glass display. I thought I was about to pass out, and turned and walked away as fast as my legs would carry me.

I tried to take my mind off Antonio's bakery. At the same time, I started to hear the sound of someone typing on a typewriter, somewhere out in the street, and particularly during the night; it still surprised me how little removed from us in time these machines are, when the sound of them seems so dated. Not that any of this meant I didn't become lost in thought at times, not that the writing didn't flow. The apartment, tubular and with a single window onto the street, conferred a rapid perspective on everything I wrote, like a person with all the run-up in the world to go and launch themselves into the empty air. Nevertheless, there were moments when my mind did veer in the direction of Antonio and his bakery, which, just a stone's throw from my apartment, I did all I could to avoid whenever some errand took me that way. Every few hours there would be the sound of people shouting in the attic above. I don't believe I've mentioned them: two individuals I can only describe as the imbeciles, students at Columbia, with whom I had no choice but to interact because we used

the same clothesline on the rooftop to hang our washing on. They'd drink and have the most monumental
arguments. Their Contemporary Lit professor lived
with them. The association, fundamentally unnatural,
and I believe sealed by the head-to-toe tattoos they all
three sported, meant they saved money for beer and, in
opposition to the Western tradition within which they
were being educated at Columbia, for eastern-inspired
books on natural living and self-help, which were the
basis of the lectures they tried to give me every time we
bumped into one another on the stairs or when hanging out our washing. I soon saw that the professor was
the ringleader; he wasn't technically living with them,
just had a room in the apartment for times when his wife
kicked him out, which was frequently. They grew tomatoes on the roof, saying it was more natural doing it up
there, which, given the pollution levels in Manhattan,
seemed unlikely. When our paths crossed and we got
talking, I tried to explain that this kind of cultivation
is altogether regressive and uncivilized, but they didn't
understand; neither did I push the point. Being rude to
them wasn't a good idea, given that they were close with
my landlady, whom I'd met through a friend of a friend
of a friend, Luis being one of the friends in this chain.
Chains of friends are something I'm very suspicious
of. As for the rooftop tomatoes, there's something else
to be said: the friends had hung the pots upside-down,
so that the tomato plants grew straight down, doing
gravity's bidding. This they claimed made the tomatoes better for you. I explained to them that growing
things in this way, in the same direction as the pull of
gravity, as well as being scientifically inconsistent, represented a redoubling of the uncivilized, given the fact
that the history of humankind is the result, precisely, of

89

the struggle against gravity, not a surrendering to the same, and that it's this struggle which has enabled the existence, after thousands of years of evolution, of fountains, which send water upwards rather than letting it flow downwards as rivers do, and of aeroplanes, which carry us from one place to another with no apparent effort, and of Columbia University itself, this inheritor of Hellenic thought, something that raised minds up rather than letting them go plunging down, but they never listened. In my view, they were a sect, and the professor the shaman, or the instigator at least. But they weren't bad people, not at all: for a very reasonable fee they let me use their washing machine down in the basement, which meant avoiding trips to the local launderette. I suppose my money went towards more self-help books and gravity-assisted tomato plants. The first and only time I set foot in their apartment, as we sat at a table which, though entirely covered in beer bottles, always seemed to have room for one more empty, they told me they were about to try growing broccoli, no easy thing on a rooftop in New York City, and that to them this represented a great challenge. As for their attire, something I found particularly unbearable was the fact the pair wore a black T-shirt – the same one, taking it in turns – which had the first line from Ginsberg's *Howl*: 'I saw the best minds of my generation destroyed by madness.' I one day said to them that the truly modern thing would be to make a T-shirt that said 'I saw the best minds of my generation destroyed by Facebook.' This made them laugh, a lot. I meant it, but they fell around laughing, laughing harder than I'd ever seen them do before, and that annoyed me even more.

2.

One morning, before setting off for the Instituto Cervantes, I called Luis to make a plan to meet up. He said that he could pick me up at five at my East River bench. I spent almost the entire morning in the library, on the first floor of the Institute, by the window that overlooks the interior courtyard and garden, with its central fountain and gravelled area, where the teachers sometimes take the students. Sitting on chairs arranged in circles, they'd play Spanish language games for beginners. I couldn't hear them through the window, but I saw their gesticulations, full of that emotion, somewhere between the histrionic and the bashful, which comes with the sense of mastering a language. I wasn't writing so much as looking up information on a subject that had been a side interest of mine for a number of years: the relationship between Manhattan Island and the creation of the atomic bomb in the Second World War. Not the most recondite of subjects, but not so well known either: parts of the city had served as centres for different phases of a project that in the end came to be named Project Manhattan. Really, at that moment my interest was to do with circumstance: seeing as Skyler's specialism was war, I wanted to have something to say for myself in case I saw her again.

Come the afternoon, when I got to my bench by the East River, Luis was already sitting waiting for me, his motorbike parked a little way off. I thought to ask him why it was that he always wore black shorts. Shorts, he said, to show off the sudden tan he'd come by when he was pumped full of the pure oxygen, and black because coming out of a coma meant having been resuscitated, having left the former Luis behind, so he was in a kind of mourning for himself. We both laughed, and saw the fishermen alongside us looking uncomfortable; holding their rods, they stayed deathly silent. The eddying water, particularly lively that day, sucked down and spat up all manner of objects. Luis pointed out the stench coming off the water, a hormonal, masculine smell, as though the East River was packed with men fresh out of the gym without a shower. 'But look, Luis, look at the way the objects all spin around and get sucked down by the water, and how other ones then instantly appear. Isn't that what New York City itself does with everything that comes within its bounds? I could spend days looking at the river churning and still not tire of it.'

I don't believe I'd finished making this point when there came a voice from behind us, and we both turned to look: 'I make that same point myself, my good men, and it all boils down to trash, blessed trash.' He was a man of about seventy, dressed in an ash-grey suit, pinstriped like a diplomat's, with a white shirt and cufflinks, brogues, blue eyes, hair to match the suit and a moustache with tips waxed to point straight upwards, a detail that made him look astonishingly like Salvador Dalí. He sat down on the bench beside us. I was about to say something, but he started talking before I could:

'My good men, trash is not a thing that should be recycled, the best thing is to leave it where it falls, one day we'll be buried by all the trash, it'll be the end of us, but not because of an excess of it, rather by default, and if we recycle it all, what will become of memory? How will we recognize our past selves if everything's already been radically transformed? Future archaeologists won't have any objects to work with, only files, computer files; oh, you'll have objects, yes, but only the ones we place in museums and other sites intended to transmit the most curated samples of our world to generations to come, and all of this, my good men, will be completely worth-less; bear in mind that everything useful we know about former civilizations is that which they left behind unin-tentionally, that which was accidentally dropped and forgotten about, the things they threw away and never bothered to gather or recycle, that's to say, their trash, it's this kind of random thing that truly tells us what past civilizations were like, and these things, the constants of the universe, are what join us to our forebears, because in the time to come there will be objects that neither change nor are capable of change, or, more precisely, and as paradoxical as it might seem, for a transformation to take place something has to remain the same, for example, in a chemical reaction everything changes, but the overall mass remains constant, and if it doesn't, the change can't take place, or, for example, consider the well-known story of Dr Jekyll and Mr Hyde, where the main character's personality changes, but his social en-vironment, his home and the city he lives in go virtually unaltered, because if that weren't so, if in that story ev-erything changed completely, there couldn't be a story, the narration would simply fizzle out, do you under-stand? Well, the same goes for trash, if we eliminate it or transform it into another thing altogether, recycle it in a wholesale way, we'll be disconnecting ourselves from history, our history, and that would mean ending up in a kind of reality parallel to the civilizations that went before us, while, paradoxically, remaining linked to them, and I really mean this, my good men, this isn't sci-fi I'm talking about, this is real life, anthropological-ly real, things that actually affect us, because if these constants cease to exist, that which we call memory would also cease to exist, for example, that bottle of wa-ter you're holding in your hands,' he pointed at Luis, 'you're going to drink it, and that will entail a transformation of that liquid inside your body, which you will then pass into the toilet at your home or right into the river here if you find yourself in need, but the only thing that will remain, the only thing to guarantee the memory of this act, of you drinking the water, is precisely the bottle, the empty bottle is the constant in the transformation of that shared water into your urine, urine that's exclusively yours, such that if we recycle the bottle and turn it into chairs or the doors for kitchen cabinets, the act of you drinking the water will be lost forever, hence why it's so important to bury trash, to create a ritual around it, conserving it in the same way we conserve the dead, that is, I mean, so long as we don't treat it the same way as we sometimes treat the dead, by which I mean cremation, because I don't know where this barbaric custom of burning bodies and scattering the ashes comes from, imagine if the Egyptians had done the same with their dead, we'd have no knowledge about their common people or their pharaohs, or no direct knowledge at least, all we'd have would be the texts they left behind, the inscriptions and papyruses, that's assuming we were able to decipher their language correctly, because we wouldn't be able to directly interpret their dead, do you see, my good men, what it is that I'm saying? So, with this onslaught of proliferating computer files and second-hand information, my idea is to create a union for the conservation of material in general, and for the prevention of recycling, because, believe me, otherwise everything's going to turn into computer files; believe me when I tell you all these text and image files we upload onto the internet really are hanging over us, they hang over us like the sword of Damocles, they're only going to come down and, wham, that'll be the end of us, it's like we're Sigourney Weaver and they're our very own Alien, such that it won't be us keeping these photos on our hard drives and computers but the other way around, it'll be them keeping us, do you see? And, I'll say it again, this isn't sci-fi I'm talking about here, I'm talking about real life stuff: Neil Armstrong goes to the moon and takes twenty photographs, the most important event of the twentieth century and there's only twenty photographs of it, but any teenage birthday party in this city, or any other city on the planet, will generate two hundred photographs-plus, is that not grotesque? Where's the sense in it? Where are we going to put all these images? In fact, by transforming them into digital files, files nobody will be able to read in a few years' time, since the programs needed to open them won't exist any more, what we'll actually be doing is obliterating those moments, they'll disappear and never come back, and what this amounts to is a slow but certain negation of material itself, nothing short of a disaster, but that's not even the worst of it, my good men, now we get to the nub, by which I mean the recycling of bodies, how we hate the body, with what furious intensity do we seek to do away with it; in centuries gone by hatred of the body only manifested in war, in killing, in laying waste directly to that which lives in the flesh, but nowadays this has moved into the realm of aesthetics, I'm referring to all the different surgical techniques employed in the name of aesthetics, all the many ways there are now of transforming the flesh, because we're obsessed with the idea that the body is something that holds back progress, that the body is, in and of itself, something harmful, that the body prevents History from progressing, and thus we seek to eliminate it, by pitching it into the mortal conflict of war, or by subjecting it to aesthetic surgery, even though this is actually the direct opposite of war: it's us imagining the body to be eternal. Yes, war and surgery are at odds with one another, but they speak to the same thing, two sides of the same coin, each being a negation of flesh and the body; this is an idea that goes way, way back, consider, for example, cathedrals, which arrayed all their grandiose architectural excess against the human body in order that, when a person set foot inside, that body would be reduced by comparison, made altogether insignificant, in order that the human body, thus overawed and outweighed, would disappear in the face of a divinity far, far greater than it, or consider for a moment any number of modern-day architectural feats, – airports, for example, they're a place in which the body seems willed to disappear, it's as though the people who design and direct those aeronautical monstrosities are trying to tell you that your body is a throwback, something primitive, something that creates a drag on the flow of events, a kind of leftover superfluity that would be better off disappearing, and sooner rather than later, and tell me, is this not terrible? We create places that do not tolerate leftovers, places in which everything must circulate in a frictionless manner, no excreta, no wastage, this, my good men, is an entirely religious way of experiencing the body – and have you ever noticed the fact that most airports are designed in the shape of a cross? If you view bird's eye images of them, you'll see, for all the walkways and satellite terminals they may have, their basic form is a plain crucifix, like cathedrals, and this is no coincidence, the idea is that everything inside them should disappear, my good men, I haven't been outside Manhattan in years or taken a flight for this very reason, so as not to confront this airport-crucifix, and what we see is that in airports, the idea is for everything to be recycled, they're places in which bodies are supposed to forget the flesh, to leave it behind, turn it into a computer file to circulate from place to place with no deterioration whatsoever, everything that goes on in there is part of a great aesthetic surgery, as if there were one gigantic body with portions of flesh being continually removed; we're at war, believe me, we're at war, it's the conservation of material versus the disappearance of the flesh, remembering versus forgetting, hence my interest in everything to do with trash, the conservation of trash, in a sense we ought to be its guardians, there aren't enough rites or temples, however big, to do justice to the waste we create, this is why when I saw you here, sitting so neatly, so diligently, so alike to a couple of altar boys in the face of something you don't even understand, sitting so symmetrically, even, before this churning river – which you gaze upon, but clearly don't understand – I felt sorry for you both, don't be offended but I did feel very sorry for you, because this great spiralling mass, the origin and destination of which are both unknown, represents the trash that's been spat out after a great deluge, that which the storm washes through, and it seems to me that the soul of trash must by necessity reside in this churning mass, a soul I go looking for, I look for it every day in the streets, I've spent years looking for it, and, my good men, I want to take this moment to tell you that I have written a great deal concerning this city, I have dedicated a number of books almost exclusively to it, and there are my memoirs as well, which doubtless you're aware of given their worldwide fame, this city makes innumerable appearances in all my work, and, every time it does, what I'm actually seeking to do is this: to find the soul of its trash. Allow me to tell you a story now, the story of what this was all like when I first came to the city, but first you'll have to allow me to go off on a tangent and make a few clarifications as well. Are you in a hurry at all?' 'No, no,' we both said, almost in unison, and not knowing very well why. 'Well, as you'll see, there are certain subjects that, by their nature, generate paradox, apparently irresolvable problems we struggle to comprehend, and one such subject is computation, something to be expected given that any union between humans and machines can't help but produce serious objections of a philosophical kind. In 1965, the computational theorist Edsger Dijkstra put forward what he called the paradox of the dining philosophers, which is simple enough, and I believe can be stated in the following way: five philosophers sit around a circular table to debate ideas and eat noodles. As you know, in order to eat noodles, you need two chopsticks, but in this case, each philosopher has only one chopstick, situated on their left-hand side. If they all decide to eat at the same time, and they see that in order to do this they each have to take the chopstick belonging to the person on their right, they'll remain eternally blocked, forever waiting, one among them needing to let someone else use their chopsticks so that at least one of the others may eat. Thus, prevented from eating their noodles, sooner or later all will die of hunger. In the field of computation, this situation is known as *death by starvation*, and it comes about when one computer is indefinitely denied access to a resource shared with other computers, so that, as occurs with the philosophers and their noodles, it's impossible for the computer to carry out its task, putting it into a self-defeating loop before it eventually burns out. But what I want to draw your attention to is the lapse before that death, the lapse during which the philosophers sit with chopsticks raised, in suspension, on pause. This *pause mode* is something I find to be of tremendous significance. When I used to fly, I'd never wear those travel pillows that get prescribed for cervical pain, and yet, many years ago, the last time I took a flight, from Madrid to New York, to be specific, in the hope of some respite from intense back pain I'd been suffering since falling off a cliff in Port Lligat, I did wear one of those travel pillows, which I'd bought at Madrid-Barajas itself, and had a rather silly design featuring a multitude of Bugs Bunnys and Tweety Birds. The flight attendants soon came round to perform their mechanical handouts of the food trays, and, hoping it would help me to sleep, and though I'm not a drinker, I asked for a glass of red wine and some water, which it was my custom to mix in equal parts when travelling. Then, when the cabin lights were dimmed, and only the emergency exit signs were left on, conferring on the low-lit space the sensation of truly being inside a temple, I decided I'd watch one of the in-flight movies. To my surprise, in among the rom-coms and kids' movies, one of the options was *The Shining*. I couldn't even remember how many years it had been since I'd seen that movie. Soon enough I was presented with the opening images in which the family, driving in their Volkswagen Beetle, come winding along the freeway in the Rocky Mountains, one of them pointing out that pioneer wagon trains had become lost in the same area, and, after months without food, those pioneers had been forced to resort to cannibalism. The trio in the car went into great, mechanical detail on that macabre story, as though they were a machine, as though, within the first minute of the movie, they were all dead already. Their conduct wasn't so different, I thought then, to that of the air stewardesses obliging me to choose between the chicken or pasta options a few minutes earlier in metallic, mega-phone voices. I believe I closed my eyes shortly before the famous part where the twin girls hold hands. I can't say how long exactly I slept for, but when I opened my eyes again the movie was still playing, and the cabin was still dark. I raised my blind a crack; it was dark outside as well. The mixture of wine and water had had its effect, the moment had come to eliminate that which the body didn't need. I pressed pause on the screen, extracted my-self from the Bugs Bunny-Tweety Bird travel pillow, and went to the bathroom. I was quick. On my return, having made my seatmate get up once again – she was trying to sleep too – I was about to press play, but the still image on the screen made me hold off. To my aston-ishment, the twins had been directly overlaid by the columns of the pause icon, columns that were also twins. It seemed such an extraordinary coincidence to me that I took a picture of it. I've got it here, look:

'I didn't dare touch it for the rest of the journey; I left the image exactly as it was. What do you think, my good men? It gives me shivers just looking at it. I'd now like to take you back a lot further in time, to 1881, when Adolphus Washington Greely, a First Lieutenant in the American navy, was given the mission of leading an expedition to the Arctic, to go and map and carry out geological studies in those latitudes, still largely unexplored at that time. On July 7, he set off from Newfoundland on board the steamer *Proteus*. After a year-long expedition, and having gathered highly valuable data on the north-east coast of Greenland, he went back the following winter as part of another expedition, this time on dog sleighs, and after a difficult journey decided to set up camp not far from Cape Sabine, where food and supplies were supposed to have been left for them by another ship. On arrival, they found twelve lemons wrapped in newspaper, placed on some rocks. And that was all. They didn't know – they had no way of knowing – that the supply ship, having offloaded these twelve symbolic lemons, in reference to the Twelve Commandments (it was usual in those days for sailors to make such religious references), had sunk before delivering the second, full consignment. This left the crew of the *Proteus* having to survive the winter with the only animal present in those latitudes – the Arctic hare – as their sole source of food. Believing this would see them through, they cooked hare day and night, but any sailor, any person at all, who fails to complement such a diet with other foodstuffs will soon enter a prolonged state of slight drunkenness, which will very soon give way to overwhelming hunger pangs, which will persist no matter how much they then eat, and which will soon lead to their death. When they were rescued several months later, of the original crew of twenty-five, only six were still alive. Nobody found an adequate explanation for such a death toll. Initially cannibalism was suspected.

The plentiful supply of hare would suggest that the eating of human flesh would have come about merely as something to pass the time, or as part of some aberrant ritual practices they'd recently been exposed to; there was even talk of a pagan religion having sprung up among them, with First Lieutenant Greely as the main celebrant. In one of its most extreme versions, the accusation took the following form: the twelve lemons recalling the Twelve Commandments had been taken by those shipwrecked sailors as a resounding symbol of negation, not only a rejection of Christianity but an all-out attack on that religion, hence the human sacrifices and hence the unashamed ingesting of the victims thereafter. One sacrifice for each lemon. Once the twelve lemons had been matched, the lust for human flesh had taken hold among the men to such a degree that the slaughter went on unabated, leaving, by the end, just those six survivors. These accusations, levelled at them for at least a year after their rescue and return, were thrown out after the ship's logs were consulted, and no mention of unnatural practices found. For their part, the accused declared that they could barely remember those lost months, as though, for them, the land and the sea had themselves ceased to be in motion. One Doctor Kern, who had attended the survivors on their return, dubbed this collective memory loss "the great pause". Over the years, the suspicions of cannibalism diminished. When he was ninety-five, shortly before his death, First Lieutenant Greely would be awarded the Medal of Honor for his work expanding and mapping the United States' borders, though the award was not without controversy given that one of the requisites is that you have to be fully aware of your actions and heroic intentions, a requisite clearly contravened by the memory loss, by that "great pause", from which he still suffered. It would take medical science many more years to come up with a satisfactory explanation for death due to ingestion of hare meat over long periods, a pathology that has subsequently been named "leporine starvation", and is directly linked to a diet of pure protein. I quote the explanation, which is in a book, from memory:

> At the onset, more and more meat is ingested, until, after a week, the amount of meat being consumed has multiplied three- or four-fold. At this moment, if fats are not also being ingested, signs of starvation will become apparent, as well as poisoning due to an excess of proteins. Food is taken in considerable quantities, but the hunger never goes away; the subject will suffer from a distending of the overfull stomach, and will experience a sense of futility and considerable disquiet. After a period of seven to ten days, diarrhoea will set in, and only be alleviated, again, if fats are taken on. Death will follow after a number of weeks.

'This fragment, which explains the wherefores but not the origin of the "great pause" referred to by the survivors, comes from the book *Good to Eat* by the anthropologist Marvin Harris, whom, as it happens, I was lucky enough to meet in this same city: a great man. Aside from this, death by protein intoxication also makes an appearance in various works of fiction, for example in *The Tin Drum*, in which one of the main characters, a woman, decides to commit suicide by shifting to a purely fish diet over a long period of time, the most radical case being raw eels – pure protein – which by the end she's eating nonstop. Nevertheless, in certain central European cultures, there's more than five hundred years' evidence of this protracted form of suicide having been a recourse for those looking for a discreet way out of this life. And then, like I was telling you, after stepping off that flight, the last flight I've ever taken, once I'd got to my apartment here in New York City, I spent several days looking at the photograph of the pause icon superimposed over the bodies of the twin girls in *The Shining* and at myself, too, in a full-length mirror, sometimes fully clothed, sometimes naked, and in either case found that I was starting to waste away, looking really not well. I'm not trying to suggest that the two things were linked, but in my mind a link did form between the pause icon on top of the twins in *The Shining*, geometric and filiform, and my haggard state. And it was during that time that I began to think of the five philosophers, whom I pictured holding their chopsticks in the air, all of them wasting away, all of them also on pause, and how they too were going to starve to death, and I felt great sorrow on their behalf. At the same time, Adolphus Washington Greely's expedition, and everything about his odyssey of the great pause and the bodies it involved, began to have a greater presence in my days, worrying as I did that I was going to suffer the same fate. But more than anything I was visited by another class of thoughts, memories, really, taking me back to travels I'd been on around the world: thoughts and memories that were of no help to me since my reflections on the subject of trash were already beginning to dominate my life, and meant that I had no choice but to stay on here, in New York City, temple of detritus. Added to that was the fact my English was finally up to scratch. And I had only started learning it a few short years earlier, thanks to a residency in Austin, Texas. My method for learning the language had been simple, but to explain it properly I need to briefly go back a couple of years further, to a week I spent in the city of Algiers, where I'd been invited to take part in the international contemporary art fair. There was nothing left of the Algiers my good friends Albert Camus and Jacques Derrida had known; not only the capital, but the entire country had been taken over by radical Islamic factions, with the educational institutions, and, consequently the minds of the populace, the first to have been captured. A process that had begun, a civil servant at the Spanish Embassy told me, with a fanatical and exclusionary version of Islam being injected into the lower classes, penury-stricken and with a cultural understanding practically null. Once this match was lit, and given the numerical superiority of this section of the population, this radical version of Islam had spread unstoppably. So, when I arrived in Algiers, women were already banned from smoking in public, there was gender separation in queues for public institutions, and come six o'clock in the evening the streets would be deserted. As for the international contemporary art fair, it boasted a large library, but 99 per cent of the books were on religious topics or indeed just versions of the Koran. This experience of mine in Algiers, and in view of the well-known facility of religious language for burrowing into most people's brains, was of use to me, as you'll see, because I could then apply this "religious method" to myself; when I then went to Texas, this entailed dividing my time between beginners' language classes and shutting myself inside my apartment to watch television. I found a couple of channels showing old, classic content, series with a fanatical Catholic edge passed through a Calvinist filter, *Rifleman*, *McMillan and His Wife*, *Highway to Heaven*, this kind of content, all very easy to understand in terms of

105

vocabulary and plot lines, and almost always taking the form of religious parables, because both things – religion and language – were in this case directly interlinked. That was a sure-fire way for me to get a grip on the English language. And my approach never varied: I'd go by a gas station a few blocks from my apartment for a litre tub of cheesecake ice cream and a can of beer, putting it all in a non-transparent plastic bag, walk those few blocks home, almost always in full sunlight, a route that would see me pass at least three or four different Austin urban subcultures. This included a white guy, very fat, who sold cassette tapes of his own music on the sidewalk. One day I stopped at the sheet he invariably spread on a corner – frequented more by tumbling pieces of wastepaper than people – and asked him about his music. He had a cassette player there so that the buyer could try before buying. He'd only let you listen to the first minute of the first song on each tape; he had one of the clocks they use in chess matches to time you. All the tapes seemed the same to me, American folk of the lazy variety, a singer with his guitar and no other accompaniment besides. In the end, out of compassion more than anything, I bought a tape for two dollars which had the words "Crime of the Century" written in childish handwriting in red marker on it, and which, to be clear, had absolutely nothing in common with Supertramp's record of the same name. The lyrics, he said, were included, printed out on photocopies inside the cassette box. This was how I first came across the story of Greely's Arctic expedition. One of the songs, the third one on the B-side to be specific, recounted the odyssey of the *Proteus*, the winter spent on Cape Sabine, the twelve lemons, the Arctic hare ingestion and the ensuing death of nineteen crew members. He sang as though it was the story of the

106

death of a loved one, but here's the thing, it wasn't written from the point of view of the explorers, but rather that of the hares. They were the ones speaking, which made the whole thing pretty strange and, if possible, even more moving. I also heard about the paradox of the philosophers and their noodles for the first time from that cassette, in a song that had a spoken delivery, while the guitar strummed a sequence of what seemed to me the same chord over and over. But that was just that one day. Generally, I went directly from the gas station to my apartment, which was on the top floor, and there lowered the blinds, and spent hours watching the series I mentioned. These I complemented with the twenty-four-hour Rosary Channel, which, as the name suggests, features an uninterrupted recitation of the rosary, with images of saints and Bible scenes and suchlike sliding past. So it happened that in six months of applying myself in this way, I'd learned more English than in years of attendance at prestigious language schools. And so it was that I found languages to be intimately connected to religion, whose intellectual representative they are, their visible, lay versions, as it were. In this way, every language is the manifestation, the reflection, of a profoundly religious structure greater than it, a characteristic that only becomes apparent through the kind of close observation, experimentation and effort I had partaken in. But what happens, I wondered, when, as has so often occurred in history, a language becomes extinct, disappears, and turns into trash which nobody can recycle? Well, what happens then is that the language enters a pause mode – or, better put, it becomes an eternal pause. This is what's tragic about a language dying out: not the loss of the language itself or even the attendant culture and all the learning that goes with it, but the fact

that the religion sustaining the language is lost; this religion enters a great and eternal pause. And this certainty
crystallized in my mind when, on my return, here in
New York City, I applied my mind to the observation of
the paused image of the twins in *The Shining*, or when I
thought about the philosophers with their chopsticks
never-endingly aloft, also on pause, or the story in the
Great Explorers book – which I bought in the Strand
Bookstore for next to nothing and sat up late reading
and rereading – of the hare meat-eating sailors on their
Arctic odyssey. And with that, it wasn't long before a
feeling of spiritual incompleteness came over me. It was
this that led me during the following months to start
paying attention to objects abandoned in the streets, certain ones in particular: those that were part of other
objects, for example nails, screws, pieces of wood, engine parts, as well as objects intended for building or
repairing other objects, for example a hammer, packing
tape or a section of rope. It was only then that I noticed
the way people, when they walk by such detritus, and
small or insignificant as the detritus may be, linger over
it and seem to want to take it with them. My sense is that
this is a natural instinct, one that means we are constantly concerned with the act of building, with being gods.
True, we human beings are fundamentally destroyers of
things – we're naturally predisposed to destruction and
we take pleasure in it, which is entirely normal – but it's
no less true that when we come across the bits and pieces
of some formerly assembled thing, we believe we feel
that Creation itself is by our side. There's no greater
pleasure for the neuronal network than to imagine the
combinatory possibilities offered by these bastard materials we've just happened to find. I then gave up my usual
habit of walking looking upwards – I've always had a

liking for the facades of buildings, for clouds, for balconies – and began walking instead always looking down at the ground: trawling that network of objects of which the ground beneath our feet is comprised. And I realized – a eureka moment, almost – that this was similar to another entirely normal activity: that of wandering clothes stores looking for things to buy, things to wear, mostly, which nonetheless does nothing to satisfy the ridiculous vanity of accumulating belongings that act as representations of our money in any of its possible versions, paper money or credit card money. I realized that this makes buying things a kind of roaming or roving or drifting that is as addictive as it is merely symbolic; to buy things is the same as picking up trash, a kind of roaming or roving or drifting over to which I, secure by this point in my mastery of English, devoted myself utterly. And at that stage of New York City's development, Soho had already become a tourist area with the highest density of fashion boutiques per square metre anywhere on the planet. I rented an apartment on the Lower East Side, less than ten minutes' walk from Soho. I immediately went in search of objects and clothing to throw my money away on: in Prada, in Chanel, in Marc Jacobs and in small boutiques so select they didn't even have names, I went around them all, buying something in each and every one, things I lost interest in after a matter of days or, even while they still held an interest for me, were at the same time disappointing – you only had to read the list of component materials to see how truly commonplace it all really was: cotton, terlenka fabric, nylon, this kind of thing. Then I went to the Zara on Fifth Avenue, unrivalled temple of vulgar pretentiousness, and bought a large number of plain grey T-shirts, the cheapest ones they had, took them back to my apartment and scrawled "The Crime of the Century" on the chests in black marker pen. I then spent a number of days wearing suit trousers, my brogues, all the best makes, topped off by one of these cheap T-shirts I'd written on, and going around the same places where I'd blown hundreds and hundreds of dollars, but this time not spending a dime. I know that the security guards were always struck by the picture I presented, and this was redoubled if we keep in mind what was written on my T-shirt, ultimately an allusion to the extinction of the human race. But even I didn't really know what I was trying to achieve with that elaborate manoeuvre. I went into the stores and came back out again wearing my T-shirt, yes, and some of the people working in the stores stood waiting for something to happen, and others' jaws hit the floor, but every time something was missing, something that would have given me a sense of wellbeing and a genuine feeling of violence or friction with these commercial outlets. All in all I failed: going into the stores and making purchases was actually far more fulfilling. I saw that I had to take it a step further: I had to unbridle myself by means of a solution that was even more radically elaborate. I put those Zara T-shirts to one side and spent a day going around all the main clothes stores in Soho, buying T-shirts in each of them, always T-shirts with some symbol or bit of writing that made it clear which brand they were. The whole operation cost me quite a bit, some $800 as I remember it. In my apartment, a studio apartment with nothing to it but an adjoining bedroom and kitchen, a single bed and a table with an adjustable lamp, I again got out the marker and wrote on these T-shirts: "The Crime of the Century". The next day, I put on the Prada T-shirt, now, as I say, doctored with my own writing, and waited for early evening, when the sun was at its lowest, making my shadow stretch further out behind me on the sidewalk: a dramatic effect I considered fundamental to that phase of my plan, although, a number of hours later, walking down Prince Street on my way to the Prada store, it turned out to be totally irrelevant. When I got there, the security guard on the door immediately recognized the transformation the T-shirt had undergone; I observed him whispering something into the mic on his headset, alerting his colleagues, I supposed, the ones hidden on the other side of the nearly fifty CCTV cameras in the shop, probably sitting in offices situated in other continents. I nodded at the man and then made for the stairs that led down to the lower floors, imagining my figure, wiry, quite elegant, under the constant scrutiny of those hidden watchers, who would be squinting at their little low-resolution screens to try to make out the words on my chest next to the Prada logo, "The Crime of the Century", and I then felt a strange charge run through me, through my muscles and internal organs, a hardening of all my bones with all the power of the Prada brand, with all its salaried employees, all the pay cheques and social security payments and work clothes that were part of the operation, the shop designs that were the most costly in the world, its courses in customer relations and all the things I could imagine and many things I could not, things we can barely begin to get to grips with when it comes to the running of major brands, yes, all the power of Prada condensed inside my body then, in my T-shirt, in my figure as I went on moving between the different sales stands inside the store. It's well known that actors and actresses, especially those who work in theatre, are utterly unbearable to be around; when you're with them all talk has to be about them, and if not

111

they'll become frustrated, there's never a moment in which they won't turn things around to the subject of them, their own bodies, nobody has an ego as brazen as actors and actresses, but going around that Prada shop, I realized why this is: they're aware that the moment they set foot on stage, the second their mouth opens, however minor or halting the utterance may be, their body is the epicentre and gathering point of effort, work, talent and money on the part innumerable individuals over the years, it's all directed at this, their body, this moment, this seemingly innocuous twitch of a muscle or apparently insignificant word. And so, feeling myself observed by dozens of cameras in the Prada store, while wearing my customized Prada T-shirt, that same feeling of power came over me. As is also well known, Americans have no sense of lying as a vehicle for humour, they take things very seriously, such that, as is the way in this country, it wasn't long before salespeople of both sexes started coming over to me and very respectfully asking if there was anything I needed, and that if there was, all I had to do was let them know, to which I replied, my English straight out of a TV series and certainly Bible-tinged as well, "No, no thank you," but that I'd keep it in mind, and then I started lingering longer than was normal over the clothes racks, the ones carrying T-shirts, to be specific, which put the security guards inside the shop even more on edge and, needless to say, the CCTV watchers all across this and other continents. After half an hour, I was really struggling to think of how to conclude my act so that when I got back to my apartment that night and found myself sitting in front of the TV with a plate of frozen beans, I wouldn't feel ridiculous. Then, deciding I'd play up to the corporation, and not knowing very well what I was looking for, I headed for the accessories section, where I went around scrutinizing the items for sale very close up, leaning in and, as you see experts doing, taking off my glasses and putting them back on in a show of trying to see these things better. Nothing took my fancy particularly, until a display featuring some very expensive walking sticks caught my eye. And the thing is, before his untimely death, the designer Alexander McQueen, in an undoubtedly retro move, and one not without a certain comedy, had developed a walking stick line for Prada, items that had quickly been taken on, taken seriously, by people with a lot of money to spend, leading to a sudden preponderance of these walking sticks, which were of course merely decorative and entirely unsuited to actually helping anyone suffering from any kind of limp or other physical problem. I picked one of them up: brown, pearly, the tip a silver metal and the handle, of the same material, featuring a miniature golden sunflower motif. $599. I asked if it was in the summer sale, they said that it wasn't; the seasonal discounts couldn't be applied to these accessories. People who know me know about my obsession with unsettling store clerks, but none of them have actually seen me in full flight since it's only when I'm on my own, when no one's there to watch, that I really do my worst, such that they don't know the heights of sadism my insidious methods are liable to reach. To explain: my opening sortie is to ask the shop clerk something banal, nothing of import, and once they've answered I ask something else, connected to my previous question but more complex, and when they answer again, again I come up with another question, and when the shop clerk thinks they've worked out my methodology, a methodology which up to this moment we could call "the arrow tip", aimed at a very specific point, I come with another question, one which, though not un-connected to what we've been talking about, is only so very tangentially, and the clerk will have to scrabble to pick up the new thread with me, after which I begin with a further battery of questions, guided by the same logic as previously, so not a completely crazy logic, more, let's say, hazy: an approach that proceeds by way of what we could call pseudo-logical blocks, always, clearly, very respectful on my part, to the point of me even making myself appear slightly bumbling. This explanation makes it seem like a futile game, an attempt on the part of a perfect idiot to embarrass people, but the experience of it is quite different, what occurs is an outright twin-ning of the store clerk and myself, a union of the materiality of the product on sale with my body and the body of the clerk, an equilateral triangle in which the three actors enter a continual swapping of roles and ex-change of emotions that are both frankly sublime and contradictory. To top it off, as I've said, Americans are excessively polite people, so that, as long as you stop short of anything really socially unacceptable, it's possi-ble to hold a completely insane dialogue with an American that seems nonetheless informed by logic, as long as it isn't you who goes first in breaking some tacit or indeed written law, all of which makes them perfect for this kind of prank. All they care about is the struc-ture of things, not the flesh, as though they were French thinkers from the post-war era, but at the same time they're utterly rustic, people guided by a military kind of logic. All of which makes them, for resilience and self-control, the best candidates for my ingenious tor-ture methods. Also to clarify, in case it ever occurs to you to try any of what I'm describing in this city, don't be fooled, the moment you slip up, however small the slip-up may be, they'll come down hard on you with a quirk native to them, something called irony, a thing hardly ever used in Latin countries but widespread in these latitudes, to the point that it's come also to be a pillar of their literature and of their politics in the last hundred years. And, speaking of lies, let me tell you something: we know that Cain killed Abel and that afterwards, so that God wouldn't see, buried him. This was the first burial in history. My sense is that what God found so unacceptable wasn't the death of Abel at the hands of his brother Cain, but the secret burial, the attempt to hide the body away, that's to say: the lie. It's also my sense that God didn't throw Adam and Eve out of Paradise for disobeying Him and eating the apple, but because they tried to blame it all on the serpent: again, lying presents itself as the worst of all forms of logic. And this and nothing else was the reason why, in the Prada store that day, I had to be very careful not to be caught in my dialectical attempts to make the shop clerk's head spin; Anglophone culture is the direct inheritor of that visceral, almost pathological rejection of lying, in direct opposition with Catholic countries, where, as is well known, lying is something utterly integral to the everyday, also providing the deep structure for all that's considered civil and decent. So anyway, the clerk in the Prada store held his own pretty well as I quizzed him on the walking stick, and while my questions became more and more tortuous and involved, delivered in my aptly biblical English. To say the clerk "held his own" – that was only really true initially, given that my sadism reached such a pitch that he himself started to enjoy it, a rupture thereby taking place of the contractually sacred and always invisible barrier of buyer/seller; in effect, the two of us became one, there ceased to be anything separating us, a seduction and confusion of market economics lasting only brief seconds, which mustn't be allowed to continue lest it ruin your day completely, to come back to haunt you in the way I've just been describing. So I informed the young man – who, it also happened, couldn't take his eyes off my T-shirt – that I had decided to buy the walking stick. When he went to put it in wrapping paper for me, I said there was no need, I'd take it as was. Using it to walk with, and not putting on any kind of limp, I crossed the store in the direction of the exit. I could imagine the faces of the CCTV watchers at their filthy little screens, trying to decipher the why and the ultimate significance of all those movements. As I was leaving, the security guard on the door whispered something into the headset mic, for a moment taking me back to old photographs in a book called *Races of the World* that I used to look at when I was a boy on days when I was off school sick: tribesmen with large pendulous earrings that were more than mere adornments, in fact denoting very specifically their status within the tribal community. When I stepped outside the store, it was practically night. With very few people around, Prince Street was bathed in the final, low rays of sunlight, shining from the far side of America and lighting up all the trash on the sidewalks. The walking stick made a light metallic tap as it struck the paving slabs. Though in reality it wasn't metallic, but somewhere between metallic and pneumatic, a noise I had never heard before, and which struck me as odd. I'm a fan of Noise music, which I know practically all iterations of, from the use of the sounds made by early computers through to the analogue approach of religious types from Asia, and taking in, of course, traditional Western rock versions of Noise, and yet I have never heard a musical note like the one created each time the tip of that walking stick struck the Manhattan sidewalk. To me, this new sound was the true stroke of genius in that object, the secret goal that, before his death, the designer Alexander McQueen had scored for so-called world music. I crossed a number of streets, kicking coffee cups from my path, promotional flyers, bags with smiley faces that looked more sardonic to me than ever. The sun moved into alignment with the rectangle of Manhattan's east-west axes, and it was then that I felt the last ray of sunlight hitting me, and the words "The Crime of the Century" ablaze on my chest, and the whole T-shirt in flames, flames that burned but did no harm. My shadow, drama-tized to the point of paroxysm now with the addition of the walking stick, joined together with the shadows of the skyscrapers, together forming an unbroken, contin-uous flame. Two Chinese men, feverishly smoking cigarettes, crossed the street at my approach. As I got closer to my apartment, very little daylight left now, the feeling of victory also began to wane as it struck me that, even though I had managed to violate, in the clearest manner possible, the honour of one of the most powerful corporations on earth, in the end, carried along by a pure exhibitionistic streak, I had still let that same corporation seduce me so that, in pure contradiction of my act, I had spent close to $600 on a walking stick, one of the most expensive and pointless products in the entire store. The whale cannot be killed from inside its belly, I said to myself; evil takes many forms, the most common being when you convince yourself you've defeated it. I imagined the hundreds of CCTV watchers, at their screens on their various continents, now send-ing one other messages, having a good old laugh at my expense. It was Sunday: trash collection day in the

117

neighbourhood. When I got to my building, I pulled open one of the trash bags piled up outside the door to the street, and put the walking stick in it. I then took the T-shirt off and put that in as well. Before tying the bag up, the light from the streetlamp allowed me to read the words "The Crime of the Century" one last time, there among food scraps and a quantity of dog food cans. Bare chested, I took the stairs. I entered my apartment, it was warm, I took my pants off. In only my boxers, I reheated some beans left over from my lunch earlier on, when the sun had been at its highest, when, as in a great pause, there had been no shadows in the city. I have been combing this city ever since then, my only desire to find that walking stick and that T-shirt, soul of my trash. They must be somewhere.'

His speech ended there. He sat gazing out at the churning river.

We should, I suppose, have laughed, said something at least, but it didn't happen. A few seconds dragged by, we stood up, said we were going.

Looking back, I saw the man still sitting there watching the water. Luis and I went over to the motorbike, I told him I'd rather walk. I watched his helmet until it became lost among the traffic. I set off for my apartment. On the corner of Fourteenth Street and Second Avenue, a few teenagers were having a fire in a miraculously undeveloped empty lot. They weren't cooking food, they just threw bits of paper and tables and chairs into the flames, and stood staring into them, the flickering blaze mingling with that of the sun, which was close to setting. Their silhouetted bodies, scrawny and underfed in the eyes of an overfed society, seemed to me figures of a very ancient culture, one even anterior to tribal rituals.

3.

Skyler and I got together again. She texted me to suggest
a trip to the cinema one evening, to see none other than
The Ballad of Genesis and Lady Jaye at Film Forum; I decided
to keep things simple and just not mention the bad experience I'd had in the same cinema. As I was going up to
the roof to get my clothes for the date, I bumped into the
two imbeciles. They were on their way back down from
watering the gravity-assisted tomatoes. They had a routine: after watering the plants, they would lie sprawled
on the asphalt sheeting and spend hours looking over
their tattoos: You haven't got this one, that one's a repeat,
you copied that one; it sometimes came to blows. They
also took photos of the individual tattoos. When I saw
them that day, they were inspecting one of the photos on
a phone, zooming in so that they could make out grada-
tions in the ink not visible to the naked eye, over which
they argued as well. We exchanged nods, no more.

A number of hours later, Skyler and I were sitting in
the front row in the seven o'clock screening; it was just
us in the auditorium. The lights had gone down when
she looked behind us and said: 'Doesn't it frighten you?'
She immediately said she wanted to get out of there.

We walked several blocks, and then got a table on the
terrace at Sidewalk. It was clear that Skyler was a naturally talkative woman, fearful of silences, as if there
was a hole her personality came spilling out through.
She told me about her travels around the world, always
linked in some way to her work as an artist. 'I first became interested in wartime relationships in 2002,' she
said, 'with the invasion of Afghanistan. 9/11 had tested
people's sanity, in that it was an act of war in which both
sides knew from the outset they had more to lose than
to gain, something that makes no sense. Ultimately, all

war is a game, in the sense that each side always weighs the real likelihood of losing something against the possible benefits, but what happened that September day, and with Afghanistan and Iraq afterwards, was a violation of this universal anthropological principle. I did a lot of fact-finding, looked at case studies of ex-soldiers from both wars, travelled from Miami to Chicago, from Austin to Boston, did an endless number of interviews with anyone I thought might add to the piece, and the conclusion I came to was as indisputable as it was surprising: the more absurd and illogical the conflict, the greater the number of relationships you see between members of the opposing sides. Every such relationship in war is a singularity that comes about through the simple necessity for a pressure valve, a pressure valve more real and intensely felt the more irrational or nonsensical the conflict: wherever the absurd mutates into outright hate, it brings with it the need to believe in human intimacy as something potentially stronger than the homeland or the state. I admit I was surprised by what I found, for all that it does make sense, and I started looking into other conflicts, like the Six Days War, like the Balkan Wars, your own civil war or the genocide of the Armenians in the Second World War at the hands of the Turks.' She paused then, and I jumped in to confess my burgeoning interest in the Spanish Civil War, and the fact that this had come about after spending some time, a year earlier, on San Simón. This was also my chance to tell her the real reason I'd visited her at the studio, which she said she understood perfectly, adding that she too was forever concocting plans and underhand strategies to get her hands on information she needed for her work, adding that it made her doubly pleased she hadn't introduced me to Antonio. There was the potential for my obsession with San Simón to short-circuit his brain, were her exact words. She then started asking me about the Spanish Civil War, questions I said I didn't have clear answers for. It was soon obvious that she knew a lot more about the subject than I did; she had an extensive and specialized literature at her fingertips, Spanish as well as non-Spanish sources. I said she ought to do a video piece or something photography-based exclusively on the Spanish Civil War, an idea with which she roundly disagreed; not even with the American Civil War would she do so. She would shortly go on to say that my suggestion had shown a lack of respect for my country, my dead forebears and my history, and while she was doing so a very specific look came over her face, a set to her lips and eyes, such that I saw the Virgin Mary in her. Indeed, it came to me that she bore a striking resemblance to an image from my childhood, one that I had very rarely, if ever, thought about. It was a postcard from my first communion, all pastels and golds, with Mary holding a baby in her arms, Jesus presumably. She gazes down pacifically, while the babe's eye is fixed somewhere outside the picture, a look charged with all the indifference and haughtiness of someone truly aware of His status as Son of God. I remember how it used to remind me of the expressions adopted by rock legends. Apart from that, that evening at Sidewalk, except for one or two allusions, neither of us brought up the subject of Antonio again. I suppose we both wondered if it might sour what was left of the evening, and what we could by then glimpse of the night. Nonetheless, in the gaps in her speech, when she paused to take a mouthful of nachos, guacamole and cheese, I did think about Antonio and the two lives he'd lived: the first as a prisoner on San Simón, and the current one as a New York City pastry-maker of some renown, coming to the conclusion that he must now be wanting to bring the two identities together. The proof being that he had lent Skyler the photos of his time on San Simón, which, however minor the gesture, suggested a move towards reconciliation with himself. It's like when you're in an aeroplane, and you see its shadow down below, separate from the aircraft, and then on landing, shadow and aircraft become one. There are times when our bodies and their doubles, having been on separate journeys, also join together once more, a reunion that generates a collision, an explosion capable of unbalancing even the more stable minds; with that, I felt slightly worried for Antonio. Skyler had asked for the bill. She put her cigarette packet in the back pocket of her trousers, and mine in another, 'To balance them up,' she said, laughing.

Intending to have a little more to drink, we set off in the direction of Houston Street. It was the time of the night when people descend in droves on the city under the light of the streetlamps. A multitude of young people from the New Jersey shore, the boys with marine-style buzz cuts and the girls dressed as if for graduation, out in Manhattan for a good time. We hadn't walked three blocks when we saw two falcons hovering in the sky above a rooftop terrace. Every x number of years the city council releases falcon couples as part of the drive to keep the rat and pigeon populations down. These two, in silhouette against the lights of a distant skyscraper, turned countless circles, trying to spot some prey, we guessed, and then, one at a time, dropped from the sky, diving for something we couldn't see from where we were. As we waited at a corner for the lights to change, Skyler pointed straight ahead, saying that if we carried on this way we'd come to Antonio's. 'There's a story people in the neighbourhood tell about him,' she said as we crossed the street. 'They say that when he first arrived in the city, he used to make cookies in the shape of pregnant dogs.' 'He still does,' I said, 'I saw them in the display.' 'Yes, yes,' she said, 'I know: I have those cookies for breakfast every single morning. But in those days they had a very special flavour, and do you know what it was that gave them that flavour?' 'No,' I said. 'Milk from humans – breastmilk. He'd pay women who were breast-feeding, and they'd express the milk for him. Funny, right?' 'Really,' I said, though I found it anything but. We passed the CitiBank cash machine with the Spanish language option; I took some cash out: my forty-dollar-a-day regime had gone out of the window with a movie plus dinner. 'Give me the fire,' I whispered to myself. 'Here, take the fire.' 'What's that?' asked Skyler. 'Oh, nothing,' I said, and she tugged on my arm. The notes had been sitting there for a few seconds already.

It wasn't long before she pointed out a bar, the oldest Irish pub in the city, which was dark and cramped inside, the walls lined with pre-constitutional flags, and full to the rafters with people who had had several too many. This was our destination and it struck me as the worst dive in all of Manhattan. Maybe it was bloody-mindedness, but we stayed there all night. At a certain moment it seemed acceptable to ask if I could call her *'Virgen María'*, to which she said yes. She didn't know what the Spanish words meant, but said she loved the way it sounded, pronouncing it herself, with a flash of those white teeth, more like *'virgenmagia'* – 'virgin magic'. Starting in on her seventh beer, she fantasized about using it as her artist name, before kissing me, her tongue reaching all the way back along the roof of my mouth, at which, as if she'd pressed a button whose existence only she knew about, I came on the spot; I put the all-body shudder down to my lack of drinking practice. 'Go and splash your face in the bathroom,' she suggested. My underwear, presumably still lodged behind the toilet bowl in that establishment.

She slept at mine; I bedded down on the sofa. She was so drunk that the only physical contact I felt comfortable with was lifting her up by the armpits and getting her onto the bed, taking her shoes off and placing a sheet over her. While she lay snoring like a boar, I, on the sofa, unable to get to sleep, went on pressing my tongue against the back of the roof of my mouth, and went on thinking about the low evening sun at the end of every day and the way it seemed to make the city streets shed their skin. Perhaps, I said to myself, it's this constant mutability that means the falcons of New York, once they have their freedom, never land again.

As I believe I've already said, during my first trip to New York City, in January 2002, it was snowing much of the time and a few blocks from my hotel I saw a young man sitting on a chair out on the pavement while another, older man, gave him a haircut. When I came back past the same spot a number of hours later, men and chair were gone, but the locks of hair and the spots through which they'd melted were still there. I took a lot of photographs of those spots. While I was doing this, a man stopped, of indeterminate age but certainly older than me, smooth-faced and with a slight tremor in his eyes that I've always put down to his extreme sensitivity; he stood patiently waiting for me to finish, before asking what I was up to. Pointing to the hair on the pavement, I told him I was interested in marks and traces of all kinds, anything evanescent, anything bound to disappear. With the easy manner innate in Latino immigrants in New York, he asked if he could take a look at the photos. So we could see better, we ducked under an awning, and I then looked more closely at him, his slight build, Jewish features and very fair, curly hair. He dressed in what, at that time, and not without a certain arrogance, I thought of as the style of an office worker: a dark, three-quarter length parka, under which a blue suit could be glimpsed, on his feet boots-cum-shoes with very rounded toes which, because they were the opposite of square, pointy-toed winkle-pickers, I decided should be called winkle-bashers. We got talking, about photography in general, and he told me he'd done a lot of photography, though in an amateur capacity, in the place he came from, Cabo Polonio, Uruguay, before coming to New York to see if he could make a go of it professionally. And he did now earn a living from it, taking pictures for a variety of different clients, among whom the *Village Voice* was the most notable. He offered to give me some pointers on places to go and ways of getting around the city. In a bar just next to where we'd met, we had cookies and watered-down coffee while he talked to me about some of the city's idiosyncrasies, and we finally ended up exchanging numbers.

We met up just two days later for a walk in Central Park. That first New York City stay of mine lasted almost three months, and we would go on to see each other at least twice a week. We liked that park, particularly going for walks around the decommissioned reservoir, the narrow paths surrounding which would turn busy every afternoon with people out jogging. The two of us, opposed to this sporting pursuit in every way, always walked against the flow of joggers, and we would watch as they came past us and say what a shame the whole thing was, especially for the younger ones who, unaware of the wear and tear they were submitting their joints to, had no idea of the arthritis their old age held in store. The water in the lake, stagnant in places and scattered with the occasional sheet of floating ice, gave off the same smell as that of New Yorkers' bodies, or so Rodolfo claimed, on the basis that the residents of Manhattan actually drank the water from this reservoir, without much filtering taking place beforehand. Looking at a map of the city one day, it struck me that the lake resembles the Iberian Peninsula in outline. Some days later, in a shop near the park that sold souvenirs and posters, I saw an aerial photo, and the resemblance to the Iberian Peninsula was even more startling than I'd thought; you had to rotate the image only slightly, and the two would practically match. I told Rodolfo about this, but had to take him to the shop to see it before he would believe me.

We usually met some time after 2 p.m., in a cafe not far from the park that no longer exists, on the same esplanade where Apple would years later put up its glass cube. He would eat pasta salad and I, a night owl, would enjoy a breakfast of eggs Benedict and coffee. At the table, which had views of the Plaza Hotel, we chatted about various things. One day he directed my attention out of the window and said: 'Look, see that man going inside the hotel? He's called Trump, Donald Trump, and he owns the hotel. It's written in the stars that he's going to be president one day.' On several occasions he told me of his dislike for the financial district, how it was his least favourite place in all of Manhattan, with the narrow, dirty and always dark Wall Street at its heart, which in his view was evil's true temple. On that street, he said, Mammon's devotees watch figures scroll

126

by on screens with the same combined devotion and absent-mindedness as the Nazis watching train carriages roll by full of bodies, flesh indistinguishable. Then, feet warm by now inside our winkle-bashers – a pair of which I, in an act of pure imitation, had also bought – we walked into Central Park, whose main footpaths had been cleared of snow, but which was otherwise impassable, and at that point the topics under discussion changed radically, as though we had entered a space reserved for us and us alone. He'd start asking me physics questions, things to do with the expansion of the universe, and I tended to tell him stories about the Belgian priest Georges Lemaître, who, a few years after the First World War, had found mathematical proof of that expansion, the consequence of a Big Bang, but I did what I could to skip that part, it being a subject I actually found boring. I imagine that our attire, at opposite ends of the style spectrum – boots aside – jumped out at the people we passed, and this, for reasons I can't explain, produced an enormous sense of satisfaction in me. He had read about the construction of Central Park, and recounted the story to me over the course of the days we met there. Rodolfo's way of telling a story consisted of what I can call a 'layer model': he proceeded not by way of the park's different areas, rather by telling me something general about the place as a whole, and overlapping with whatever he'd told me the previous day, and so on successively. It began, he told me, in the mid-nineteenth century, with the city authorities having to turf out thousands of people – African-Americans, mostly – living in huts and shacks in the midst of the deep, dark forest that lay at Manhattan's centre in those days: more than two thousand individuals who faced a fate which, to this day, nobody has bothered to investigate. A few

years later, in 1857, the landscape architect and ideo-
logue for the park, Frederick Law Olmsted, had begun
a detailed study of the subsoil, taking samples from as
far down as it was possible to go and working upwards,
with the idea of designing the park and all it would go
on to contain 'as a direct reflection of that which lay beneath the ground'. I wasn't that clear about the way in
which this replica of the subterranean layers could have
been put into practice, but it is true that all the different kinds of trees in the modern-day park correspond
with fossil species found at depths between 300m and
500m, and all the animal species in the park, including
the insects, are none other than living versions of the
fossils found 200 to 100 metres down, and so on, such
that I came to understand that what we were seeing on
those walks together, what we were treading on, was
a kind of Noah's Ark in replica, there on the island of
Manhattan. 'What they didn't bother to make a replica
of was the top layer,' I said sarcastically, 'the dwellings
the African-Americans were ejected from.' After that,
Rodolfo confided in me that he had been in the park
shortly before they closed the gates, at which time of day,
it being winter, the place was nearly deserted, and that
he had seen Federico García Lorca walking the reservoir, in precisely the same manner as the two of us when
we did so – slowly, deliberately, no hint of a jog – and
that he would disappear into the mists almost as soon as
he had appeared, 'because, you know, the Spanish poet
was a great walker, famous for walking the length and
breadth of this island, even sometimes getting lost along
the way, something he didn't mind at all.'

One afternoon, under clear skies – only a few clouds
to be seen in the far distance over Ground Zero – we
were meandering across one of the park's many raised

terraces when he saw a bird at the top of a tree, stopped and started whistling to it; it was a falcon. This was how I first learned of the existence of urban falcons on the island. Such habitués of the city are these birds that they never go over the park: they avoid all wooded areas, hence why Rodolfo was so surprised to see one coming to land on a tree. 'The falcon is one of the animals the Bible expressly forbids the consumption of,' he said, 'and I know it's crazy to ban the eating of something that features in no known diet anywhere in the world, but there it is, that's what the Bible says. All sacred texts have crazy stuff like that, I suppose that's why they're sacred.'

A number of days later, at our usual cafe, as I mopped up the last yolky streaks of my eggs Benedict, Rodolfo said Central Park was all very well, but what he really loved was the Cloisters. It was the first time I'd heard it mentioned, and he explained that, as the name suggested, it was a series of cloisters, real-life cloisters, originally medieval, on the north-western edge of Manhattan, a long way up past Harlem, on a hill with views of the Hudson River in the little-known neighbourhood of Washington Heights. In the early twentieth century, he told me, these cloisters had been brought, stone by stone, from different places across Europe, and then pieced together again. 'The result is a medieval abbey made of pieces from France and Spain. The subway would get us there in a little over half an hour...'

We got on the A train at Columbus Circle. Next to the platform was a graffiti mural showing streets busy with people, represented in oblique projection whereby the figures faded into a background of skyscrapers and what appeared to be rainy skies above. During the subway journey, I asked Rodolfo about the Cloisters. I learned then that John Rockefeller Jr. had donated several hectares on the banks of the Hudson to the city in 1925 for the building of a museum; he wanted it to hold the medieval art collection belonging to the American sculptor and collector George Barnard. Rockefeller Jr. had simultaneously donated a strip of land in New Jersey, on the banks of the Hudson directly opposite, stipulating that this be left undeveloped, guaranteeing unobstructed views from the museum-to-be. Then, in 1930, Rockefeller Jr. would go on to employ Charles Collens, an architect whom he had entrusted with other projects, to build the monastery today known as the Cloisters, using pieces from various medieval constructions, such as the monastery of San Miguel de Cuixá, the abbey at Saint-Guilhem-le-Désert and the Benedictine Monastery of San Pedro de Arlanza, all of which had been brought over the sea by boat. We came out of the subway onto a street crowded with Jewish and Black people, though more than anything it was Latinos here, and bordering a leafy hill with the Cloisters at the top. It started to snow. We made our way up a winding concrete footpath. In the areas of the hillside park not covered in snow, a kind of vegetation had taken over that, I said to Rodolfo, reminded me of the sort you'd see in Galician woodlands. Rodolfo, tired from the climb, actually gasping for breath, told me that the gardens had been designed to emulate those of medieval monasteries. There were almost 300 species of plants that had been brought, in a sense, directly from the Middle Ages. This included certain medicinal or sacred plants nowadays almost extinct. Many were the same as those seen on the unicorn tapestries inside, because, he continued, as we approached the front entrance, the Cloisters have a permanent exhibition on the myth of the unicorn, including some fifteenth-century tapestries from Holland, depicting that animal being hunted by the nobility of the day. They have the creature's supposed horns on display inside bullet-proof glass cabinets, the pressure and temperature inside which are kept constant; the horns are whiter than ivory and a metre and a half long. We went through the main entrance and were surprised to find it just as cold inside as out. I read in an information brochure that the collection comprised some 12,000 objects, all the product of George Barnard's mad-cap acquisitions across Europe. There were display cabinets with objects from Germany, ivory carvings brought from French colonies, goblets supposedly from Alexandria and entire altarpieces that had been plucked from Spanish churches. The exhibition spaces, as we advanced through them, did not disappoint. Remarkably, the incredible gallimaufry of the exhibition didn't drive us out of our minds.

After nearly two hours we decided to sit and have a rest in the cafe: metal chairs and tables arranged under the arches of a fifteenth-century cloisters originally from the Carmelite convent of Trie-en-Bigorre, near modern-day Toulouse. At the centre of the cloisters, a small garden with a very tall palm tree, and four radial stone paths set out between the kinds of plants as appeared on the unicorn tapestries. These led to a fountain at the very centre which wasn't at that moment spraying any water. We ordered coffee. Before the waiter came with the order, Rodolfo said he missed Uruguay, but that he couldn't go back because he was in the US illegally. If he were to go, he'd never be able to come back to New York, at least not until changes to the tough new laws brought in after 9/11. He was from Montevideo originally, he pointed out, not Cabo Polonio, the latter, he added, being the most beautiful and rugged place he'd ever been, and unique in his experience as somewhere that had undergone a process inverse to what was usual in nature: having been an island in the past, geological shifts over time had seen it join up with the mainland.

'As soon as I was able to leave home,' he said, 'I rented a cabin on that Cape, no electricity or running water, but a place where the wind is constantly rushing around and the skies are unimaginably full of stars. The fields are all lush green, and the rocky coastline slides directly into the Atlantic, which is always stormy, such that you don't know where the land ends and ocean begins. I started going to Cabo Polonio on weekdays, my work as a video game designer permitting. I came to hate my job at one point, and I'd jump in the car and go and hole up in my cabin every chance I had. I painted it all different colours; it looked like one of those Nordic houses. My brother, who's a marine biologist, owns it now; I sold it to him before coming here. Such was the way I decorated and furnished it, some friends who came to visit would say it resembled a dwarf's house, not as in a miniature house, but as in one belonging to a dwarf, and I didn't get this at all, only later on seeing that the furniture was all slightly too big for the dimensions of the rooms, producing this effect of apparent dwarfism, so I painted a sign on the front gate saying "The She Dwarf". I killed time while I was there taking photos, using a telephoto lens. But my favourite thing to do was look at the stars, I even got to a point where I was able to tell the dead ones and the living ones apart – the light's slightly bluer when they're dead. And I mapped out that whole sky, the dead stars in particular, real constellations that I sketched. I left those sketches behind, they're among the many things I miss. I also spent a lot of time looking out at the island off the coast there, less than a kilometre out, so flat they actually call it "Flat Island" – *Isla Rasa* – and where a sea lion colony always gathers, so that it's easy to take photos of them. I had a solar panel to power my few appliances and my computer; I didn't have a TV, just books: stacks and stacks of books on world history, filling up the dining space, the kitchen and the little bedroom which served as the bathroom as well. The sea lions formed such a thick carpet – I guess they still do – that you couldn't see the surface of Isla Rasa; all mounded together in piles, you can easily mistake them for rock formations. Of everything I read in that cabin, apart from the books on the history of Europe and the Americas, my favourite was *Kaleidoscope* by Ray Bradbury, to the point that I reread it at least three times; certain passages I know off by heart, like the one in which the spaceship splits in two at the arrival of a gigantic tin opener, and the four astronauts on board are sent flying off into space, all in different directions, and the empty space sucks them away into unknown orbits or means their bodies themselves fly off in different directions. The only thing joining them together are their radio transmitters, and then, the book says, "instead of men there were only voices – all kinds of voices, disembodied and impassioned, in varying degrees of terror and resignation." Might this not be a description of the way we approach history's abyss, truly like time-travelling astronauts? I then tried to imagine what those four astronauts would see looking down at our planet, what kind of strange miniature the Earth would seem like to them, the Earth as a simple keyring, a beach souvenir. But also, in their dramatic disappearance into outer space, those astronauts appeared to me like those stars which, though they're already dead, shone down on my cabin porch night after night. And when the weather was bad and I couldn't sit out at night, I'd go and surf on rudimentary web pages – portals that had already ceased to be active – and this was a kind of archaeology like any other. On my last day there, sitting outside, I had a supper of macaroni with some clams my neighbours had brought for me, and I stayed out until very late gazing at the blue of those dead stars. When my eyes had adjusted sufficiently so that, cat-like, I could have hunted bats if I'd wanted to, I went inside the cabin and sat down at the computer. Having looked around lots of places in Manhattan, searching for information and areas that could be useful to me on the journey I was about to make, I came across a page that, as it so happened, talked about the Cloisters,' Rodolfo paused here, gesturing around at the place in which we were sitting, me following with my gaze, 'and I couldn't help but dive into a lot of what was contained there, particularly the story of the workers who built this abbey, men who were mostly white, not a single African-American involved because the people in charge had the pretty out-there idea that a job as European and as noble as the reconstruction of an abbey had to be executed by the white man only, with his more refined genes. Indians and Black people were used only for modern, vulgar constructions: freeways, skyscrapers, hanging bridges, steel and concrete. The white workers were chiefly from Ireland, Uruguay, Spain, a little bit of everything; they'd been in prisons in their homelands, not so many on charges of violence, and they worked in exchange for bread and board. Not that it made the work any less gruelling, seeing the way it brooked all building logic: starting at a central point where the chief engineer placed the stone he considered to be the geometric centre, the work would proceed outwards from there in a succession of rooms, doors, passages and

134

halls, until they came to the outer edge, where the walls would be put up. But before this, the terrain, which was pure granite and basalt, had to be dynamited using unprecedented quantities of explosives, even more than had been needed for Central Park. How many workers lost their lives, I don't know. They slept on-site, at first in the walkways of these cloisters, later in improvised lodgings set up in the halls once these had been built. You can still see some of the writing they etched into the walls around the entrance, questions and answers, the closest thing you'll see to the kind of scrawlings you get nowadays in public toilets. Typhus was pretty common; there's an estimated hundred or more bodies buried on this hillside. Nowadays, this neighbourhood is physically linked to the rest of the city, but as it was then, New York City was just a speck of light in the distance. Those workers must, over time, have felt increasingly lost, also drifting in an interstellar space, a place both amoral and completely comfortless.'

Half an hour had passed since Rodolfo had begun his story. I think we were both cold. We returned the way we'd come and the exhibition spaces seemed somehow changed. Coming to the unicorn tapestries in which the creature was shown being held captive inside a fenced garden, one very similar to a child's playground, we stopped. I pointed out the mistake in the rendering of the unicorn's mouth: 'If unicorns only eat grass,' I said, 'they can't have canines like those. You only need to look at an animal's mouth to tell whether it's a herbivore or a carnivore, and what it's able to digest. For example, the fact that humans nowadays have only four canines, which are the teeth for incising meat, out of thirty-two teeth, means we ought to have a diet that keeps the same

135

proportions: eight plant-based to one of meat.' Rodolfo nodded, laughing; it was the last time I saw him laugh. Minutes later, with the streetlamps lighting our way, we were going back down the path towards the subway stop again; it had stopped snowing. I paused at the subway entrance and looked back at where we'd been. The stone abbey, up on the hill with snow banked all around it, had the look of a ground-down molar, one more piece in the, as it were, row of rotting teeth that is Manhattan. We waited a few minutes, the train came. Half an hour later, at Columbus Circle, we said goodbye, and never saw each other again. When Rodolfo failed to show two days later for our usual Central Park walk, I called numerous times but got no answer; I left voice messages. On the eighth day someone with a Uruguayan accent, claiming to be his brother, picked up, and said Rodolfo had died eight days earlier following a heart attack in his apartment. His mortal remains and all his belongings had just arrived back in Uruguay. I thought of the messages I'd left during those days; my voice speaking on a dead person's answerphone. The brother brought the conversation to an end almost immediately, though not before mentioning that the emergency services had found a whole community of falcons in Rodolfo's apartment, which had been under his care. 'News to me,' I said, at which, looking onto the street outside, I saw a falcon launch itself from a rooftop before melting away into the late afternoon sun.

When, many years later, Skyler, semi-unconscious after all those beers, fell asleep in my apartment, she woke to find the hearty breakfast I made for her and which she barely touched, still drunk, seemingly, or maybe just pensive. I made the same joke as the previous night, about her looking like the Virgin Mary, but she wasn't laughing now. I asked if she was hungry, no reply. I asked again, and in the end, pressed with still further questions, she confessed that it was the first time she'd ever been out with someone and not had it lead to sex, and that she found this somehow troubling. She'd had so many sexual encounters, she said, that she'd lost count. Something drove her to sleep with all men, regardless of her personal taste, sometimes even in active contravention of it. I asked her to expand, and she said it was a simple case of trying to find something to love in each and every man who crossed her path, not in the sense of a challenge but rather a way of testing something out: a way of seeking the part inside every man, small and hidden away though it may be, worthy of being loved, but then to make her departure, not let herself get stuck in that part of the man in question. With me, for the first time in her life, she'd found nothing. I pretended I found this upsetting; in fact I didn't mind. She then said that she avoided this thing we generally referred to as being in love, out of a fear, she said, of getting trapped inside another person's dreams. 'Falling in love means letting another person have you inside their head,' were her exact words, 'which is a place you can never escape from, and the precursor to them coming up with their own stories about you.' Her few lasting relationships had been purely out of a need for economic stability. 'I might seem selfish, egotistical even,' she said, 'but to me it's the most sensible way to be, and the most honest as well. It's tough at first, or not much fun at least, but you quickly get used to living in this ongoing eradication of your own feelings – it's like what immigrants experience when they go off to distant places looking for economic stability, and they prosper and grow in this very eradication of their feelings, and that gives them strength for the rest of their lives. An immigrant is something invincible. When it comes to relationships, I am as well.'

She didn't stay for long. She left her half-drunk coffee cup on the tablecloth, the piece of toast with the smallest bite taken out of it, her knife and fork in a perfect cross on her plate, like the blades of a fan, which, this being a way of saying you haven't finished, gave me hope that I might hear from her again in the not too distant future. I didn't clear the table until the evening, and when I came to do so, just as I was about to throw her leftovers away and make space for my dinner, with the cup in my hand I felt the need to drink her coffee, and to eat the toast she'd barely nibbled and the eggs she hadn't so much as touched, and it was then that a low feeling came over me, it was then that the fact she'd been unable to find anything in me to love made me feel like some leftover thing, residuum, a lump of flesh destined to go out with the rubbish.

I didn't see Skyler again during that stay. She didn't answer when I called, and I chose not to push it. A few times, particularly in the final weeks of my stay, I went on her website, which had details of the travels she'd been on for work, her observations on other artists' work and the opinions of various gallery owners and journalists on her own. Also photos of parties at her studio, and of her most recent pieces. One of these was a photo of a kitchen table with a breakfast on it, comprising the following elements: a half-full coffee cup, a piece of toast with a small bite taken out of it, a plate of scrambled eggs with the knife and fork next to it, this time in parallel, this time in the having-finished position. Next to the technical details of the photo, the title: 'Spanish Civil War'.

4.

I kept almost exclusively to my apartment after that. I sat at the study desk, facing the hallway, with the window behind me, and outside the sound of the gridlocked city bubbling away. The typewriter noise I heard coming from somewhere out in the street demonstrated that, unlike in the countryside, in a city the streets and the interiors of peoples' homes all meld together to form an unbroken mass of smells, textures and sounds, and this even goes for the flora and fauna, given that the same cockroaches I'd see on the pavement outside would later show up in my kitchen. I sometimes felt a tremendous urge to go out and search all the buildings one by one for that typewriter, so I could then take it and throw it out of the window. I remember that I didn't reply to any of the messages Luis left for me, and that he came by one day, rang the doorbell for a while, then banged on the door, before leaving a bag of food for me out on the landing. My thoughts were soon full of the rats, large and brownish-grey, that I had been seeing since my arrival and that would emerge in the twilight to root through the rubbish. And of the local homeless as well, whom I watched from my window also picking through rubbish bags, to my mind recalling zombies picking through a person's body for something edible. I inevitably drew parallels between all of this and the abnormal shrinkage undergone by the bodies of humans, and the no less abnormal mushrooming of the rodents' bodies, that had occurred on Flores Island. There are rats at the polar stations as well, I said to myself, human beings cannot consider a place conquered until the rats have got in on the act as well, and on this basis the moon can't really be said to be ours; it belongs only to itself. And so the two imbeciles in the apartment above seemed to me: two rodents

I'd hear arguing and stomping around above my head. Many a time I felt like going up and tearing down their gravity-assisted tomato plantation. One of them, I don't know which, would recite, at a shout and at all hours, the opening of the poem printed on that T-shirt of theirs, 'I saw the best minds of my generation destroyed by madness, starving hysterical naked, dragging themselves through the negro streets at dawn looking for an angry fix,' and my thought would be: what on earth did these two know about destruction, or starvation, or madness? I often thought of the Oroza line, 'It's a mistake to take the things we've seen as a given,' and the image of Rodolfo would immediately rush in, his body all those years before, gravity acting on it while being borne along in a coffin inside the belly of an aeroplane travelling from north to south across the Americas, and his mobile phone ringing among his belongings, and my voice being contained inside that: 'You didn't show up yesterday,' it said, 'is everything okay?' Come night, I'd get up from my desk and see a man in the building across from mine who, standing there in his underpants, would heat up frozen beans in a pan. America is a very sad place. All there is there is sadness.

One day I felt an urge to be down by the East River again; I hadn't been for weeks, since I'd stopped going to the Instituto Cervantes. Half an hour later I was sitting on my bench gazing out at the water eddying past. It was peculiarly inactive that day – far fewer objects being spat out and sucked back down – and so I shifted my gaze, looking up at the far side of the river and the Williamsburg skyline. Minutes later I felt someone tap me on the back and looked up to find that big moustache with its upwards-pointing ends before me. I asked if he wanted to join me – what else could I do? After a few niceties, I mentioned the intense stink of the river, like male hormones, and he said he'd noticed it too, especially when the eddying waters were at their most active. Fearing he was about to launch into his story about trash and the soul of trash, I said the first thing that came to mind: 'Did you know García Lorca appears in Central Park close to nightfall some days, when the gates are about to be shut? A Uruguayan friend of mine said he saw him there.' 'Of course,' said the man nonchalantly, 'he comes to see me. We often talk together. We meet by the gate on the side of the park nearest the Met.' 'Really?' 'Sure, sure. Central Park is his domain; it's Federico's and nobody else's. All night long he walks around the Reservoir – which, by the way, is the same shape as the Iberian Peninsula. The rest of the city, meanwhile, is mine; that's how we've divvied it up. And we sit down right at that gate, him inside and me outside, and we have a conversation through the bars, sharing memories of our turbulent younger years. Dear Federico was an extraordinary creature. For example, during our time together in Madrid, and as I've recounted already in my memoirs, he staged his own death at least five times a day, he could never sleep at night if we didn't all go in as a group to put him to bed, and then, once he was lying down, he'd always find a way to drag out the most poetic and transcendent conversations of the twentieth century. He, at the end of his "Ode to Salvador Dalí", makes an unequivocal allusion to his own death and, in passing, tells me to waste no time in following suit: that the moment my life and work started to flourish I should follow his lead, at which point I'd become not just world-famous but famous for all the ages – which, as you know, young man, I am. The last time I saw Federico alive was in Barcelona, two months before the outbreak of the Civil War. Gala, who hadn't met him before, was utterly taken with the phenomenon of total, if affected, lyricism that was Federico. The feeling was mutual. Federico spent three entire days doing nothing but talking to Gala, spellbound. And one evening, at dinner in Barcelona, at a restaurant called El Canari de la Garriga, a small insect appeared on the tablecloth; it had an awkward way of moving, a sort of goose-like waddle. Seeing it, Federico cried out and, without appearing to think, squashed it under his thumb. Gala and I were amazed to see that, when he lifted his thumb, the insect had disappeared, no trace of it whatsoever. Pure magic. And you must believe me when I say that this insect may have had a considerable hand in Federico's fate, and thereby the whole history of Spain, because Gala, truly astonished at the way he'd made the insect disappear, asked him to come and spend a few days with us at our home in Port Lligat. Federico spent the following three days agonizing over whether to come or not; he'd have a change of heart every quarter of an hour. His father, at the family home in Granada, had a bad heart, and there was a worry he'd soon be dead. In the end he left for Granada and promised to join us in Port Lligat once he'd visited his father. Federico was lined up and shot a few days later – the irony being that his father outlived him. I've always regretted that we weren't insistent enough on him making the trip, which is one of the reasons why I come and see him at Central Park, when he brings me things he's found in the rubbish bins or that have been dropped on the sidewalks, things he thinks might help me get closer to the soul of trash, which he knows I'm looking for, while I bring him things to eat from different street-food places – he's so thin. All our talk is of the past, but still I implore him to come with me to see the real New York City, outside the park, and then he asks why don't I wear my "Crime of the Century" T-shirt any more, he liked that T-shirt a lot, he says, and I can't bring myself to tell him that it's been years since I threw it away, and that that very T-shirt *is* the soul of trash I've been searching this city high and low for. During these talks of ours by the gate, a point invariably comes when Federico squashes an insect and, as I look on, repeats that incredible feat by making the creature disappear. He's happy staying put, he says; he'd rather just walk the Reservoir as usual; it feels peaceful to him, the way its outline matches the Iberian Peninsula's. The canteen he always carries, containing water from that lake, is in constant use, he's forever taking sips from it; the water does him no harm, which is because his body purifies everything it comes into contact with. One night, while I was talking to him about how great life is here outside the park, he began idly picking up gravel stones and throwing them into a hole some telecoms workers had made in the ground earlier that day, in the ditch that lies between the park and the sidewalk. Seeing him doing this, I joined in, picking up a slightly bigger stone and throwing it in, and then he picked up a bigger one and threw that, and I found an even bigger one and threw that. A few minutes later, between the two of us, we'd lifted a stone off the ground, a small boulder really, the size of a suitcase, and took it and tossed it into the hole in the ditch. We heard the noise it made as it landed on the stones we'd already thrown in, a sound like dry bones crunching. That was one deep hole. Federico, the veins on his arms bulging after the exertion of it, said to me: "Salvador, I've a feeling we're not on the island any more."'

After the encounter with this Dalí of ours, I started going out even less. There was a book in the apartment I guessed had been left by the previous tenant, *The House of the Dead*, one of Dostoevsky's short novels, a first person, semi-autobiographical account of his time in a Siberian prison camp. On one of the pages, heavily underlined in pencil, we're told of the prisoners dreaming aloud, constantly crying out in their sleep, babbling things about knives and hatchets and the cutting off of heads. The next day, when the narrator asks them about their dreams, they reply by saying: 'We are broken, we are dead inside, and this is why we shriek in the night.' I read this passage over and over, fearful that I was on course to suffer the same fate. Some weeks later, I made an astonishing discovery: in the word processing software on my computer, the blank document had the same dimensions as my apartment – it was a scaled-down version of the very rectangle in which I was existing, and from then on I started, when I was writing, to play around with making the words move from the bedroom to the kitchen, down to the toilet, over to the shower; they would then follow suit and make supper, watch television, sleep, have nightmares, everything. I also played with making the margins of the document narrower, because, I said to myself, words are always looking for the limits of things; it's indisputably the case that words want to go to the places nobody and nothing has succeeded in going, and, as a result of shrinking the margins in this way, the words started straying into the adjacent apartments, and going for a walk through the East Village and the whole Lower East Side, off to see the sights; indeed, my words began to magnify, in the same way the eyes of falcons soaring over the city magnified;

144

I was my building's falcon, my neighbourhood's falcon,
New York City's chief falcon, this animal the Bible expressly forbids the killing and consumption of, and this
in turn made me into an untouchable body, somehow
above it all. And I remember the sun, above all a great
deal of sun, oval-shaped and eccentric even by morning,
and at that hour of the day being able to take photos of
the people on their way to work, because, I said to myself, just as Dostoyevsky said, bodies are decimated at
night; the night makes mincemeat of our bodies, and
when the sun comes up, and on the way to work, we go
along putting ourselves back together again, and I, with
my camera, halted this reconstitution of the flesh, setting it down forever in photography. And some weeks
later the page in Word had started to take in the smells of
the building and the surrounding neighbourhood, and
then I remembered what Luis had told me and felt afraid:
that the last thing you experience before you die is a
smell, a smell from the deepest-most place in your memory, the smell of the first cell you ever were, or something
along those lines, anyway. Although in my case it was
the opposite, in the sense that the range of what could be
smelled expanded: first I could smell the stairwell, followed by the door onto the street and its immediate
vicinity, then the whole street, and, as in one of these
meteorological maps with its isobars and so on, and
without setting foot outside my apartment, I had begun
creating an expanding smell-map comprising iso-smell
curves and lines, as it were, and reaching even as far as
my bench by the East River and the intense smell there
of male hormones, a smell no deodorant could ever hope
to mask, a smell that – I remembered – I had come across
on innumerable occasions previously, inside mountain
huts, principally in the French Alps, where I'd spent

145

time in my student mountain-climbing days. And, in those Alpine climbing huts, the difference between the smells given off by people of different nationalities in a pre-globalized world was so evident that, even when they were sleeping, lying wrapped inside their sleeping bags, you could tell which country they were from by their body odour, which was all down to diet. After having something for breakfast, we'd set off at dawn to tackle ascents of varying difficulty. At least a couple of times a year someone wouldn't make it back. It took the rescue workers an average of three days to find the bodies. In most cases, the best the French authorities could do was present the remains in a package the size of a plastic bag, a package that, having been secured and then placed inside a semi-translucent plastic box, would be handed over to the family. Strange as it might seem, this is how the bodies of people who have fallen from heights greater than 300 metres are returned to their loved ones. The families, who came from all over Europe but principally from France, Italy and Germany, found the meaning of this packet impossible to understand. They come back to me now, those people, as if it were happening right now, holding the semi-translucent box to them, walking around the large table in the mountain hut, while someone from the court presented them with forms to sign, and they struggled to comprehend how it could be that something until so recently possessed of a form and an outline not only perfectly recognizable but actually unique, could suddenly have become nothing more than this mincemeat parallelepiped. It was the pilot of the rescue helicopter usually given this unpleasant task who, in 1986, inside the aforementioned hut, recounted all of this to me. There were times, he said, when it was impossible to land on the snow, either because it was too powdery or because the body had landed on an unstable blue ice serac, or on a declivity so steep that any approach by air was simply unthinkable, meaning that the bodies of the dead mountaineers would remain where they lay, littering those slopes, until summer came round, or until another mountaineer happened upon them and, in a single or several goes, dropped them onto an ice shelf lower down, from which they could actually be recovered, and I say recovered because what occurred after that could no longer be called rescue. The kind of people who do this work are tough, not insensitive souls as such, but unquestionably hardy, which also gives them a certain sense of humour; this particular pilot had a joke about bringing the bodies down off the slopes as their very own form of Alpine golf, and when he said it he gave a smile that I couldn't help but plaster my own face with, though it wasn't an idea I found funny. On one occasion this pilot, whose name was Francesco, an Italian living in Chamonix who by rights should have retired by now, between servings of an ad-hoc supper consisting of macaroni and a tomato sauce with a sprinkling of rosemary and oregano he'd collected in a meadow far up in the valley, told me that, being nearly eighty-five now, he'd flown all manner of aircraft previous to settling on rescue helicopters. He'd worked for Alitalia at the time when pilots could still fly for up to twenty-four hours without a break. 'The good thing about passenger planes,' he said, 'is that when you're all that way up, you don't see a thing; it's like you're just floating, and even more so at night. You look at the stars and it feels like you could almost reach out and touch them, as if you were just another star. I've never crashed a passenger plane, but I did crash during the different wars I was in before that,' and he went on to say that the worst war he'd been involved in was the Second World War, in which he'd had to drop bombs over Normandy, in the days when there had been no thought for civilian casualties, or the idea of collateral damage as a war crime. The craziest war, though, the one he found hardest to comprehend, had been the Spanish Civil War, and in particular the time he'd been sent to drop bombs on the town of Guernica, and I remember feeling nothing, nothing at all, when Francesco said the words 'Spanish Civil War', given that for a young Spaniard in the 1980s that war was a complete abstraction, a concept with no content whatsoever. All of this meant, Francesco continued flatly, that his career had comprised a singular progression from laying waste to human life to, in the present day, saving it, though it was often the case, such as the one that had brought him to the Chamonix shelter that day, of doing no more than making up a package of bones and meat to then give to the family. He described to me the smells given off by this shredded meat, and said how incredible it was to see, after several months, a lung or a heart so perfectly preserved by the snow that it was as though those organs had been removed from the body only minutes before, and how, because of the low temperatures, they would come to be infused by the smell of rosemary and oregano, and feldspar and the mica contained in the granite, and of the winter flowers nestled deep in the snow waiting for spring, as if everything were imitating everything else, 'because smells stick to things, they mirror one another, that much is beyond doubt,' he said, 'dead bodies dispense with their original smells, they take on the smell of the place in which the death occurred, which, as it happens, is the exact opposite of rubbish, because rubbish smells the same the world over. I've been all across

the world and I can tell you for certain that rubbish always smells the same, no matter where you go.' I couldn't
help but ask whether the rosemary and oregano in the
pasta sauce originated in one of these trips; he didn't answer, and if he did, it wasn't a clear yes or no. A number
of days later, in Chamonix, I, along with a Galician
friend and a German guy who'd been milling around
the shelter looking for someone to latch onto, would set
out with the intention of climbing the granite needle
known as the Petit Dru, taking the American Direct
route; this was known as one of the great climbs in those
days, and a year never passed in which it didn't claim a
number of lives. We departed at 4 a.m., and before we
reached the foot of the wall, a blizzard suddenly moved
in, forcing us to stop, though we then tried to carry on,
whether walking straight or around in circles there was
no way of telling, all the while being lashed by genuinely
knife-like particles of airborne ice. We decided to make
camp for the night, shovelling a snow-hole for ourselves
in the side of a ridge. Huddled together like rabbits in a
warren, facing in, our feet jammed up against the improvised stove of one another's testicles, we spent close to
two days with next to no sleep, until a point came when,
having assumed the worst, a shaft of sunlight broke in,
illuminating the interior of our snow hole. We climbed
out and, looking back down from the vantage point at
our footsteps in the snow, sunk so deep that not even the
blizzard had covered them over entirely, it became apparent that two days earlier we had only walked around
in a figure of eight: the footsteps came repeatedly back
around on themselves, like a boomerang flying through
the air, creating this outline of a number eight. At that
moment I interpreted it as a sign of stubbornness, the
product of a survival instinct gone badly awry. It would

149

be a number of years before I came to study, as part of my professional training, the basics of so-called Chaos Theory, at which point I learned that, both in drawings on paper and in computer simulations, far from being anything to do with stubbornness, the figure eight comes about in response to the very opposite, namely an object being given almost complete freedom to oscillate at will, endlessly, between two points it never touches. And so it was during my stay in New York City thirty years later that, after more than a fortnight not setting foot outside my apartment, tired of wandering the neighbourhood just to shrink the margins of my Word documents, tired, too, of mapping out iso-smells, and in the grip of what I can now see was a nervous breakdown, I started going out at night with my single aim being to walk, to, I believe I could say, roam with no destination in mind, and, looking back at a map of the routes I took, it so happened that, up and down Manhattan, and with no intention on my part, my footsteps led me in the very kind of figure-of-eight or figure-of-boomerang I have just been describing. I'd usually set out at around 11 p.m., when all the restaurants closed and the only places left open were the 24-hour diners, tables populated by taxi drivers, street cleaners and a random assortment of insomniacs, establishments I would hurry past in search of quieter streets, not stopping, always with a certain resolve in my step. I soon found that it's possible to walk the length of the city in a single night, a city surprisingly empty except for the colonies of homeless people who, under sections of dismantled courier company cardboard packaging, huddled together in the CitiBank cash machine booths, such that, as I think of them now, they seem identical to my companions and I in that snow hole on the approach to the base of the Petit Dru. I was usually back at my apartment by 7 a.m., buying a punnet of blueberries from a girl no older than ten who stood barefoot on the corner selling that fruit and that fruit only to passers-by. It struck me then that children are caught in a constant daydream, they ask nothing more of life, and I found this profound and continuous capacity for abstraction, which is what keeps them from the temptation of drugs, endlessly amazing; people get into drugs when the innate reflex for imaginative dreaming is lost, usually at the shift into adolescence. That little girl sold her blueberries at three dollars a punnet, and I would give her a five-dollar bill and immediately walk away, hoping the fact of the single bill would prevent her from noticing my charity. And every day it felt as though that little girl's dreams were going to come to an end that same day.

On one of my night walks – which had already begun to overlap and mix together in my mind, as if all part of one single night – I felt an irrepressible urge to jump the fence at Central Park. I chose the section near the Met, where I knew the fence was lower than elsewhere. Walking over fruit fallen from the trees, which burst when I stepped on them, I went deeper into the park, until coming to the bench on which Rodolfo and I usually sat on all those years before. I spent a number of hours listening to the hundreds of animals the names of which, in my ignorance, I don't know, a low murmur overlaid with the intermittent bursts of ambulance and fire engine sirens, which seemed to me the alarm calls of a planet now too distant. I was surprised to hear myself whisper the words: 'Rodolfo, I've a feeling we're not on the island any more.'

As for the two imbeciles, they stopped saying hello

to me. The last time we spoke, they accused me of repeatedly banging on my ceiling with a broom, as well as having spoiled their broccoli crop, the first ever broccoli crop to prosper on a rooftop in this city. I did bump into them once more after that, actually, in the deli on the corner; I was buying fruit, they were buying ice cream. In what I took not as a sign of peace but at least as one of ceasefire, they came over as though nothing was wrong. They said I should feel free to come by any time: 'We'll have a few beers at the infinite table,' they said, which was the joke name they'd come up with for the table that never seemed full no matter how many empties you loaded it up with. They both laughed; I didn't. Pointing to the notepad I had under my arm, which contained the notes I made during my walks, they asked me what I did with my days, what was with all the walking and all the time spent holed up inside the apartment? I was writing, I said. 'Anything about tomatoes or broccoli?' they asked. 'No,' I said, 'it's a murder story, and a horror story. A story of immense terror.' Clearly excited, they asked if New York City featured, to which I answered that it did, adding: 'This street's in it too, and your apartment, you two are in it, and a friend of mine, a woman named Skyler; she's going to commit a series of murders purely for the pleasure of seeing blood spilt.' At that, they made themselves scarce. That was pretty much the last time I saw them.

5.

Somehow, autumn arrived in New York City. My night walks grew colder and, if anything, more forbidding. Cities that experience very hot summers and very cold winters seem to me like bags of frozen food, frozen and defrosted over and over again: you need only tear open the plastic to see how inedible the contents have become. And that's precisely what I think my walks amounted to: a way of wearing down the outermost layer of the pavements, the skin, eventually to have it rip open of its own accord, so that I could then take a look inside. I thought I saw Luis's friend once, Lucy, the artist turned carpenter. She was making a bed for herself among some cardboard boxes, alongside a group of homeless people, and wore the same work overalls and the same oversized checked jacket as when we'd met. It was as though her place in society had been dragged down to the level of the clothes she wore – and not the other way around – which troubling thought I found myself unable to shake for at least a couple of weeks. I saw, as I went on walking at night, cameras made from toilet rolls, asbestos sheets emblazoned with stars and stripes, a dog whose ears were almost parabolic, videogames that seemed like the entrance to a sewer, a prefab sheet-metal patenting office, a duck's kidneys exploded on the pavement, many public lavatories overflowing, a window display in a design shop with a pair of solid gold representations of the Twin Towers just after the planes hit; sooner or later, every civilization creates reproductions of its own defeats in gold. For me, New York City was already the last medieval city of the Modern Era, like seeing Pompeii just before the volcano erupted. I often walked past the doors of Film Forum, which was showing, among other things, *The Warriors*, a film about battles between New York gangs for which I've always had a weakness. When the first snowflakes began to fall, I bought myself a pair of winkle-bashers identical in all except colour to the ones I'd bought in imitation of Rodolfo all those years before, and generally quickened my pace in a bid to combat the cold. I'm not sure how I came to have a tote bag hanging over my shoulder, a Strand Bookstore one, in which I carried a water bottle that I would refill from the tap, chocolate bars, a spare jumper, pens, and flyers and pages from magazines I found strewn around. I'd arrive back at the apartment at dawn, collapse into bed like a dead falcon, and immediately fall asleep. I started to have dreams that, on waking, I'd remember in great detail, for the fact they were unlike any dreams I'd had before: the images combined in my head with the texture, grain and colouration of a video recording. I was dreaming in video, almost. At first the dreams consisted purely of wide shots that went on for hours, the most frequent being one of a street with nobody on it, nothing going on at all, but I knew my dream wasn't on pause from the fact a light breeze moved the leaves in the trees, or the occasional sight of somebody opening one of the windows in a hive of buildings, looking out at me for a few moments and then disappearing behind a curtain. A night came when the dream changed and I saw a street busy with the comings and goings of people, and I seemed to be enjoying the hustle and bustle of the place only for everything to then stop, I was still dreaming in video but it all came to a halt, and then I glimpsed *myself* walking through the paused pedestrians towards the camera. I was wearing my winkle-bashers, the Strand tote bag was stuffed full of bits of paper and I was carrying the small bottle I invariably filled with tap water. How long the dream stayed like this, with nothing moving, I'm not sure. And then suddenly it started moving in reverse, very quickly – the tape was rewinding – and I watched as the people I'd already passed came by me again, and it went on; night fell in this street and the dream fell dark, there were only taxis reversing and the very infrequent pedestrian walking backwards, though within a few seconds it was daylight again, and again people streamed past, and that day turned to night, to the previous night, and a long sequence ensued, successive years unfolding in reverse, and I saw a great pile of bricks come back up again in a mass of airborne dust, turning into two twin towers, and I saw the filming of dozens of movies that everyone's watched, though I won't say which, and I saw child crack addicts and yuppies getting into limousines, and hippies protesting and Ginsberg's beard and Susan Sontag's mane of white hair among a knot of young people, and young black men shooting guns at white policemen, and a cavalcade of astronauts with confetti all over them which could have been falling from the sky or rising from the ground, and then men in post-war hats and women in Chanel dresses, and US troops, and manual labourers putting sandwiches into lunchboxes when in reality they were taking the sandwiches out, and on it went like this until, coming to a sunny morning, it stopped, and there, among the crowds, directly alongside a young man selling magazines with headlines that read 'Stock Market Crashes: Thousands Ruined' and 'Save America', I saw him: he had a black suit on, a hat and bowtie, a pair of winkle-bashers, an elegant shirt, a tote bag over his shoulder and a canteen in his left hand. I saw that he was on his way to Wall Street to take the pulse of the dramatic events unfolding there, the Great Crash that had just happened, possibly seeking inspiration for a poem. He then came over to me and, like a baton being passed, he handed me his canteen, which I imagined to be full of water from the Reservoir, and I handed him my plastic bottle, which contained tap water. An electric shock ran through me, a dazzling burst, a tongue of fire. The image turned grainy, horizontal stripes appearing across it, as though the dream-video were readjusting itself on the screen, and then, as the image began to fade I saw a look appear on his face, one of solitude and sorrow, the look of someone when they realize their interlocutor is going to wake up, is going to open their eyes and not remember the moment at all. I woke up. The midday sun cut a swathe through the dust motes hanging in the air. Not wanting to forget what I'd just seen, I went over to my desk, barely as big as a school desk, and transcribed the dream as fast as I could. Once that was done, I relaxed, glancing out of the window. The man in the apartment across the street, wearing the same underpants as ever, stood before a pan, his diet of frozen beans apparently unaltered. He turned his head ever so slightly, for the first time allowing me a glimpse of his face: on his upper lip, a moustache with tips pointing straight upwards.

A few days later, very late at night or very early in the morning, my wanderings took me in the vicinity of Penn Station, and I went inside to warm up a little. Standing looking up at the departure boards, I was reminded of a moment I'd forgotten altogether: my first arrival into New York City had not been on an aeroplane but on a train, from Boston, where I'd flown on a cheap flight from Madrid, and I had sat down on one of the very benches now in front of me. I remembered that I had been wearing unusually formal clothes for someone on a long journey, and had a rucksack, which in those days I preferred over suitcases. I sat and waited for a friend who was supposed to be coming to pick me up. I remembered the course of the following hours, how I'd worried I might miss my friend if I got up to go to the toilets or to buy a bottle of water. I believe I sat on that bench for over three hours; except on television, I had never seen so many people pass by me while not moving anywhere myself. I had then tried calling my friend from a phone booth and got no answer, and so tried the number of a friend of this friend's, which I had with me as a fallback, but they didn't pick up either. The feeling that comes over you when you're in a city you don't know and nobody's picking up is very close to that of abandonment; the numbers of the phone keypad become like something out of a bingo game, and the winning combination impossible to land on. When the wait became unbearable, and it dawned on me that my friend wasn't coming, I tried to leave the station, only to become quite lost; I rode a number of escalators without being clear at all whether they were going up or down. It was the same sensation as opening up a computer and looking at its circuit boards for the first time, seeing those Piranesi labyrinths which, properly considered, carry all things inside them. Once I managed to exit the building, I asked a taxi driver to take me to a hotel; it didn't need to be nearby but it did need to be cheap. He ended up leaving me in the East Village, on the far side of the city. And it would be the very next day that I would come across those shorn locks of hair in the snow, followed by meeting Rodolfo, who proved not only to be the saving of those several months from what I believe would have meant unmitigated solitude for me, but who would, two months later, go on to die, in a sense in my arms, as a way of communicating something to me. It was on this return to Penn Station in 2015 that I realized Rodolfo's death must contain a message; it simply couldn't be otherwise. Impelled by this feeling of certainty, I left the station having suddenly decided to take the subway to the Cloisters, and from there walk the length of Manhattan, a walk of some twelve miles as the crow flies, and closer to fifteen with the twists and turns entailed if you cross Central Park. Because I now saw, in visual terms, the instruction Rodolfo had given me all those years before: I was to set out from that which was spiritually perfect, from the Good constituted by the abbey of the Cloisters, and move south over the island to the Bad, to Iniquity, to the origin of all wars and contemporary conflicts, specifically the narrow Wall Street, always in shadow, and the adjacent and no less macabre Ground Zero, where some class of revelation would await. This route and no other, I said to myself, was the one Rodolfo had always been suggesting I take, a suggestion that I, with unforgiveable insensitivity, had failed to interpret. And so it was that I rode the subway up to the Cloisters on its hill, closed at that time of the morning, and set off south the moment I arrived; it would have been 8 a.m. I walked into Harlem, a part of the city I was unfamiliar with, and on through it as the businesses in the various neighbourhoods, Jewish, Latino, African-American, opened their doors; they spoke in low voices, and in an argot completely incomprehensible to me, as I passed by in my parka with my Strand tote bag over my shoulder and my boots on my feet. You actually didn't need to look at a single one of the inhabitants to tell which neighbourhood was which, you could simply listen to the music coming from the buildings and vehicles; a kind of iso-phonia, this. As you moved from one neighbourhood to the next, this music, always blaring from some parked car or another, grew considerably louder; this I took to be a way of marking territory. After nearly three hours it began to snow very steadily. I reached the north side of Central Park, over which I saw falcons flying; they appeared to be accompanying me. The snow forced me to pick my way through the wooded parts of the park, I became lost more than once, before exiting through the south gate onto Fifth Avenue, next to which stood the cafe where Rodolfo and I always tended to meet for breakfast. It would have been one o'clock in the afternoon when, not having slept for twenty-four hours by this point and doubtless looking worse for wear, I started along that drag, where it was very clear to me that the further south one advanced into Manhattan, the more profoundly the Evil began to penetrate the shops and hotels, the people slipping and sliding chaotically along in the snow, the smells emitted by the buildings, the exhaust pipes of cars, the very mouths of the New Yorkers I passed, where this evil took the form of their condensed breath in the air, grey, dull, altogether a synthesis of negativity that, in short, only if you have come on foot from the Good is it possible to perceive in its entirety. I turned onto Second Avenue, less busy, where the snow lay so thick that, except for tourists from warmer countries, laughing and throwing snowballs, nobody was out. The falcons always overhead. I soon found myself following a set of single footprints that led towards the end of the street. Going on, I saw a woman taking money out at the CitiBank cash machine with its Latin keypad – give me the fire, take the fire, I whispered to myself. I walked by my apartment, aware I was nearly there because the sound of the typewriter that had been tormenting me for months now struck up; through the window of a mezzanine floor apartment I saw the little blueberry-seller girl hammering away at that very typewriter; she simply pummelled the keys, no apparent regard for where her fingers landed, and with such energy that she seemed to be making up a whole book on the fly. I saw the window to my apartment, choosing not to linger over it in case I found myself tempted to abandon my mission. The footprints in the snow led me to some streets I couldn't remember having walked down before, Victorian redbricks on either side with lace curtains thick as walls. On I went until the snow-covered awning of a cafe unleashed a sudden blast of memory in me. I stopped dead. It was the place where, on my first trip to the city, I had seen a man having his hair cut on the pavement. Seized by an emotion, an overwhelming feeling of memory regained, I went over and, on an impulse, started digging down to see if I could find any locks of hair buried in the snow. My heart then shrank to half its normal size: looking up, I saw the neon sign over the awning: 'Antonio's'. Until this moment, with everything snow-covered as it had been twelve years before, thus recreating the same composition, I hadn't seen that this was where Rodolfo and I had met: outside Antonio's bakery. I hadn't seen that it had been Antonio's bakery where we'd taken a table and had our first coffees together, along with some cookies – they now took form in my memory – that were in the shape of pregnant dogs. I looked inside. Antonio, deep in thought, sitting at the same table as always, looking like a character on a postal stamp, apparently staring off into space. But it was me he was staring at. I stood stock-still. I stopped feeling the snow landing on my face and hands. From that moment on, for almost a year, all trace of me is lost. A period I have no memory of whatsoever.

PART THREE

1.

Skyler stared out of the window as green, undulating hills rolled past, studded with the occasional farm and other rural construction as the Cabo Polonio-bound train left them all in its wake. She broke her silence to say: 'I feel like Uruguay's got more insects than the United States.' And then was silent again. A number of minutes later, she suddenly turned to me and said, 'And is the manuscript somewhere safe?' I answered with a resounding yes, patting the satchel between my feet. The train rumbled along at no more than 50 miles per hour.

What had happened, after taking a flight from New York City to Montevideo, is that we'd spent a number of days in that city, a first for the both of us. We spent our time traversing the Rambla, a promenade that runs for miles along the River Plate – the fact it's so long is, I think, why so few people go there – with small but powerful and astonishingly consistent waves rolling in. There was the odd fisherman spending a morning or an evening at the water's edge. We watched them from the hotel, the main entrance of which gave directly onto a groyne. Skyler said she wanted to go and speak to them, claiming that 'nobody pays the slightest attention to people who go fishing in cities, but they're the best tour guides there are.' Fine, I said, I'd try, but then when we approached – put off I think by this tilted posture fishermen assume, which gives them an air somewhere between executors of some primitive kind of office and Zen masters – I ended up saying nothing, but just stood, like them, gazing out at the waves and the horizon, beyond which nothing was visible, no land, no nothing, and I then couldn't understand how it was possible that what I was seeing was a river and not the ocean. She, instead of having the hotel breakfast, went to one of the taverns in the streets behind the hotel, in the Galician quarter, composed of an assortment of small brick houses, which were either half-built or halfway through being demolished, there was no way of telling. She'd come back very pleased with herself, having been given a Galician empanada for free. I had to laugh; in the Southern Cone, anything gets called a Galician empanada. We spent those days walking as much of the city as we could, almost always climbing up away from the waterfront, heading towards what looked to us like a mountain, or several mountains. Some nights we saw bonfires being lit inside lorry tyres on the bare concrete, people introducing planks into the flames and standing warming themselves; none of them spoke, and Skyler inferred from this that they were fishing for something too, only inside the fire. At least twice a day, she, in genuine concern, would ask: 'Are you sure the manuscript is safe?' To which I would invariably, and without checking, answer yes.

We saw the Palacio Salvo which was on the city's Independence Square, and about which we knew nothing until reading a tourist handout. It is a tower nearly one hundred metres tall, opened in 1928, the work of the Italian architect Mario Palanti, and until 1953 the tallest building in Latin America. Corbusier said of it: 'It ought to have been demolished the moment the final stone was put in place.' It looked to my eye like a cross between Art Deco and Portuguese Late Gothic. At first glance it gave the impression of being both a completed building and still under construction, or, in Skyler's words, in that inimitable American way of explaining everything by way of domestic references: 'Like a cake that's been taken out

162

of the oven five minutes early.' The same architect had been responsible for an identical tower, this one's twin, in Buenos Aires, both inspired by *The Divine Comedy*. The handout said there was a third tower somewhere, though the location was unknown, creating some kind of esoteric triangle that was neither of us could comprehend; any three points not in a straight line always form a triangle. What was interesting to us was the way this Montevideo tower housed people from every stratum of society; it was like a country in miniature: on the lower floors, small, asymmetric apartments slotted together as in a game of Tetris, and the upper floors held apartments that verged on the stately. The paradox was that, the higher up the dwelling space, the less natural light it received. That same day – we were there at about noon – we tried to get in, claiming we were going to the travel agency inside. The porter, sitting at a desk that was very long, but not in comparison with the enormous foyer, said that if we didn't have an appointment we could show him proof of, we weren't allowed in. While we argued over this, an old man, really very old, tall and with the palest of skin, stepped out of the lift, a bag in his hand stuffed full of what looked like clothes. There was something of the zombie about him. He walked past us and out onto Independence Square, heading for the opposite corner, where, I now saw, there was a building that looked very similar, if not identical, though on a smaller scale, to the United Nations in Manhattan. Some minutes later, sitting in a cafe, Skyler said: 'That old man with the bags, he was like an older version of you – you forty years from now.' I made as though I wasn't interested, or hadn't heard her. Leaning over, she brushed her nose along my neck, kissed me and, detaching her lips from mine, said the guys at the place she'd been going

163

for breakfast had invited her to a party the next night in the back of the bar. This started an argument; I didn't want to go. It was our first serious falling out since the trip began.

The following day, we each did our own thing. I sat in the hotel lobby reading local magazines and watching the fishermen down at the shore. At one point I was filled with the paranoid sensation that Skyler, to get her own back for my refusal to go to the party, had taken the manuscript that was supposed to be in my care. I didn't think she was planning to lose it on purpose, just that she had it with her, and I couldn't stand the idea that the principle reason we'd made this trip was out in the streets, at the mercy of pickpockets or even just the weather. I ran up to our room and, after keying in the safe code, saw the manuscript was safely where I'd left it. Taking it out, I lay down on the bed. I flicked through the sheets of paper – there were no more than fifteen. Seven poems from García Lorca's *Poet in New York*, transcribed by hand, and dated 1937. Each one was underlined, some with green, some with blue, others red, and there were occasional notes in the margin, all in the same handwriting.

What had happened, weeks before this, in New York City, and having vanished for a year not only from the world but also from myself, is that I had appeared at the door of Skyler's studio on a sunny June morning. She opened up to find me standing there with the Strand tote bag at my shoulder, inside of which, as well as a large number of cookies in the shape of pregnant dogs and flyers and pages from magazines I guessed I must have picked up over the course of my year's wanderings, and a canteen full of water I only had to sniff to tell it was undrinkable, was this manuscript I now held in my hands, with a note inside asking if I would kindly take it to Rodolfo's family. It was Skyler who, thrilled at the find, convinced me of the importance of undertaking the trip.

Skyler came back to the hotel at noon very frightened; she'd been down at the old port and a group of teenagers had tried to rob her. When I told her the paranoid vision I'd had, she laughed. 'I haven't come all this way with you to go messing around with the manuscript,' she said. With that, taking a shoe off, she immediately squashed an insect on the wall. Since our arrival in Uruguay she'd been killing insects on a constant basis, squashing any she saw; a predatory side to her that hadn't been apparent in New York. She undressed before stepping into the shower. Her knickers were enormous in comparison with her bra, which I found extremely attractive. I took a shower after her and we got dressed to go to the party.

The party was at the rear of the bar, which had imitation-wood plastic sheeting lining the walls. The host, a young guy with a wispy beard and very dark eyes, gave us each a beer by way of welcome; handing one to Skyler, with a half-smile he called her 'our punk Virgin Mary', indicating her spiky hair and immediately explaining for my sake that she'd told him how she'd come by the nickname. There was a table groaning with bowls of potato salad, smoked meats, carrots with a vinegar dressing, Uruguayan wine, beers and snacks. Through the back in the building's interior courtyard was a garden where a barbecue was being prepared. The people were of all different ages, and peculiarly mixed too in attire and aspect; Skyler, whispering in my ear, said it reminded her of something out of a Fellini movie. I spent a few minutes looking over the decor, little wooden busts from Java on top of the dishwasher, machetes from the Amazon next to the fireplace, your typical shop-bought Indian figures standing in a row and candles, candles everywhere. The host came over and said: 'All this belongs to my parents.' We went and sat in the garden. It started raining heavily, and through the fence we saw lightning over the river and over our hotel. We went back inside, the rooms now bursting with people. I felt a tap on the back and turned to find a young guy with a great shock of frizzy hair, a peach-coloured shirt and fingers covered in grease from the barbecue meat he'd just introduced into his mouth. 'So,' he said, 'you're from Spain. So cool you could be here.' We shook hands, with the corresponding transfer of barbecue grease from his fingers to mine. We talked for a few minutes, I couldn't say what about, before he said:

'Did you know it's the Brexit vote in three days?'

'It's what?'

'In three days, they're having the vote about Brexit.'

'No, I had no idea. I'm not sure I know what Brexit is.'

'Ok, cool. And have you noticed the way people always talk about large numbers of people migrating in terms of migration "flows", them "flooding" an area, a "stream" of immigrants, that kind of thing?'

'Pardon?'

'I just mean, the language always tends to be liquid-related – "flows", "streams", "floods" – like it was water, light or wind being talked about. I sometimes wonder what would happen if we referred to movements of people in terms of what they are, which is to say a succession of real, solid bodies, the sum of a whole lot of particles all independent of one another – don't you think that would change everything?' I stuttered a response, something even I didn't understand. 'Doesn't matter,' he said, 'listen, the real reason I came over was something else. That Yank girlfriend of yours, she's been killing insects since the moment she walked in here. You need to break it to her, okay, it doesn't matter if she's the high priest of all punk Virgin Maries, you don't do that kind of thing in this country.'

Some hours later, when we got back to our room, she said: 'Check the manuscript's where it's supposed to be.' This time I did. When she got out of the shower she said she was going downstairs for a cigarette without asking if I wanted to join her, just disappeared through the door. I looked down from the window and saw her compulsively sucking on her cigarette and pacing around the flags outside our window, I don't know how many flags there were but most pertained to made-up countries. Beneath these made-up flags she stopped for a moment, dropped her butt, and was about to stub it out but squashed an insect instead. When she came up to the room, I was already in bed. She got in wearing the same undershirt she'd worn that day. Putting her arms around me, she fell asleep almost instantly. We were due to take a train the next day to a station just past the city of Maldonado, where we were to pick up a hire car and drive the rest of the way to Cabo Polonio.

2.

The manuscript was still in the satchel between my feet and the train taking us to Cabo Polonio was chugging along without ever exceeding 80 kilometres per hour. The landscape outside had changed, rolling hills giving way to flat, rocky expanses. Skyler said Uruguay seemed to her a mineralized country, timeless. Moments later I would experiment with something that always happens to me on trains: if I look out of the window on my side, the landscape appears bathed in morning light, and then if I immediately turn and look through the window on the other side of the carriage, it looks like the light of an afternoon or evening. This is a tremendously mysterious effect, and I went on playing with it, thinking to myself of the train carriages as the hands on a clock stuck on midday. After that, while Skyler went on gazing out of the window, I flicked through the train magazine, something about hurricanes. At the different stops the train was alighted or boarded by locals, almost all of whom were functionaries who topped up their salaries with farm work. I whiled the time away trying to decipher their conversations. I found people in this part of the country hard to understand, their Spanish issuing from a long way back in their throats. The inspector came around to punch tickets, doing this every time somebody got on, as though each new passenger modified or reset the conditions of our journey. It started to rain. The flat expanse outside the window, lacking, as I've said, anything to give you a sense of scale or depth, meant you could only tell it was raining if you focused exclusively on the drops hitting the pane of glass. The train's forward motion sent the raindrops horizontally back along the glass; the whole thing resembled a multitude of spermatozoids emerging out of nothing onto the glass only then, within a second or two, to disappear into a different nothing. The genetic make-up, to put it one way, of a world parallel to the one Skyler and I, and the rest of the passengers, were inhabiting.

The thing is that travelling has always provoked

visions like this in me, which, far from being moments of delirium, far from hallucinations, only diverged very slightly from my normal perception. For example, the most panic-inducing thing for me is being in a city I don't know and having the unshakeable feeling I'm going to turn a corner and be confronted with someone exactly the same as me, and the two of us will look at one another but not say a word, and then both go on our way. Hence why, when I'm in an unfamiliar city, I cross the road continuously, and I walk quickly, and try to stop as little as I can. Anyone crossing my path might think I'm on the run from something, but it's quite the opposite: it isn't being followed that I'm afraid of, but the prospect of suddenly finding myself face to face with somebody who is also me. This was why, when Skyler had mentioned the likeness between me and the old man leaving the Salvo Palace with all his bags, my heart skipped a beat, unimaginably for Skyler, unimaginably for anyone: my double was getting old, speeding up, getting away from me. I was surprised to find that I lamented this loss.

Or, for example, a few days earlier on the plane from New York City to Montevideo, when I'd sat looking at the emergency instructions they put in the seatbacks. These had a picture of a woman looking out at you from the sea with a flotation device in her hands after an apparent crash-landing. She reminded me of Venus in Botticelli's *The Birth of Venus*. Maybe it was the look in her eyes, or the way the wind tossed her hair, or her facial features, which were surprisingly similar, or her unsettling calm. As though, instead of having just been in plane crash, she'd that very moment been born out of the waters.

169

And of course, I then remembered the myth and the fact Venus was born after Chronos castrated Uranus and threw his father's testicles into the sea.

Or like on another occasion, when I was in Rio de Janeiro for a literary summit: one morning, after breakfast, I stopped in front of an information panel in the reception detailing the day's events in the hotel. One of the rooms, the Velázquez Room, was going to be in use: a workshop was being given on beauty make-up, so a sort of link to painting. But the rest of the rooms were going to be empty. I didn't mind any of this, the non-use of those spaces even struck me as logical, all except for the Lorca Room. That bothered me. I couldn't understand the reason for this gap.

The people at reception told me that the Lorca Room kept flooding, that was why it was out of use; they couldn't even use it for storage. The thought of a mass grave then came to me, but an empty one. Throughout that day, as a taxi driver pointed out Ipanema beach to me, as the radio talked about the demolition of one of the city's symbolic buildings, as I watched a skater fly headlong into a palm tree, as the organizers of the summit welcomed me, as we had a coffee break together, as I sat in on a talk about contemporary Arabic literature that I wasn't very interested in, and then on another about Spanish literature that I was even less interested in, as I ate the *feijoada* dish I was served, as a little favela boy asked for 100 reais with hands outstretched, hands that seemed to me like those of an adult, as the coach took us back to the hotel and the rain beat down so hard it felt like being inside a boat, as, that's to say, the day ran its course, I went on thinking about the Lorca Room standing empty – an emptiness that at moments seemed almost immeasurable to me. I asked to have dinner in my room that night. While I waited, I used the time to count how much money I had left for the last four days of my trip, and it was then that I had what seemed to me an inspired idea: to write on each of the notes a word from a García Lorca poem, any of his poems, so that my remaining twenty-three pieces of Brazilian currency would then always carry part of the poet with them. I looked up his poems online and picked the one that seemed the best-suited to a country like Brazil – 'Dawn' – and wrote out the first twenty-three words on my twenty-three notes:

Dawn in New York has
four muddied columns
and a hurricane of black pigeons
splashing in the putrid waters.
Dawn

172

I took the notes, arranged them on the bed and made a photo-document:

I could see no better way to make up for the emptiness and disuse of the Lorca Room (which happened to be directly below the room I was saying in) than to put this fragment into circulation, meaning that the poem could potentially range to the farthest ends of the country.

Or like when, shortly after this trip to Brazil, I went to Turin with the fetishistic intention of recreating Friedrich Nietzsche's tragic experience in that city by literally walking in his footsteps. On the morning of 3

January 1889, Nietzsche is known to have left his Turin residence on Via Carlo Alberto, intending to walk into the city centre. He'd gone barely two hundred metres when, coming onto the Piazza Carignano, he pulled up at the sight of a recalcitrant horse being flogged by its driver. Nietzsche approached and, throwing his arms around the beast's neck, whispered something in its ear that to this day remains a conundrum: 'Mother, I am stupid.' He immediately went back home, where he lost the power of speech and soon passed out, not coming round until a decade later, a few days before his death in 1900.

A period Nietzsche would have no memory of whatsoever.

I had gone to Turin to cover the same short distance the philosopher had walked that day, from his home (A) to the square (B).

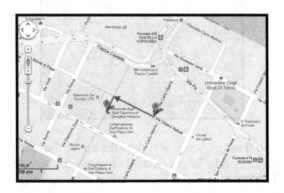

I went along Via Cesare Battisti, approaching what had been Nietzsche's apartment. It's on a corner and not difficult to spot.

I stopped for a moment by the café that nowadays occupies the ground floor. Looking up, I saw the window of Nietzsche's room. I took a photo, zooming in all the way.

The fact the window had the proportions of a golden rectangle jumped out at me. In the nineteenth century, this ratio, this privileged geometry, was a mark of a fine home, the thinking being that the people in charge of society ought to be in balance at all times – ought, that is, to be golden. I felt certain then that Nietzsche, before setting out on his final walk, had looked out from this window at the men and women responsible for the construction of civilizations, with their perfect countries and their perfect cities, and that when he looked out on returning from his walk all he saw were the dead, the piazzas strewn with corpses: he was seeing the future of the twentieth century, in which golden ratios would play no part whatsoever. And that it was this contradiction that made him fall silent forever. His own personal disappearance.

I went over to the door and took a photo from the pavement.

There was a confusing piece of graffiti on the wall: it looked like three number nines with a crown over them. A piece of paper had been stuck up inside the glass, advertising a room to rent. On the second floor, to be precise – Nietzsche's floor. 'For more information, call the porter's office.' My forefinger hovered by the bell; in the end I didn't press it. And if I had, I now think, I'd have become a different person. I went back to the corner with the café on it and started along Via Cesare Battisti.

It was a relief to be walking in the shade. The paving was set out in a rhomboid pattern – to drive the walker on, to make you feel less tired, and therefore buy more things. The same principal as in the colonnades of old, which were designed to prevent fatigue in those traversing this new landscape of shops.

I counted the bicycles, I counted shopping bags, I counted estate agents' posters. Here, everything was for sale. There weren't many people around. At the end of the street was a bookshop. I like looking at the window displays of bookshops in foreign cities; I have a habit of fantasizing there might be a book of mine there. A woman was coming towards me from the left, talking to her friend about some piece of local politics, something about the dismantled Fiat factory, I think, and she was so angry about it that she threw her hands about manically and didn't notice we were about to pass; her bag hit me, she said sorry.

I went up to the display, which was organized according to theme. There was a mistake: the Bible was in the tourism section.

I turned to the left. Ahead of me the street opened out into the piazza that was my destination.

I came to the exact spot where the philosopher had embraced the horse. There was a group of workmen there. I went over to them.

I asked what they were doing. One in a checked shirt said they weren't doing anything, they were eating, taking a twenty-minute break before going back to work; they were doing renovations on the car park beneath the piazza. From their accents they were clearly Romanian, illegal immigrants possibly. I told them they were sitting in the exact spot where a philosopher had spoken his last words. The men looked at the ground, as if looking for something. I looked, too.

I asked what their names were, how they'd come to be there – what was it that had brought them to Turin and not Madrid or Rome – but none of them said anything. Then they started laughing. I asked what at. The one in the checked shirt said not to take it the wrong way, they were just laughing, he said, my questions seemed funny to them, they were just there doing building work on a car park, they were something like an earthing element, another said, pointing at the floor, the world's own earthing element, and they laughed again, or the world's placenta, said another, the place we all come from, and they laughed even more. I asked if they minded me taking a photo of them, they said no problem. One asked for a cigarette and I gave him one and then turned and walked away. And I can now see when I look at the photo that one of them, holding some yellow sticks in his hands, is wearing a T-shirt on which someone has written in marker pen: 'The Crime of the Century'.

'Want anything from the refreshments carriage?' said Skyler, putting a sudden end to my reverie. A few minutes later our stop was announced. I jumped up to go and find her; opening the door to the next carriage, I found her hurrying back to join me. We had just enough time to gather our jackets, hand luggage and respective mp3 players, which neither of us had so much as touched. Stepping down onto the platform, it was clear we were the only ones getting off. With a beep, the train doors shut. We watched it roll away. The platform, with a covered building to one side no bigger than a bus shelter, stood out in the middle of a muddy upland. There was a hut on the other side of the road which, judging by the signs for ice creams and refreshments, was supposed to be the café. Your first thought in this kind of situation is to assume you've gone wrong, taken the wrong train, been given bad directions, misheard the voice announcing your stop. We crossed the tracks nonetheless; our wheelie suitcases didn't like the stony ground. We sat down on a couple of very dusty seats under the awning of the former café. We strained to listen for cars. Skyler picked up some newspaper and wiped the dust off the flat shoes she was wearing. I remember I fixed my gaze on the horizon, so flat here it was like it had been drawn with a ruler. A flyer for a Montevideo department store that had got caught under my feet flapped in the breeze. I wondered what tornado or hurricane had brought it to this place. Skyler put her headphones in. 'What are you listening to?' I asked. 'Sparklehorse,' she said. 'Does anyone know why the singer killed himself?' I said. 'No,' she said, 'but they said in *Pitchfork* his songs are so surreal it's hard to imagine they could be metaphors for anything.' 'I can see that,' I said, watching Skyler as she scanned for insects. Almost that instant she stamped on a dung beetle, or what looked like a dung beetle. It was then that a dust cloud appeared on the far horizon, and grew in size, approaching until it came to the spot where we sat. The driver pulled up next to the platform.

Following the obligatory pleasantries, he told us he'd take us to the place where the road met the motorway, half an hour away, which was where our hire car was. We left the shelter and drove along a mud track. The darkness in that moment was total, the car headlights sweeping across expanses of yellow grass which, with the wind blowing through it, looked like liquid gold. We passed a cowshed, one wall of which was covered in a confused mass of graffiti; I just had time to read a part that said: 'God doesn't fear the news. God is the News.' We saw a chapel a little further on with a cemetery; I didn't know if the creature lying outside the entrance was a dog or coyote. Driving at night is a question of trying to see things before you reach them; by the time you do, the headlights have moved on to something else. This same anticipation, I said to myself, applies in life generally given that life is a journey through darkness at the end of which, in dying, you emerge into the light of day. Skyler was fast asleep; mud and small stones drummed against the underside of the car – it was like a reinforced music box. We passed a series of industrial warehouses, there were a few signs of civilization now; one of the warehouses bore a red neon sign, I think it was the first time I'd seen a real-life bordello. Eventually we came to a properly asphalted road, though it had no markings and there weren't any pavements, and this then brought us out at the motorway. Then, at a crossing, we came to the other car. 'Keep going straight,' said the driver, 'and you'll come to Punta Chica. You'll be able to spend the night there. Keep on straight after that, tomorrow you'll be in Cabo Polonio.' And it was true, half an hour later Skyler and I came into Punta Chica on its main street, the strange wideness of which seemed out of proportion with the low buildings on either side. Closed bars and

181

shops. We came to a set of traffic lights as they were turning red, and stayed red for at least four minutes; we sat and waited, in spite of the absence of any other vehicles on the road. The idling engine was extremely quiet and we could hear cicadas. We looked around for greenery but saw none. We did see, down an alleyway, the sign for Hotel Punta Chica. At reception, a young man, his hair gelled into a quiff, asked for our IDs. 'Ask about the safe,' Skyler said, three times, and each time I explained that the man had said there wasn't one, and didn't the town and all that lay around it seem like enough of a safe? Once we were up in the room, both worn out, we decided to go straight to bed. 'Still wearing that undershirt?' I said as she undressed. We made love, and, unusually for us, the sex was undemanding. Afterwards, Skyler, with a sentimentalism that was very much unlike her, said what a strange thing falling in love was, how strange to pick just one person out of the possible millions, separating this one body and taking on its feelings, a bet on one single card, which from any point of view is a bad bet, and nonetheless throughout our entire lives it's the one thing we think about, 'Nobody, absolutely nobody,' she said, 'dedicates as much energy to any one thing as to finding, and then keeping, a partner; it's the most radically political and at the same time sentimental act there is.' She sat back against the bedhead, and declared that this kind of love was something totally new to her. She lit a cigarette. I got out of bed and opened the window to let the smoke out. She went on: 'People are nothing in and of themselves; identity is a delusion, a hallucination on the part of the ego; we only stay in love with someone if we love the things that surround them: their friends, their work, their family, the things they do in their spare time, their religion. Its childish to think otherwise.' 'What are the things around me that changed to make you want to be with me?' 'I don't know, I think you seemed slightly dumb before.' 'Dumb!' 'Yes, a little.' 'Me, or the things that came with me?' She thought for a moment: 'Both.' 'What do you mean, both?' 'Just that, there wasn't any conflict in you; I didn't pick up on any wars in your lands; you seemed to move around in a world that wasn't so much virtual as unreal, which is worse. It was only when you showed up at my door last month, all ragged, broken – like you'd stepped out of a war – with that tote bag and this manuscript, only then did I see that you and your lands might be worth exploring.' I said nothing to this. 'Does it bother you that I say all this?' she said. 'No, no,' I said, 'I was just thinking.' And it was true, I was just thinking.

3.

The coffee they gave us with breakfast was the best we'd had since being in Uruguay. It would have been ten o'clock when, having consulted a roadmap, we set out from the hotel; as I turned the key in the ignition, Skyler was still finishing her toast. The asphalt of the roads we drove along was a very dark blue, the kind that resembles a boiled sweet and makes you want to pop it in your mouth and eat it. Skyler said she'd just remembered it was her birthday. Many happy returns, I said, and then wondered how I could say that to a person I wasn't sure I knew at all. Suddenly she smacked the inside of the windscreen, making me flinch; she'd squashed a mosquito under her thumb. 'Finally. I was starting to think the insects in this country don't have any blood inside them,' she said. 'It isn't their blood though, remember.' 'What does it matter if it's from a human or an animal,' she said, 'blood, it's like money, it comes and goes; it only belongs to whoever happens to be using it at the time.' She carefully wrapped the insect in a bit of paper and put it inside her jacket pocket. After driving for nearly an hour over flat terrain we entered a steep gorge, the road dropping down between narrow cliffs and bringing us out onto a plain identical to the one we'd left behind, though the light here was different, more coastal. 'Tell me,' said Skyler, 'what was your favourite thing about Rodolfo?' Considering my answer, I turned to look at her. 'Look out!' she cried, and as I turned back to the windscreen I just caught sight of a rabbit running out and had to swerve, almost landing us in the ditch.

After turning off for Cabo Polonio, we passed through an area of such sandy terrain that we wondered if perhaps we'd gone wrong. We kept going until a scattering of structures appeared in the distance, what could barely even be called huts. We parked and left the car on an esplanade: the closest thing we found to a town centre. Soon we were amidst these brightly coloured structures, with TV antennae and chimney smoke alike winding up out of them. The porches had little windmills in the shapes of fish and tubular bells which knocked together almost harmoniously. We started asking locals who, sitting out on their porches, were chatting to one another or involved in domestic tasks, but Rodolfo's name meant nothing to them. We soon came to a beach, the long sweep of it empty of people. In the distance was a silhouetted hut with a lifeguard flag. Walking just inland from the sand of the beach and, passing this hut, we took a path that had been carved between the rocks. This brought us out at a row of seafront structures that were newer and more robust, what looked like holiday homes. There were some children playing in a car park. They were kicking a ball against a wall with a large Argentinean flag painted on it. We asked them, and a very small boy came over to say there was a hut, a little further on, with 'Rodolfo' written on the door. Someone shouted at the children from inside the hotel. As we walked off, an older boy came out and told them not to speak to strangers; he looked over, and our eyes briefly met. 'What is it?' said Skyler a few moments later. 'You've gone completely white.' 'Oh, nothing. That boy just reminded me of a waiter I met a couple of years ago, when I was on San Simón.'

Within a few minutes we were standing outside a pastel green hut, a garden of weeds and sand standing between it and the rocks on the shore. On the fence, in small, faint lettering, it said 'Rodolfo' and, below that, 'The She Dwarf'. Out across the water, covered in a mass of sea lions, we could see what we guessed to be Isla Rasa. We went through the gate and up to the front door. A piece of paper stuck on with a nail read: 'I'm in the SOS hut'. This, we guessed, must be the lifeguard's hut we'd just seen on the beach. We looked in through the windows: the interior was crammed with an array of nautical paraphernalia. 'It's like Isla Negra, Neruda's place,' said Skyler. 'I saw photos of it once.'

Going back the way we'd come presented no difficulty, but the sand on the beach was less easy to walk on; Skyler took her shoes off. The lifeguard's hut was raised above the sand at the top of a ramp, though this was so slippery I couldn't see how anyone could hope to get an injured person up it. We knocked on the door. 'Come in,' said a stern voice, and Skyler pushed on the door. A man sitting in a chair turned to look at us. On a table, a pair of binoculars, a plate with some leftover food on it, and a tablet with a videogame on the screen and some lively music coming out of it.

'Good afternoon,' I said, 'we're sorry to bother you, but we're looking for the family of a man named Rodolfo. He had a hut out here. We saw a note on the door. We wondered if you might have been related.'

Blue eyes looked us up and down before the man answered:

'Who are you?'

'Well, Rodolfo and I met in New York, and I've come to deliver something of his. My friend here's come with me.'

Without getting up, and continuing to stare unblinkingly at us, it was a number of seconds before he answered:

'Yes, I'm Rodolfo's brother. You'll know of his death, then.'

'Maybe you won't remember, but I called you a few days after, from New York – I hadn't been able to get hold of him and was getting worried. I think it was actually you I heard the news from.'

'No idea. It was a horrible time; repatriating an illegal isn't the easiest thing in the world. If it wasn't for the fact our grandparents lived in the States for a long time, and the friends we've still got there, I think my brother's body would have been dumped in some mass grave in that country.'

Relaxing somewhat, he got up from his chair. He had khaki combat trousers on, a checked shirt and beach sandals. We each shook his hand; a solid steadiness unmistakeable in his handshake. He was taller than Rodolfo and slightly older; close up, you'd put him at about sixty, though he wore it well. Fair, shoulder length hair and, as is often the way with people who live on the Atlantic, weathered skin.

'Would you rather we met somewhere else later on?'

He thought for a moment.

'I've got some work I need to finish. You go to the hut and wait for me there, I won't be more than an hour. It isn't locked.' Turning back to his tablet, he said: 'Help yourselves to coffee. There's a percolator in the kitchen, it should still be warm. Did you know the Brexit side won, by the way? It's just been in the news.'

I think it was Skyler who said we had no idea.

The cabin was as Rodolfo had described it to me. A single space made up of a living room, dining room and kitchen. At the back, a tiny bedroom with a mattress resting on four tree stumps. Next to that, an equally cramped shower space, with what we thought was probably just a hose sticking through the wall. The overall sensation was indeed that of a dwarf house. Skyler and I poured ourselves some coffee, though the sugar was nowhere to be found. Then, as we waited for Rodolfo's brother, we went around separately and – our silence taking me back to the times I'd quietly sat on the bench looking out at the East River, at all the things carried along and spat out and sucked back down by the waters – we inspected the many objects, with which all the walls, shelves and little niches were carefully crammed. They seemed to be organized into things come from the sea – a starfish skeleton, for example, went together with a shark's jaw-bone or a simple oar mounted on the wall – and those that hadn't but were still nautical, like a smoking pipe in the shape of an anchor, a coffee cup with a whaling ship depicted on the side, or a couple of pages inside a picture frame, from what appeared to be the instructions for a videogame, the title of which, *The Cloisters Under the Sea*, stopped me in my tracks. '*The Cloisters Under the Sea*,' I whispered to myself. Skyler came over. It was she who took it down from the wall, this set of technical details that, though incomprehensible to us both, we studied with such absurd intensity that she burst out laughing.

'What's so funny?' came a voice from behind us.

We both turned to find Rodolfo's brother standing there. He came over and tore the picture frame from Skyler's hands. She, red as a tomato, apologized profusely. I translated what she was saying.

'I don't need you to translate,' he said. 'I understand her language.'

Hanging the picture frame back in its place, he added:

'These are from the last videogame my brother ever made; two years later he was dead.' He paused for a moment, composing himself, before going: 'It was one of the great games of the early 2000s. It wasn't a commercial success, but programmers consider it a cult game. It was Rodolfo's homage to our grandfather. Would you like another coffee?'

Skyler, in shorts, her undershirt and a woolly jumper, wrapped her knee-length parka around her; it had turned suddenly cold. Rodolfo's brother still had his combat trousers and sandals on, and a jacket on top as well now which, blue, double-breasted and with golden buttons, added to his assertive manner to give him an extravagantly masculine air. As he moved about the kitchen looking for the sugar, which he couldn't find either, we completed the introductions. He was called Tomás, and he lived there six months of the year. He wasn't a lifeguard, but a marine biologist. He used the lifeguard hut in winter to study the sea lions on Isla Rasa.

'Okay, then,' he said, pointing us to a couple of armchairs facing out to sea. 'So tell me to what I owe the visit.' He was perched on a kitchen chair, which looked far from comfortable.

Now, I couldn't see how to start. I found myself hesitating and, not knowing where else to, decided to begin at the end:

'Well,' I said, 'it's a long story, and you probably don't need all the details. The reason we've come is this.' I opened the satchel and took out the sheets of paper. 'It's seven of Federico García Lorca's poems, transcribed by hand.'

Tomás jumped in:

'Underlined in colour, with notes in the margins?'

'Yes...' I said and, glancing at Skyler, handed them over.

He read the pages carefully, notes in the margins included, taking several minutes over it. Once he'd finished, he got up and went through to the bedroom, where we heard him rummaging and moving boxes around. After a few minutes, he came back with a bundle of letters.

'These are all from my grandfather,' he said, 'letters to his Montevideo family from when he was living in New York. Have a look and tell me the handwriting isn't exactly the same.'

We could see from a glance that it was. Tomás put manuscript and letters to one side:

'Where did you get these?'

'An old man in New York gave them to us, a Spanish guy called Antonio. He wanted us to bring them to you. Well, it didn't happen exactly like that, but... they just appeared in a bag I was carrying, including the note telling us what to do; we think it was this old man called

Antonio who wrote it. That's all we know. Your brother and I were good friends, I felt I had to bring this in person.'

'Antonio the baker?' he asked.

'Yes.'

'He's still going then?'

'Yes, he's there, like lots of other refugees from the Spanish Civil War who settled in New York.'

'Refugee? War criminal, more like. Real piece of work, that guy: he was a warden in one of the harshest prisons there was. A place called San Simón.'

'What do you mean, warden?!'

'Exactly that. It was my grandfather – Tomás, I'm named after him – who fled to the US after being held prisoner at San Simón. Antonio, who was his friend, was on the side of the Nationalists.'

I translated for Skyler. She was so taken aback that, still gripping a compass in her hands – I thought she might be about to crack it – she broke out in unexpected Spanish:

'But I've known Antonio for years,' she said, 'I go to his bakery for breakfast every day, and he's shown me lots of photographs of when he was in Spain, when he was a prisoner on that island, always with a warden standing next to him.'

'Well,' Tomás said, himself switching back to Spanish, 'he's tricked you or you've got mixed up. You so wanted to think the person you'd met was the one you identified with morally; you assumed he was the prisoner. But no, the prisoner was my grandfather. By the way, is Antonio still making those cookies, the ones shaped like pregnant dogs?'

'Yes,' Skyler and I said in unison.

Tomás got up and poured himself another cup of

coffee. He still couldn't find the sugar. Sitting back down, he clasped the cup for warmth, as though to squeeze the heat out of the porcelain itself, and proceeded to tell us how Antonio had helped his grandfather to escape from San Simón, and that, though he didn't know every single detail, Antonio certainly organized a boat and the grandfather, who, having been to university, had been given a job in the prison offices, had claimed there were some documents and office materials coming in by boat, and then only needed to get down to the jetty, where Antonio was waiting for him. The pair had rowed all night, heading beyond the estuary and out to sea, where a boat full of refugees bound for the United States picked them up. Tomás said his grandfather had a line about how simple it is to escape when there's somebody from the other side there to help you; you only need one, and all your problems are solved. He knew nothing about Antonio's motives for leaving the country, given his comfortable warden existence, but he had been aware of a collection of poems, eight of them, written out by hand, that during the grandfather's time in prison created a bond between the pair; the grandfather would read them out loud, and Antonio always found them moving.

'But there're only seven poems here,' I said.

'Yes, one's missing,' he said, putting them down on a side table next to him. 'In any case, my grandfather really missed having this manuscript. When we were little, on more than one occasion he told Rodolfo and me that Antonio had stolen all the poems from him.'

'And what about the prison escape?' asked Skyler.

'Well, the boat they thought was taking them to the US was actually bound for Cuba, but having made it that far they didn't really care, so long as it meant getting as far as possible from San Simón. Then, in Havana, with hardly any money except what Antonio was able to provide, they rented a room in one of the poorest areas. It only had one bed, which they took turns sleeping in. They both started in the sugar business, and it went well for them; it was a good time in that industry. They began at the bottom, working in the fields, and ended up with their own plantation, which, even if it wasn't one of the biggest, meant they were able to live comfortably. My grandfather stayed in sugar all his life, but Antonio gradually moved on to other things, eventually opening a bakery in Havana, followed by two more. We've still got photos of Grandpa in his first linen suit and a dark tie, sitting on the terrace of a cafe in Havana, with a neon sign behind him saying "Antonio's, Bread & Coffee". Grandpa's sitting between Antonio and a young Cuban woman, Paquita, who would later become my grandmother. They married three years after that. And it was then, after the wedding, when Antonio said he wanted to have nothing more to do with them, though nobody understood why. Not long after, 1945, my mother would be born in a hospital in Havana. Around the same time, Antonio got engaged to one of the girls working in his bakery. Antonio had some political connections by then, and started pulling strings in order to ruin my grandfather, who then decided to take my grandmother and mother and go to the US. In those days, pre-Castro, it was easy to go back and forth between the two countries. They arrived in New York and, like so many other Cubans and Spaniards, set up on the other side of the Hudson in New Jersey; my mother was four. Grandma got a job as a cleaner, she'd be up at five every morning to cross the tunnel that runs beneath the Hudson, leaving my mother in the care of Grandpa; he didn't have a job, and talked afterwards about looking out from his house at the abbey known as the Cloisters, on the other side of the river, at the northern tip of Manhattan. The abbey reminded him so much of ones in Spain that he went one day and asked for a job, anything they had going, accounts, doorman, he didn't mind. Given his experience on the land, from the plantations in Cuba, they set him up as a gardener. They were medieval gardens, and he was supposed to make sure they were conserved in keeping with the original designs, a job he immediately took to. He told Rodolfo and me a very entertaining story about how he'd started making innocent changes, for example planting a kind of fern in one of the cloisters that was native to San Simón Island, some of the immigrants having brought seeds with them to New York. And so it began, like a game, until within a few months he'd hatched a plan whereby, within a forty-year period, the gardens would have every species of plant he had seen on the island of San Simón. It was his own way of secretly paying homage to the old men at that prison, who, he'd told us with tears in his eyes, used to wander the gardens of the island until they died of starvation. Naturally, he never managed to make his vision a complete reality, but my brother Rodolfo told me that there, in the Cloisters, in a garden intended as the replica of another that appears in a tapestry of a unicorn being hunted, there's secretly at least three or four species of plant identical to one on San Simón, even including a certain type of palm tree. Grandpa did it in such a way that the differences wouldn't be too obvious, or, if they were noticed, possible to put down to the natural evolution of the different plants featured in the tapestry, all of which were from the fifteenth century. Well, Grandpa had to pass the time somehow. Grandma, though, didn't adapt so well to the new setting – the kind of cleaning

193

work immigrants were expected to do was pretty punishing – in actual fact they were made to sweep the streets: she told us about sweeping every square metre of those paving slabs with infinite patience, and about the amazing objects she sometimes found, and even the dust, the dust of that city is amazing, she said, it's unlike any dust anywhere else in the world. She later got a cleaning job at the United Nations building, which was great, diplomats are very clean people, but was sacked after six months, something to do with budget restrictions apparently. Then, convinced that my mother, who was still tiny then, would have a better future in Uruguay, she came up with the idea of sending her here to live with some of Grandpa's family who'd emigrated from Galicia before the Civil War. Grandma said she and Grandpa argued a lot over this; over his dead body, he said. In the end, Grandma, using what little she'd saved from her cleaning salary, booked passage on a boat for just her and my mother, bringing her here and leaving her with the family, who, like most Galicians in Uruguay, had set up in the bar and restaurant business, specifically the bars around the back of the Montevideo Rambla. And back she went to New York. That passage would last a total of thirty days. She arrived to find Grandpa extremely angry; not a word was spoken between them for another month. Once all that had passed, Grandpa told her that when she was away, one afternoon, on a walk through Manhattan, he'd seen a bakery with a sign over it saying "Antonio's". He was amazed to walk in and find Antonio sitting at one of the tables; apparently he'd been in the city for a year, having escaped Cuba after Fidel came to power. For the rest of Grandma's time in Montevideo, they'd seen each other almost every day. From what I understood, it was at this time that Grandpa

194

lost this manuscript you've now brought to me, though there were only seven poems in it at the time. Antonio asked to borrow it, saying he wanted to reread the poems that had done him so much good on San Simón, and Grandpa let him. He was never to lay eyes on the poems again. This was incredibly hard for him; he said that reading them was like having the poet there whispering in his ear, transmitting the same harsh New York to him that he was now experiencing. Somehow those poems helped him to become part of the city, to make it his own. Often, he'd tell Grandma he was going to Manhattan to buy seeds for the Cloisters gardens, but what he was really going to do was walk around in what he thought, from his reading of the poems, were Lorca's footsteps. He kept a map in his locker at work so Grandma wouldn't get wind of it, marking down all these routes in green, blue and red, to correspond with the same underlining on the manuscript. During her life in New York, Grandma never learned of the map, or about Grandpa's walks. He showed us the map when he was very old. He got me and Rodolfo together at our aunt and uncle's bar, sitting at the bar itself, the two of us on stools with feet dangling off the ground and him on the other side of the bar, as though about to get us a drink, and, reaching down into a discreet sort of bum bag he always wore inside his boxer shorts, he showed us those routes through Manhattan, all intertwined and overlapping; I remember them as braided lines of all different colours, like an alternate subway map, and he said to us: "Look how lovely it is, all the routes come together to form this figure of eight." One of those days, at the bar, he recounted an episode from his time in New York, something neither Grandma nor our mother had told us about: late one day, after finishing work at the Cloisters, he walked down to the stop he usually got his bus home from, but, he said, as he did he could feel his legs carrying him towards the street that leads into Harlem and on in the direction of Central Park, and so he kept on going, straight past his stop, and ended up walking that whole night, through Harlem, a pretty hairy place at the time, until he got to Central Park, which in those days didn't shut at night, and which he walked the length of, mechanically, not stopping for anything, and all the while there were falcons above him in the sky. That particular route didn't feature in any of the Lorca poems, but Grandpa said he thought maybe they linked to an eighth poem which had disappeared – a poem he had given Grandma as a present when they met in Cuba. She had been so zealous about the safeguarding of the poem, and had put it away in so many different places, that when it came to their move to the US, she couldn't remember where it was. And Grandpa, the night he walked the length of Manhattan, as it was nearing dawn, believing himself to be approaching Wall Street, or what is now Ground Zero, finds himself outside Antonio's, much to his amazement. Standing on the sidewalk, he can hear the bread machines kneading the dough inside. The blinds on the front window are down, but there's a gap in them. Putting his eye up to it, he sees a group of young women inside expressing milk from their breasts, pumping it into these brass bowls. And it's at this moment that the darkest, strangest episode in the history of our family occurs: he doesn't know whether he loses consciousness, or what happens, but Grandpa disappears without trace. Not even he knows what happened in the following period. A year later, there's a knock on Grandma's door, and she opens the door to find Grandpa there, haggard, emaciated, looking like he's just stepped out of a war, and holding a bag. Grandma, who had given him up for dead by now, let out a scream, then fainted, the neighbours came rushing in, and he, as though nothing had happened, opened the fridge, poured himself a glass of milk, took a canteen out of the bag and some cookies in the shape of pregnant dogs, which he tried to eat but found they were too hard, they must have been at least a year out of date, then said he needed to have a rest, his day was due to start at the Cloisters. Naturally his job had already been given to someone else there. For several months thereafter he's completely out of it, disappearing every night and not returning till dawn, and the whole time Grandma in a state of high anxiety. He mutters about needing to get the manuscript back, about how Antonio still has it, and he recalls events from San Simón, talks about a noise, a noise that stopped them from sleeping at night, and which he says he's started to hear again there in Manhattan. My grandmother takes it upon herself to go and talk to Antonio, who says he doesn't have the manuscript, that he gave it back to Grandpa over a year earlier. It's then that she, unable to cope any longer, decides to take Grandpa and return to Uruguay for good. Surprisingly, she has no trouble getting him onto a boat, simply telling him they're going on a daytrip to the Statue of Liberty, for a picnic, and Grandpa boards the liner, spending the crossing walking the upper deck, talking about the lost manuscript and saying he can already see the Statue of Liberty in the distance. They arrive in Montevideo, the family welcomes them with open arms. My mother, still only really a teenager, cries for three days straight, sleeping next to her father, who, in a daze, keeps to his bed almost the entire time; they're worried he might be about to die. After six months of being looked after, he seems to come round. My mother said that Grandpa didn't mention the manuscript ever again, or anything about his time in New York until we were born, first Rodolfo and then me, two years apart. We never met our father; he died in the gold mines in Corrales, in the north – not an accident but a fact of life, as we say here when somebody dies down a mine. Everyone thought I was the eldest: Rodolfo always seemed younger than me. I used to say that was because of the machines, that the machines kept him sprightly, because from a young age he was always interested in drawing different machines; he could spend hours studying a washing machine motor picked up in a scrapyard, or drawing one of Leonardo da Vinci's machines, he didn't mind which: he'd sit and draw any mechanism that was put in front of him. Grandpa would spend whole mornings watching him doing his drawings, using these precision illustration instruments and magnifying glasses to get all the tiny details right, and he'd sit completely silent as he did so, like he wasn't actually there, like you'd imagined him. Years later, when PC computers appeared on the market, he got into programming, and he was amazing at it, but he got tired and decided to buy this hut; he'd come out here and do stargazing, and draw constellations he said he'd discovered, – I've got them somewhere, all clipped together, I haven't been able to bring myself to look at them since his death because, according to him, they were constellations of dead stars. And then, before going to the US, he did his final job as a programmer, the Cloisters videogame – the instructions for which were what you had in your hands when I came in. Sorry, what was your name again?'

'Skyler, my name's Skyler,' she said, without taking her eyes off the ground.

'That was it, Skyler. Sorry, I'm terrible with names. More coffee?' We both said no. 'So, like I was saying, Rodolfo made this videogame; the main character's a gardener in the mid-twentieth century who gradually changes the gardens at the Cloisters, like Grandpa would have done if he'd been able to follow through on his plans. Grandpa died in his sleep, a month before the end of the century. The videogame was something he never got his head around, but it made him proud that his grandson had used it to finish the job he'd started in real life. He wasn't at peace when he died: till his very last day he missed this manuscript, and I think, secretly, Antonio as well. I suppose you're here because Antonio regretted stealing it after all. I so appreciate you coming all the way here to do this thing.'

Tomás was silent, still clasping the coffee cup his hands; cold by now, I imagined. Skyler sat saying nothing, sunk down in the sofa with her parka wrapped tight around her; she was still turning that compass over in her hands, it was like she wanted to demagnetize the thing. I saw some fishermen walk by on the path outside carrying empty baskets and their fishing rods, and children trailing behind them.

'Don't mention it,' I said. 'Now we know the story, it's even clearer that we had to come.'

'That's not all.'

'Oh?' said Skyler.

'No. I'll tell you. Not long after Grandpa's death an Argentinean surgeon, from Rosario to be specific, started coming into the family bar, having married a young Uruguayan woman. He came in three days a week for something to eat, and a coffee and mineral water afterwards. Grandma chatted with him, given how unusual it was to see a doctor in a bar like ours, more the kind of place the local fishermen went to meet up. She quickly found him to be a trustworthy sort of person, and she took the bold step of telling him about Grandpa's case: the strange episode in New York of him passing out and apparently vanishing off the face of the earth for nearly a year. The surgeon didn't believe a word of it, to the point that Grandma almost lost her temper. He carried on going to the bar to eat, but they never touched on the subject again. Then, after a few months, he said to my grandma that he'd given a lot of thought to Grandpa's case, and in actual fact over the course of those months it had been the only thing he'd thought seriously about in a scientific sense. Having consulted dozens of psychiatry manuals, and looked into theories about madness, none of which threw any light on the problem, he'd come to a solution, surprisingly in the field of surgery itself. When he ran Grandma through it, which took over an hour, she said she didn't understand a word, and asked him to come back the next day to explain it to Rodolfo and me. Naturally, we made sure we were there. The four of us sat at a table at the back, so the customers wouldn't hear, and the surgeon talked to us about a French physiologist from the nineteenth century named Pierre Flourens who, among other things, had been the first to show that the mind resides in the brain and not in the heart. But the truly important part, in terms of Grandpa's case, was that Flourens had been a staunch opponent of the use of anaesthetic in surgical operations: he claimed that when they get you on the operating table, give you the anaesthetic and open you up, the body experiences pain, an incredible amount of pain, and the brain simply forgets it when you wake up. The significant thing about this is that it would mean anaesthetics don't actually do anything about the pain experienced when you go under the knife, only the memory of the pain: they erase it. So anyway, this was his take on the year of Grandpa's New York disappearance: something awful had happened to him, leaving him in shock, anaesthetized, but with his motor functions still intact. It meant that as he'd wandered the city those weeks and months, Grandpa *had* suffered, he'd suffered a lot, but when the shock went away, his mind simply forgot, just like when you wake up on the operating table. That was why he looked the way he did when he got back to the house in New Jersey, seemingly back from a war, nothing but skin and bones; these stood in for the bruising you see on a person's body after an operation. The surgeon saw it every day in the operations he was carrying out: contusions in places they hadn't so much as laid a finger, skin discoloured for no apparent reason, eyes bloodshot as if the person had been crying for hours, sudden weight loss and so on, with lots more possible examples, he said. So that's a summary of the conclusion the surgeon came to; Rodolfo and I weren't sure how seriously to take it. Grandma said it sounded exactly right to her, and from that day on let the surgeon eat for free, said he could have whatever he liked from behind the bar as well, though I never saw him drinking alcohol, which he claimed to be the worst anaesthetic there was. A number of years then passed, Rodolfo was in New York by this time, and Grandma started to feel nostalgic for the country she was born in. Any time there was any mention of Cuba on the news, she'd well up. Walking by a travel agency one day, one of those with photos of the Malecón in the window, she stopped to look; she wouldn't say anything, but you could see her turning it over in her mind. My mother said she was concerned what Grandma might then do; if she'd been intrepid enough to bring her to Montevideo, alone, in the fifties, what wouldn't she do? Not long after that, Grandma started talking about memories from her childhood, details that gradually took on more and more prominence until a day came when she said she wanted to go back, wanted to walk the Havana streets again, see whether the houses she'd lived in were still standing. She started coming to my apartment every evening – it's behind the Rambla Hotel – and she'd sit in my living room drinking coffee; we'd talk about this and that, but she'd always come back to this idea of us making a trip to Cuba; we had to, she said. She even made me buy some Cuban rum and she'd have a small glass every evening. I told my mother that Grandma's trip to Cuba had to happen, and that she should go with her, but my mother wouldn't hear of it. I went over to my Grandma's one day and, not telling her where we were off to, took her to a travel agent they've got on the mezzanine floor at the Salvo Palacio, in Independence Square, and bought two tickets, one for me and one for her. When the guy working there handed her the tickets, it was the first time I'd ever seen her cry, and the last as it happened. When we came out of the Palace, she pointed to the building on the opposite side of the square, saying had I noticed it was an exact replica of the UN building, just a little smaller. Every time she passed it, she said, she saw herself inside, down on hands and knees scrubbing the floors, as she'd done in her younger years in New York. A month later, in December, low season, we flew to Havana. She'd made me compile a list of the addresses of all the places her family had lived; I'd bought her a notebook for that purpose which she kept in her handbag. I bought her a mobile phone as well, one of those dumb phones, big buttons and a screen you can see easily, in case she got lost. She put the notebook and the mobile phone in her handbag, and sometimes mistook the one for the other when she put her hand inside, which I found funny to begin with, but which started to irritate me over the course of the days. She was so uplifted, so rejuvenated, the moment we stepped off the plane in Havana, she'd start talking to strangers any chance she had, and even though she was ninety then, always made sure her hair was nice, put lipstick on and this glitzy necklace I'd never seen before. She wanted us to go for strolls in the nights, and to sit out on the cafe terraces, which she remembered being just the same, but older; "Only a little bit older, like me," she'd say, putting her hand on mine. I had a great time too. There were plenty of people who took me for the younger lover, in it for the money, and I wasn't at all comfortable with that but she found it hilarious; I think she even tried to encourage people to think it was the case. Being there also brought out her obsession with shopping and bartering, which I couldn't remember seeing in her before. I found it genuinely embarrassing. And she started being uppity in certain ways, like, we'd be in a restaurant and she'd demand they bring her another steak, saying hers was cold, even though it was clearly piping hot, or she'd ask for another glass of wine, claiming the one she'd been brought was dirty, even though neither the waiter nor I could see any marks on it. I think she remembered Cuba as a place of gringo opulence, fancy cars everywhere, and she couldn't accept that all of that had disappeared. She didn't mention Grandpa even once, and if I brought him up, she'd just change the subject. I remember us taking a taxi once: we were being charged an extortionate amount on the meter, and we were on our way to the house she was born in, where she'd lived till the age of fifteen. The radio was on really loud and she kept on telling the taxi driver that Spanish National Radio must be somewhere on the dial. That day, apart from her handbag, she also had a beach bag with her, full, I was later to find out, with bars of soap, little porcelain figures, sweets and suchlike to give as presents to the people in the houses we were going to visit. The first one was in Havana itself, the name of the street escapes me now. She knocked on the door herself and told me to hang back. A white woman came to the door, and my grandma gave her a potted version of her childhood in that house. The woman was open to the whole thing and invited us through to a courtyard, and Grandma, fairly shouting, said, "Look, there's the table we used to eat at," and, "I remember chasing your uncle through the house one day, slipping and cracking my head open on that door," showing us a scar on her head, and, "We used to play catch around here, I can still see myself haring after my cousin." The woman whose house it was listened attentively. Everything was just as my grandma remembered it, and the woman still used some of the kitchen appliances my grandparents had left when they moved. There was still a portrait of our family on the dining room wall, and when my grandma asked why, the woman said they'd always liked it because of the funny clothes everyone was wearing. I took a closer look at the photo: my grandma can't have been older than twelve in it, and she was wearing the same necklace she had on now. I turned around to find her standing by the sofa, saying to the woman: "That cushion on the right, if you turn it over you'll see it's been sewn up on one corner. That was the first piece of sewing I ever did." The woman turned the cushion over, and there indeed was a patch, the stitching along

204

the edges all wonky. The woman seemed slightly uncomfortable to me – I suppose I'd have felt the same in
her position. All of a sudden there're two guests in your
house who, in reality, have always been there. As we
were leaving, standing on the doorstep, my grandma
asked her if she had any children, to which the woman
answered that she did, and grandchildren too. Grandma
sent me off to the taxi for the beach bag. She took out a
packet of sweets for the grandchildren, and some porcelain figures for the woman, which she thrust into her
hands like they were some kind of contraband. We set
off for the second house, some 40 kilometres to the east
of Havana, a hacienda with a few trees around it, set out
in the middle of a huge expanse of sugar cane fields; we
could see it up ahead in the distance as we approached.
Clouds moved in, my grandma said she felt cold; the taxi
didn't have any heating. She put a jacket over her shoulders and told the driver off for not having heating. We
started along an earth track. I was surprised at how
clearly she could remember the way, she got every turning right first time, didn't need the notebook with the
addresses in it, or the little sketched maps she'd made,
her hand wonderfully steady, the previous night. The
taxi pulled up outside the main house, which was white
with a white garden wall all the way around – you could
see a courtyard just beyond it. Pointing to the gabled
roof, she said it was all for show, pure folklore, she said;
there was asphalt roll under the thatching; your grandpa
put it down when we got married. She took her handbag;
I took the bag with the gifts in it, and we got out, went
through to the courtyard, and she shouted out a couple
of times in what she intended as greeting. A middle-aged
couple emerged, the man black and the woman white. I
did as instructed and again stood a few paces back, and

she did the talking. Man and wife were both barefoot, some people always feel hot, or enjoy that direct contact with the earth, I thought, as my grandma told them about having lived in the house in the prime of her life, and her wedding being held there. The couple seemed to find it all slightly strange, but they let her in. I went back to the taxi, I was feeling cold too, I asked the driver if I could wear his jacket, which was blue, with golden buttons – it's this one I'm wearing now; the guy took a shine to me and let me keep it. When I went inside the house again, they were already up in one of the first-floor bedrooms. I thought I'd save myself the spectacle of Grandma's memory parade, and just stayed put in the reception room. Then the man appeared from upstairs, saying my grandma needed me. We went up to one of the bedrooms, it was very light and airy in there, she gestured for me to go over, took me by the arm and said: "Look, this is the bed where your grandfather and I conceived your mother." She was really emotional as she said this, almost like she was conceiving her again. I forced a smile and went back down to the reception room, where I then stood looking at a photo, a studio portrait of a girl no older than three, whose face reminded me of Franz Kafka's as it is in one of those stock images of him. It looked like it was from the late nineteenth or early twentieth century. She was sitting on a dark bundle of something. Then, incredibly, I realized that the bundle was a person, an adult covered with a dark sheet. I'd never seen anything like it; the little girl seemed oblivious.

'I took my camera out of my pocket, and was just taking a photo of the photo when the husband came into the room. The photo wasn't theirs, he said, they'd come across dozens just like it in another house, one that had subsequently been knocked down, and he liked it for the fact the girl reminded him of one of his granddaughters when she was little; she'd died four years earlier, he said. I wasn't going to pry, but the man told me about the girl's death without me asking: she was one of a large group who all drowned trying to cross to Miami. She was sixteen years old. While the man recounted his granddaughter's awful fate, I couldn't take my eyes off the photo. I kept staring at that little girl because, I think, I wanted to understand the story that stranger was telling me, the story of his granddaughter, a bit like I was trying to get inside the body of one dead person via another. Our minds are full of things that are dead and yet that we live for and couldn't live without, I said to myself as my grandma went on looking around upstairs. The man explained that in the nineteenth century, when they wanted to take a photo of a baby, it was usual for the mother to be covered up like this. The child, sensing the mother's warmth and the smell of her, would feel safe. In those days, the exposures took several minutes and, without the mother there, the child would be sure to crawl off or start crying, and the picture would be ruined. The photographer would then crop close around the baby so that the contours of the mother wouldn't be recognizable, she would just look like background cloth. This photo was the step prior to that cropping. The man took out lots of very similar photos from a box, holding them in his long, very dark fingers to show me. Far from getting used to them, the more photos of concealed mothers I was presented with, the more intensely incomprehensible they seemed to me. It happens sometimes: a repetition doesn't bring about a law or a norm but instead makes the repeated thing all the more singular, like the species evolving in reverse. I heard my grandma coming down the stairs. She was carrying a typewriter, it was my great-grandfather's, she said, and she had just bought it from the wife. Before we left, my grandma got the beach bag of gifts out; I found the whole thing with the gifts really quite testing. We said goodbye at the door, the wife embracing us warmly. The sky was clear now and the midday sun was right overhead;

I remember because as my grandma walked across the courtyard she didn't cast a shadow. Then it happened: looking over at a tree we were passing, she stopped in her tracks. For a few seconds she seemed lost for what to do, then she went over to this tree, murmuring something that I failed to catch. Standing beneath it, she studied the trunk, knelt down and then started ripping out the grass at the base, and then digging up the earth. When the hole was some three hands deep, she stopped, exhausted. With everyone looking on – in amazement, as you can imagine – she got up, wiped her hands off with some grass, walked over to the taxi and said: "We can go now, young man." When I asked her a few minutes later what was under the tree, she said there was nothing there, she just thought she'd remembered burying a wooden box under the tree with a poem inside it before they left for New York, one that Grandpa had brought with him from Spain. What poem, I asked? She told me it was called 'Dawn' and, with interruptions from the taxi radio, recited it to me:

Dawn in New York has
two muddied columns
and a hurricane of black pigeons
splashing in the putrid waters.

Dawn in New York groans
along vast staircases
seeking in its angles
a cure for the anguish described.

Dawn arrives and nobody takes it in their mouth
because neither morning nor hope are possible there.
Sometimes the furious swarm of coins

cleaves and devours abandoned children.
The early birds know in their bones
there is no paradise to come, nor unmitigated love;
know they are bound for the mire of numbers and laws,
and for mindless games and fruitless tasks.

The light is buried beneath chains and noises
in the impudent challenge of rootless science.
And crowds stagger sleepless through the boroughs
fresh, seemingly, from a shipwreck of blood.

'At the end, the taxi driver let go of the steering wheel and, clapping, cried: "That's Lorca!" In the days that followed, she hardly left the hotel: we'd go for a short walk in the streets nearby and within five minutes she'd be asking to go back to the cafe or to her room. When I asked her what was going on, she said the island was suddenly lacking in something, the motor that drove it on, the mains switch or something along those lines anyway. She kept up with her swims in the pool – they had a swimming instructor there and he got her working out, and not just her; there'd be like thirty old folk in the water with her. When I went to go and collect her, the surface of the water would have this pink film on it from all the lipstick, hairspray and lotions they used. Well, Grandma being down in the dumps like this gave me a chance to have a break from her. I made the most of it and went to the Marine Museum, where I met up with some marine biologists I've actually gone on to work with in some of my research. I kept thinking about the buried poem episode, kept on having an urge to take a taxi out to my grandparents' old house to dig around under that same tree, but I never got around to it in the end. Not that I regret it; I think it would have been a bit of a betrayal to go and do that without Grandma's say-so, a bit like trying to steal one of her memories. When we got back to Montevideo I bought the *Poet in New York* collection, and a few times got her to recite the poem to me again. And everything was the same except for one detail in the first stanza. So when Grandma said:

Dawn in New York has
two muddied columns
and a hurricane of black pigeons
splashing in the putrid waters.

My copy said:

Dawn in New York has
four muddied columns
and a hurricane of black pigeons
splashing in the putrid waters.

I asked about the deviation, and she assured me that the version of the manuscript Grandpa gave her had said "two muddied columns," not four, she was absolutely certain of it, and to her this was completely normal because "it's clear that Lorca was seeing the future in this poem, you only have to read it to realize that the two columns are the Twin Towers, and the black pigeons are the planes, and so on to the end of the poem, which is like a point by point description of what happened on 9/11". As you can imagine, I was dumbfounded hearing all of this. We never talked about it again. And that's everything. If you're planning on staying on in the country, you should come to Montevideo; I'll introduce you to my grandma. She'd love to meet you; she'd love it if you were to hand over these things to her yourselves.'

Skyler and I took a deep breath. More than two hours had passed since he'd begun his tale. We'd seen the fishermen come back in again, their baskets full, and the setting sun lighting up the bodies of the sea lions on Isla Rasa. Feeling the cold myself now, I got up and took my jacket down. Skyler put the compass that she'd been playing with on the table, I imagined it not only demagnetized but re-magnetized by now, though toward which latitudes I didn't know. We said we ought to be going, we needed to find a hotel for the night. Tomás said hotels wouldn't be open at this time of year. He had to work through the night in the beach hut; we were welcome to stay and sleep in his room. He set about making supper, something special, fresh eels, just bought, to celebrate the return of the manuscript, he said. Skyler and I went and perched on a couple of rocks in the garden for a cigarette. The pungent aroma of grilled eels drifted out from the kitchen window; 'Smells like pure protein,' said Skyler as she scanned the ground for insects. I looked up at the sky, so many stars that some among them must have been dead; I imagined lines between certain ones, stringing them together. A rat went by outside the gate, and then another one, which stopped less than three metres from us and sniffed at the earth. 'Did you know rats can't see more than twenty centimetres ahead of them?' I said to Skyler. 'No,' she said, 'I didn't know that.' The rat disappeared into the darkness. Skyler rested her head on my shoulder. I pointed up at a constellation of dead stars. 'They're in the shape of a pregnant dog,' she said. From the hut, Tomás called out: 'Five minutes till supper!' We were about to get up and go inside when a message alert came through on my phone, the vibration startling me. I read it immediately: 'It's a mistake to take the things we've seen as a given.' I looked up at the sky once more. There was no way of telling which stars were the living and which the dead.

BOOK II

USA
(Mickey Mouse grew and grew and turned into a cow)

1.

It's one in the morning, there's a glass on the bedside table, two minutes ago it contained two fingers of vodka. I know that my name is Kurt and that I'm lying in bed. I look up at the stain on the ceiling, it's grey, fractal in shape, looks like the side of the moon we don't see from Earth, or possibly the totality of the moon, I don't know. An ambulance goes wailing by outside, its lights sweep the room. I know that it's 1975 and Niki Lauda won the Formula One World Championship this year, and that's about it. I know from the home hardware catalogue that always drops through my letterbox, which has a page dedicated to sports – around here the national sport is following sports. Often I think of a golf ball that goes sailing out as far as the earth's exosphere and doesn't stop there but just keeps on going. I hear the shrill buzzing it makes: the shrillest, most piercing sound ever. Another ambulance goes by, followed by the alarm on the microwave going off. I sit up, lift myself off my air force-issue mat, drop my air force-issue blanket to one side. I shuffle forward, I think. The single room in my prefab home features a kitchen that consists of little more than a counter jutting out into the living room. I go over to the kitchen. A faint trembling in my Achilles tendons. Everything appears to me in a slow-motion kind of blur. My collection of astronautics books is on the bar cabinet. Another ambulance goes by, red and blue flashing lights, here for a second, gone the next. Out of the corner of my eye I see my model F-105, the plane I flew in Vietnam. How many more ambulances could possibly go by, I don't know. The microwave is going off, it's unrelenting: it sounds like it's about to explode. I rest my elbows on the countertop, sweep the plates aside, open the microwave, grab the vodka glass off the revolving

217

plate and down it in one. An insane pounding starts up in my temples. I take a seat on the couch. My eyes come to rest on a newspaper cutting I've had framed, with the words: 'Edwin E. Aldrin said today: "The fact we made it to the moon wasn't for study reasons or to bring back soil samples, it was to overtake the Russians in the Space Race. That was all."' Another ambulance goes by, but it isn't another ambulance, it's the fifth cop car to park directly outside my front door. This I know because somebody then knocks on my front door; I go and open it and see my neighbours peeking out through their curtains. There's a cop standing there, he's got a flashlight in his left hand and a gun at his belt. 'You've really done it this time, Kurt,' he says. 'We're taking you in.'

Yes, it's me, Kurt Montana, the fourth astronaut on Apollo 11, which Armstrong, Aldrin and Collins supposedly took to the moon and I supposedly did not. The Three Little Pigs, I call them, though I don't believe I've ever said it out loud. It just came to me the moment I first laid eyes on them: the similarities with the sweet little animals of the tale were just so striking. I won't say which of them lived in the solid brick house, which in the house made of sticks and which of them in the shitty sty made of straw. In fact, for the avoidance of misunderstanding, and to prove I bear the guys zero ill will, I won't ever call them that again – the Three Little Pigs – though I will just point out that they each invited me into their homes on numerous occasions, though no boiling vodka shots were ever drunk there. I'm the fourth little pig, not purely because that prefab home of mine was less sturdy than any of their abodes, but because I have been redacted from all the official accounts. I feature in none of the photos of the lunar expedition, the reason being that it was always me taking the photos.

The arrest at my prefab home was a long time ago now,
in San Francisco in 1975. I'll come back to it, but for now
I want to recount how, years before that, at the beginning
of the 1960s, when I was just out of my teenage years, my
father came back to the house one day and announced
we'd won the lottery. It was clear from his belly and his
dress sense that he was involved in cattle-farming: the
kind of man people in the 60s might have referred to as a
modern-day cowboy. We lived in Montana. My mother
wasn't at home that day; she had a weekly meet-up with
her girlfriends at the county social club, a run-down
wooden shack situated more or less at the midway point
between the ranches in the area. It was never completely clear to me what she and her friends did during those
get-togethers, I'd just see her coming through the door
at 9 p.m. with leftover carrot cake in a paper bag and a
bottle of some liquor with nothing but a sip left. 'Here,
Kurt,' she'd purr, 'kept you a little cake.' And I must have
been in my first year of university; by my estimation it
was summer vacation the day my father spoke the magic
phrase, the phrase of the twentieth century: 'We've
won the lottery, folks!' It sounded like he was repeating
something somebody's fairy godmother had told him.
Then he took off his sheepskin jacket, which he'd tanned
himself in his youth, and hung it on the coat stand by the
front door, never to take it down again. I have a memory
of the Hollister boys – seven in total, all of them white
as white can be and doughy-looking – coming a few
months later to take away the stuff we didn't want, saying they'd take everything except the jacket, which was
green by then, with a layer of bacteria swarming across
the hide. My mother took the lottery win badly. She had

no desire to leave Montana, while to my father the wind-
fall meant the future of the family clearly lay in Florida,
which was then the up-and-coming place. In the mean-
time I enlisted, though without much hope that I'd end
up taking part in the first Vietnam offensive, only then
to be sent out after all. First an aeroplane reeking of co-
logne flew us out to Hawaii, from there a plane dripping
with male hormones took us to an island on one of the
Japanese seas whose name I can't now recall, and last of
all a shit-smelling boat dropped us in the conflict zone in
South Vietnam. I remember a kid from New York who
came and sat next to me on the first day, and ended up
sticking to me like a limpet until hostilities ended, saying these words: 'Don't sweat it, Kurt, these smells, the
way they're just getting worse and worse, it *ain't* a sign
of things to come!' Upon arrival, since I had some flying experience – there was a ranch near our own back
home, the McCormac's, and they had a little prop-plane,
which me and the McCormac boys took out on occasion
– I was trained up, and within four months found myself
flying F-105s, which it turns out is a cinch. I didn't take
down very many of the Vietnamese fighters, but I can
say with certainty that I had a knack for dodging their
missiles. I can also say that I took my anger out on the
civilian population. Not something I can reasonably put
down to drugs or psychiatric issues, not like the jokers
who came and joined later in the war – and don't even
get me started about the guys in Iraq, an all-expenses-
paid vacation if I ever saw one. No, in my case it was
sheer pleasure, iniquity for iniquity's sake, the kind of
iniquity that manifests when you get away from yourself
completely, and suddenly every single moral injunction
you grew up with is just spinning around your head like
the pieces of a junked machine. As for the recent war

in Afghanistan, and the even more recent one in Syria, both of which I've only really half-followed on TV, I've seen recruits trotting out the same self-deceiving crap: more excuses. Excuses: the great issue of our time. Truth is, in war, same as when you play the lottery, the mind just goes empty, and that's the drug that nullifies all reasoning. You get to a point where you think you're on the sequence of vessels that took you to Vietnam again, but in reverse, starting with shit and ending with the finest perfume, when in fact you're bowling headlong down the track to total dissolution. The one thing I did come away with was the surprising ability to read Braille with my tongue. This I believe merits an explanation: we came to a town in what had been designated Zone 4 – the country had been divided up into Zones 1 through 10, with the lower numbers supposedly being the easiest areas to subdue. The infantry had already done their thing in Zone 4, so everyone assumed it would be easy pickings from the air. That turned out not to be the case. It took a full three days of low-altitude sorties to take out all the surface-to-air missile sites, manned by no more than five hundred Viet Cong armed with rifles, basically hunting rifles, but as accurate as the bows and arrows of Chinese archers. We improvised a runway in a jungle clearing and headed into town by jeep. Everything, as far as the eye could see, had been decimated; the whole place was one flattened shitheap, except for the one old building which looked half-Chinese and half-colonial, and which turned out to be the leper hospital. We found them in the basement. Mutilated corpses are a sight you don't forget, but the mutilated bodies of the living, those still capable of holding a conversation, are something else altogether. We dragged them out and got some food inside them. There was one blind guy whose hands had been eaten away by the illness so that you couldn't tell whether what he had left were arms or lamb's hooves. We ended up staying in the strategically crucial Zone 4 for six months. We were sent on bombing missions in other Zones, Zone 0 in particular, but always wound up back in Zone 4. This blind leper of ours spoke English, and I believe I was the only one who took an interest in him. I found him reading Braille one day: bringing the book up close to his face, he explored the characters with the tip of his tongue; there was nothing, he said, that he couldn't read, given enough time. When I asked whether it had been a challenge to learn, he said, No, not at all, and that in fact the tongue was better suited to reading than the tips of your fingers – far more sensitive – and that he'd be happy to teach me. It was kind of a dumb thing to be able to do, he'd say after a few drinks, but at the same time pretty extraordinary: very few people in the world could boast such a skill. 'And,' he said, 'if you do learn it, you could make a lot of money in your country someday, they give people money for all kinds of crazy stuff there.' Within twelve months I could make out short phrases pretty well, simple things. It's of absolutely no use to me, I know, but it still makes me proud to have come away from that war with something to show for it, more than any other idiot, no matter what they say.

My father took that million-dollar cheque and hid it under the bed. He thought it would be safe there. My mother had by now categorically stated her intention to stay put in Montana, that Florida was out of the question. She'd read in *Reader's Digest* about a kind of cattle farming that people said was the future, a future she wanted a taste of. All of a sudden, it seemed like the future was just about the only topic of conversation in our house. There hadn't been that kind of talk before, but now 'future' was being repeated the way a child repeats words for things it can reach and yet still seem mythical, like 'regulation football,' say, or 'Superman'. Whether we were mid-dinner and the meat had been seasoned with exotic spices, or the clock on the oven chimed at the same time as the radio, or while we gathered around the radio for the game and the pitcher unexpectedly turned his cap backwards and the crowd was amazed, or times when I was filling my parents in on my early aeronautical studies, in one way or another 'the future' was forever in the air. In my last year at college one of our professors, a woman from Czechoslovakia who had emigrated in the 1940s, told us about an art movement they'd had in Europe called Futurism, which went tearing through those lands, but the future we spoke of at home was different: a future you could smell and touch, one that was actually real. I've always had weak lungs; pneumonia and never-ending bouts of bronchitis were like my stock in trade. I'd be in and out of the hospital every month, I don't even know how many x-rays of my thorax there must be in the archives of that hospital. This became something much-discussed as well: saying 'x-ray' was the same as saying 'velocity' or 'acceleration', and when we said it we thought about light travelling through the body and about unimaginable diagnostic images, hitherto hidden from all the world, the preserve of God alone. In other words, when we said 'x-ray' we were also saying 'future'. I would look at those images of my lungs and even in those days be thinking about the side of the moon we don't see.

My mother showed me the *Reader's Digest* article and said that thinking magazines are less important than

223

books was the greatest show of ignorance imaginable. 'Magazines are always ahead of books: they get to everything first. Books just gather past knowledge, things that used to be the future.' She'd underlined the entire article with both red and blue. It went into descriptions of the revolutionary principles of certain new cattle-farming methods. There were some unclear maps and blueprints that looked like photocopies of photocopies of something which wasn't genuine to begin with. Given my studies in aeronautical engineering, and seeing as my father appeared hell-bent on Florida, she asked if I would help her build the shed in the article alongside the farm buildings. That day, I remember, she'd had her hair permed and was wearing it in a high ponytail. She looked like the wife of an astronaut, and she had three colouring pencils, one red, one blue and one green, poking out at angles from her hair like a star or a snowflake. She was sipping liquor through a piece of straw she'd pierced at one end. I also remember my father coming back that same night and having a new sheepskin jacket on, a professionally tanned one. I went back to MIT and my studies soon afterwards, and the cattle-farming methods and the sheepskin jacket began to fade from memory, mine and that of my parents as well. When, years after, the cop stood in the door of my prefab home, shone his light in my face and said, 'You've done it this time, Kurt', he enunciated my name with the same delicacy my mother had on her return from the social club: 'Kurt, son, I kept this bit of cake for you.' It never ceases to amaze me how well this country treats its former heroes.

Now I want to think about the belly buttons of the majorettes, twirling their batons as they go by, the batons

224

twirling constellation-like, and their purple nails and their high-heeled boots, and beyond them a black Cadillac with the top down, three men riding in it covered in confetti, three men who set foot on the moon, three satellites floating through the streets of Washington DC: a sensation of eternity that little by little seeps out into the multitude of onlookers. I'm there too, filming everything. If you weren't in any of the photos on the moon, they said to me minutes before the procession set off, you can't be part of this either. You just film it. You do the filming: your country will repay you.

This memory often comes back to me in my dreams. Dreaming a memory is a strange thing.

Also, here in the Home, my roommate, Semicolon, tells me that I'm always saying 'Smirnoff' in my sleep, but this isn't because of any particular liking for Smirnoff, rather it's because of a commercial I've seen: in it, a golf player strikes the ball and it flies off into some trees, but does he care, no, he isn't going to pick it out of the rough, he stands and waits for his Smirnoff and orange, with which his scantily clad wife immediately presents him. Semicolon and I get along OK, though we disagree over TV shows, all he ever wants is the ball game or to see how Hillary's polling against Trump. Semicolon likes Trump, he's come up with a nickname for him, 'the true hyperbole', because he's capable of achieving not only everything he suggests, but more than it's actually possible for him to suggest. Hillary he calls the 'metaphor for all that will never be'. But what really gets Semicolon going are Sarah Palin's glasses; he misses her and is flabbergasted that she hasn't been given at least a walk-on role in the campaign. In any case, I can't imagine a better old age than this. And now Semicolon is asking if I'll teach him to read Braille with his tongue. The same thing he asks me every night before bed. 'No problem,' I always say. 'Tomorrow's the day'.

To go back to that 1975 night in San Francisco: I put on my mirrored sunglasses, the cop swept the interior of my prefab home with his flashlight and then, putting the cuffs on me, led me over to one of the five cop cars parked outside, and then straight to the District 7 precinct. By then the prefab was all I had left of my father's, he'd gifted it to me a few years before he died. I sat in the waiting room with the other arrestees, until I heard my name over the PA. That's the way they do it: just your name, the more familiar the better, like they already know all there is to know about you. They never say, 'Come through into the interrogation rooms now,' or, 'Come to Room 2,' it's just first name, last name – like you're expected to know the way already. It was the same on the ranch when my father and the farmhands went around shouting, 'Gloria!' and 'Ruth!' and 'Pinta!' to make the cows come in. On my way to be questioned, I went past a line of guys in cuffs, whom I imagined having been stripped of their surnames too. I'm no believer, but as my name rang out over the PA again, my parents came to mind and I hoped they were in a better place, far from people like me.

My head was still pounding from the vodka toddies when the officer started asking about my activities of the previous night. I told him the truth. I'd left my prefab home at 9 p.m. and, like every night, gone by the Barbarita multiplex, or the photo booths there, to be precise, to take four near-instantaneous passport photos, 'You see, Officer, I like seeing the evolution of my face,' I said, 'the straggly hair at my nape, those bags under my eyes, bluish, kind of like bruises. Then what I do is I take the printouts, cut around my face and then stick my current face onto a photo I've got on the wall back at home, a photo Armstrong took of me, a private moment you understand, something the public has obviously never seen: it's of me walking on the moon, but the helmet on my space suit is obviously mirrored, which means you can't tell, that's why I stick the photo booth pictures of my face on it. Means I actually get to see myself on the moon for once.' 'Try to answer the question, Kurt.' 'Sorry, Officer, of course... So, after the photo booth I went for a dozen eggs and a six pack, drinking one of the beers on the way to the Flamingo Bar, and when I got there, no sooner did I step inside than I was presented with a shot of heated vodka. I remember, Officer, just before I got to the bar having to fight my way through this crowd of cameras, film crew people, they were shooting some TV show, *Starsky & Hutch* I think somebody said, looked about the dumbest thing I ever saw. As I was going by, one of the cameramen, hanging half out the back of a pickup truck, offered me something, it appeared to be LSD, Officer, but I declined. My brain's had quite enough LSD in it since birth. At about 11 p.m., and after a number of encounters with young ladies not really worth mentioning now, I left the Flamingo having drunk my fill, my plastic bag with the dozen eggs and the five beers in hand.' 'Wasn't it a six-pack?' 'That's right, but remember the one I drank one before getting to the bar.' 'Oh, yes. Go on.' 'I went walking. I walked for a good long time. Not down to the beach, most people's destination when they've got no particular place to go, but heading for the city limits, the Sacramento road, in particular, and as I went along I made sure to check in the ditches, I've always had a soft spot for ditches, for the way they don't seem to belong to anybody; if you should ever find yourself walking along in a ditch, well, that's a lot like walking on the moon, in the way that when you're on the moon you're a human but simultaneously you're way outside everything that's human, do you see what I'm saying?' 'Sure, sure. Go on.' 'Okay, so I walked and I walked, a good few miles, and hardly any cars passing, but then one pulled up and asked if I needed anything, which I didn't, and a few bikers came by soon after, sounded like Choppers to me, those drifter sons of bitches didn't even stop, not that I would have said yes to a ride, but they could have at least asked. I went on walking, maybe an hour or so more. The thing that's both good and bad about freeways is that once you're on one, there's just no turning back. Something pushes you on, and though there's the headache of all the inter-changes and junctions – you above all people must know about that, Officer, how mixed up a person is liable to become – I happen to be blessed with an excellent sense of direction, a kind of inner compass I've had since my flying days which has never left me, so I had no prob-lem finding the right fork in the path, if you will, and I soon found my way to a gas station. I decided I'd stop in for a drink, and the guy working there tells me that nobody takes that route any more: there's a new free-way now, wider and better laid out. I had a chocolate bar and that drink, me and the guy were shooting the breeze for a while, and he ends up telling me that in fact I'm walking parallel to the coast and in the exact opposite di-rection to the way I think I've been going. Hell, I think, the night is cool, the stars are out, and all I want is to be walking some place, plus the moon was waxing and just about bright as day. I didn't look directly up at it, mind: ever since I came back from the moon I've avoided that, hence if you ever see me out at night I'll be keeping my

eyes on the ground and I'll have my mirrored sunglasses on. Anyway, eventually the guy says to have another
drink on him, and he gives me another chocolate bar for
the road, here, I've still got the wrapper in my pocket, I
can show you...' 'Don't worry about that now, Kurt, go
on...' 'Okay, come 5 a.m. I'd had just about enough of
the freeway, so I turned down one of the exits, onto the
coast road proper, and away in the distance I could see
a town with some docks, and after a few miles of this
winding road, green meadows either side of me, I came
to a "Welcome" sign, passed the first few houses, and sat
down on a post at the end of one of the jetties. Behind
me was a series of brightly painted shacks, stores selling
fishing tackle and whatnot and bars with "Closed" signs
up, and in front of me a bunch of leisure boats. The sun
was coming up. I took a beer out of my bag, cracked one
of the eggs, swallowed it down raw, had the chocolate bar
and beer as chasers.' 'But hadn't you already eaten that
chocolate bar?' 'I had eaten one, Officer, but there was
the other one the guy at the gas station gave me.' 'Fine,
go on.' 'Sure, so the boats were rolling slowly, or heavily,
on the waves, they reminded me of the bellies of the cows
in Montana when they're asleep, the sea going on puls-
ing as far as the eye could see, or as far as my eye could
anyway, which after that third beer, on top of everything
else I'd drunk, wasn't all that far, and I cracked another beer, and another egg, then another beer and another
egg, and it was then that I spied, at the far end of the bay,
a house that immediately struck me as being the one out
of that movie *The Birds*. There was no doubt in my mind,
so then I realized I was in the movie location. And what
happened next, if somebody else told me about it, I sure
as hell wouldn't believe them: at first it was a dot, nothing but a dot on the horizon, which gradually started to

grow but at the same time to atomize into smaller dots, and I then saw that these dots were birds, birds flying out of that same house on the other side of the bay, headed straight for me, Officer, making a beeline, and then I'm trying to beat them off; I'm swinging my arms all around, there's thousands of them, too many for just one man, and then one of them, a seagull, came hurtling at me, it was coming to pluck out my eyes, and I threw the first thing I could lay my hands on, the last of my beers, which I still hadn't opened.' 'Right, Kurt, and just at that moment a Dutch gentleman, hearing you shouting, pokes his head out his porthole, and that beer of yours hits him square on the skull, knocking him out. Right?' 'That's right, Officer. Pure coincidence, I promise you.'

Here in the Home, I have a plastic flower in a vase on my bedside table. It's a memento, a memory of a time and place, and those are things that I do all I can to preserve. My roommate Semicolon is currently channel-hopping, constantly switching back to Fox News; new election polls are popping up every twenty minutes. For now, Hillary's ahead of the True Hyperbole in Montana as well. Where the hell is Sarah Palin, Semicolon wants to know – that's all he cares about. Now the TV is showing shots of the capital of Montana, Helena; now, a shot of the plaque outside the town hall: 'Last Chance Gulch', it reads, Montana being the last state before a person gets to Canada. An interview begins with the head of Yellowstone Park; he doesn't say who he's voting for but does emphasize the fact that, whatever happens in the elections, Montana is the United States' third largest state, but number forty-four in population figures: all the open prairies and mountain ranges are so incredibly vast that it means 'We're in God's hands here, the new

230

president has to do something about it, bring people in to populate all these empty spaces, build a whole new water system; those inmates at Guantánamo would be ideal up here, all they're doing inside is wasting decent taxpayer's money, and you get nothing back. We could sure do with them round here.' In the background a group of tourists toss sandwiches to some bears, while children record proceedings on their cell phones. My antennae go up, I wonder if there might be any mention of the county I come from, or any shots of our former ranch, and just when I feel sure my childhood home is about to feature, Semicolon's cell phone rings, the ring tone so loud it drowns the TV out. Beside himself with excitement, he says it's an alert from the National Car Chase Company, who provide a service he's subscribed to these two years past. Any time the cops start a car chase – usually it's some dime-store hoods, they tend to be Black and not very well armed – they notify the company. The company sends out its helicopters, which film the chase, which in turn is broadcast in real-time on your smart-phone. The cops try to drag things out, make more of a show of it. (Or so people say.) Semicolon, glued to his cell phone now, gives little jolts and kicks, and jumps half out of his armchair every now and then. 'Hey,' I say, 'I've got to be up at seven, turn that crap down, wouldya?' And when I come to turn out the light he's still there, the light from his cell phone bathing his face, which for some reason also appears pixelated. After a little while the warden, Encarna Low, pokes her head in; Black and with a body that is literally round, and forever breaking our balls, she tells Semicolon to turn off the cell phone. 'Breakfast's at half past seven, we're on summer schedule now, and I don't want either of you boys being tardy.' After she's gone, Semicolon, making a tent of his sheets, goes on watching in bed. 'What about them tongue-Braille classes then?' he says. 'Sure,' I say, 'tomorrow's the day.' The last thing I see before drifting off is my plastic flower in its vase. The last thing I hear is gunfire and the rumble of a helicopter ripping away into the emptiness.

It's pretty nice here. You get all kinds of people: retired non-combatants, the kind who didn't much like the prospect of soya gruel all alone in their homes, widowers who come hoping for a second chance in love, or housewives whose children have palmed them off and who here develop mean addictions to a combination of amphetamines and the shopping channel. In Semicolon's case, after divorcing at seventy, he became obsessed with his granddaughter's Barbie dolls and, in an act he still holds to be the bravest thing he ever did, got involved with a woman several decades his junior who was no stranger to cosmetic enhancements and who piloted the speedboat for retiree daytrips in the Keys. She took him for every dime he had. I can never recall Semicolon's actual name, which is my fault: a result of all the drinking. We call him Semicolon for the way he's always stopping mid-sentence, halfway through making a point. He pulls up short, mouth open, apparently never to speak again; if you're lucky, after an hour or two he might pick up where he left off. Encarna Low has a joke about Semicolon's family, about them having a single brain cell between them and taking it in turns to use it. They're easy targets, but it also happens to fit the reality of the situation like a glove. The joke first came about on a day when Semicolon's family happened to be visiting at the same time as Encarna Low's boys – four Black kids, sharp as tacks, who sat slowly eating their way through

a collection of chocolate jumbo jets. These they extracted from a see-through plastic bag which also contained
chocolate rabbit heads and chocolate Baby Jesuses. And
the second they laid eyes on Semicolon's family (the
daughter necking what appeared to be morning-after
pills; her husband, who had a Clinton & Co. Insurance
badge on, Semicolon's ancient ex-wife, who wore not
only a Lakers sweatshirt but the beanie to boot, and
the granddaughter, thirteen years old and still pushing
her Barbie around in a life-size stroller), they instantly
dubbed them the Genius Squad. Encarna Low's public
response was to tear a few strips off the boys, but, later
on, with all the visitors gone, we had a pretty good laugh
about it. I like Encarna Low; she's made of the same stuff
as soldiers are: however challenging a situation, she'll
just stop and think for a moment, seeming briefly to
gaze into thin air, and then will suddenly know exactly how to proceed. And proceed she does. Semicolon
came here of his own accord, whereas my case was more
complicated. I'd been in and out of dozens of rehab clinics in different states, but because I'm a national hero,
because of my Presidential Medal for Freedom, the
Distinguished Service Medal given to me by NASA,
and my Air Medal from the US Air Force – among quite
a few other honours – I get preferential treatment and
they can't just throw me in a cell the way they can all the
other scumbags. And, being retired, military law can't
touch me any more. So I was given a choice: take a job
as staff at a psychiatric hospital near Cape Canaveral, or
one in the kitchens of this retirement home in Florida.
I figured it's easier to hide a bottle of vodka in a large-
scale kitchen than it is in bare padded cells. Plus, Florida
always makes me think of my parents.

So, alongside Semicolon, sweet, insolvent Semicolon,

I have the task of prepping the residents' food trays. We have a list marking out each resident and their respective meal plans; all we have to do is put the right food in the right tray sections and then put the lid over the top, seal the trays with this hermetic lid, and then they are like wide, shallow boxes: the coffins, we call them. We line the coffins up on trolleys to be distributed around the Home, and that's all there is to it. It's harder trying to explain than it is just to do. One by one, the trays or little boxes or coffins, three times a day. By dinner time I sometimes get the meal plans mixed up because if I've been out in the gardens hitting a few golf balls then I might forget to take my sunglasses off when I come inside and I can't read the words very well. Then we get an outbreak of inexplicable stomach complaints, diarrhoea, dormant ulcers being irritated and blood tests going haywire. Something I like doing is writing notes to go out with the meals. I get a piece of paper and write things like, 'Chin up, not long left now,' or, 'Nice forecast today, make the most of it,' or, 'Little birdie tells me your hip's going to mend just fine.' I have no relations with the recipients of my messages; I don't know if they have broken hips or lung cancer or if they're healthier than Sarah Palin; essentially these notes of mine are very simple messages of hope, a universal balm that manifests in the kind of good mood only humans can bring about in other humans. When the Three Little Pigs and I were on the moon – oops, I'll try that again... At one point when I was on the moon with my three astronaut colleagues, filming Armstrong float-walking around, he started waving at me to get my attention, and eventually he stopped and walked on a little, leaning forward, arms heavy at his sides. He was imitating a monkey. The mime was to make the point that we were the first settlers of this land, the original primates of a world to come, and this, as well as being the first joke ever cracked on the moon, gave me a real boost for a few moments. Back on the space shuttle later that day, he explained that his breathing apparatus had stopped working properly: he hadn't been getting the correct amount of oxygen, and gradually began to feel dizzy, which culminated in some light hallucinations – objects flying at his face – and he'd begun flailing his arms around to defend himself. This is what I mean when I say a person doesn't need to understand a signal in order for that signal to be a balm to them: errors can be effective, even explosively so. That's the reason I'm so open to the operation of chance in the distribution of my food-tray good-mood notes. Aside from that, the garden of the Home overlooks the sea, and an electric fence separates us from what we might call the world. This mortal fence isn't there to stop us getting out – nobody's here against their will – but rather to stop all the criminals around these parts from getting in. I once saw a photo of a portion of the Earth as it is today. It was a photo of an aerial image from Google Earth, and I came across it in one of the free magazines that do the rounds here. You could clearly make out the Home and the adjacent fields and smallholdings. I'd never imagined that Google Earth saw everything with such clarity; when I was in space, the planet looked way blurrier. For example, on the way back down, as we were about to enter Earth's atmosphere, we saw, at the eastern edge of Turkey, what was undoubtedly a soaring, snow-covered mountain, out on its own in the middle of a desert, and on top of it there was the silhouette of what appeared to be a boat, a very big one; the silhouette was faint, like the kind you see on x-rays, so the boat seemed to be buried a little way down in the snow. A great number of speculations and comments, and even one or two private jokes, filled the ensuing minutes, things the four of us would go on to recall and laugh about at the annual NASA reunions. We later found out that what we had seen was the silhouette of what experts have claimed to be Noah's Ark. Semicolon is a firm believer in God, and I mentioned this to him one day, and he said: 'Shut up and put this tortilla in that Tupperware. By the way,' he added, handing me the quarterly magazine produced for the Home, 'have you seen this? Isn't it the gal you got together with last year on the outing to the beach?' There was an interview with a woman who owned a souvenir store in the area, and when she was asked what she liked best about her work, she said: 'People need memories, we all do, and that is what these things I sell are: machines for reconstructing all that people have lost.'

2.

The exams at MIT are no walk in the park. It's sink or swim. The students were housed in bungalows on a campus out in the middle of dense forest. An icy wind blew almost constantly, originating in Newfoundland and stopping off in the urban mesh of Boston before it hit us. There was a superstition among the students that if you could survive a night completely naked out in the forest, you were guaranteed a decent degree: a strange supposed link between physical hardiness and intellect, one I never attempted to verify. Vietnam meant I deferred my second year two years running, and, predictably enough, I had little interest in the freezing temperatures the pristine New England forests around the campus may or may not have reached.

In the run-up to Easter vacation, fifth semester, I receive a telegram. It's from my parents. As tends to be the way with Montanans who go away to study, I've only seen them once over the year, at Christmas. My father was still in the prefab homes business then. I know he'd tried his hand at several new ventures and none had gone that well. Now they're in Florida. 'Come quickly, something to show you, something that changes everything. Love, your parents.' I'd never been sent a telegram before, least of all one from my parents, and still less one like this. Generally, they would either talk nonstop or clam up for months at a time.

One day in March I take an early Greyhound from Boston to Penn Station in New York City, from there a taxi to JFK, and then a flight on to Orlando. My father comes to get me from the airport. We drive in his Cadillac to the place he's currently residing. We get there, I see it's a motel. My mother emerges from a side door and comes running over to kiss me, a trowel in one hand and bits of grass in her hair: she doesn't tie it back these days, and she is radiant. My father puts an arm round her. Events then go more or less as follows:

They show me around. My father's itching to give me the lowdown on his new hotel, which he has it in mind to turn into a timeshare resort. This he points out as we go down a wide, winding staircase, newly installed, which comes out at the reception, a half-floor below the main entrance. You don't need to look very hard to see that several of the lights have blown. My father's summary of the works continues:

'I added a patio with ocean views,' he says. 'Designed it myself. The quotes from the landscape architect were steep as hell.'

It's immediately apparent that almost every single

room still needs work. None of the kitchens have been installed and, stopping in the doorways and glancing in, I see large holes in the walls, the result of the latest group of students to come and wreck the place. We keep finding air conditioning units lying on the floor with missing blades. My parents have requested a loan to help shoulder the costs, and things are on the up. For now, only one or two of the rooms have been taken, but the first floor is being wallpapered. Just yesterday the new roof was put on, my father says, pointing to some carpets piled up in a corner that look to be water damaged.

'I'm looking to make it a really high-end kind of place,' he says. 'Give it a real upgrade. No more students, no more lowlifes.'

The person in charge of these works is Buddy. My father found him standing by the highway, in the place labourers line up every morning, waiting for someone to drive past and give them some work. A buck an hour. Seeing the look on my face, my father says wages are a lot lower here in Florida. My mother says Buddy is so strong: she finds it incredible, given his size, how he carries cement blocks around all by himself. I think she says something about a 'mini-Hercules'.

We go around a whole array of different units destined to become convention rooms. They are identical, but being so run down, no two actually look alike. I nearly tear a handrail off just putting my hand on it. This happens in Florida. I ask what the smell is. My father, going ahead up another flight of stairs, says nothing. I try again, this time more discreetly:

'Usually when somebody buys a place as big as this, they get a soil sample done. Could find yourself sitting on a toxic dump.'

'It smells the same wherever you go in Florida,' my

mother says. She is wearing dangly earrings which sway as she talks.

We come to a hallway, dimly lit by a few wall lamps and with a green runner extending down the length of it. My father leads the way. My mother has been nudging me constantly, and only now do I see why: my father's gait is odd, he clearly needs to do something about his back. But instead of doing anything about it, he'll just take himself off for the occasional soak in a hot bath in the en suite they share, Room 308. A trolley bearing mops and cleaning products suddenly emerges from a room, and we narrowly avoid being run over. The person pushing it is a large woman of colour whom my father doesn't seem to know; he carries on past her. My mother gives a little singsong hello, but the woman just gazes back.

Close to halfway down the hall, a small balcony appears on the right. 'There it is!,' says my father, as we step outside. I remember looking out towards the ocean, the darkness of stormy seas that I love, but he's referring to the patio just below. We look at the swimming pool with its very blue water and the smattering of tiled dolphins, and the recently acquired lounge chairs beside the pool, and beyond them a crescent of palm trees that looks, frankly, pretty damn nice. For a moment I see it all through the hopeful eyes of my father: works being completed, tourists out sunning themselves, children splashing in the pool, men with their bellies on display, women's bellies hidden under swimming costumes, and the business really ticking along nicely. Buddy appears down below, I don't know where from, with a very large bundle in his arms.

'Buddy,' my father calls down, 'that palm tree isn't looking so good. Did you tell the tree guy he needs to

239

come see it?'

'Yes,' Buddy calls back, 'I called him.'

We look at the palm tree. It's one of the smaller kinds, my father says: the larger ones cost a whole lot more.

'I prefer the larger ones,' I say.

'Is that right? The royal palms? Smaller, bigger, to me it's all the same. But don't you worry: when things are up and running, we'll be sure to get a few.'

None of us says anything for a short while as we look out over the patio and the ocean which, as it is everywhere in Florida, is a deep, almost purple blue.

'When it's all done up,' my mother says, 'we'll be millionaires. At least.'

'No doubt,' says my father.

After the million dollars my father did win on the lottery, he went on to buy property in Fort Lauderdale, which he later sold at a healthy profit. The move to Miami came not long after, and there he set about repeating the trick. He got his light aircraft pilot licence, bought a twin-engine aeroplane, the Cadillac and a decent-sized boat. He could have called it quits and retired, but, in keeping with the modern, entrepreneurial spirit that moved him, he started travelling the length and breadth of the country buying up more land and property. He was in great form in those days: every single day he came home from Texas, a bunch of yellow roses for my mother. But none of his ventures went well for long. In the space of a single day, and due to a scam cooked up by an associate of his, the North Carolina ski resort he'd acquired went bust. The ensuing lawsuits were not cheap. In a panic, rather than sticking with what he had, he opted to go into the prefab homes business: they were like mobile homes, he said, only much better. Plus, once you got them up, they did look truly homely. The whole

240

country was one big construction site in those days, you had unskilled labourers going wherever the work led them, which was just about anywhere, and there was a lot of demand for family homes that could be thrown together and taken back down again in the time it took to draw up a contract. According to my father, the prefab homes business was set to outdo even fast-food, which was coming up at the same time.

Two years ago, on Christmas day, when they were living in an apartment very nearby, my father took me to see the first one. He made a surprise of it for me. After a big breakfast and opening the presents laid under the tree the night before by my mother, he said he wanted to take me for a spin in the Cadillac. We soon left behind the beaches and modern buildings, the areas of the city I knew. The road bisected fields and small rural communities. I remember how run-down the houses were, and I remember the trees. I'd never seen trees completely covered in Spanish moss, which hung from the branches in abundance. I remember being reminded of my mother's earrings. After a couple of hours, we came in sight of a water tower, the kind that resembles an onion raised up on its own stalk. It had OCALA painted on the side. Taking a hand off the steering wheel, my father shot me the 'OK' sign. We soon entered Ocala proper, only to drive clean through it.

'I thought you were saying it was in Ocala,' I said.

'No,' he said. 'Not much further, though.'

Again we were passing through uncultivated fields, more of the moss-black trees and the houses with the shoddy paint jobs. After about fifteen miles, we came to a vacant lot. A muddy, vaguely circular clearing, bare of all trees and plant life, and at the far end stood the prefab home. Fair to say, it did look every bit a real home. We walked over to it. This meant stepping around a whole host of potholes: the county was laying water pipes. All the while my father was looking around and saying: 'This'll all be grass.'

The front door was a foot and a half clear of the ground, so you had to clamber up into it. The porch would happen after Christmas, my father said. Everything inside shook when you moved around, and the flooring seemed just as flimsy as the walls; I half expected to go tumbling through it. My father, leaning on the small kitchen counter, pointed at the ceiling:

'This one they call "cathedral ceiling". Ten feet high, eh? You could shoot hoops in this puppy!'

The homes did not sell as well as he hoped. He worked for a while in a bank, but wasn't cut out for it, so went back to the personal enterprises. A guy came and knocked at my apartment one day and asked if I was the vice president of some real estate company or other. I already had half an idea where this was headed, and just answered yes, and he handed me a summons. I put it in a drawer along with numerous others and promptly forget about it. My father had been quick to shift focus. For example, and always with the promise that the eventual proceeds would come down to me, he made me vice president of a number of companies covering a wide range of industries. He sent me forms; I signed them. At intervals, the summonses would rear their heads again. One day my brother told me that our parents were deep into our mother's pension money. It was then that they went around asking the banks for loans and, somehow, got given one. In a final push to get back on track they bought this abandoned hotel, the Palm Beach Resort, with the idea of doing it up and going full tilt at the fledgling timeshare market.

We stay out on the balcony. Poolside, Buddy is struggling to prise the lid off a colossal pot of paint. In the distance, the vast ocean is still that same deep blue-purple. My father says something about wanting to show me the model of the timeshare resort, of what will later be a timeshare resort. I'm not really listening, but I turn and follow him back inside.

We go along the same gloomy hallway, coming past the cleaning lady who does not appear to have moved, and who acknowledges us this time. We take the stairs down to the ground floor, and my father uses the master key to open either Room 101 or 103, I can't remember which. The moment I step inside, I feel as though I've been here before, everything seems eerily familiar. Then I see why: the colourful striped blankets, the bedside tables with their round legs and copper-tipped antlers made into wall lamps. I see furniture from my childhood in several of the rooms. It's like years of uninterrupted rain have combined to shrink our old house to this.

'It's all your old things,' I say.

'Look good here, right?' my father says.

'What are you using for a bedspread now?'

'Regular bedspreads,' my mother says. 'The same as in the other rooms. Hotel issue stuff. They're OK.'

'Here,' my father says, 'come into the living room.'

It takes him a moment to find a working light switch. Casting around, I find none of the furniture here familiar. We look at a painting on the wall depicting the skeleton of a boat washed up on a beach.

'Got almost a hundred of these from this one warehouse. Five bucks a pop. Pretty nice, huh? They've all got the seaside theme going on: shells and lobsters, that kind of thing. And no two the same, all of 'em real oil paint, all done by hand. Whaddya think?'

I say nothing, he answers for me, I seem to remember him saying something about Picasso, something I then instantly forget. He is smiling as we go back out of the room. He'll show me Apartment 207 shortly, he says, my room. He has taken to calling the rooms apartments, to distinguish them from the motel rooms they used to be. Mine has a small kitchen, and a balcony overlooking both freeway and ocean. I know for sure I'll end up spending time watching passing cars. My father put a poster up in the entrance announcing an irresistible offer: any guest who stayed the night would automatically receive free sunscreen. So far, nobody has gone for it. Apart from Judy, the secretary, a native of Ohio who wears her hair in a long plait, kind of a high school look, only a few elderly couples are currently residents. They go down to the swimming pool every day. There's the woman in her motorized wheelchair and her husband, with his very pale face and lumberjack shirt – Minnesotans, I think. They complain that, past a certain age, you just can't get a tan any more.

Ever since I can remember my mother has had premonitions in her dreams, and in this new life she and my father are leading in the hotel they have been happening a lot. She dreamed about a hole appearing in the roof, and a number of days later, one did. She dreamed about the skinny cleaning lady from Tallahassee upping and quitting, and the next day the skinny cleaning lady from Tallahassee had. Another much-discussed dream was about a young man who came to stay and broke his neck diving into the pool, which had been drained. A number of days later they had to drain the pool because of a fault in the filter motor – a motor, according to my mother, that never, ever broke. She tells me this one day when my father's off on an errand and the two of us are in the pool – me swimming, her sitting on the side dangling her feet. She's never learned to swim. I don't remember the last time I saw her in a swimsuit, her excuse being that the sun is dangerous for her freckles, which practically cover her entire body. She joked in years gone by about every freckle being a star, which made her skin a whole night sky. I have the fleeting feeling of being at swim lessons again, the way I used to feel when she came to pick me up, but then, seeing the dark hair on my chest, the thought feels wrong. There is the sound of hammering from elsewhere on the property, Buddy must be busy with something, but a little while later I see him go by carrying a wrench about as big as one of his arms. My mother, swishing her feet, says the reason for all the dreaming is she feels like such a fish out of water. They wouldn't be so frequent, she thinks, if only she had a place to call home. She runs me through all their peregrinations, all the hotels and condos they've stayed in, including one place I haven't previously heard about: a recording studio my father bought for next to nothing which, she says, was almost the final straw. And then this: all her things, all her new dishes and cutlery, and the family photos too, in storage.

'I dream about them every single night, all packed away.'

'Something happens to them?'

'Nothing. They just stay there: untouched, unlooked at.'

Another thing we could call a constant in my parents' lives – a definitive feature of my mother and father – are the surgical procedures they are always planning on having, and always postponing. My mother is always talking about a facelift, the classic kind, stretching the skin back at the edges, but with a twist: there is a new technique that also means an alteration to the roof of the patient's mouth. Her upper palate has been drawing back over the years, and her top teeth don't fit against the lower ones any more. The idea is to pay for the work with the proceeds from the prefab home venture. For his part, my father needs an operation on one of his spinal discs to at least alleviate the pain that makes him walk with a stoop, sometimes at a right angle. There is also the slated prostate intervention, intended to widen his urethra; in spite of his trouble passing water, he doesn't seem to mind the twenty trips to the bathroom daily. Or it's that the prospect of the surgery just frightens him: he has it on good authority that this is one uncomfortable operation.

'Your father's stream,' said my mother, 'isn't so splendidly musical as it once was. You live with someone, it's the kind of thing you find out.'

I realize I am in need of some new shoes, something more suited to the unique climate in this part of the country. I brought some with me – black leather, black laces – perfectly good for walking in the woods around MIT, but sandals would be more the thing here. There are nights when I take my father's Cadillac Florida Special, the one remnant of his big-spending days, and on my way to a bar for drinks pass a souvenir store with dolphin T-shirts and straw hats in the window, and sandals hanging symmetrically and on the basis of some mysterious colour scheme. I haven't been in yet.

One day, on going down for breakfast, I stop by the office and see Judy looking all worried, chewing on the end of her ponytail.

'Your father's had to get rid of Buddy,' she says.

One of the guests then appears and starts complaining about a leak: he's in a fury, having, he says, been up the entire night calling reception and no one answering. His room is still one huge puddle, and to top it off he suspects bedbugs, though he'll leave that for a later, separate complaint. Then my father comes in with the tree surgeon, and the two of them are arguing. So now my father has the leak-complaining guest in one ear, and the tree surgeon in the other demanding payment for palm trees already planted; it would seem that the dwarf palms have dried out completely. Happens sometimes to dwarf palms in Florida, he says, and nobody knows why, but it sure as hell isn't his fault. And he needs to get paid. At this my father loses it completely, starts shouting that nobody ever told him about dwarf palms sometimes drying out in Florida, and the guest is still there demanding his refund, and me in the middle quieter than the bird just passing over our heads, and which seemed to me to be about to come crashing straight into our heads.

In the end I think my father offered the man a free night's stay. As for the tree surgeon, I'm not sure how that played out. In any case, he manages to shake them both off and asks me to go for a drive. Once we're on the road, he tells me what happened with Buddy. He was drinking on the job. Apparently he spent the entire morning in room 106, lying under a broken air conditioning unit. My father had been about to say something to him, but then the 'palm tree moron' showed up, they went out to look at the trees, and at that point my father forgot all about Buddy.

'When I get back I find him still underneath the carcass of the air con unit. Not so strange considering what a tiny guy he is. He's always been able to reach the parts us normal-sized folks can't, that's one of the things he's got going for him. But it also hits me that he's still in the exact same position as when I left. I go over, and I say something, but he doesn't answer. I give him a shake, "Hey, Buddy," I say, but still nothing. Then I see he's got his eyes shut and the cooling coil that comes off the motor is in his mouth. And the coolant, okay, is alcoholic. This scumbag's been fixing air con units the entire week! From the look of it he'd gotten some pliers and snipped the coil and, since it was copper, all he needed to do was twist it around a little and he could drink his fill. The ambulance came and took him this morning – he'd passed out. Could have been in a coma for all I know.'

This my father tells me as we go along Route A1A. Pre-10 a.m. is the ideal time to find one of the highway labourers. You can tell them by their deep tans, acquired courtesy of Florida sun and salty air. It is a mystery to me why my father discounts some at a glance. He pulls up at one guy wearing a T-shirt that could not have been more typically Florida and chewing half-heartedly on a vegetable, possibly raw cauliflower. Trying, I guess, to impress him, my father presses the novel electric button to wind down the window. The man, mouth still full of cauliflower, leans in, and he and my father, speaking some inscrutable shared patois, come to an agreement, and the man climbs in behind us.

There are nights when, while the hotel sleeps, I take the Cadillac and drive into town. I don't know if I've said this is all in Daytona Beach. Unlike other places my parents have been on their wanderings, Daytona Beach has bars frequented by blue-collar types and bikers. There is one topless place I usually go to. Not really topless,

248

given that the State of Florida bans women from showing their breasts in full, a technicality they get around by covering their nipples with stickers that glow under the lights, or sometimes with a small pom-pom. There is a miniscule aquarium set into the back wall with a shark inside it; it reaches one end, bumps its nose against the glass, and barely has space to turn back around again. It never stops moving. Some of the girls will take you through to a member's room for $10; there is a no touching rule on the customer's side, but they rub against you for as long as the song lasts. I sometimes ask if their boyfriends mind, the answer to which is that they don't mind the money. On my way back to the hotel, almost always drunk, I get melancholic. The music on the country and western station reminds me how far from home I am. I drive past a multitude of uninhabited hotels and resorts – Easter is still a couple of weeks away. There is the Viking Lodge, where you check in without getting out of the car, and then park in a carport right underneath your room, Nordic-style. I also like the Polynesian place, which is still open. My father sometimes says that ours isn't necessarily better than the rest, but that certain touches put us up a level. Like the vanilla-coloured gravel in the drive: my father is a great believer in first impressions. To one side of the gravel drive is Bob MacHugh's office, someone I haven't mentioned yet, and I don't think I will again. He's in charge of showing prospective buyers the future timeshare apartments, and to get them set up on the calendar. He hasn't brought anyone in yet.

I park the Cadillac. It's rained while I was in the bar but not sufficiently to make puddles, which means the gravel is doing its job, something I consider a miracle, considering everything else going on in this place.

Judy's light is on, while the rest of the hotel is completely dark. I briefly entertain going up and knocking on her door, asking how she's doing. Leaning on the hood of the Cadillac, and looking out to sea, thoughts running through my head, I play the scenario through. But then Judy's light goes out, and the hotel is plunged into darkness. I keep one hand on the hood, which is still warm – a warmth that transmits a sense of security. It is the only thing that seems to belong to me.

'This way,' my father says. 'There's something I want to show you.'

He's wearing shorts that look odd to me: he wears them for playing squash, he says. On our way, and without him having told me where we're going, we stop by a court. Using these weird rackets, we spend a few minutes hitting a tiny rubber ball, but he quickly runs out of puff and we call it a day. It seems squash wasn't actually part of his original plan; there's something else far more important. I follow him up to the third floor, his body more twisted than ever as he walks. A narrow staircase I haven't seen before leads us to a door; for the first time I see him use not the master key but one specifically for this door. It opens onto a roof terrace, asphalt sheeting underfoot, and out in the middle is a construction that has the look of a bunker, except for the dotting of windows.

'Exactly what I hoped for!' he says. 'The look on your face. Your mother and I are going to move into this penthouse once everything's done.'

There is a 'Welcome' doormat outside. You can't see the adjacent buildings from up here, only the sky and the ocean. Turning, I see a barbecue set up by one of the penthouse walls. It looks handmade by my father.

'We'll have a cookout tonight,' he says.

My mother appears at one of the windows, making me jump. She is cleaning the glass using the same yellow rubber gloves she used in our house back in the suburbs. Inside is full of all kinds of junk, though the doorway is clear, and, going in, I see that my mother has installed a telephone next to a plastic chair. I spot an oil painting. I recognize the style it's done in, like the ones bought at the warehouse, a still life with coral and seashells.

'It's like heaven up here,' my mother says.

'Plus the fact you don't see a soul,' my father said. 'Fully private, sky and ocean all to ourselves, and we don't even have to leave the comfort of our own home. When everything's paid for, this is going to be the family home for generations to come. You can come any time you like, come and spend a bit of time in your Florida penthouse, what do you say?'

'Great,' I say, and I mean it.

When it's dark, the humidity forces us inside. They aren't sleeping in the penthouse yet, but my mother, not wanting to leave, tries the lights. One comes on at the third attempt, though dimly, like it's running on batteries. I help her get the rubber gloves off. Then I put my hands on her shoulders.

'What did you dream about last night?' I ask.

She looks into my eyes. I know, in this moment, the thousands upon thousands of miles separating us.

'It's better you don't know,' she says.

I go into the bedroom. The furniture here is the same as in the rest of the hotel, though it seems different, more homely. The bathroom door is ajar, and I catch sight of my father standing there, though he doesn't notice me. Standing at the toilet, briefs around his knees, he is punching himself repeatedly in the lower gut. And eventually the urine comes, in a halting trickle. I am briefly aware of the existence of a problem that, sooner or later, I too am going to have to solve.

I go back to the living room and find my mother just where she was before, rubber gloves in her lap. She is gazing at something, I can't tell what. The seashell-and-coral painting is a little askew, and for a moment I think I'll straighten it, but then think it isn't really my place yet. I go out onto the roof terrace. Going to the roof's edge, through the darkness I can see the Hilton, the Ramada Inn, the tropical shack bar and, further off, the Viking Hotel. They are all lit up, but ours isn't; ours is as dark as the ocean. I notice that my right foot is wet, there are puddles everywhere, I still need to get myself those sandals. In spite of this, I have the sensation that, when I go back inside, the world goes with me. My father's on the phone. I can't tell whether he's having an argument or just talking loudly, but what I do know is that he's working to leave me a decent inheritance. Which is far more than I'll ever do for anyone else.

This was what happened that March after the telegram at MIT. Well, more or less. The story I've just told is what I can remember of a short story by Jeffrey Eugenides called 'Timeshare'. And though it's from memory, I have tried to render the original as faithfully as I could. I've read it hundreds of times, but at the same time it's also true that my memory isn't fit for any grand expeditions nowadays. In any case, I came across 'Timeshare' in a magazine that did the rounds in the Home in 1997, and from the off could hardly believe what I was reading: nothing short of a blow-by-blow, word-for-word account of the time I spent in Florida that March, except one or two small circumstantial details, plus one or two other things that I will call, simply, 'slight deviations from reality'.

The circumstantial details: 1) My father never worked in a bank; 2) I'm an only child; 3) the man who delivered the summonses, generated by my father's ruinous business ventures, did not bring them to an apartment but to my room at MIT; 4) my mother couldn't have cleaned the windows of the apartment on the rooftop terrace with rubber gloves identical to the ones she used to clean the windows at our residential neighbourhood home, because we never lived in a residential neighbourhood.

As for the 'slight deviations from reality', these are: in my father's case, next to his timeshare property complex he built a decent-sized golf course. In reality, this was his prime motivation and not the apartments, which to his mind were less likely to turn a profit than a golf course. On the night I saw my father punching himself in the gut, I did indeed go out onto the terrace, and my mother was sitting having a rest beneath the seashell-and-coral painting, which was askew on the wall. As I've said, I asked her what she'd dreamed about the previous night, but when she said I was better off not knowing, I didn't in fact leave it there, and, working on her in the way only a child can a mother, in the end got her to say: 'I dreamed something strange and terrible,' she said, 'something I can't fathom at all.' That was as much as I could whee-dle out of her. After that, as I looked out across the dark expanse of the ocean, I remember feeling a golf ball in my pocket. My father had given it me the previous day when the two of us were out walking, not far from what he referred to as 'future Hole 5', then still nothing but a big muddy tract – a fairways in waiting. My father had pointed out that the sprinklers weren't working, and that Buddy, no longer in his employ then, was the only one who knew how to fix them. I remember him stopping by the future Hole 5 – my feet on soil remarkably firm, him with shoes a few inches deep – and handing me the golf ball. It was like the golf ball was a baton, or some kind of container I had yet to fill. 'Son,' he said, 'whatever you do, don't let this ball go to waste, and don't you dare spurn it. This golf ball is your future.' And when, the next day, looking out across the ocean from the roof terrace, it occurred to me to take it out and throw it into the dark, use it to pierce that nocturnal wall, creating a hole that would make my parents happier than they currently were, and send them back to Montana, to the days when 'future' still meant something. I don't know why I didn't throw the golf ball: it's something I've always regretted. Then I heard my mother screaming. My father was in the bathroom, bleeding to death. All that time he'd spent punching himself in the gut had led to some kind of haemorrhage, something important breaking inside him. I found him arched over the bidet, like a bridge from one side to the other. At the Beach Hospital they told us that, by the time we got him into the Cadillac a few minutes later, wrapped in a shower curtain with 'Palm Bay Resort Timeshares' emblazoned on it, he was already dead. I've thought about his death every day of my life since. It's something Semicolon and I have argued over: he disagrees with my idea that the only death worth dying is one that people are going to remember. To him that isn't the point. All those petty criminals he sees being gunned down on his cell phone, nobody ever thinks about them again, and *that's* beautiful: things being forgotten just as soon as they take place, which is especially true of death. But, I always say, imagine having to tell a mother that her child has died, and then imagine this mother suffers from an illness that means she only has a fifteen-second memory span. Would you

254

tell her that her child's dead? She won't remember. Does it make sense to put her through fifteen seconds of infinite suffering, only for it to pass from her memory in a few moments' time?

3.

Semicolon just crept in, far more stealthily than he usually does; I thought he was about to come out with the same question as always about our tongue-Braille classes. Instead, he took a sheet of paper from the back pocket of his shorts and unfolded its sixteen folds: I saw that it was a page from a magazine. It's folded so many times that it looks like a mosaic stuck together at the back with some kind of glue. Crazier things have happened. You come across people, gambling types and junkies I mean, who get into this very thing as therapy: they cut the pages of magazines up into tiny pieces and then go through the painstaking process of sticking them back together again. This isn't what the page just shown to me by Semicolon is – gluing together the two halves of a porno magazine page would clearly be beyond him. It's just the two of us in the kitchen, and yet he glances nervously around while I take a look at the page. His hands, with his tapered fingers – chubby at the base, pointed at the tips – crowded with rings bearing the coats of arms of supposed European monarchies, hold the page gingerly. Half of it's taken up with a colour photo of a figure – man or woman, it isn't clear – throwing themself from one of the windows of the Twin Towers. While I look it over, Semicolon, beside himself, fills me in on his incredible discovery. The photo's old, from 1987, and the caption says that the person captured committing suicide in it is a girl called Kate Springs. Semicolon gets another sheet of paper out of his pocket, this one folded into sixteen as well, and unfolds it with hands still trembling. Again a photo from a magazine, again in colour. It's lower quality than the first one, but not in fact older: the person pictured jumping from the Twin Towers in this one did so on 9/11. Semicolon, his finger like a cursor, points me to a part in the text: 'Kate Springs, impelled by the encroaching flames, throws herself from a window.' Semicolon looks me in the eye:

'Tell me this, Kurt: how can a person commit suicide twice, and to cap it all, in the exact same place. I don't get it. Do you?'

I say nothing, making as though I'm studying the two photos.

'It's the discovery of the century, Kurt. And I discovered it, me.'

Taking a handkerchief from the sleeve of his jersey, he flicks his wrist to unfurl it and then mops his brow. In comes Encarna Low, her cell phone around her neck and the squeaking of her thighs chafing together announcing her approach.

'What's happening boys?' she says brightly. 'Some kinda problem?'

Now I'm going to think about the woman named Kate Springs, better put, going to think about her brain, the labyrinth of its gyri, a labyrinth that's one hundred per cent Kate Springs, that could bear a sticker on it with her name, Kate Springs. And it gets me down. A brain that falls, a brain plummeting to earth at an accelerating rate of $9.8 \text{m/s}2$, a brain that to the few square feet of sidewalk it's about to explode on is soft like a punctured ball. And she falls and the acceleration causes her brain to be displaced, up, back, barely a fraction of an inch, but enough to change the way it's functioning. This induces a hallucination before she touches down. I remember when we landed on the moon the first thing I did wasn't to look at the horizon, but to glance instinctively at the ground, an absolute attraction being exerted on me by the ashy soil, something akin to wishing I could throw myself into the void from my normal standing height, to get down and lick that soil, a totally physical and hypnotic sensation I've never experienced again. I've always felt sad I didn't try that moon soil. And now I'm going to think about those star-crossed towers – twins they most certainly were not, their personalities could hardly have been more different, genetically speaking. For example, in one, the button for the elevator on the fortieth floor was broken into three separate pieces, and the corresponding one in the other tower was intact; that's the kind of thing I mean. There's no such thing as identical twins, but this apparent doubleness makes them seem invulnerable to us. On an unconscious level we seem to believe that two twins can be added together; what I mean is that each possesses the other's life force, as well as having their own, and, like a pair of rice sacks dropped onto kitchen scales, they can be made into one single quantity. But sameness is not a thing that can be added together. I'd actually go further and say that sameness is a thing that reduces and weakens. I lived in New York City for a while, 1980 to 1982 approximately, and when I arrived they'd just finished putting up the second of the towers; work was officially completed in 1973 but there were still a host of finishing touches to be added. I crashed for the first few months with my friend Frank, whose Armenian parents had emigrated in 1915, fleeing the upheaval of the First World War, when Armenians were rounded up and shot en masse by the

Turkish army. Frank's apartment was in Brooklyn but he worked in an abattoir in the Meatpacking District, an area in west Manhattan, and in those days not a nice neighbourhood. Frank didn't get to handle the saws or electrodes, or to dress the meat – he was a nightwatch-man, which came with added risks. He was also friends with all kinds of artist types, how this came about I don't know; I sometimes thought he must be a government infiltrator in that bohemian scene. Various of Frank's artist friends had studios on the top floors of the taller of the two towers, thanks to a grants scheme run by a certain millionaire who used to boast he fed his favourite dog better than he did his chauffeur. Frank was discreet, but also liked to talk. You don't often find guys like that. Whenever he started a conversation it felt like he was desperately searching for something; some people are like that, searching for words, words of all kinds. His favourite topic was Armenia; he dreamed of going there one day and being able to recognize his forebears' lands. And when he said 'recognize', he meant it in the strictest sense: to walk through the few remaining ruins in the hope that some signal would rise up out of the depths of history and grant him knowledge of that which was somehow, as he put it, 'already in me but very far down, as though sleeping'. A few times he talked to me about Mount Ararat, the perpetually snow-covered volca-no that is the country's symbol: 'Noah's Ark wound up there,' he said, 'when the waters began to recede after the Flood. What's left of it is there, under rocks and volcanic material the earth's spewed out over time.' I never men-tioned having seen the Ark on my way back down from the moon; at that time, I was pretending to Frank that I was a window cleaner. One day he told me about his theory of the global union of humankind: 'Kurt,' he said to me, 'all human beings, no matter how far apart and unknown to one another they may be, are in fact joined by one war or another, the six degrees of separation that sociologist proved all those years ago, it would actually be cut to just four degrees if we took into account the wars that unite us all. And this doesn't only go for the present, but joins us to all the dead as well, as far back as cave people. Like the stars, shining down on us even though they're long dead, we're a legion of the living and the dead, joined by the self-same thing: destruction and war.'

One day in November 1982, I said to Frank:

'Frank, take me to see those towers. I've never been up them.'

'I'm guessing you don't have a problem with heights,' he said. 'What with the window cleaning you used to do in San Francisco?"

'No, no problem with heights at all.'

We left my apartment, which wasn't far from Frank's, in Williamsburg – the run-down Brooklyn neighbourhood where Scorsese shot *Mean Streets* in the seventies. We went by the Salvation Army store to buy me some shirts and pants to match the occasion, I put them on there and then, standing between the racks of coats and jackets; I jettisoned my ex-astronaut clothes, dropping them in a corner, and we headed to Bedford Avenue for the five-minute subway ride to Manhattan.

After making ourselves known to a disinterested super, we rode the elevator up to the 107th floor – the top floor. Carlos, a Spanish friend of Frank's, was there to meet us, he'd just gotten in from Madrid, he was sporting a New Romantic look, which was like Punk but more sophisticated – his words. He said something to Frank in praise of my attire, but not so praising about how old I was. I, keeping up the former-window cleaner charade, tried to put on all the tics, physical and verbal, of that kind of individual, but I guess I wasn't fooling anyone. This Carlos spoke about Madrid like it was some new Mecca for the arts and music, it reminded me of the way people in California had talked about San Francisco in the seventies. I nosed around his studio. The views were decent, but not really all that; not a patch on the horizon-simulation room at Cape Canaveral. I took a seat on a battered old sofa in front of some sculptures he was obviously still working on. With Frank and Carlos behind me, and music coming from somewhere, a song in Spanish, the only part of which I could understand was, 'What sticks in the memory... is the melancholy' – over and over – I sat looking at a series of life-size clay men. Dressed in what seemed to be togas, they had jumbo jets flying into, or through them, one half sticking out on either side. Their faces had a look of simultaneous suffering and ecstasy. I sat for quite a while like that, nursing my beer, until eventually a voice came from behind me:

'What do you think?'

'Not bad, I guess. Look like they're in pain.'

'Right,' Frank said, joining in. 'They're sculptures of Saint Sebastian.'

'Saint Sebastian's big in Spain, see,' Carlos continued. 'Usually you see him with all kinds of arrows sticking out of him. I've gone for jumbo jets instead. Works better.'

'Got it,' I said. 'Very suggestive.'

'So, Frank tells me you used to be a window cleaner.'

'Right. People don't think it's much of a job, but

260

there's worse. The things you see. Women getting out of the shower, for instance.'

We had a laugh about this, a few laughs in fact, and once we'd drunk a little more those Saint Sebastians started making complete sense to me.

Frank and I were saying our goodbyes when there was a knock at the door. It swung open to reveal a guy about the same age as me, skinny and shy-seeming, and wearing an old-style suit, peasant-style, no tie. We were introduced. His name was Carlos as well, and he was Carlos's best friend. As we rode the elevator back down Frank told me that this was Carlos Oroza, a Spanish poet who was friendly with Ginsberg.

'Just a few weeks back, here in this very building, he was sitting at the studio window, and as he looked out at the unsurpassable sunset you get from up there, he spoke the words: "It's a mistake to take the things we've seen as a given." And he instantly got a pen out and wrote it down.'

When I got back to my rented apartment in Brooklyn that night, I started to hear the shrill buzzing of a golf ball, again that buzzing on the far side of the exosphere, and birds began to appear in my mind in their thousands, raining down, coming straight for me. I thrashed my arms to fend them off, I started throwing things loaned to me by the landlord, objects seemingly extracted from a collection of absurdities. My downstairs neighbour Kitty, an Irish woman who spent all day every day drunk, took her broom and started whacking it against her ceiling, my floor, until eventually I pulled myself together.

Now I want to talk about Kitty, who lived with her youngest son – little more than a baby then – and who was constantly down in the Polish bar telling anyone who would listen about a present from her husband, Ryan: a set of teeth with the words KITTY & RYAN IN LOVE etched into them. As a way of showing this off, she'd order a slice of meringue pie from the Polish bar lady, take a bite out of the biscuit base and then proudly show off the result. The base indeed showed that message of love rendered in Gothic type. The surprise came when she flipped the biscuit base over and you saw the indentations from her lower teeth, which read: FUCK YOU RYAN BYE BYE. The lower message she'd done herself, she said, after he walked out. Whenever there was an episode like the one that night, and once she'd had enough of battering the ceiling with her broom, she'd start screaming up at me to quit it otherwise she'd climb up the fire escape and into my kitchen and come and use those teeth to bite my balls, give me a lasting reminder of that love/hate message. She was a good woman, but I did worry the day might come when she'd follow through on one of her threats. I couldn't get to sleep that night. I remember when it got to sunrise, and as I looked out across the East River at the Twin Towers, thinking about something much-discussed between Frank and me: what would happen if they were one day to come tumbling down, if they turned out to be less sturdy then the abodes of the Three Little Pigs in the tale. Inevitable to think that kind of thing, when you're presented with those two giants. In a certain sense, all the disaster movies in those days were preparing us for it. In the America of 1982 there was the general sense that nothing lasted, certainly not forever. Reagan, the greatest president this country's ever seen, had taken it upon himself to foster this very idea, this simulacrum that keeps you on tenterhooks, and which, as a reaction to the fear that comes with it, makes you strong: the fortitude brought about when you're constantly sensing threat from absolutely every quarter. Reagan was onto something: some years later the city would be filled with the mixed smell of burnt plastic and roast chicken, a smell that lingered for a couple of years in the south of the island. 200,000 tonnes of steel, 325,000 m² of concrete, 55,000 m² of glass from 43,600 blown-out windows, 198 elevators, each of which had an average capacity of 55 people, 71 escalators, 930,000 m² of office interiors, 3,000 humans, all reduced to dust. I was installed in the Home by then, but people say that particles, both organic and inorganic, got into every single corner of the city, into people's lungs and homes, into their food and their mattresses. It must be pretty strange knowing you've got particles of people's spleens inside you, particles of pens and hair, of Turkish rugs and asbestos, of the glasses formerly worn by young graduates, of silicon from people's breast implants, of adipose tissue, cockroaches, mosquitos, rats, sirloin steaks and trout from the Great Lakes. Pretty strange, truly, to go around in the knowledge that this entire superstore of destruction is inside you, and always will be.

Semicolon, whose knowledge of subjects never surpasses that of the generalist magazine, says the same thing every time New York City appears on the TV: 'Here we go,' he says, 'let's see if your old apartment makes an appearance.' He's forever saying this, and he's just as unshakeable in his belief that my time there was split between a loft apartment on Park Avenue and levitating on sidewalks. The only thing that can possibly wrench Semicolon out of this closed loop ('Your old apartment... your old apartment...') is if his cell phone rings and it happens to be the National Car Chase Company. When that happens, I turn over in bed and try to sleep with the sound of helicopters raging at my back.

4.

A little further back now, to 1975, which was when I got out of San Francisco – on the day *Starsky and Hutch* first aired. I know this because I was in my prefab watching the first ever episode, and I remember laughing when I saw them driving the same car as I did, a red Ford Torino, though mine obviously didn't have that unsightly white stripe along the sides. I'd spent the previous night staring at the small ceiling stain, so like the surface of the moon. I think I'd also drunk a good number of my vodka toddies, which meant I wasn't much use for anything. It was during one of the commercial breaks that I heard the knock on the door. 'Open up, Kurt,' came a man's voice. 'It's King, with the police.' We knew each other already because a few weeks earlier, on one of my night escapades, I'd been in the midst of demolishing a public phone booth using only the receiver of that same booth, and he, driving past in his patrol car, had pulled over intending to take me in, but, seeing who I was, took mercy on me. He was a little younger than me, somewhere around twenty-five I'd say, but as a teenager he'd been a dedicated collector of the stickers that went to make up an album of the lunar mission, and though I obviously didn't feature in any of the footage, he said he couldn't have cared less. He planned on holding onto his album so he could leave it to his son, when he had one. Blonde, tall and healthy-looking, there was something elemental about the guy, you'd look him in the eyes and see the reflection of that quintessentially wild Americanness,

264

which nowadays has been lost completely.

'You gotta get out of here, Colonel Kurt,' he said – he always called me that, although I'd never risen higher than sergeant. 'They'll be here any minute to take you in, Sergeant says he intends to lock you up and throw away the key, no bail. Says he intends to lean on the DA.'

The honest truth is that I don't remember what it is they wanted me for this time. Some minor offence, most likely – the straw breaking the camel's back. To thank him, I gave him the photo I kept on top of the TV set, which was of me on the moon, striking an odd pose, a photo Armstrong had taken of me on his personal camera, one that never graced public channels. I handed it over, and King gave a whistle. I started throwing a few things in a sports bag, whatever came to hand, while at the same time scrawling out a dedication to the young officer on the back of the picture, using the same pen he'd used to write me up for God knows how many fines. As I handed him the photo, a silence fell between us, not very easy to explain. Putting it in his inside jacket pocket, he gave me a firm handshake, the firmness of true gratitude, and said: 'God bless you, Colonel Kurt.'

It was a clear night, the lights in my neighbours' houses flickered on and off; the sequence, considered for a moment, was like a long snaking line of fairground lights. I slipped my sunglasses on and set off. So it was that in a red Ford Torino, window down, one August night in 1975 with the moon overhead as bright as day, I left San Francisco, never to go back. I passed the last traffic signals in my neighbourhood, taking in the raucous sounds of crickets I'd never noticed.

I don't know if I've said this already – I don't have much of what you could call a memory – but soon after my father died my mother had used the money from the timeshare resort sale to get herself a small apartment in Miami. There was no chance of selling the prospective golf course as such because, though the irrigation lines were partially laid and other amenities in place, it turned out to be over a swamp. A speculator from Ocala took it on, putting in a tree nursery that sold the only thing anyone could grow around those parts: dwarf palms. The mortgage on the timeshare resort was bigger than my mother had expected, and with the little she made she took this third-floor apartment in a Miami suburb. This being the case, as I and my red Ford Torino left the Bay Bridge behind, I devised a plan: I would go and hole up in this apartment. My mother too was now a few years in the grave, having died pretty unspectacularly, while sleeping in her bed – what did she dream that night, I've always wondered? – and the property was mine, in a sense. It had been confiscated on account of some unpaid taxes, but I'd kept a copy of the key, meaning I just needed to get inside the compound and then, once in the apartment, make sure I kept all noise to a minimum so as not to alert the neighbours. Reaching inside the sports bag beside me on the passenger seat, I checked my funds: I had close to five thousand dollars in mixed denominations. That would last me for the journey plus a few months' living costs. I ran my fingers over the bills, slowly, pleasurably; if there's one thing that shows the US to be a true democracy it is the fact our banknotes are all the same size. A homeless man pulls out a dollar bill to buy himself a can of soup, and at a glance it could be the same as the hundred-dollar bill Hillary Clinton hands over to pay for her lover's dry martini at the Hotel Plaza. It fortifies our great democracy, and makes it unique. I took a bundle of cash and

266

slipped it into the front pocket of my brown sweatpants. I had a pair of Nikes on and, on top, a check shirt the sleeves of which I'd cut off at the shoulders. My reasons for removing the sleeves were simple, but still worth recounting.

A short time before, Barbara, the only woman I have ever truly loved, burned these sleeves off – on purpose – with a lit Chesterfield cigarette. Basically, Barbara hated being contradicted. When a man becomes famous, it isn't unusual to receive the attentions of large numbers of good-looking, submissive women, all of them armed with condoms doctored beforehand with razor blades. The moment I met Barbara, I knew she was different. The fall of 1970, it must have been, I was still living in San Francisco but had gone to New York City for a reception at the French embassy, a three-storey building on East 53rd Street which isn't there any more. It was your classic Franco-American love-in and, as tended to be the way in those days, once the speeches were over I started drinking. Not going crazy, but a bit harder than was appropriate at a soiree like that. I found myself in a group near the drinks, which included the ambassador himself, who had come from DC especially, his wife, who was a twenty-two year old nymphomaniac with brightly painted toenails and had just, she said, flown in from India, a country where, she did not say, she'd started dabbling in Class As – she would later die of an overdose in the bathrooms at CBGB's – a guy who claimed to be a writer but to me came across like one of these utterly tedious linguists – specifically, he reminded me of Noam Chomsky, whom I'd had some run-ins with during my MIT days – and a woman impossible to put an age on who was there on her own. At one point someone, I can't remember who, brought up a piece of tittle-tattle that was doing the rounds at the time: namely as to whether, the year before, I'd walked on the moon while in a state of inebriation, and whether in fact my omission from all records had been down to certain poses I'd struck, an unjustifiable display, not to mention the denigrating of a national hero. They badgered me about this for a seemingly endless half hour, there were moments when the conversation seemed to be heading in another direction but it soon came back around to me again. Denying everything, I then excused myself, saying I was going out to the terrace to see a friend, though I actually went downstairs and sat out on the front steps, doing a little sidewalk watching. I lit a cigarette. End of September, the breeze sharp, I turned the collar of my suit jacket up, placed my vodka and ice down on one of the steps, and at first I couldn't see her clearly, but there she was, sitting in a car parked right out front. She turned her head and our eyes met. She got out, slamming the door after her. She was wearing a tight sheepskin coat, I remember thinking it was a bit over the top given it wasn't really cold, plus bell-bottoms and a pair of square-toed platforms. Her hair fell in dark ringlets over her sunglasses. She asked if I had a light.

'You get bothered by lights at night too?' she said, pointing to my sunglasses.

'Yeah,' I said. 'Goddamned streetlights.'

I started coughing, and had to explain my longstanding lung problems.

'I'm here to get some x-rays done. DC hospitals have the latest high-tech stuff.'

She, making no sign she'd understood, nodded at my drink:

'Can I have a sip?'

I, making no sign I'd understood, asked:

'What are you doing out here all alone?'

'Oh, waiting for a guy, but he hasn't showed. Can I get a sip or not?'

'Sure,' I said. I held out the vodka and she sat down next to me.

She took small sips, too noisily if you ask me. Then, in a bold move – entirely out of character for me – I said:

'Instead of us sitting here on this step, why don't I see if I can get you a drink some place?'

'Okay,' she said, 'but dinner first. I'm running on empty.'

We wound up at a nearby bar, an imitation Midwest diner, with walls made of metal and booths to sit in. Barbara told me she was an exorcist. I laughed out loud, couldn't help it. She was a little angry. I'm sorry, I said, I really am, and once she calmed down she admitted it wasn't true, in fact she was studying textile design and dressmaking at a college on 14th Street. Then a guy walked in the door, an older guy but dressed as a Mod (something she clarified for me later on; at that particular moment I had no idea what a Mod was), who came over to our booth and started calling Barbara a whore – shouting, 'Whore, whore,' over and over at her. I went to intervene, but the guy said to me, 'Stay out of it, hillbilly motherfucker, this doesn't concern you.' Now, when I joined the army I signed something saying I would never use my hand-to-hand skills on a civilian, but I got up and hit the guy, a roundhouse with my right, and before that had even landed followed it up with a left-hand jab, and then another to the gut, which put him out of circulation. He was floundering against the bar, not a squeak. The customers inside cowered behind their tables. Then, possibly on account of the red lights in the place, or possibly the alcohol, I felt dizzy for a second, a second the guy took advantage of to smash a bottle over my head. Next thing I know, I'm waking up in the morning in a Lower East Side apartment I've never been in before, the smell of toast and instant coffee in the air and a cassette tape playing 'A Day in the Life'. Barbara and I were inseparable from that day on.

The guy, I found out, was her teacher at the fashion school, and it was him she'd been waiting for outside the French embassy. He was married, and that didn't help the relationship, though it had more or less run its course anyhow. But a while later I also found out that her exorcist claim in fact hadn't been a joke, though the kind of spirits she worked with were even more out there than you might expect. It happened a number of months later, when she came to San Francisco with the intention of continuing her studies in a college in my neighbourhood, and she started telling me about rites and all kinds of olden cultures. I was earning a living conference-speaking: gigs I'd sign up to a long way in advance but half of which I never went to; I preferred being with Barbara. I made a serious effort to cut back on the drinking and between us we fixed up the prefab. She decorated it in a special way, making a hippie den of the place with 'underground' ornamental details that looked like products of Warhol's factory – something I first read about in the mail order fashion magazines Barbara received. One day she planted flowers in my prefab home. Little esoteric female figurines came later on, things that left me pretty cold. There was also the fact that we experienced our first true orgasm together, which I know was life-changing for the both of us. I remember finding her sitting on the ground out back of the prefab one day. She took a small lump of brown paste out of a metal case, placed it in her mouth and began to chew. What the hell was that, I asked? She then gave me my induction to something that would go on to play an important role in our time together. Eating mud, she said, which people in Europe had done during the baroque era, had multiple benefits, being both a proven contraceptive and, when ingested in high quantities, capable of engendering mystical experiences. Though she, in fact, ate mud for its nutritional properties, having once been on a trip to Utah and seen the poorest communities surviving on mud biscuits. I couldn't get my head around it, to me you might as well stuff your face with desiccated dung, but she insisted we go gather mud from a bog a friend of hers had mentioned, up near Mill Valley, and that we bring it home and do some mud-biscuit baking in the oven. Naturally, I said she could count me out. Eating mud dredged up in the outskirts of San Francisco didn't feature in my life plan. One afternoon, I came across a copy of a magazine called *Health and Spirit* in the drawer where Barbara kept her latest arrivals. It featured a piece all about mud-eating. Barbara insisted she be the first to read her magazines, and not me, but she was in class so I went ahead and read all about these ladies at court in seventeenth- and eighteenth-century Spain eating a special reddish clay known as *búcaro*, a practice forbidden by the Church. *Búcaro* came from Portugal, and the article quoted the late seventeenth-century writings of one Madame d'Aulnoy, in which she claimed that the eating of Portuguese clay was a favourite pastime of Spanish nobility. The crude pottery made from this red clay belonged to the dark side, the secret, underground aspect of upper-class life during that time. The article included a contemporary letter in which a nun confessed to having given way to temptation and eaten *búcaro*, following, she said, the example of one Marquise de la Laguna. It spoke about the mud as acting on the skin to make it paler, how this was desirable because it distinguished noblewomen from the peasants who worked in the fields, and its capacity for inducing low-level hallucinations. Big Spanish writers of the day, names like Cervantes and Quevedo, had also written about the practice, including the crafty ploy of some women to drink water from jugs made of the red clay, thereby ingesting it by drinking the trace amounts dissolved in the water. Sometimes the water was flavoured with things like orange blossom, rose, cinnamon, sugar or red wine vinegar. Other times, having drunk the water down, and already addicted by this point, they would take a bite straight out of the jug. The piece said numerous remnants of jugs had been un-covered in Spanish palaces with great big bites taken out of them – not the gnawings of rodents, as they were initially thought to be, but those of people. Next to the deathbed of the Spanish painter Velázquez, a multitude of such jugs had been found, leading to the supposition that he too might have been a *búcaro* addict. My immedi-ate thought was to wonder if this had anything to do with the urge I'd felt the moment I set foot on the moon to get down on the ground and start licking it.

We were having a drink at the Flamingo one eve-ning when Barbara, seeing some younger guys playing pool at the back, said to me: 'Kurt, you gotta change your look.' She had a point: wherever we were going, no matter the occasion, I opted for the grey pants and blue shirt that were part of my cocktail and events outfit – events I was being invited to less and less, just about never in fact – and they both had butter and oil stains all over them, and the remnants of wine spillages and semen too. My nice shoes had seen better days as well,

272

and I never cleaned them. So there it was, a shopping trip for Kurt. I remember stepping out from the fitting room and her looking up at me, ringlets twirled around one finger. Thumbs up, or thumbs down. All I ever saw in the mirror was the twin you're always trying to flee. We went through large numbers of sandals with flowers on, flares exceedingly tight at the crotch, shirts you were supposed to leave unbuttoned as far down as the navel, and all kinds of other juvenilia, before I wound up getting myself a lumberjack shirt and leaving it at that, the kind you'd see guys out in Minnesota wearing, checked pockets and pearl-effect buttons. 'Wasn't exactly what I had in mind,' she said, 'but anyway it beats those air traffic controller shirts.' We paid for the shirt, but when we went to leave, the store alarm went off. They checked the shirt, but the antitheft sensor had indeed been removed, and having patted us down they let us go. The exact same thing happened in the other stores we went in that afternoon, the alarms going off both when we entered and when we left each and every one of them. We got home and inspected the shirt, but couldn't find anything. I wore it a couple of days later, and off went the alarm at the superstore, and the same in all the other stores I went in thereafter. Barbara then came up with the idea of *her* wearing the shirt; maybe it was something between me and the shirt, she said, some kind of adverse reaction, like you can get with medicines. But no, she went into some stores, and it was the same story. 'Put it in the trash,' I said, tired of the whole thing. 'It's just an imitation farmer's shirt; I had a whole bunch the same in my youth.' It made her angry to see me give up so easily, and she took it personally. Then she told me about a friend of a friend who was an exorcist specializing in alarm systems. He'd been studying at Barbara's previous college and claimed to be a sorcerer. From what she'd heard, he had experience of other such cases, they were actually becoming quite frequent, and he was able to exorcize the electronic spirit trapped inside any item of clothing. These were the words she used: electronic spirit. Barbara was so into the idea that I just gave her the shirt and said to do whatever she wanted. The guy lived in a commune on the outskirts of Sacramento at the time, and that was where she would need to go to see him.

She got a ride from some people who came by before sun-up one morning in a blacked-out van. She put the shirt in a bag, we had a long kiss goodbye, and said we'd see each other on the terrace at the Flamingo five days later. Five days went by, and Barbara didn't show. I went and found a friend of hers from college, the skinniest woman I've ever laid eyes on, to ask if she'd heard anything. I waited for her after class, and she came out eating from a supersize tub of ice cream, using what seemed to be a flame-blackened spoon, but she just strode past me saying she couldn't talk. She just kept on repeating this, robotically, and when I finally gave up, letting her go ahead at a crosswalk, I secretly hoped for some civil servant to press the wrong button so that the lights would go green with her still only halfway across.

Two months later there was a knock on the door. It was the postman with a package for me. A cardboard box with no return address, tied around with knotted esparto grass, as though recycled from a million other packages. Inside was the shirt, neatly folded, and the sleeves covered in dozens of cigarette burns. Taking it out, there was a mound of Chesterfield butts underneath, the unmistakeable violet-pink of her lipstick on the tips. And a note:

Mission accomplished, Mr Kurt.
Regarding Barbara, she's going to be staying here with us.
Peace, nothing but peace.

I never saw Barbara again.

I cut the sleeves off and put them out with the trash. It was four years before I wore the shirt again, the night of my departure from San Francisco, a night of flooring it in the Ford Torino. In the passenger seat, the sports bag containing a few thrown-together items, the first things I'd laid my hands on after signing the photo for the young cop, King, the photo in which I, Little Pig #4, struck a golf ball on the moon with a 7-iron, the same golf ball my father had given me, up to his ankles in prospective golf course mud, on the soupy-aired Florida afternoon before he died.

5.

The night my father's body was taken to Beach Hospital wrapped in a shower curtain with 'Palm Bay Resort Timeshares' emblazoned across it, I was surprised to see tears rolling down my mother's face. She wanted to bury him at the unfinished golf course. Negative, I said: we had no way of knowing whose hands the place was going to wind up in, and I wasn't exactly taken with the idea of having to pay entry and rent a buggy and golf clubs in order to visit the grave. This was an excuse. In fact I just didn't want to have to set foot in Florida again, or anywhere else if it meant visiting my father's grave; if I'm honest the man had been a ghost to me for years, ever since he'd entered that lunatic spiral of trying to build on his lottery win. I intended to have him cremated and then throw the ashes in some Montana river. My mother was against this, at least partially. She agreed to the cremation, but insisted the ashes go in a Perspex urn and that we bury this at Hole 5, which was the last thing my father had been working on when he died. It was a hole he and Buddy had actually played; they'd installed the porcelain cup that sat at the bottom of the hole itself to receive the ball. We agreed that along with the coffin and his body, his sheepskin jacket and the winning lottery ticket – a laminated photocopy of which they'd kept – ought to go in the incinerator, and indeed that his body should go in with the 'Palm Bay Resort Timeshares' shower curtain wrapped around it; after all, the business had been his last and final dream. Another candidate for incineration was his good-luck fob, a small block of pinewood he'd gouged out of his own father's coffin and always kept his keys attached to. To clarify: it's tradition in my father's family for the oldest son in each generation, in the presence of all available adults on the day, to extract a portion of wood from his father's coffin, only a small portion so as not to break the coffin, and then to carve it into a fob, in any shape or motif that should occur to him. The keys to all the houses and properties he went on to own were supposed to be attached to it for the rest of his days. The tradition dates back farther than I know for certain, but I do know it started before the days of political parties as we now think of them. 'We are our dead past, all the coffins that go before us': so my father said to me one spring afternoon when I was nine years old, as we stood in the kitchen at the ranch, him jangling the keys on his familial fob – a pinewood rectangle the same size and shape as a dollar bill. I remember a cow outside the window stooping to drink from a meltwater stream – the winter ice was melting – and how it licked its lips and lowed as if to make light of my father's words.

276

I naturally didn't have it in mind to show up at the funeral home with a hammer and chisel and start taking chunks out of the box containing my father. The golf ball he'd given me was still in my pocket, I ran my fingers over its pitted surface constantly, and I thought it would more than suffice as a fob to satisfy the family tradition. My mother took this badly, said she'd just do it herself. I believe that deep down she thought the whole thing garbage as well, but still felt obligated to follow through on what was, after all, my father's final wish. And so she did, robotically, as I looked on. The man taking charge of the cremation was mystified at the sight of this woman taking a swing at a five thousand-dollar coffin. The correct tools not being to hand, she tried a flathead screwdriver, bashing the handle with a hefty glass ashtray that the funeral parlour secretary discreetly removed from a drawer when my mother went and asked her for 'something big and heavy'. As it turned out, she managed to get the screwdriver head into the wood, making a kind of jimmy of it and yanking sideways, and before she knew it a crack had opened in the side the length of the corpse. At this point I stepped in. But she still wound up with a slab in her hands almost five feet long. She leaned it up against the wall, forming a hypotenuse with the ground, and, stamping down on it a few times, came up with a largish sliver. And that was that. As the wooden coffin rolled into the furnace I asked myself why we were doing this, and what was with the barbarity of burning a loved one until that loved one turned to ash, anyway. We headed out to Hole 5 that night with the Perspex urn in a bag. My mother refused to take off her high heels or to change out of the red flares she'd worn for the ceremony.

I was telling Semicolon all this a few days back, while

277

he sat flicking his cell phone on and off. He wanted, he
said, to try to get one over on the phone makers by turning it on and off, and on and off, quicker than the light
from the screen could keep up. I told him to quit it, he
was going break the thing.

'Did you know that as foetuses we're 72 per cent
heart,' Semicolon said, 'and at that point the heart's outside the actual body?'

To which I said:

'Did you know that the brain itself doesn't experience
pain, so if someone shoots a bullet into your brain, you
feel nothing? You just wind up a dumbass, like you.'

'Know the only creature on earth that never gets cancer is a shark?'

'Know some planets have two suns, meaning it never
gets dark there?'

'Did you know there's a guy in Miami who requested
to be cremated and then for his ashes to be sold in a souvenir shop down at the beach?'

'Did you know that homo sapiens and Neanderthals
will one day meet again?'

'No, Kurt, I did not know that! How could I? Jesus,
are you batshit or what?'

We both sat and thought for a few moments. Then I
started my story again:

So, the night of my father's cremation, on our way
out to Hole 5 on the yet-to-be completed golf course, my
mother refused to take off her high heels or change out
of her red flares. It's never actually dark at night in that
part of Florida, too much light pollution from the nearby towns and cities, but in the small, semi-impenetrable
forest you had to cross to get to the golf course, you
were tripping over roots and bumps just about every
other step. 'Get your lighter out,' said my mother, 'shine

it over here.' 'Sorry, Ma, I just quit.' 'It had to be just now.' 'Yes,' I said, 'just now.' The Perspex urn in the bag, me holding tight to my mother's arm. She suddenly pulled up short, seeing something on the ground a little way ahead, light spilling out of it. I kept moving forward. I quickly saw that it was a small battery-powered television, propped against a tree. The picture was completely white, though not because it wasn't getting signal, and the sound was off. I looked behind me, my mother can't have been more than ten feet back, but the darkness was so complete that I couldn't make her out at all. Her voice floated forward, I heard her say the television was my father's; he had a habit of taking it places and forgetting about it. Doubtless he'd ventured out here in recent days for a little peace and quiet, to watch the ball game without her or the hotel workers to bother him. 'So this was where he came,' she said, 'this was his little man cave.' I heard her approaching, turned and saw the red flares nearly upon me, only for my mother to catch her toe and go tumbling to the ground. I was surprised at how hard she fell.

'These heels!' she spat, sitting on her backside.

I went back and tried to help her up.

'I can't!' she cried. 'It's my ankle! Goddamn heels, goddamn roots sticking up, goddamn forest, goddamn Florida! Your goddamn father!'

'Don't say that, Ma. You loved him.'

'Sure I loved him, but fools fall in love! God knows how you made it through a war, you still haven't got a clue about anything.'

I got her to her feet. Draping her arm over my shoulder, I took her over to the light of the television, sat her against the tree and rolled up the pant leg. The ankle had blown up immediately; it was as wide as the hem of her flares.

'Let's have a breather,' I said. 'You should rest.'

'Nonsense,' she said. 'I'll lean on you, we keep going.'

'The forest's pretty dark, Ma.'

'The forest's your father's prostate, boy; I know my way around it perfectly well.'

I went and found a branch for her to use as a walking stick. Hanging between the improvised walking stick and my shoulder, she managed to hobble on. The light from the television was soon lost behind us, but after several minutes' walking the end of the forest still seemed nowhere in sight.

'How big is this fucking thing?'

'Not 200 feet at its longest edge.'

'You sure?'

'Sure I'm sure, the golf course is all around it. Your father and I came through here like a hundred times.' The bag with the ashes swayed as we went along. She stumbled several more times. 'Can you see the sky, son?'

'No. I can't see shit.'

She soon asked for a rest. We sat down by some clumps of high grass, her leaning back against a rock, the bag on the ground between us. Neither of us said anything for a while, with her gazing down at the bag, me up at the starless sky, and then the television set came to mind: how long had it been since we'd left it behind? Five minutes? Ten? A half hour? It beat me. A squirrel came scampering past, stopping to sniff the bag for a second before going on its way.

'Take as long as you need, Ma. We've got all night. There's nobody waiting for us and Hole 5 isn't going any place.'

'Your father's last and final dream is waiting for us at Hole 5,' she said. She closed her eyes and, in that dropping of her eyelids, I saw the vast and endemic tiredness of a mother.

'Tell me,' I said, 'what was the last dream you had?'

'I told you already, it's better you don't know.'

'Tell me anyway.'

'I will not. I can... tell you about another dream I had, years ago, when I was a little girl. How about that?'

'Fine,' I said. I wasn't even slightly interested, but she'd forget about the ankle for a while at least.

'Okay, do you know what colombophilia is?'

'Pigeon fancying.'

'Right. Well in this dream, there's a Spanish town, by which I mean a town in actual Spain, the country. And there's a boy, couldn't be any older than ten, and this boy has a little sister. There's also an older brother, and there's a Mom and Dad. They live in a big house, big like a house on a ranch, but it's all Spanish, and they have a maid who's Portuguese. The kids sit in the kitchen to eat, bread and milk, and the father goes off to work in a factory, he's the overseer there or some such, a managerial role, you know. The factory is a long way away but they can see it from the house: some big industrial ovens, a metal foundry, or at least that's how it seemed to me. The mother never gets out of bed in the morning, it's the Portuguese maid who wakes the children and makes sure they're fed. Then the older brother takes the two younger ones to school on the back of his motorbike before driving on to the factory, where he also works. The father wanted him to start at the bottom there and work his way up: he's an assistant on one of the ovens, something like that. This son often takes his girlfriend to the factory at night: the ovens are blisteringly hot, you can be naked a hundred feet away and still keep warm. Now, this older brother keeps homing pigeons in a dovecote next to the house, and the two younger siblings have a real thing for them. Sometimes, if he travels to the city on an errand and it's going to keep him there for more than a day or two, he'll take one of the pigeons with him and send a message home. So the two younger ones are fascinated by the pigeons, but the dovecote's out of bounds for them. They're forever spying on it through the holes in the walls. A day comes when their school-teacher gives them a class on the digestive systems of birds, and the boy spends recreation poring over the page in question from the textbook, running his finger along the digestive tract the food travels down. It fascinates him that birds should expel everything through one single orifice. There's clearly something in this, he thinks, having just that one orifice – or one, that is, for things to go in, and one for things to go out of. That, he thinks, must be proof of the existence of a single God. Then one morning he gets up and hears some kind of commotion in the house, splashes his face, goes down for breakfast, and to his surprise finds his mother up, standing there in her pom-pom dressing gown with her hair down, and she's slumped against the father crying. The little sister is clutching her hand, and the maid's crying too, but over to one side. Somebody says: "No school for you today, Mikel." The older brother soon appears, and he's got a soldier's uniform on. Looking out of the window, the little brother sees an army truck, full of young men also in uniform. A light rain is coming down. The older brother says his goodbyes, a hug with the mother, a firm handshake with the father, a stronger hug with the maid, before the two siblings swarm him and start asking where he's going. Somewhere far away, he says, but he'll be back soon. They ask if he'll take some pigeons along and write them, and he promises that he will, once a month he says, they won't miss a thing, and then says it's up to them to look after the dovecote while he's gone. With that, out he goes to the truck. As it's driving away, Mikel feels the mother's hand begin to shake, and again she breaks down. After that the brother and sister spend every waking minute in the dovecote. They take turns up on the roof after school, watching for incoming pigeons. A mission as straightforward as avian digestive tracts. Months pass and nothing. The girl starts to get tired of all the waiting, but not Mikel, who does the majority of the looking out now. But one lunchtime it's her up there, and she cries out, "Mikel, Mikel, pigeons, I see pigeons!" Mikel leaves his sandwich on the open page of the illustrated encyclopaedia, open at C for colombophilia, and is up the stairs in a flash. They both stand and watch as the flock approaches. The girl hops about with joy; Mikel stands stock-still, eyes fixed on the horizon. A few minutes pass, and the pair fall into one another's arms, shielding their eyes so as not to see Guernica in flames.'

My mother fell silent.

'Is that it?' I said.

'Yes, that's it. I was ten when I had that dream.'

'And is it a real town?'

'It is. I looked it up at the Montana library a few days after.'

'But how did you know the place was called Guernica?'

'I had a clear memory of being in the dream and looking out as the army truck drove away, and seeing a road sign with that on. Guernica, it said.'

The squirrel came back to check out the bag again. I flicked my foot at it as a discouragement and suggested we get going. My mother stood with the help of the ad hoc walking stick. The swollen ankle wasn't getting any

283

more swollen. We walked for another quarter hour, going in circles till we spied a light through the trees. Not a portable television this time, but the moon glinting on the golf course, which was waterlogged. We picked our way through mud and puddles. When we got to Hole 5 my mother went and knelt down by the hole and started digging with her hands, madly scrabbling, hamster-like, like she intended to dig something up rather than deposit it. The porcelain cup was soon exposed, and my mother carefully pulled it out, trying not to destroy the cavity it sat in. She then placed the urn inside that cavity, and then the porcelain cup on top of it. I replaced the excavated mud and went around stamping it down, over and over, as though I was trying to stub a cigarette that never goes out. My mother stood at Hole 5 and wept; she was done with possibly her life's most important task. Death is a piece of shit and crying is a piece of shit and everything in that entire place was one shitty piece of shit piled on top of another piece of shit, so you could hardly blame her. To the rest of the world there would be nothing down there but a porcelain cup and a whole lot of soil.

6.
We're relaxing in the garden, poolside, and Semicolon's cell phone rings. It's the National Car Chase Company. Semicolon sits bolt upright in his lounge chair. The helicopter, they inform him, is currently located over Manhattan. Information scrolls across the bottom of the screen. The commentator says that today's offender was seen shoplifting at the Prada store in Soho; he stole a T-shirt with this season's Prada slogan on the chest: 'The Crime of the Century'. And that as he made his

getaway, by car, things turned ugly: he's already crashed into a set of traffic lights, knocking them clean over, and run down a pedestrian on the corner of Houston Street and Broadway.

'Come and watch, Kurt!' cries Semicolon. 'Let's see if they show your old apartment!'

Me and a few of the old folks gather round. It takes some of them a minute to reach us because of the weight of their diapers, wet from the pool; there's a rule saying they have to wear them even in the water. Today's offender gets to Williamsburg Bridge and crosses it into Brooklyn. He's slammed into a truck already, spinning it round and leaving it stuck sideways across one street. We watch, from the helicopter camera's bird's eye view, as the car enters the Hasidic neighbourhood, mowing down everything in its path. Some of the residents say they don't get it; they've seen this movie already, they say, turning and going back to the pool to continue with their water aerobics. One of the attendants comes over, laying a hand on Semicolon's shoulder and saying: 'That's how you get a group of people to join together, boys. Nothing else comes close.' We're both quite a bit older than him, but he calls us 'boys'. And then the thing that I have so often feared would happen, and that Semicolon has hoped and prayed for, happens. The car tears back up along the East River, up Bedford Avenue, heading north, taking out an ice cream van, screaming straight across the baseball field at McCarren Park, clipping the batter – the commentator says this has to be the most spectacular chase of the year, today's offender the most utterly brazen – and eventually coming onto Franklin Street, before slamming on the brakes and doing a U-turn: it's a dead end, he's cornered. This dead-end street leads to the back of my old apartment. This

I tell Semicolon, who lets out a squeak, saying: 'I told you, I told you.' I believe he might be about to explode. The helicopter camera zooms in, we see today's offender shinning up the fire escape at the rear of the building. He's unarmed, the commentator says. Reaching the second floor, the man trips on a doll, almost certainly a doll belonging to Kitty the Irishwoman, who I expect is still leaving her signature mark on meringue pies: KITTY AND RYAN IN LOVE; FUCK YOU RYAN BYE BYE. I point this out to Semicolon, telling him that Kitty used to collect dolls. Semicolon grabs me by the arm, and he's so het-up that his rings, with the heads of all those unknown European monarchs on them, dig into my bicep. The new burst of excitement draws a number of the residents out of the pool again: 'It's Kurt's old apartment, it's Kurt's old apartment,' Semicolon repeats, breathless, mechanically jabbing his forefinger up at me. The camera has zoomed all the way in now, we see the man smash the window to my old kitchen and climb inside. There's a brief lull in tension, but then they throw the heat sensor on, and we see a red figure advancing through the apartment. The commentator does his best to spice up proceedings: 'We are dealing here with a criminal so completely callous, it's entirely likely he's now helping himself to the contents of the refrigerator'; and, 'Now it looks as though he's got in the shower: see how the red of the heat map is fading... My god, the sheer, unmitigated callousness of it.' After a short while the red figure, standing still, disappears altogether, at which the commentator falls silent, not choosing to explain it, no one chooses to explain it, it's as though the shower water has swallowed up the offender. A couple more minutes and, with nothing to see, the residents start drifting away again, I do as well, everyone departs except for Semicolon. He's convinced today's offender is going to reappear, and sits glued to the cell phone screen until dinner. It's starting to grow cold out, someone has to go and tell him to come inside, he's still there in his dolphin-pattern swimming trucks, lying in the hammock, one testicle poking out the side, staring at the screen, mouthing something at it.

Semicolon had such a thing about the time I spent in Brooklyn that the same night, after lights out, I told him the following story, about something that took place in that same apartment a number of years before I moved in:

'Okay, so one evening after dinner, Clara and Peter, a couple who lived there previously, are watching TV. The news comes on and Clara, having zero interest, gets up, gives Peter a kiss and says: "I'll go and do the ironing, honey. There's a whole pile of it to get through." Peter, entranced by the news, doesn't even look up as Clara disappears out the door. After a quarter hour, he calls out: "Clara, don't forget my baseball jersey! Game's tomorrow!" He gets no answer. "Did you hear, Clara?" Still getting no response, he thinks maybe she's annoyed at the shouting – the apartment is no bigger than 150 square feet, and she's only in the next room. So he tries calling out again, this time more gently, cooing somewhat. Still no answer. He gets up and goes into the next room. As well as being the place where the ironing gets done, it's where they stack their bicycles and shoes, and hang up laundry, as well as being the place Peter hides his collection of bullets from Vietnam, where they keep a closet for the toys they bought the baby girl she had to abort just after he was sent to war, and generally the place to dump all the clutter that builds up over

287

the course of a marriage. He sees the half-ironed pile of clothes. There's steam coming off the iron, but Clara isn't there. He searches the rest of the apartment: the door onto the street is still locked from the inside, all the windows are still bolted as normal too. He calls for her a couple more times, and nothing. He goes and looks in the room again: nothing but the iron with steam still trickling out. Eventually he has to accept it: it isn't that Clara has left the apartment, it's that she's disappeared. Like the shoplifter disappearing on screen today. Are you listening, Semicolon, are you listening?'

But Semicolon was sound asleep.

I stayed in Williamsburg from 1980 to 1982, and only went back to the neighbourhood in 2016. I arrived on a Sunday morning at the beginning of May. It was a hot day, with a light drizzle coming down, and I pulled my blue Samsonite wheelie suitcase behind me, so completely different from the tote bags of the young guys crowding the sidewalk on Bedford. It was nothing like it had been in the early eighties. Its shabbiness was studied now, and I passed some gardens I remembered always being occupied by junkies and lowlifes, now in the throes of what I later learned is known as 'hipster' culture. One of the saddest things was finding out that the trade unions based in the nearby factories had thrown in the towel in the interim, which meant all the shops were open on Sundays. I had to dodge all manner of these hipsters, none of them looking where they were going, all fishing for epitaphs in the depths of their smartphones, and to a one dressed as if the Ramones were on a trip to India organized by some Mods. The old ice cream van came by, its dollhouse jingle ringing out. That, in some way, felt comforting to me. I'd arranged to

288

stay in my old apartment, with the landlady away visiting her daughter in California. I socked the side of the mailbox to unjam it, took out the keys and headed up the stairs to the third-floor apartment; it was an old wooden Victorian building, I don't think I've mentioned: no elevator. Immutable as the image on the side of a dollar bill, it hadn't changed one bit. I was met by murmurings and cooking smells as I climbed. I put the key in the lock. The narrow hallway inside curved to the right, leading into the kitchen, where I was presented with a note from the lady of the house in red pen, and at the top the line: LIFE, A USER'S MANUAL. It had instructions for how to turn the gas off, how many air con units you could use at once without blowing the fuses, which neighbours I should and shouldn't trust, things like this. As though I didn't know. She had also written down the addresses of a number of people who'd be happy to show me around the area. Pretty much everyone I'd met during my time in the city had departed, and I'd lost touch with those who were still around. A banging started up downstairs, and I recognized Kitty's voice, hoarser now than it had been three decades before. She was probably drunk. She was shouting at her son in Irish. The apartment was covered in dust, layers upon layers of it, on top of which somebody had daubed a thick coating of varnish. I couldn't remember if it had always been like that. The floor was covered in piles of rugs, rugs upon rugs, so it felt like you were walking around on a trampoline, and it gave the place the intense smell of stables too. I suddenly regretted having said yes to the commission to write something about Williamsburg; a magazine called *Moon & Wine* had contacted me about doing something for their regular Reunions feature, for which astronauts and other NASA staff would revisit a place they'd lived

289

in the past and then write up the experience. The letter had come to me at the Home, and nobody batted an eye-lid when I asked for a month off. They didn't appear to think I was in any danger of relapsing, while to me going on a trip and jotting down a few thoughts seemed a pretty good way of making some cash. The magazine offered me a hotel room in Manhattan but I thought I'd be better off staying in my old place: more immersive. I turned on the portable TV on the kitchen table. Taking a can of Polish beer from the refrigerator, I downed it in two gulps.

Frank and I got together the very next morning. We sat out on the steps of a place on Bedford Avenue and drank coffee through straws. I remember it clearly because it was then that I made my confession to Frank: 'The only window I've ever cleaned,' I said to him, 'was the one on Apollo 11. It was smaller than the windows the clerks sit behind at the post office.' Frank didn't seem at all surprised – it was like he either knew already, or just still didn't believe me. In spite of my seventy-one years, I'd got on board with the neighbourhood look already: I had a white pair of thrift-store All Stars on, skinny jeans and a Minnesotan lumberjack shirt, with a badge that read: 'Sylvia Plath Was Right'. Any time an acquaintance of Frank's came by, he introduced me as the neighbourhood's 'first ever hipster', saying I'd been at it all the way back in the eighties. The sun went behind a cloud for a moment. We heard the unmistakeable jingle of the ice cream truck, now stationed next to the park. 'Let's go for a chocolate and pistachio,' said Frank. On our way over there we saw a guy with a foldable white stick, and Frank said: 'Look, it's Blindman Bob. Say something; see if he'll give you an interview.' He didn't.

A number of days later, as I went up the stairs at my building and was going along the landing on the second floor, I had a feeling Kitty was watching me through her front door peephole. I don't think she recognized me. Putting water in the filter so I would have some ready for breakfast, I noticed black filaments swirling in it. I was reminded of the oil spillage they'd had in East River all those years before, and then I thought how I'd been seeing a minimum of one rat a day during this visit, out in broad daylight, bold as brass. You could have taken as many photos of them as you liked and they would have carried on about their business. Not like the local artists, none of whom would agree to have their picture taken. They could talk, my God could they talk, but good luck trying to get a photo of them – it was like the old Indian idea, like they were worried a camera would steal their souls. Though that would be to assume they had any. I tried to sleep, though it was like an oven in the apartment, even with the air con going full blast. The carpeting gave off the accumulated heat of the day, combined with the intense smell of the stables. The next building along was a live music venue called Studio B, and the noise from the concerts, especially the bass and the drums, shook the walls so hard it was affecting my heart rate. I got up, lit a cigarette, read some of the things I'd been writing, notes for the article, which wasn't going all that well. Again, the heat of the carpets and rugs, my feet sweaty. I'd had enough: I got down on my knees and lifted up the rug, which looked like it might have originated in Peru – the top rug, that is: I found another one underneath, this one with geometric motifs. This second one down was harder work, but I managed it with a little elbow grease, and was then presented with a third carpet, this one coffee-coloured and pretty worn out, and fastened with tacks. I thought it was fastened to the floorboards, but found yet another one underneath, covered in pictures of what looked like cartoon characters and tacked down even more securely; I went and found some pliers, and these I had to really dig with to get at the heads of the tacks. Next was a series of bathmat-type rugs, sewn together along the edges, creating a multi-coloured checkerboard, full of hairs and other particles that, whatever they were, were part of the carpet now. I ripped up this succession of floor coverings and came to what was in fact the final layer before the floorboards, some thick lino, with a series of very worn footprints tracking across it. I followed where the footprints led: they petered out on arrival at a wardrobe. Opening the wardrobe, I found a bundle of baby clothes inside, never worn, and masses of rifle cartridges that I instantly recognized as being the kind we used in Vietnam. For a moment I even wondered if some of them hadn't been fired by me. After that I dragged out the whole mess of rugs and carpets and lino as best I could, leaving them in a big mound midway down the hall. Four in the morning. The last of the Studio B concert-kids were traipsing by outside the window. I sat down on the bed and took a long drink of filtered water. I stared at the mountain of carpets and rugs, it nearly touched the ceiling, blocking my view of the front door. Neither the heat contained in it nor the stable-smell had dissipated. All that had happened was these things being moved to and concentrated in that single point. A little like what my mother did in her dreams, moving things from one place to another, I thought. I fell asleep thinking about the universality of this flow of ideas and bodies, common both to the functioning of the most modern satellite and the water in a river.

292

The article was a struggle. I decided to take a day out and head over to Manhattan. It's a single subway stop to get there, but I thought I'd join the people crossing Williamsburg Bridge on foot instead. Hoping to avoid the worst of the sun, I set off early, about eight, which meant the streets were quiet. The one thing I remember from the day is the huge bolts on the bridge supports, big as my head; I'd never seen head-sized bolts before. I didn't make it all the way across either – the sun was too intense. That night I was relaxing in the kitchen, eating bowls of corn flakes with a little vodka added, when the TV transmission started picking up interference. Every time a plane bound for JFK went overhead, the picture started breaking up. I waggled the antennae around, to no avail. I was in the middle of a truly excellent National Geographic scene in which it wasn't clear which were the humans and which the monkeys. I heard Kitty bawling at her set, and her son trying to calm her down. The kid I'd known as a six-year-old was in his thirties now, he had an obesity problem and went around Williamsburg with his shopping bag of sketchbooks and his hands covered in felt tip ink. He sat in McCarren Park and did his drawing, or watched the baseball players running around and around. The picture wasn't going back to normal; Kitty carried on bellowing at it. I pictured the son getting out of bed, putting the sketchbooks aside for a minute, dragging his huge frame – well over six feet and fifteen stone of pure sausage meat – into the living room, where Kitty was really starting to lose it now. I imagined him in his grey Bermuda shorts and round-toed sneakers as he said: 'Wait, Ma, just wait for the plane to go by.' Then I wasn't imagining it any more – I could hear Kitty shouting, 'If you don't fix it this instant I'm coming over there and I'm gonna bite those greasy thighs of yours, give you something to remember me by!' The exact same threat she used any time he was naughty as a little boy. The son shouted back, she started shouting his name – Tom, that was it, he was called Tom. Then I heard Tom start to cry. Kitty went on shouting. A few moments passed, and the plane must have finally gotten out the way of the satellite in question because the picture on the screen was suddenly clear as day once more.

After a fortnight that passed in a rapid whirl of ice creams and beers with Frank, and saw me make zero progress on the article, he took me to do an interview with a guy called Joe Ferguson who lived among the rubble of what had been his home. He slept in a rusted-out car on the lot. Soon after his wife had left him, the house had collapsed because of a subway tunnel that was being built right underneath. The official version said that it had been down to structural issues. He decided to stay on and still have a home there; at the end of the day the lot and the rubble now piled up inside it were his property. He took his car inside and got himself a couple of dogs for company. He'd been battling the town hall for years to make them accept responsibility and do a complete rebuild. He went around in cut-off denim shorts in summer and winter alike. Every morning he took himself down to the park at dawn to do Tai Chi. We found him moving in slow motion in the early morning mist. Frank said we were better off leaving him to it, and we headed to his place to wait for him, stopping off first at Ron's for breakfast. Bellies full, we got to Joe's, his two dogs forming the welcome committee. Fatboy and Not-so-Fatboy they were called, though both were the size of blimps. We sat ourselves down on a pair of beach chairs. Joe had filled in the cracks and then painted the walls, painted the piles of rubble and joists as well, such that it put me in mind of the Palace of Knossos on Crete, a place that Aldrin had regaled us about during the lunar mission – his honeymoon on Crete, the great wonders of the Palace of Knossos, how it knocked Vegas out of the park; truth was I didn't listen all that closely since at that particular moment I was watching some kind of fire spreading across this one tract in Africa.

Joe soon showed up. He held out a hand for me to shake, apologizing for his sweatiness: 'Tai Chi's more anaerobic than it might look.' He said he'd make tea. He got a television screen out, leaning it against a crumbling cement pillar – the unevenness meant the screen wound up at an angle – and hooking it up to a car battery. While Frank filled him in on the *Moon & Wine* piece, I watched as on-screen somebody dunked a coin into some kind of liquid, and where it went in all scuffed and dirty, grubby as hell, it came out shiny; this was my first ever sighting of a Cillit Bang commercial. Joe couldn't have been happier to recount his story, which he proceeded to do, thinking it'd be a way of getting the public to sit up and take notice. Poor wet-behind-the-ears dope, I though. The world's full of them, I thought. I asked him if he had any Williamsburg tales, anecdotes, things specific to the neighbourhood, at which he pointed at my shirt and said:

'I got one about a Minnesotan lumberjack shirt, just like yours.'

'I bought this a couple of weeks back, here in Williamsburg.'

'Right, right, that's what I'm saying,' he said. 'One day a guy called Benny, the owner of Glass & Glass – you know him, Frank – buys himself a shirt just like it, same brand, in a store in Manhattan. He was over there

295

on a little shopping spree, so he's going into stores all day long, but now every time he does, the alarms start going off. He gets frisked like a hundred times by the store guards, but of course they never find a thing. At like the fifth store, they finally decide it's gotta be the shirt – gotta be, right? But the shirt's clean, the anti-theft gizmo, that's obviously been taken off. And anyway, so that's that. From then on, any time he decides to wear the shirt, he goes around and he's like this store alarm trigger man, right? The shirt winds up living in that wardrobe of his, never getting worn. But then one day he meets a guy who tells him about an exorcist for store alarms, tells him he isn't the first to suffer this particular fate, it's a more frequent occurrence than people think. When I met Benny he told me that the exorcist had actually just burned the shirt. Kill the dog: no more rabies, he'd said. Then, as a kind of grace note, the exorcist guy made Benny go round all the stores in Manhattan with the ashes in a bag. So Benny, as well as now having no shirt, loses a hundred bucks to this jerk, and the ashes of the shirt still set off the goddamn store alarms! Right? It's like *things* have got a soul, and you can burn 'em all to hell, turn 'em to ashes if you like, but that soul doesn't go anywhere. Know what I mean? Want some more tea?'

Lying in bed that night, I thought about my exorcized shirt, the one I'd worn the night I left San Francisco in my Ford Torino. I also thought about Barbara. What had become of her? I had a dream about a mountain of carpets and rugs barring the hallway and beeping forever, on and on, in a never-ending alarm.

Three weeks in, it was clear there wasn't much for me to write about in Williamsburg. Joe and one or two others aside, hipsters were more tight-lipped than I'd imagined, and it was hardly worth sticking around. But then again, given it was all expenses paid, I thought I might as well. By day I went walking, trying to strike up conversations in the streets, so my only memories of the apartment are of being there at night. Frank couldn't always come with me. He still had a job as a nightwatchman, though not in the Meatpacking District abattoir now, but in Williamsburg itself, in one of the big tech warehouses on Franklin Street. He could pilfer just about anything he wanted and the managers never caught on. While I was in town he was busy trying to procure TV screens for some video installation. This, I now found out, was why he'd been friendly with so many artists in the eighties: he procured materials for them to work with, and charged nominal prices. 'Artists tend to be pretty out of it,' he said to me one day as we sat drinking Sierra Nevadas, 'and the ones who've already made it would far rather use their money for booze and partying, the net result being that most works of art made in this city use the crappiest materials you can imagine. Most fall apart if you so much as breathe on them – toys made in China are sturdier. How many years these pieces will last, I don't know, but not many I'd bet. You watch: art restoration's gonna be a booming industry in no time at all. A lot of those crappy materials come direct from yours truly: I'm pretty well-connected now – in a way, you could say I've single-handedly fostered the collapse of contemporary arts in this country, though that's never been my motivation. For me it's always just been a bit of extra pocket money. So like in the eighties, my abattoir days, all the artists went in for the whole *materiality* thing, everything was blood and guts, you know, and it was down to me to procure meat for them – both to feed themselves, there were always offcuts from the processing machinery, and for the work they were making: pig heads they wanted for models, cows they'd slice in two and use as moulds for sculptures. That kind of thing. I got a bunch of pigs and cow thoraxes for Francis Bacon, the great Irish painter, though at the time I had no idea he was British or great. Oh, and do you remember that Spanish artist we went to see at the top of the Twin Towers that one day?' 'Yeah,' I said, 'Carlos.' 'Well remembered! And do you remember his Saint Sebastian pieces, with the jumbo jets crashing into them?' 'Sure I do. He was inspired by that poet friend of his. Spanish. What was his name?' 'Carlos Oroza.' 'That was it.' 'Well, Carlos, the sculptor Carlos, he died in the Twin Tower attacks. He was sleeping in his studio at the time.'

On one of my many sleepless nights, on account of another concert at Studio B, I got out of bed and, like I used to do in the eighties, went and stood at the open window to contemplate the Manhattan skyline. Minus the Twin Towers now of course. The thought of Carlos the sculptor made me shudder: really, he'd been practising voodoo on himself. I noticed the ice cream van parked on the sidewalk opposite, lights off, music off. Presently a woman in high heels and a miniskirt walked up to it, knocked on the back door, a hairy arm helped her inside. I heard her ask for the cash upfront. Moments when the mysteries of this neighbourhood struck me as more and more profound.

I headed to Rum Bar to meet Frank, whom I hadn't seen for a week at that point. I wanted to show him the draft of my article, not much more than an outline really, a page and a half tops. I took a shortcut across McCarren Park. The sun was just dipping behind the tops of buildings.

I saw Tom sitting in the bleachers on the far side of the diamond, and went over. Seeing me, he looked up from his sketchbook.

'Tom, right?' I said. 'Kitty's boy?'

He started casting around, seemingly hoping for company other than mine in the sunny empty ballpark.

'Sure,' he said reluctantly, 'I'm Tom. I live on Franklin Street.'

'You won't remember me, but I knew you as a little boy. How's it going?'

'Who are you?' He carried on glancing around.

'Don't worry, Tom, I'm a friend. I lived in the apartment above you, years ago now. Kurt's my name. Do you remember me?'

'Kurt the window cleaner?'

'That's right, Kurt the window cleaner.'

'You look completely different.'

'So do you, Tom, so do you. I'm in town for a few days, trip down memory lane and all that. How's your mother?'

'Worse than ever. Between the booze and her arthritis she can hardly stand up. She doesn't go out.'

'Okay, well it's nice to see you. See you around, okay?'

'Okay, see you around.'

Frank showed up an hour late. Enough time for a couple of Sierra Nevadas. I was about to give up and go home when he appeared, visibly flustered. 'I was this close to the homeware section manager catching me with this old plasma screen. Jeez, it was awful. I've never had that before.' This seemed a fair excuse. 'Next round's on you,' I said, 'I'm going to the bathroom.' 'Another one of these?' he said, pointing to the empty bottles on the table. 'Yeah,' I said.

Coming back to the table, I found him staring at the label on the bottle.

'These snowy mountains remind me of Mount Ararat, in Armenia,' he said. 'I met this woman artist last year, lives in the East Village, hot as anything, blonde but with Eastern European features. Her work always had something to do with war, and she told me about a piece she'd done about the Armenian Holocaust. The two of us talked for hours. I told her my idea about there being no two people on the planet not joined by some war or another, that the six degrees of separation everyone talks about are actually four if we take into account all the wars that have taken place. She told me about some studies showing that the six degrees of separation in friendships have been cut to four as well by social networks.'

I jumped in then, pushing the fledgling article across the table:

'Would you have a look, tidy it up a bit for me? I'm no good at typing.'

He took it, saying he'd be delighted. Then, seeming to notice something on my shoes, he whispered:

'Don't move...' Getting up, he lunged forward, squashing a cockroach under my stool. He soon made his excuses – the plasma screen was in the trunk of his car and he had to get it to the artist in question. He couldn't tell me who the artist was – too famous, he said.

I started out home. It was dark. It was a moonless night but I still put my sunglasses on, just in case. I came back through McCarren Park, going in at the corner where the ice cream van usually parked, through the small wooded area and across the athletics track, leaves swirling about my feet in the gentle summer wind. Tom was still in position, gazing down at his sketchbooks

300

under the floodlights. I went over to him.

'What's up, Tom. Still here?'

Startled, he put the sketchbook to one side.

'Yeah, I don't want to go home. There's gonna be planes flying over.' Rolling up the left leg of his pants, he showed me his quad, which had KITTY & RYAN IN LOVE scarred into it. He didn't need to show me the back of his thigh.

'I understand, Tom.'

'Earlier on, after you stopped by, I started remembering things. How you used to go on about flocks of birds flying straight at you, raining down on your head. I believed you, I spent years scanning the sky, I couldn't sit down to draw without having to glance up every thirty seconds. I also remembered seeing you go out in the evenings and then hearing you come back, how we'd hear you walking around your apartment, we'd know when you were in the kitchen, when you were in the bath or in bed, and how I said to my mom one day that we ought to do a picture in chalk on our ceiling of your tracks through your apartment, a map of you, and how that was the best way of getting inside a person, like a diagram of your soul's movements or something. I grew up without any toys, and it was nice having you around the place. You showed me a bunch of boxes with x-rays of your lungs, you said they were like the surface of the moon. I believed that as well.'

'You remember it all, then. Here, let me have a look at the sketchbook.'

'No, no. It's just doodles, none of it's any good.'

'Come on, man. I've known you since you were yea high.'

He handed it over. The pictures were all of houses. I flicked through the pages; there were some amazingly

301

realistic renderings of the interiors of houses, seen through windows, from street level. He'd created a picture of the entire neighbourhood, one page per building. Like polaroids, but handmade.

'I got dozens of sketchbooks back at home,' he said, seeing my surprise. 'That's why I'm always out in the street.'

I lit a cigarette.

'Why do you draw so much?'

'I feel completely certain that, one day, homo sapiens and Neanderthals are going to meet again.'

'But, Tom, the Neanderthals all died out.'

'I don't believe that.'

'Fine,' I said, 'so the Neanderthals didn't all die out. What of it?'

'Nothing, really. It's just my hope that I'll capture the historic meeting through one of these windows. When it comes, I want to be the first one to get it down. Like those old cave paintings, all the buffalos and hunting scenes and all, but in the here and now.'

What I didn't say was that I had one of those very meetings every day of my life, in the place I was now living, with Semicolon. I looked at more of the sketches. Domestic scenes, featuring a lot of people I felt I knew. Then the streetlights in the park all went dark, followed, a moment after, by the floodlights over the ballpark itself going out one after the other. We were in complete darkness.

'It's like being in a Neanderthal cave,' I joked, holding up the flame of my lighter.

I came to a page depicting Frank in bed with a woman. She had short blonde hair.

'Do me a favour, Tom. Don't mention to your mom that I'm staying upstairs.'

'Sure, Kurt. No problem.'

After eating the first thing I found in the refrigerator, I went and sat by the open window, hoping the night air would clear my aching head. The streets were particularly quiet, except for a few young guys working on a car under a streetlamp, banging on it every now and then with hammers. They didn't talk much, but when they did it was the kind of speech you hear middle class people use when they want to make it seem like they're from the projects. I picked up the phone and dialled Frank's number. I wanted to tell him about Tom's drawing of him, and I wanted to ask about the blonde woman. He didn't answer. I looked out of the window again, the young guys had taken the car into a garage, and the hammering was ongoing. They were all men and all of them, like me, produced semen. Their semen was the same as mine. Disgusting thought.

4 July. The neighbourhood awash with stars and stripes. The fireworks were about to go up over Manhattan, any second now. Everyone was up on their rooftops waiting for the display. There were parties going on, cookouts and beers, and it would all keep on going on until everyone was plastered and wending their separate ways home. I was ironing some clothes. I heard footsteps up on the roof, heard the charcoal sizzling. I got dressed, clambered over the pile of carpets and rugs, headed out. The landing on my floor gave onto a ladder that led to the roof. I went up it. Things were already getting lively up there. The whole building was in attendance, Kitty included, and I saw that Joe Ferguson had been invited – he had Fatboy and Not-so-Fatboy in tow. Somebody handed me some barbecue; they were using pages from

the *New York Times* and *Village Voice* as plates. I sat down on the asphalt roofing, away from the crowd, next to the air conditioning pipes. I put the newspaper on the floor; the meat glistened in between my legs. I took a swig of cold beer. The fireworks got started. I'd never seen a firework display as impressive, and that includes the 1969 show in DC when they celebrated our return. Every time I went to take a mouthful of the meat, the light shone on an article in the Arts & Leisure section, the subheading of which read: 'Antonio's, the popular East Village bakery, to shut. Locals yesterday paid homage to the owner, a war vet. The property is due to be turned into a branch of Citibank.' When I finished eating, I balled up the paper, and took a shot at the barbecue: three points. A big flame shot up for a second. I took another swig of beer. A girl I'd never seen before came and sat down next to me, we stared at the sky in silence. The light in the sky illuminated our faces in flashes.

'Kurt,' I said, holding out my hand for her to shake.

'Clara,' she said, not shaking it.

Neither of us said anything. It was a few minutes before she broke the silence:

'Have you ever been in a war?'

'No,' I lied.

'Well,' she said, pointing up at the fireworks, 'it's more or less like this.'

Silence descended between us once more.

When I turned to look again, she'd gone. I looked around the roof party, but there was no sign of her. It was a few minutes before I realized: she hadn't left the party, she'd disappeared.

7.

I'm sitting on a park bench in the city of Miami; the paving slabs beneath me are inlaid with dolphin and mermaid tiles and they are the closest to Paradise I can currently hope to get. We're out on one of our monthly day trips, which I always sign up to, and, the moment we arrive at our destination, whether an amusement park, a mall or a swamp with unsurpassable panoramas and obese crocodiles lazing in the sun, I pretend I need the bathroom and make myself scarce. Always for at least fifteen minutes (long enough for two cigarettes) but no more than thirty, thirty minutes being the time the residents can last without needing another ice cream or slush puppy or to use a bathroom themselves, and therefore the juncture at which a headcount will be carried out. And if I'm not there at that moment, all hell breaks loose. Example of hell breaking loose: with Sarah the resident harpy leading the way, all the old folks start to shout and make a fuss. Sarah the resident harpy isn't our tour leader, she's one of the residents, though she isn't actually so old, only wishes she were, wishes it with all her might. She's on record as saying the worst thing that ever happened was her wearing odd socks to Holy Communion, an event that explains all she's been through since: her inability to ever find herself a husband, and general man trouble besides, the endless visits to psychics and the line, or lines, she bought about love always being just around the corner, having to re-mortgage her home several times to pay the psychics, and, last but not least, what she refers to as The Loss: the loss of her ankle-high dog, Spider, who one day ran out under the wheel of a passing car, the bodywork and upholstery of which, according to her, were the same colours – a pale red and an intense, fiery red – as the

non-matching socks she'd worn to Holy Communion.
Which isn't to mention the hue and cry that will come
from Semicolon specifically if he notices I've gone. He'll
start hopping about, stomping on the spot, the real reason being that he's courting Sarah the Harpy, fawns
over her constantly, does anything he can to please her,
and that would include ratting on me, stealing the plastic
rose from my bedside table to give her as a present or
even paying for a whole year's subscription to the National Car Chase Company should she give the slightest
hint that this is her desire, which has never happened.
Not that this stops Semicolon who, any time one of our
excursions takes us to a mall, hides behind a pillar or
partition, or among clothes racks in the woman's garments section, and when Sarah the Harpy approaches,
jumps out in disguise making a noise that sounds like
'coo-coo'. I don't mention this out of any kind of spite for
Semicolon, but because he did this one day, one day he
did precisely this: he jumped out with an old-style cowboy hat on, got up in a frankly incomprehensible
disguise, so incomprehensible it would require several
pages to describe, pages I naturally don't intend to waste,
while making the 'coo-coo' noise and blinking his eyes
open and shut, accompanied by a slow back and forth of
the head, as though he was pecking at some kind of fruit
in slow motion, at which Sarah the Harpy screamed so
loudly and with such piercing stridency that the security
guards came rushing over, and Semicolon almost burst
into tears. It was dramatic; I couldn't stop laughing, but
it was dramatic. The tour leader that day encouraged
me, as his roommate, to have a word. I took him off to the
coffee room used by the staff at the mall, the place they
went to put their feet up and gossip, and I sat on a stool
facing him, which put me a full foot and a half above

him. Once it was just the two of us, we began to talk, or rather he began to talk, he was sorry for what he'd done, he said, sobbing, but it had just been so long since he'd felt anything like what he felt for Sarah, he was a useless good-for-nothing, he said, going on to explain how his family had disowned him following his elopement with the plastic-enhanced younger lady, and the people who came to visit him every three months weren't his actual family, they were some random people he paid to come and see him: first, he said, counting on his fingers, there was the daughter who necked contraceptives all day, he'd found her in a pole dancing place; second, this daughter's supposed husband, the one with the Clinton & Co. Insurance badge, he'd come across him working as a parking attendant, the guy had been on the verge of getting fired for stealing hubcaps; third there was his supposed wife, the ancient lady who sat on the sofa inside the entranceway way in her Lakers paraphernalia, he did actually have some history with her, she used to clean his house in the time after he left his real wife; and as for number four, the thirteen-year-old granddaughter with the baby-less baby stroller, he said he'd rather not say where he found her. He was still sobbing. The coffee room was a bare, rectangular box, one of these places that belongs to nobody, a sort of addendum to the public world of American consumerism, not much more than a table with empty coffee cups on it, an overflowing ashtray in spite of the No Smoking signs, a sofa the bottom of which had fallen through and a Bruce Willis poster on the wall, which can be accounted for by the fact that women outnumber men four to one among the staff at all large malls and stores in this country. And as Semicolon went on with his tale of woe, I instinctively started checking for a hidden camera, not because I

307

thought this might be some candid camera show but because I felt an incredibly strong urge to do something to him, something unpleasant, I mean: slap him, call him a useless good-for-nothing or force him to drink the dregs of the cups on the table, mixed together with the contents of the ashtray. Since coming back from Vietnam, where I took my anger out on the civilian population in a series of acts that, though people could easily imagine them if they tried, I have never talked about and never will, I'd never felt like this. It was the first time in fifty years that the desire, almost impossible to resist, had come over me to do something iniquitous for the sheer hell of it, whether a recurrence or a hangover of my war experiences, I don't know – experiences that come bubbling up out of a place you thought had ceased to exist. Semicolon looked at me, searching for some kind of approval, and said, 'What are you looking for, Kurt?', and I saw the shame in his eyes and his fearful, anxious quivering cheeks, and still my urge failed to dissipate – the opposite, it grew even stronger. 'Nothing,' I said, 'I'm not looking for anything,' and, helping him up, I patted him on the back and we went back out to the mall where the group was waiting, everyone except Sarah the Harpy, who had gotten on the bus already, was sitting there alone and profoundly upset. So, yes, all this and more Semicolon would be willing to do for her, which is why I know that right now, as I sit on this bench in this Miami park, if I were to take longer than thirty minutes before going back to the group, Sarah, an obsessive when it comes to order, will absolutely lose her shit, at which Semicolon will instantly forget the day I sat and consoled him in a coffee room hidden away at the back of a mall, that I dried his tears, spared him the cruelties that a part of me, a part of my nature, wanted to inflict on him, and that I even in a way saved his life that day, given how easy it would have been for me to end his life there and then, how incredibly easy, get one of the sofa cushions and press it down over his face, 'He had a real weak heart, Officer, plus what with the obesity and all, I don't know, suddenly he was down on the ground, nothing I could do: the door was locked and I couldn't break it down, these oak veneer doors, they're tougher than they look, and the music they were playing out in Homeware meant nobody could hear me calling for help, yes, Officer, America is a great country and even the lower quality items turn out to be incredibly robust when least you expect them to be, nothing opens right when you need it to, I even tried doing mouth-to-mouth, I did, but everything I tried came to nought.' It had been well within my power to end his life that day, but I know that if I now spend more than a half hour away from the group, he'll have no mercy, there'll be a big ruckus and him and Sarah the Harpy will be at the heart of it, which means that now, sitting on this park bench in Miami while everyone else admires the views and the colossal, redwood-sized crocodiles, a park we only just got to and the name of which I don't even know, nor do I believe I ever will, I know I ought to keep a careful eye on the minute hand of my Rolex, far more careful than I was when, in full view of millions of earthlings watching on TV, harmless spectators who stupidly adore you for no reason at all, I walked on the moon, spectators who, unlike the group from the Home, never kick up a fuss, swallow just about anything they're presented with. I now notice a tree by the bench with an electrical outlet set into the trunk, a plastic cover to protect it from humidity and rain, and I feel like I want to plug my laptop into this electrical outlet-tree, since I always bring my laptop with me on our day trips, and it seems this city provides electrical outlets for businessmen and others who, like me, find themselves at a loose end and choose to connect to the Great Beyond while eating cones of freshly chopped fruit; this is a good leisure-time philosophy, I say, to eat fruit chopped by the hands of strangers, and going online requires a huge leap of faith, the willingness to believe in the existence of something you'll never physically encounter, so I decide to do it, I get my laptop out and plug it in, and I see the battery icon on my laptop begin to charge, and I ask myself where this energy comes from, and my thoughts also inevitably turn to the sap of the tree, a communications satellite and a churning river of information now flowing my way. Most things, if you think them through to their endpoints, wind up fitting into one of two metaphors: that of the communications satellite, and that of water flowing in a river. And, now that I am aware of this tree's electrical energy – I'm utilizing something that it seems there's a surfeit of in this city, vampirizing it – and a man walks by pulling a shopping cart behind him, I'm suddenly put in mind of epilogues – I've never thought about the epilogues of things before, of what comes after – and it occurs to me that every time you re-read a book or think about a book you read once upon a time, you're writing an epilogue for it, and that everything that deserves to be in existence has been created to be seen at least twice, and I think that every time you watch a movie for a second time you're also filming its epilogue, and that the more you think about a book or a movie, the more epilogues you create for it, layers and layers of epilogues, a big seamless slab of epilogues piling up. And I think about cities as well, because I'm sitting in a city park and because, I don't mind admitting it, I prefer cities over both books and movies, and I wonder: What would the epilogue for a city be? Or, better: What is the epilogue for a country? I don't mean countries that have ceased to exist, like Yugoslavia or the USSR, or pre-genocide Armenia or the state of Texas before it was part of America, no, I mean countries that really do belong to us, the ones we're in the process of building right now, and I could go on and think about all of this, it's a good idea to think about this kind of country, but I don't, I really can't be bothered, which often happens: you have an idea, you know it's going to be a colossal idea no matter what, you see it rearing up, but you drop it anyway. For example, although I dream about Barbara every single night, I never stop to think about why she left, and neither do I intend to do so now, sitting here on this bench in Miami. And I suspect that the epilogues of countries are all the stories and myths, varyingly fantastical, told by later generations regarding said countries. One way of putting it would be to say that they're the imaginary aspect of things already in existence, like when we went to the moon: that was real, we were physically there, but it wasn't all shown on TV; I myself didn't feature in the TV footage, not for any special reason, only that it's technically impossible to hold a camera and be on camera at the same time yourself, but back home the idea immediately sprang up that we never made it to the moon, that alterations had been made to the footage, cuts and redactions, and that it had all been a big scam, but that wasn't the case, of course we went to the moon, and yet this did nothing to prevent the idea from gaining currency, from becoming real, as an epilogue in the popular culture of our country. And I have no idea why I'm thinking about epilogues at this moment in time, maybe it's because I'm sitting on this bench in a Miami park and there's a tree next to me with an electrical outlet, and when I unplug my laptop the battery immediately starts to drain, it's dropping at a significant rate, like the financial markets in 2008, whose charts resembled ski slopes, or like when my mother crashed to earth in the woods the night we went to bury my father's urn, he must still be there I guess, my father turned ash; yes, I'd say my laptop battery is collapsing, and I wonder where all this energy goes, and then suddenly it's me experiencing the energetic loss: something takes hold of me; I myself am being vampirized by the city; the entire country is vampirizing me and it isn't going to stop until I pass out on the paving slabs of this park, with their inlaid mermaids and dolphins which are the closest I'll ever get to Paradise. And the cemeteries in a city, I wonder as I fall to the ground, what kind of epilogues are they?

8.

I know that I'm lying on the ground in the park and that my eyes are open because I can see blue sky and faces around me looking down, all of them stock-still until I blink a few times. There are both women and men in the circle, most of them young folk, they look like paramedics, and I see a few of the residents among them as well. I am lying on the ground, that much is clear, and the tiles depicting mermaids and dolphins are digging into my back. There's Sarah the Harpy, looking down like I was some frog ripe for vivisection, and wearing dangly earrings that point directly at my eyes. There's a female paramedic leaning over me, her straight, chestnut hair so long it almost brushes my cheeks, but that feels less of a danger than Sarah the Harpy's earrings. There's a male

312

paramedic, and he's got nothing hanging off his head: he's got a buzz cut, but he does have a chain around his neck with a tag dangling down over my mouth, though I can't tell if it's a religious symbol or just a tag. There's one of the old ladies from the Home, she's staring at me pretty intently, and dangling down from her, an inch or two from my face, are her two pendulous breasts and colossal cleavage, and it occurs to me that a cleavage is lovely not because it's easy on the eye but because it's exclusive to the human race. Deer, chicken, eagles: none of them have cleavages, and as a comparison I try to think of what it is we men have that the males of other species do not, but nothing occurs to me. There's Semicolon, the skin on his face sagging down, jowly cheeks especially, but I don't stop to think about Semicolon's face, far too much in that for a moment like this, a moment when the array of faces and things leaning and drooping over me join together to create – I already said it – a circle with the blue sky at its centre, or the purple-blue sky, to be precise, given that constant purple tinge to Miami skies. A plane flies overhead, white vapour trail behind, and it makes the overall composition look to me like it's empty. I hear voices, Sarah the Harpy starts saying she would like to give me a foot rub, and the male paramedic says that isn't going to do it. The tiled dolphins and mermaids digging into my back. I shut my eyes.

And open them again. No faces above me now, but a cream-coloured ceiling. Looking down, I see a drip attached to my left arm, a see-through catheter. I bring my right hand up and rub my head, which I find has a bandage around it. The room has a muted feel, verging on the serene, like all Miami clinics. The slatted blinds, half open, let in a diffuse, feathered light. There's a telephone on the bedside table, also cream-coloured, and at the foot of the bed a blue armchair for visitors, and beyond that an open wardrobe with lots of hangers but no clothes, which puts me in mind of a room for keeping dead people's bones – an ossuary. The bedside table also has a vase containing flowers of different colours. I wiggle my toes: not paralysed. I look out of the window which is to my left, see small buildings slotted between a series of buildings that start tall, seventeen storeys high at least, and descend in height, descend or cascade, and have very nice-looking roof terraces. I see people on these terraces, and inside the apartments as well, domestic scenes mostly based around the eating of food, looks like it must be lunchtime. I see a brown leather bag hanging on the blue armchair at the foot of the bed; I don't know who it belongs to, it's just there, hanging, stationary – as am I. How is it, I wonder, that there can be two things in the world so utterly at a standstill, so completely static and frozen? The door opens and in comes a small woman in a white nuclear gown. She chirps a hello and comes over, starts doing something with the drip, opening and closing valves and pressing the number keys on a control panel. She asks how I'm feeling; I don't know what to say to that. What happened to me, I ask? Oh, nothing, she says, just a bang to the head, but the doctor thought it might not be a bad idea to come in for tests, a CAT scan and, if anything shows up on that, maybe an NMR. What's an NMR, I ask? Stands for Nuclear Magnetic Resonance, she says. But it could be nothing, she says. I tell her I feel fine. I say this twice – it always seems a good idea to say things twice: I've heard of languages that don't have the plural in the way we think of it, and which create multiples by repeating the singular, so 'get my bags' would be 'get my bag bag', and 'the surfer surfs the waves' would be 'the surfer surfs the wave wave'. And so on. The nurse starts telling me again how they're planning to take some scans: she says I'm due to have a 'CAT scan, a CAT scan, a CAT scan', as if the nurse, having gone beyond the singular, wanted to exceed the plural too, but, I wonder, does anything beyond the plural exist? I'm thinking about this as she goes on with her 'CAT scan, CAT scan, CAT scan', before suggesting I get some sleep, some sleep, some sleep. She goes out, pausing in the doorway to point out the binoculars on the bedside table, so I turn and look, I haven't yet turned in this direction, still less at such a steep angle, and I see them, a pair of black, medium-sized binoculars. They're for when I'm up and about, she says, in case I feel like looking out of the window. I had a visitor, a kind man, she said, who asked after me and left the binoculars while I was still asleep. She shuts the door, I hear her go away down the corridor. I feel bad I ever thought ill of Semicolon, ridiculous and awkward as hell though he is, and though when he dies the planet won't register the loss in the slightest. At least he bothered to come and see me, bothered to bother about me, and left these binoculars, which is a very Semicolon kind of thing to do: completely pointless, but nonetheless the kind of thing I say to myself I ought to be conscious of in the future. I feel the call of nature, bladder needs emptying; I get up, take the wheelie drip pole along with me, the wheels don't spin round so well: they make a scraping noise like galvanized roller skates, like the ones we used in elementary school in Montana. We rolled around and around in the covered bus park, 'roll' was a word people loved using in that place of geometrically fenced-off lands: Montana looks like a chessboard from the sky, in reality the entirety of the US looks like

315

a chessboard, this is our game, North v South and every state a square, though it's a game I still don't think we've actually learned to play. I go into the bathroom, lift up the toilet seat, empty my bladder, this is what I'm up to right now; we're always all up to something, I say to myself, and I at this particular moment am up to emptying my bladder, and my back hurts, and when my urine hits the water it creates bubbles, lemon-yellow bubbles that are in constant flux, and in the little motion picture made by the moving outlines I think I see something pink-yellow, like when you look out of a train window and glimpse a flower and it stays put; it's lost to you forever and you'll never know what becomes of it; roses are something people have always talked a lot about, still do, I'd even planned to plant one on the moon; roses are the most famous flower, and my urine is currently creating a yellow rose inside the toilet bowl. My bladder empty, though my penis isn't erect, I suddenly find myself coming, bracing against the wall with both hands, the sensation only lasts a second or two, no semen is produced, or at least not real semen, my semen has been nothing but simulation semen for years, pure theatre props, but I do experience pleasure – it takes my breath away. Having your breath taken away, being made to gasp, is the most degrading voluntary bodily response – it reminds me of a rabbit being hunted, scrabbling to get away from the inevitable – and I gasp and feel shame just for briefly gasping. On the way back to the bed, pulling the drip pole with me, I stop by the double-glazed window, which muffles the sound of everything going on outside while giving a very clear view of it. On the roof terraces of the descending or cascading buildings I see a bikini hanging on the back of a chair, and I also see a dog sleeping under the palm tree in the gardens

316

separating this hospital from the descending or cascading buildings, and I also see surfers surfing waves, and a beachfront hotel, the Double Beach Hotel, and though it's midday and the Florida sun is shining, the hotel still has its neon sign on, and this is such an incredible waste of electricity it's beyond me, and I can now see that my room is on the fourth floor because I count the corresponding floors on the building opposite, one, two, three, four, and it occurs to me that the world is perfect to the extent that it lays itself bare, gives up its details, but I know the opposite could also be said to be true: the world is imperfect to the extent that it gives up its bare details, though the truth is I'm someone who only ever picks out harmonious details, good details: for example Semicolon coming and leaving me the binoculars, or the ceiling being painted the colour of vanilla ice cream, or me having a sumptuous orgasm but nothing coming out of me, or the fact that there's a series of buildings across from my room that descend in a kind of cascade; what more can I possibly ask for. I go back to bed. I shut my eyes.

I open my eyes. I don't know how long it's been since I closed them; I have slept, that's for sure, but I don't know whether for minutes, hours or days; I don't think I've ever slept more than seven hours consecutively my whole life, maybe today's a first. I notice a stain on the ceiling: it looks like the stain on the ceiling in my prefab in San Francisco, a stain that in turn looked like the moon, and while I'm looking at it I start to hear 'A Day in the Life' playing in one of the rooms along from mine, Barbara's favourite song, the song I woke up to all those years ago in an East Village apartment with the smell of toast and coffee on the air, an awakening that happened to follow another bang to the head, though in that case courtesy of Barbara's previous lover. Barbara was pretty: she often went around with a plastic rose in her hair, a rose I keep on the bedside table in my room at the Home. She and I once visited Alcatraz together, the tourist boat dropped us at the little jetty, it was cold but the sun was shining, I remember her going inside the cells on the prison visit and when she came back out each time being a different person, people will think I'm making it up but she was different every time, and only when she came out of the last cell was she actually herself again, we then went and sat on some rocks while the boat waited for the rest of the tourists to come back, the sun was setting over the rim of San Francisco Bay, and down below we saw some men in uniform pulling a dead body out of the water, somebody said it was an illegal immigrant, we looked at the body and said nothing, made no comment except to say 'Time to go', and the next day she told me that the thought had occurred to her that the clothes of people who drown are more durable than the flesh of people who drown, this seemed an incredible thought to me, but it left her feeling extremely low, she said, because she was studying textile design, or possibly it was dressmaking, I never did get my head around the name of the course, and from that day on every time she went to cut the shoulder section of a jacket or part of a trouser leg the thought would come to her that she was really making a fabric coffin for someone who had drowned, isn't this an incredible thought? Only Barbara was capable of thinking things like that. What I could really do with now is a cup of coffee: I'd sure like to go get myself one, there must be a coffee machine somewhere in the hospital, there always is, and a dollar goes a lot further in the coffee stakes in hospital than it does out in the real world, a hospital isn't the real world, or it

318

half-is, nothing bad can happen to you inside one, I've sometimes thought hospitals are these limbo spaces hovering an inch off the ground, such a tiny clearance that nobody can tell with the naked eye, but hover they do, and I've also thought that this uterine quality becomes apparent the moment you set foot inside one of them, becomes even more apparent when, like me, you've been admitted to one and you're at the mercy of all these tubes and wires, at the mercy of hospital manager and nightwatchman, at the mercy of middle managers who in turn have to follow medical directives, at the mercy even of the building itself with all the objects it contains, all of them pretty weird for your average person, at the mercy as well of the more normal objects like beds, armchairs, floor tiles, restrooms, vases, clothes hangers and coffee machines, objects that here in the hospital take on a different identity altogether: they're appendices to you, they're organs belonging to you, for all that they are separate from you: they're your 'abstract self', yes, these beds, armchairs, floor tiles, restrooms, vases, clothes hangers and coffee machines are the portrait of you as an invalid, but painted by an abstract painter, because all these objects have one single purpose now, which is to serve you, which means that in a hospital we get to be a VIP guest for a short space of time, like millionaires, I say to myself, and 'A Day in the Life' is still playing in one of the rooms, perhaps not one of the ones next to mine but one of the ones next to one of those, and it's the very last thing I'd expect to hear in a place like this. I feel completely at peace listening to this song. I stare at the ceiling. I shut my eyes.

And open them again. And again I can't tell how long I've been asleep for, days, minutes or hours; the light doesn't appear to have changed, though 'A Day in the

Life' isn't playing now, all is quiet, a spongy quiet, I don't exactly know what the word 'spongy' could mean when describing a kind of quiet, but I can't think of any other way of putting it, and then there's the sound of some-body clearing their throat and I jump out of my skin, it happens again, twice, three times, I ought to look down the bed, see who's sitting in the blue visitor armchair clearing their throat, but I don't, I don't know why but I don't, instead I go on thinking about Barbara, because though I dream about her every single night I never think about her in the day, and now that I'm awake I don't want the image I have of her to fade. I always woke in her East Village apartment to the smell of fresh coffee, God knows how many times I must have mentioned this, and it was several days before I worked out that she didn't make the coffee herself, she went and got it from the hospital across the way, pinning back her bangs with her plastic rose, taking two cups from the kitchen and, still in her pyjamas, crossing the street, pressing the but-tons on the coffee machine, ground floor, Minor Burns department, and coming straight back, steam still rising off the coffee on her arrival, and it was then that she would put 'A Day in the Life' in the cassette deck and open the curtains in our bedroom just a little ways. I'd get up when the song ended, and she told me that the or-chestral part in 'A Day in the Life' had been created by getting all the instruments to start at their very highest notes and play down to their very lowest and then taking the recording and playing it in reverse, back to front, and now, hearing this same song start up again in one of the nearby hospital rooms, it strikes me as a brilliant idea, that of reproducing things in reverse, properly considered this is how memory functions, colossal or-chestra that is my mind in this current moment. I shut my eyes. Open them, I've slept but again don't know how long for. It's getting dark outside, there's nobody sitting in the blue visitor armchair, the bag that was hanging on the back of it has disappeared. I get up, the neon sign on the Double Beach Hotel incandesces against the sky, when I look out through the binoculars I see that the letter 'e' has blown, I've only just noticed, it means the sign spells out Double Bach, a mistake that brings a smile to my face, the lights inside the descending/ cascading buildings are on, I can see the people in their homes, isn't it funny how, viewed from outside, people walking through their homes appear to leap from one window to the next? The surfers on the beach are calling it a day, Barbara comes to mind once more, what I wouldn't give to be with her right now, I don't know why I never made any attempt to locate her, and now, when I try to recall her face, I find that I'm unable to, not because of the distance between us but because of the thing that happens, whatever it is, that makes it hard to remember the faces we're most familiar with, I mean even though you can recall an object perfectly well, you can't recall a face, it's weird, though I have had it before. The first time it happened I was on the bus home from high school, and I tried to remember my mother's face but couldn't, simply couldn't conjure it, whether in a moment of her handing me a slice of carrot cake, her bun with three coloured pencils sticking out of it, or even the different parts of her face, not a single feature I could conjure, an inability that, sitting on the bus that day, upset me so much that I started trying to invent a new face for her; I started superimposing on her a different face altogether, and that got me even more upset. That was until I managed to call to mind a photo we had in the living room, of her standing in front of some French gardens smiling – the French gardens were one of the local photographer's props, you could also have chosen the Coliseum or the Empire State Building if you wanted – and I could recall this photo in perfect detail, her face as clear as if she were sitting on the bus beside me, and ever since then, any time she went off to one of the other ranches in the county to play cards with her girlfriends, or when I was in Vietnam, or during my studies at MIT, and even now that she's dead, I only have to think of this photo and her face appears before me; it could have been any photo, the thing functions just as well with any photo at all, but it's always this one I choose to think about, and now it's completely dark down on the beach and I really can't be bothered to go all the way to the light switch, and sitting in the dark hospital room I go on trying to remember Barbara's face, but I can't, I haven't got any photos of her that would work, she and I never took photos of ourselves together, I wouldn't have minded it but she, being a lot younger than me, thought that taking photos of ourselves was the kind of thing old folks did, people who live in the moment don't take photos of themselves because they don't think they'll ever need them, they think they'll be young forever, so said Barbara, my goodness, 'always' was a word she used a hell of a lot, she used it for everything and yet nothing about her was forever, more than that, I'd say that everything about her was singularly transitory, it seemed like I was the only constant in her life, the only solid thing for her, and she, to repay me, put a lot of effort into fixing up the prefab, never once attempting to scrub away the stain on the ceiling with its strong resemblance of the surface of the moon, quite the opposite: she looked after that stain like someone looking after the best-in-show flowerbed, and she put my Apollo 11 photos in frames she got at Barnes & Noble, wanting, she said, for me always to have a way of remembering it, and she also brought an ice-making machine so that I'd start drinking my vodka cold, since she thought vodka toddies were the kind of thing old folks drank, very passé, something belonging to the days before commercials for alcoholic drinks, when everyone used to fix their drinks in their own peculiar ways. The 'e' in the neon sign now makes a recovery, coming briefly back to life, only to fall dark again, Beach becoming Bach once more, and my mind turns to the plastic rose which at this very moment in time is in the vase on my bedside table at the Home, and how, with me out of the way, Semicolon can get his mitts on it if he likes and, if he likes, give it to Sarah the Harpy as a gift; it wouldn't surprise me if he did, or if her response was to fling it immediately to the floor, vase and all, and even to start stomping on the rose; or possibly Semicolon will decide to take the batch of x-rays I keep beneath my bed and give them to her as a gift: he'd claim they were his, images of his own lungs, and he'd say that once upon a time the inside of his body worked as well as those images suggested, and that if she would only lend him a hand he'd be able to get the pecs back that in former days he was so wellknown for, but doubtless Sarah the Harpy would throw these x-rays to the floor as well, and stamp on them, and then maybe they'd all go out in the trash the same way the letter 'e' from the Double Beach sign is going to if the guy I've just seen appear on the roof of the hotel doesn't fix it, he looks like an odd jobs guy who's been tasked with lighting up that letter 'e' in the Miami night once more, I get out of bed, pick up the binoculars and, training them on him, see that he's blocking the letter 'e' from sight, that he has a tool bag at his feet, and every time the letter lights up I see his body impaled by the bright light; the guy kneels down, puts his tools away, disappears down a hatch, and the letter 'e' then takes a little over a minute to go out again. I sit down on the blue visitor armchair, I see a cruise ship, how haven't I noticed it before, a light drizzle begins coming down, dark clouds move in over the beach, the cruise ship must be at least fifteen storeys tall, it's almost square, a square prism, a combination I find troubling, and now as I watch it starts moving out to sea, exits the bay and makes for the horizon, at the edge of which a few glimmers of sunlight can still be seen, a cruise ship wet from the rain, I say, and I don't know whether it makes sense to call a cruise ship 'wet', that's a boat's constant state, but I still say it, it's like wondering whether a fish drinks water or experiences thirst, I've never felt I've had decent answers to these questions, waves ripple and spread in the wake of the cruise ship, it ploughs on, parting the sea only temporarily, everything immediately going back to how it was, the sea is the strangest thing I know, you can hit it, you can make holes in it, you can even shoot a gun at it, do just about any unpleasant thing you can think of, but after a certain amount of time it'll go back to its resting state, there's no way to snap it out of that. Black clouds move in over the descending/cascading roof terraces, the beach and the Double Bach Hotel, sparks now flying from the 'e' of the neon sign, due to the rain I guess, and the guy with his tool bag is back, he's sure to get himself electrocuted, I'm watching him and there's nothing I can do to make him stop, any moment now he's going to get fried on the letter 'e', true Miami barbecue, fare for tomorrow's breakfast buffet at the Double Bach. The cruise ship goes on out to sea, I too was the sea, Barbara's sea, not her swimming pool but the stability everyone needs,

and then one day she upped and left, that's just what people do when you treat them well, right? And here's the
great mystery of couples, a mystery even more profound
than the origin of matter, we're so proud and arrogant,
nothing's ever good enough, and now the cruise ship is
so far out I can only just see it, those on board will be
sipping martinis on the loungers by the covered pool,
gazing up at the sky through the transparent roof cover,
fixing their sight on the night clouds in an attempt to find
answers to the questions they've been pondering their
entire lives, questions they hope to solve in this voyage,
and here I am, taking it all in with a single sweeping
glance, I am a lasso, I snare objects and then bring them
inside myself in miniature, the human gaze is capable of
such things, shrinking the entire world so that it fits onto
your retina, the sparks flying, pouring now from the letter 'e', if somebody doesn't unplug that neon sign, I'll say
it again, we're going to have us one chargrilled man,
maybe even a building fire, but all of this is yet to happen, sometimes nothing happens at all, we always want
something to happen, we wait and hope, we don't know
what for, only that we've waited in vain. The cruise ship
is nothing but a speck in the far distance now, a boat formerly moored on land, it was built on land and will
never reach land again, isn't this the most terrible thing?
Like a bird that took to the air and had to stay up there
forever, forever beating its wings, never allowed to land.
I shut my eyes.

And open them again. I don't know how long I've
been here, it's just struck me that I still haven't left
this Miami hospital room, there aren't any magazines,
there's no TV, or no good one any way, there's an old
Zenith set mounted on the wall with a coin slot to make
it work, but I don't have any coins, I really ought to go

and see if I can get some coins and while I'm at it figure out what's going on outside these four walls, see if I bump into another nurse, or into the girl in the room next to mine whom I've heard talking on the phone a few times, and heard wheeling her drip pole around, I've heard her talking about getting out of here one day, seems she thinks she will, she's convinced of it because she's young and because somebody who's utterly in love with her is waiting for her. She has no idea she's never actually getting out. Young people in this country are the most innocent, and the most strange, of all young people, until the day I walked on the moon with the Three Little Pigs – sorry, I'll try that again – until the day I walked on the moon with my three astronaut colleagues I was an innocent young American as well, something I've thought a lot about. I once happened on a book called *The Labyrinth of Solitude*, it was by a Mexican author whose name I can't now recall, but I remember his photo on the back, he had a toupee on that made him look like Tintin, and I felt intensely drawn to this image of him. We were given the book on a trip to Mexico City; the president of Mexico gave it to us at a reception held in the US embassy there. And that book was our gift, though for all I know a poisoned one, and I read it over the days that followed, or flicked through it really, sitting on the roof terrace of the hotel they put us up in, near a big square I remember being called Zócalo. I could hear the murmur of people down in the square, a murmur similar to the hum of the simulator for the second motor on Apollo 11 just before blast-off, a moment when you feel the motor's full force, its forceful intent to depart, to make a break with everything once and for all, but it never does, never blasts off, because it's only a simulator, the idea being to test how you stand up to the fear you're inevitably going to experience come the day of the actual launch, and in the same way the murmuring of the people down in the Zócalo never blasted off, but remained an eternal, ancestral murmuring; there was the feeling that something was about to happen, to suddenly change, in that goddamned square down below, though not, being completely honest, for me, because while on that hotel terrace, while, as I say, I was reading, or rather leafing through the pages of *The Labyrinth of Solitude*, a Mexican waitress kept bringing me mescal to drink, mescal with segments of orange in the glass, and it was in that alcohol-infused moment, indissolubly linked with the reading of that book, that my life as a drinker began. Until then I'd only ever drunk at parties or cookouts on the weekend. It was then that I entered the state of perpetual drunkenness I would only occasionally abandon thereafter. The book read:

When I arrived in the United States I lived for a while in Los Angeles, a city inhabited by over a million persons of Mexican origin. At first sight, the visitor is surprised not only by the purity of the sky and the ugliness of the dispersed and ostentatious buildings, but also by the city's vaguely Mexican atmosphere, which cannot be captured in words or concepts. This Mexicanism – delight in decorations, carelessness and pomp, negligence, passion and reserve – floats in the air. I say "floats" because it never mixes or unites with the other world, the North American world based on precision and efficiency... When I arrived in the United States I was surprised above all by the self-assurance and confidence of the people, by their apparent happiness and apparent adjustment to the world around them... It seemed to me then, and it still does, that the United States is a society that wants to realize

its ideals, has no wish to exchange them for others,
and is confident of surviving, no matter how dark the future may appear.

That was how *The Labyrinth of Solitude* put it, and it had
a point, in this country we do have this insane faith in
our own survival, so much so that when it comes to
these terminally ill young men and women of America,
the ones I hear trailing their drip poles around with
them, seemingly fresh as daisies, brains completely see-
through and the map of the United States inscribed in
their faces, no one ought to tell them that the wheels
on their drip pole are making that noise for reasons far
darker, far more sinister, than a lack of oil or low quality
bearings, we're better off letting them keep their minds
firmly set on their American futures, letting them go on
thinking that the drip they're taking around with them
is a prelude to the oversized skateboard which will very
soon carry them back out onto the streets of Miami, that
they will in fact get out of this hospital alive. And, okay,
I know I'm not getting out of here alive either. Which is
why there's one last story I want to tell, an exceptional
story nobody's ever heard, something truly remarkable
that happened to me in Los Angeles at the end of the
eighties.

It was at the corner of Hollywood Boulevard and Laurel
Avenue: I was waiting for the little man on the traffic
light to put his green clothes on, it was the middle of
the day and the sun was particularly piercing, I was the
only person on the street except for a couple of bums
sheltering from the sun in their cardboard boxes, they
looked like gigantic chrysalides that would never turn
into butterflies. It was in the days when, out of a simple

desire to not do what everyone else was doing, I was going against the unwritten Los Angeles rule whereby you have to drive everywhere, I'd said to myself I was going to get to know the city on foot; however long it took, I was determined to go wherever I needed to go by dint of my own bones and muscles alone. I think I saw myself as the last legitimate explorer of that city. Freeways, boulevards, projects and side streets, I consumed it all on foot, and all without the first idea of the risk I was running: any pedestrian in Los Angeles is liable to make a lot of people fearful and suspicious, but I had this desire to feel the sidewalk burning my soles, the non-conditioned air of the streets, to leave my mark on the half-melted asphalt. I won't say that walking those streets was as transcendent as walking on the moon, but it wasn't far off. I saw all the oil wells dispersed throughout the city, pygmy oil pumps folk had built in their back yards, six feet high at most. Los Angeles is situated on one of the United States' largest oil fields: you go along the sidewalks and see all manner of pumps on the other side of garden fences, even in the smaller gardens. When you drive around, you're too low down to see them; you have to be on foot to get a view of these seesaw-like backyard pumps swivelling lazily around like steel herons, pecking at the ground in slow motion, and when you get several of them in a row then it looks like these dancing creatures are responding to a musical score welling up out of the ground. I even saw one oil pump between some graves in the middle of a cemetery; this was unusual but actually not illegal, strangely enough all a person had to do was pay a little extra in order to be granted rights to the several square feet of air over the grave as well. And people went by every day to extract a little of the oil their ancestors offered up, making jokes about it as a kind of involuntary inheritance. Yes, exploring Los Angeles on foot meant seeing all kinds of things I never would have from the seat of a car.

So, during the afternoon walk in question, as I waited at the corner of Hollywood Boulevard and Laurel for the little green man to let me cross, a limo appeared, approaching from my left, mustard-coloured, a serious-business kind of limo, nothing flashy. Though the light was green for vehicles, it slowed down and came to a stop on the opposite side. The person in the back rolled the window down, and it was George Bush Sr., I recognized him instantly because in those days, in the run-up to the Gulf War, he spent his every waking minute on TV appealing to the spirit of the nation. Before the window was even fully open he stuck his head out, he seemed to be in tears, and then, after retching a number of times, he proceeded to vomit all over the asphalt below. Eventually a hand came out and grabbed him by the jacket, pulling him back inside, and the limo screeched away, heading north. The little green man lit up but I stood rooted to the spot, truly staring in wonder, trying to work out if the whole thing was a setup, if some hidden camera crew was watching me, but couldn't see a soul. A few months later, somebody told me there had been another person present, a writer named Jerry Stahl, who'd been on TV talking about exactly the thing I'd seen. He must have been hiding in the bushes or just somewhere outside of my field of vision – I couldn't see a soul. My shock began to subside, and with the little green man showing again, I crossed, stopping in the road next to the patch of vomit. A mustard-coloured splash at my feet, semi-solid and speckled with what looked like some kind of meat, plus some kind of vegetables, plus a whole mound of unchewed grape seeds, a hell of a lot of grape seeds, all in one big sludgy pile. It was the same shape as Australia, I swear, and the tips of my boots fit pretty snugly against its southern coastline. The stretch of road I was on had been asphalted only months before – there was still a hint of freshly laid asphalt in the air – and so the top layer wasn't completely impermeable and absorbed the vomit like a sponge, starting at the more liquid outer edges. I stood for several minutes watching it being absorbed. There was no traffic at all; I stood exactly where I was, and at my feet Australia ceased to be, becoming an abstract shape instead, and then coming to resemble the outline of an animal, a big bellied dog that lasted long enough to have its moment in the midday Los Angeles sun: a cute little pregnant dog, I thought, even cuter than the dogs we drew on the fuselages for every enemy fighter we shot down in Vietnam. Soon the asphalt had sucked down the entire liquid component, leaving only solids. In between the chunks of meat, half-digested beans and the huge quantity of grape seeds, I now spotted small scraps of a strange blue material: some kind of plastic, it looked like. I got my water bottle and poured it carefully over the remaining vomit, with circular, swilling movements to separate the bigger pieces from the smallest. Two litres proved plenty to separate it all up, and I winnowed out the pieces of shiny, dark blue plastic, a blue that was almost purple, and which I then saw were – unbelievably – lots of tiny scraps of an x-ray printout. Using a stick I picked out of a nearby hedge, I separated these scraps completely from the half-digested food. They were very small, each no bigger than a fingernail, and the edges, rather than having been torn, were clean, like they'd been cut up with scissors. I put them inside a paper KFC bag that I found in a trashcan right next to the traffic lights, and headed back the way I'd come. I needed to get back to the apartment and inspect the scraps. I walked past the homeless guys, chrysalides still under their cardboard boxes, and kept the pace up for several more blocks. Rather than going the direct route through Beverly Hills, I went down to La Cienega, and from there all the way without stopping to Venice Beach – where I was staying in a place overlooking the ocean. I let myself in and crossed the apartment block's communal gardens, with its lawns and flagstone paths, to my apartment. I dropped my backpack on the carpet and opened the blinds. I opened the window, which looked out over the highway between my block and the buildings on the waterfront. The ocean air gusted into the open-plan living room and kitchen – the bedroom was separate, accessed by a short hallway, no more than six feet long with a Spanish-style arched ceiling. I took a 7-Up out of the fridge and collapsed on the sofa. My legs felt like lead and I had a slight headache, doubtless a touch of sunstroke. I shuffled out of my pants. Sitting in underpants and shirt, I stared down at the rucksack, which was still on the floor by the door. I did not turn on the TV which, given the fact it never gets truly cold in LA, had been fitted inside the fireplace – one of the many nutty things the previous inhabitant had done to the place, and something I never bothered to change.

A few days after I moved in, I'd improvised a living room table under the window, getting a five-dollar door I'd bought from a local carpenter and setting it across a pair of sawhorses. The door's peephole was still intact, glass and all, and the previous tenant had painted rings on it to make it look like a dartboard, and a multitude of puncture holes had been left behind by the tips of the darts. Sometimes I would sit at that table having a drink, and horse around looking through the peephole at the floor and my feet, which looked oddly deformed. I put the rucksack on the table, opened the zip and took out the KFC bag. This I took over to the sink, turning on the faucet and tipping out the scraps from the x-ray printout. Within a few moments George Bush Sr.'s remaining gastric fluids had washed down the drain, destination the Pacific, immense on the far side of the highway. Picking the scraps out of the sink, I took them back to the window and placed them on a towel on the aforementioned door-table, being careful not to damage them. The empty KFC bag I left on the floor. I got myself a beer and cracked it open. I was a reformed individual in those days, going at life with a new kind of structure and discipline, so as well as moving on my own to a city where I knew absolutely no one, I had a rule of two beers a day max. I didn't fall asleep, but I did go into a trance for a while – a couple of hours, by which time I felt ready to get up again. I had a look at the x-ray scraps on the towel, which had dried out. As if the day hadn't had enough shocks in it already, I now saw that the printouts had writing on them, writing that had been x-rayed: every shred was covered in letters and words. I pulled out a chair and turned on the lamp to inspect them in the light, wondering how I was going to put it all back together again; I've never been one for puzzles. The letters were truly miniscule. I found the four corners – rounded corners, as you often get with x-rays – and made a start on trying to fit the pieces together, to start assembling legible words and sentences. It seemed like I was on a hiding to nothing, but I only needed a few minutes before I was manipulating those scraps like a card dealer. I soon found that I wasn't in fact looking at one, but two x-ray printouts: eight of those rounded corners materialized. Any hope I'd begun to entertain was now dashed. There was an added obstacle: the lettering on both printouts was the exact same font and size, nothing to distinguish it. I changed tack, placing the eight corners down on the table and looking for the pieces that would attach to the inside edges of each, trying to work inwards, implosion-like, towards the centre of each printout. The problem was I had no way of knowing whether the corners were correctly placed in relation to one other. After a couple of hours, the task struck me as beyond impossible. The sun was starting to set, I looked up and watched beachgoers packing coolers into car trunks, a couple of my neighbours walked by and we exchanged hellos. This included Nash, the carpenter, who said something about the door-table and who laughed when I got up to greet him wearing only my shirt and underpants.

At 11 p.m., and having made zero headway, I turned on the TV and then the stove in the kitchen. I got out a frozen meal of beef and potatoes and dropped it straight in the pan. It smoked quite a bit. On the TV behind me, a presenter was going around interviewing average-Joe types. On this particular day the piece was on freeway brothels; I stirred the beef and potatoes with a slotted spoon, heard the presenter ask one of the prostitutes: 'What are you proudest of, Sherry?' And her replying: 'Love is a tough gig. Loving is the hardest thing I've done in my entire life.' I got one of the plate-bowls down and emptied the contents of the pan into it, since there was no other crockery – another of the previous tenant's quirks. Pouring myself some 7-Up, I took my dinner over to the table by the sofa, where I sat watching that night's news. A hurricane was tearing up the Florida Keys. The Berlin Wall was on the verge of being torn down, maybe it already had. Some teenager had run amok with an assault rifle in an Oregon superstore. George Bush Sr. also featured, he was talking about Saddam and the American troops, and he was wearing his metal-framed sunglasses; he looked in good shape, far better shape than me; nobody would have guessed he'd been crying his eyes out and projectile-vomiting somewhere in LA just a few hours earlier. The table lamp, which was behind me, projected my shadow onto the wall. Leaning forward over the table like that, eating my dinner, something in my resultant shadow made me think of a primitive creature: a Neanderthal scratching around for something to shovel into its mouth; I felt disgusted and afraid in equal measure. George Bush Sr.'s speech ended, the sports news came on. I went back over to my worktable and sat down. It was so dark outside that the ocean on the far side of the freeway was invisible.

Daylight woke me. I lifted my head, looked out of the window. People walking along the street. A few minutes after midday. I'd fallen asleep with my head on the x-ray printouts. I turned on the coffee machine. Putting on my pants, but not changing my underpants or socks, I headed down to the bakery for a loaf of bread and a couple of the incredible cupcakes they sold there, which they dispensed individually in cellophane wrappers. I came back along Pacific Avenue, parallel to the seafront. But rather than head back directly, I decided to stretch my legs; I had no particular place to go, and I felt like being among people. Leaving Pacific Avenue, almost back at my street again, I came past the Erwin Hotel. I went inside and walked up to the reception desk. A Chicano kid welcomed me with a smile, asking what he could do for me. I requested a room with sea-views; what the hell I was up to? Did I want the bellboy to go get my bags from the taxi, he asked? To which I said I didn't have any, and that there was no taxi. A few minutes later I was being led into the hotel by another young guy, also Chicano. We stopped outside Room 486. Seeing as I didn't have any luggage, he joked I should hand over the bakery bag so he could hand it back and thereby justify the tip. Still smiling, he went back down the hallway. The door shut softly behind me: the 'clack' of the lock made me think of a spinning gun cylinder. I inspected the bathroom, which had a mix of low-quality tiles and better quality marble. There were old-style imitation light switches. The sink had two bars of soap standing vertically by the faucet, like the then still-standing Twin Towers. I lifted the toilet seat – an American Standard, wide berth, just the best. I took the wrapping off one of the bars of soap and washed my hands. On the wall opposite the bed, above the TV screen, there was a print of *Las Meninas*, the Velázquez painting. I went over to the window, opened the curtains, saw that I had a view over a back alley. To the left, above the adjacent buildings, I could see the tops of some palm trees belonging to another beach hotel, and a row of flags snapping in the sea breeze. Most of these flags pertained to no nation. I thought about whoever it was that made up the flags for countries that don't exist, how it must be a bitter sort of task, profoundly marginal, spending your days thinking about borders and rivers and dynasties and mountains, and for the fruit of your labour to wind up snapping in the breeze above the heads of tourists who will never give your work so much as a second thought. Over to the right, not 150 feet away, I saw my apartment, the living room window open and the table lamp, which I'd forgotten to turn off, lighting up the x-ray scraps. I worried they might be getting overheated. An elderly couple stopped right below my window and kissed, the kiss lasting several seconds. I could see my apartment and I could see them kissing and I thought I sure would've liked to know where this kiss was heading. When you kiss someone, you never know what they're thinking about; a pretty frightening thought. I stepped back from the window. I recalled the 'clack' of the door shutting. I went over and opened and gently shut the door several times, leaning in close, trying to hone in on the sound, to focus on it to the exclusion of all else. 'Clack, clack, clack': I did it quite a few times, until it occurred to me that not only did hotel doors go 'clack' when you shut them, all the doors I'd come across in the state of California did. This struck me as a very clever subliminal way of maintaining social cohesion. It was beyond me to say who'd come up with it, but there was no doubt it had to be a superior sort of mind; when it comes down to it, I said to myself, doors are everything. They are security, they are the beginning of a journey and the end of one as well, they somehow stand for, and before, the very thing we're all in search of: hearth and home, the wall that opens just for us and keeps all the bad things at bay. It means that when a Californian enters their home, shuts the door and hears that same 'clack', it links back, by a secret sonic thread, to the doors at their offices, the homes of parents and friends, the bar where they go to watch the Super Bowl once a year, the bank where they deposit their pay checks, even to the White House itself. This world is full of so many doors, I said to myself, we rely on them for life, and that goes especially for California because Hollywood is in California and Hollywood has led people to set a paranoid kind of store in the security of their homes, as well as in hotels, places of work, and even the more humble kinds of abodes, huts in shanties and favelas included, all of which combine to multiply the number of doors in the world just as nightmares multiply the number of labyrinths and satellite dishes. Indeed, you could go right across California using this sound-thread as your only guide, clack-clack-clack, thousands of gun cylinders spinning around at once, and in that same instant discover both the peace of being in your own home and the memory of the forging of the small kitchen-garden that is California: courtesy, that is, of the Ferris wheel of fear that is the cylinder of a gun.

I lay down on the bed and, though I didn't usually watch TV before evening time, switched it on, turning the volume down low. I stayed in that position, horizontal, weighing up my new discovery, while looking at the Velázquez picture above the TV screen. After twenty minutes I got dressed, left the room and got in the elevator. The receptionist asked me if I wanted breakfast, to which I said yes. I crossed the street and, going into my apartment, couldn't help but notice the clack-clack of the front door as it opened and shut. I poured myself some coffee – cold by then – from the pot I'd left brewing. I turned off the lamp. Seeing the KFC bag on the floor, I remembered the bag from the bakery: I'd left it back at the hotel, on the bed. I drank the coffee standing next to the door-table. The wind had blown some of the x-ray scraps out of position, but given I'd hardly made great strides in reassembling them, I wasn't that concerned.

Sitting down at the door-table, I applied myself once more to this strange puzzle, glancing out of the window from time to time; my hotel room was right across the way. When it started getting dark I turned the lamp on, the old couple I'd seen kissing earlier came past again, this time hand in hand on the sidewalk opposite, I watched them go down the street until the window frame

338

got in the way and I couldn't see them any more. My parents came to mind: surely they'd been like that couple at one time or another, I'd never witnessed it myself, but they must at some point have had their moment in the sun, before throwing it all away – the love, the money – on the phantom of a timeshare resort. I hoped they were in a better place than the one I was in, far from people like me. I am certain that when a person disappears from our lives, whether they've died or you've simply lost touch, we replace them with a part of our body, an organ that doesn't just take the place of but immediately *becomes* that disappeared person. My father, for instance, is my prostate. Over the years, as relationships run their course and friends and family fall by the wayside, your body stops being your own and becomes the sum of all the people you've lost. My mother is my hands, somehow it's always her who holds the glasses I drink from, who opens the door for me, who lights a cigarette, who was putting these scraps of an x-ray printout in the correct order. Barbara is my lips, that much is certain: it's her, any time I kiss someone, who does the kissing. And the same goes for people we've hated and lost, only in that case they become identified with disposable elements of the body, our hair, our nails, vomit, or the forest of dead cells that covers the epidermis. So it goes: by the end of our lives our bodies are taken up completely by people who aren't around any more. And this explains why we don't want the people we're fond of to leave us, or to die: it's pure egoism. We don't want to be stripped of our own bodies, to be conquered by other bodies courtesy of 'affection', that total scam. It was quiet on the street outside, night had fallen completely. I got up and, before getting into bed, went and opened and shut the door. Clack-clack. I put an extra bedspread on, it was the end of August and the Pacific nights were growing cool. A routine was established, a routine is always established. Getting up, going to the bakery for bread and a couple of the cupcakes, going over to my room at the Erwin, opening and shutting the door to check the clack-clack was still unchanged, lying in the bed and looking across at my apartment window, leaving the room at 2 p.m., getting back to my apartment and drinking the coffee I'd left to brew in the morning, and working into the night, in vain, on the x-ray printouts.

In the hotel room one day, I looked over at my apartment and saw the window half-open, the curtain drawn and the lamp lit, and on the table a can of beer, precisely as I'd left it however many hours earlier. And then it happened: the curtain fluttered in the sea breeze, once, twice, three and four times, more, until I saw that it had nothing to do with the breeze, but that there was somebody in my apartment. A person, though all I could see was its shadow. My mind went into overdrive: it had to be on account of the vomiting incident, I must have been seen inspecting the vomit that day on Hollywood Boulevard, and someone had been assigned to follow me. They must have been watching my movements and worked out my routine. I still couldn't see the person, I stood watching their shadow. I checked my watch, 1.27 p.m., and looked up at the sky – when something confusing happens we always check the time and look at the sky. Then, as I looked on, the intruder came to the window. My body turned rigid. It was me, I was over there in my apartment. I mean, it was me I could see, not 150 feet away: the person sitting at the door-table in my apartment, trying to reassemble the x-ray printouts, wearing different clothes to the ones I was wearing just then but nonetheless an outfit I recognized as my own – sleeveless lumberjack shirt, light blue Wranglers – was without a doubt me. I saw his, my, face. And, astonishingly, I didn't feel afraid, in fact I felt nothing, it was like I'd turned into a living, breathing CCTV camera, or like my entire nervous system had been extracted except for the optic nerve, which, as is commonly known, documents but does not feel. I went back inside the hotel room, feeling sure that if I went to look for a second time the mirage would have passed. But no: I went back to the hotel room window, and there I still was in the apartment window, working on the x-ray printouts, sipping my beer, shortly to get up and turn the TV on – holding the remote in my left hand, a habit of mine in spite of being right-handed. I moved back from the hotel window again. And I didn't leave the hotel at my usual time, I stayed on watching myself in the apartment, only leaving the hotel window now to go to the bathroom or to tear off a hunk of bread or get a cupcake to eat. There were moments when I left the apartment window, I guessed I must be fixing something to eat in the kitchen, and when I moved off to the left hand side I knew I'd be taking a shower or having a brief lie-down – which I always did if I was working intensely on something. It grew dark, the moon rose over the flags of the made-up countries. I saw myself move away from the apartment window and come back a little while later with a plate-bowl of food, sitting down on the sofa with my back to me, leaning in over the table by the sofa, the lamplight magnifying my shadow on the wall, making a primitive creature of me, Neanderthal, that body and my own joined by the self-same animality, I thought, my own personal missing link, a thought that disgusted me. In that moment, with that disgust, I began to think of the person in the apartment as 'him', not 'me'.

Not waiting for him to finish eating, I went back inside again, feeling I'd seen enough. I turned the TV on, lay down in bed, there was a programme about constructing hanging bridges, under normal circumstances I'd have paid to watch that programme, but instead I took a hotel pad and a pencil from the bedside table and, on an unstoppable impulse, started to draw what I'd just seen. It had been years – since Vietnam – since I'd felt the physical urge to create a drawn document of something. Some need to confirm that I was still myself, I think. I didn't want to take a photograph, if I'd had a camera to hand I wouldn't have used it, what I felt instinctively compelled to do was create something completely my own, something that definitively did not belong to the individual I'd seen in the apartment across the way. In Vietnam, I remembered, we didn't take photographs of the planes we'd shot down, but notched them up by painting pictures on our fuselages – a heart, a bird, that sort of thing – and it was this itself that began to fuel our desire to go up and get in another dogfight. I think that in the end we weren't fighting to win the war but simply out of a desire to draw another picture on a fuselage. Sometimes the rhetorics pertaining to good and evil are indistinguishable. I decided it was time for bed, took one last look out of the window. The moon was afloat over the tops of the made-up flags, in my apartment he was turning off the lamp and going through to the bathroom, then I saw the bedroom light come on. I'd seen enough, I got into bed. I tossed and turned, I heard the person in the room next to mine opening their minibar, the unmistakeable sound of a cork popping, and this was a brief distraction. Feeling hot and sweaty, I went into the bathroom, turned on the tap. One of the Twin Towers was finished and though the other was untouched, I didn't want to touch it, so I just splashed my face. This face, the one I saw in the mirror, seemed more unlike me than it ever had. I went back to bed, turned the light off and the TV on, thinking perhaps some channel-hopping would help get me to sleep. News bulletins on repeat, the latest episodes in long-running series, documentaries: I lay watching for a long time until I came upon a live news item on the first ever KFC to open in Shanghai. And suddenly the picture froze, not dropping out but freezing on a close-up of a man dressed as Colonel Sanders, smiling into the camera. I waited. The picture remained frozen, and I began to fall asleep with the image of that old man's face for company. I was very nearly asleep when the phone on the bedside table rang, giving me a jolt. I reached over and picked it up:

'Hello?' I said.

Silence.

'Hello?'

After a few moments, I heard a man's voice:

'What do I do with the KFC bag?'

'What?'

'I said, what do I do with the KFC bag?'

Now it was my turn to freeze, before immediately hanging up. I thought about the KFC bag I'd put the x-ray scraps in and then left lying on the floor in my apartment, by the table. The old man's face was still there on the TV screen, still smiling; a smile, I sensed, directed at me alone.

Getting out of bed, I started pacing the room. The sound of my footsteps, as I unwittingly kicked baguettes and the cupcake cellophane from my path, added to the combined hum of the air conditioning and the electricity powering the TV. I looked sidelong at the screen, where the old man, with his plastic-rimmed glasses and red apron, didn't bat an eyelid. TVs are treacherous like that, I thought, endlessly projecting images, all the images in the world coming funnelling through their innards and out, when what they're really looking for is something outside themselves to mirror what it is that they project, even if only for the briefest of moments, that's what they were invented for, that and no other thing has always been their sole reason for being: to uncover their equal and opposite out here in the real world. Shifting my gaze to the Velázquez, I saw that one of the ladies-in-waiting was holding out a jug to the Infanta Margarita Teresa. The jug was red. Here, I thought, was the red clay Barbara had talked about with its hallucinogenic properties, the *búcaro* so highly thought of by the Spanish court in the seventeenth and eighteenth centuries. Indeed, this particular lady-in-waiting wasn't hoping the Infanta would drink from the jug, she wanted her to eat it, to take a big mouthful out of it, either because she was having murderous thoughts or because she wanted to make her brain trip out for life. Before my eyes, and before the eyes of the millions of people who would be looking at a reproduction of the same painting in that moment, a crime was being perpetrated that only I had noticed – and this thanks to the old man on the TV screen, whose apron was the exact same red as the *búcaro* jug. Velázquez, this old man and me: a trio or confluence, I thought, the union of which the world had perhaps been waiting centuries for. I went and found my Marlboros. There was only one left, I smoked it down to the filter. I thought I'd seen a vending machine in the lobby. I went out along the hallway, dark at that time of night. I took the fire escape stairs, running my hand along the handrail all the way, down to the ground floor. Going into the lobby, I saw rental vehicles parked in a row on the far side of the street. I passed reception, no-body home. The 'ding' of a microwave and the smell of soy sauce in the air announced the presence of a security guard in the back office; if one was there, they didn't see me. I went through to the lounge, a glass cubicle with seating and views over Pacific Avenue, and of the low city skyline, which gave a sense of someone having gotten hold of LA at either end and pulled on it, stretching it out flat. I put the coins in the machine, the cigarette pack dropped down. Getting to my feet, I looked out at the street again, spinning the cigarette packet between my fingers. Dawn was still a while off. As tends to be the way in LA, the powerlines were overhead rather than underground, big tangles of them gathered at the tops of the poles, knots of plastic and copper not dissimilar to the ones I'd seen on top of the poles in Vietnam, where Charlie, in moments we cornered them, had sometimes shimmied up those poles and wrapped the wires around themselves, hoping to put an end to it all by electrocution. It almost never worked, instead they just made sitting ducks of themselves, and we gunned them down at will. Their bodies would stay tangled in the cables for days. By night you'd see sparks flying off them, they were like fireworks, nobody dared to climb up and free them, for fear of being electrocuted themselves, until someone took pity on the bodies and cut the supply, throwing a switch at one of the mains the location of which only the natives knew, and the families of the dead could then bring them down, usually half-rotting or having been pecked clean by the birds. I can still see a flock of tiny birds descending on one of those bodies, with an additional swarm hovering in a circle around them waiting their turn, since the body had no more spots left to land on. I once shouldered my rifle and started firing at one of those flocks, it's a strange thing to be firing bullets into something that has no body, a semi-fluid, nebulous kind of structure that just flaps about. I dropped a few of them, but the cloud remained intact, it was like I hadn't fired a single shot. If you never set eyes on the enemy, if they remain forever at arm's length or more, you wind up coming to think the enemy doesn't exist, and, from there, irremediably, it's a short hop to assuming that you yourself are the enemy, and in our time out in those Vietnamese jungles that was what really drove us out of our minds, and one upshot was that when we saw those bodies swinging at the tops of those pylons, we jumped at the chance to shoot them down: they were right in front of us for once, like enemies should be. And fundamentally that was something I couldn't take about Vietnam, because death has to generate something, whether it be more life or more death, but something, and unloading your magazine into a body that's already dead means bringing about no change at all to the state of the world; that, without a doubt, is a crime. It one day happened that I put my helmet down and sat on it, propped my rifle up next to me, its barrel still a little warm, yanked a few leaves off a tree to clean the gunpowder from my hands and, loosening the laces on my boots, sat watching the birds pick and peck at the body I'd just riddled with bullets. The avian chatter was deafening, and one of the birds broke off from the rest, flew down and landed on my head, which it proceeded to hammer with its beak. I'd only just managed to swipe it away when a bunch more of them, I couldn't say how many exactly, came raining down on me, grabbing my hair in their talons and trying essentially to peck my brains out. I thrashed about to get them off, they let me alone a moment, only then for me to look

up and see the entire flock now lining me up. It was the
sheer incredulity, I suppose, that stopped me from jumping up and hotfooting it out of there – this I only did
once the whole swarm had transferred itself from the
suspended cadaver onto my head. I sprinted over to a
group of my buddies, who had found a little shade to rest
in. My head was all bloody when I got to them, and I
came to a rest against a tree trunk, casting a look back at
the birds, which had turned their attentions once more
to the cadaver. None of us had a first aid kit; I cleaned the
cuts out using a few eucalyptus leaves. I was okay, but
the squadron leader said I could've contracted something – from the dead body. The idea terrified me, not so
much the prospect of fever or whatever illnesses might
come my way, but that the person I'd just been firing at
like a crazy person – with no justification whatsoever –
was now inside me, was now coursing through my veins,
a journey that naturally took in my brain along the way.
To this day I still occasionally suspect that microscopic
enemy of being inside me, and then feel afraid and incredibly remorseful all at once, as though I want to
throw up everything that lies beneath my skin, puke
myself up, so there'll be nothing left of me but an empty
sack, a vessel some other material might then be poured
into. When I start having these thoughts, I often see
birds raining down on me again, and then I lose my shit,
forget who I am completely – if, that's to assume, I'm
anything at all. In those moments I believe I have it in
me to commit murder. That day in the jungle, the squadron leader suggested we head back to base pronto. The
airbase was nearby, and though we were never supposed
to go out on foot, for all that it could have landed us a
court martial quicker than we could say Ho Chi Minh,
we flouted the rule for the odd escapade, a little light

347

entertainment. We headed along the path up the hillside, the base peeking out at the top. To begin with, the vegetation had hidden us from Charlie to the same extent that it hidden Charlie from us. It thinned out the closer we got to the base, which made us easier targets but at the same time made Charlie an easier target, making the end result the same whether we found ourselves in thickest jungle or on exposed ground: always this symmetry. Everything there was so static, so unchanging, something that if I ever stopped to think about it would also cause me to lose my mind. We came to the summit, an ashy grey light hanging over the valley, at the centre of which we could see the Zone 4 town. The towering leper's building, the only building still standing, was at the northern edge, and it was a sight to behold, very moving in the midst of such desolation, for the simple fact of still being in one piece. To the south of our hangars stood the runways and the barracks. In the small clearing outside the barracks a group of airmen were milling around, there was some foofaraw we were still too far away to make out; someone said maybe there'd been a heart attack. We descended the last short stretch to base. There were no guards posted. When we got to the clearing we saw soldiers thronging around a grey-brown cow, lop-eared and with huge curved horns. Some of the guys were yanking on it to try to get it off-base. It had shown up in the morning, just after engine cleaning, and gone and stationed itself outside the barracks, refusing to budge all day. Guys were saying maybe Charlie had put a bomb up its ass. And that didn't seem impossible; we'd employed stranger tactics ourselves. Then a soldier cocked his rifle and shoved it in the cow's face: the two stood looking at each either, neither of them blinking. Seeing the soldier's trigger finger start to squeeze, I yelled out: 'No!' The soldier glanced over at me, the cow kept on staring at the soldier. 'What?' he said. 'There's nothing inside this cow you need to worry about, soldier. It's just pregnant.' 'You sure?' 'Sure I'm sure.' He lowered the rifle. From the many calvings I'd seen growing up on the ranch, I knew that the mother always wants company as the moment nears, the more creatures, warmth and movement around her, the better; they find it calming. And in the case of this mother cow, her swollen udders and the wide barrel of her belly were unmistakeable. She soon lay down, somebody went and got the doctor, who on arrival confirmed my hypothesis. She started to foam at the mouth, opening and closing it. The sky was still grey, the clouds were turning more geometric, sharper-edged, which in Vietnam means a storm's brewing. The base commander showed up just as the cow began making noises the likes of which none of us had ever heard before, me included, but in the same way that all cars and all household appliances have their own particular sound, every different kind of cow also has its own vocal characteristics. The cow then suddenly jumped to her feet, to everyone's surprise, the soldier once more pointed his rifle at her head. The doctor waved an arm for him to stand at ease. The cow then wandered into the nearest hangar, and we all followed her, nobody saying a word. She went clumping forward, her hooves leaving S's on the ground, but at no point did she pause or stop, making a plodding beeline for an F4 Phantom, a state-of-the-art fighter-bomber that had yet to see any action, meaning she was a 'clean' in our airman jargon. The cow dropped her head, ducking under the fuselage and folding her legs as she lay down by the landing gear, threw her head back, gave another series of moos, the doctor got himself right in behind her, the

349

calf's hind legs were showing, the doctor got a hold of them and yanked but his hands slipped right off, he gave it another shot, getting a good purchase on the hooves and really pulling this time, the mother swinging her head from side to side, her mooing growing louder all the time, her horns knocked repeatedly against the underside of the fuselage, each time making a hollow 'tang', two materials coming into contact for probably the first time in history, probably the last too, now the doctor squatted on his haunches so he could pull even harder, the cow's sex continued to dilate and, like her tongue at the far end of her body, to exude a white foam, then the whole of the back legs were clear, quickly followed by the trunk, and when the head came everything glistened brightly, a kind of bright glistening I'd seen on lots of occasions as a boy and that always made me think of my mother's carrot cake. There was afterbirth on the cement, the cow swivelled around and started licking the calf – that's a sight. I looked at the placenta, a sac several feet long and still connected to the uterus inside. I expected the cow to start eating it, as they always do; all those essential proteins and nutrients it's got. And yet she didn't – she left it dangling out of her behind. She wandered around the base for a number of days and nights trailing the placenta after her with the calf at her side. Then we woke one morning to find her gone, and the calf and placenta. A cop car drove past outside the Erwin Hotel, bringing me out of the memory. It was going slowly, no sirens, taking thirty seconds or more to pass the glass-fronted lobby, more than a cop car it seemed like the ghost of a cop car. And it was then that the thought occurred to me, or struck me I should say, given that it was a thought so indisputably true: any time any creature gives birth, it in fact does so to two different beings: 1) a recognizable being, of the same species, and 2) an occult being, in the form of the placenta. The placenta contains the twin each of us has, deformed or diminished, but a twin all the same, and, once in the world, it departs to some unknown place and takes on a different shape, growing and growing all the time. The placenta, I said to myself, is the distorted mirror of our world. Everything, the vegetables and the minerals, even the objects around us, and the water, the air, it's all been birthed at some point, and so has its corresponding placenta, worlds that overlap only rarely. A shudder ran through me. It was starting to grow light; LA seemed to me a city of wild vegetation, a place that, if it weren't for the constant road-building and construction projects, would within a few short months be an exact match for the jungles of Vietnam. I put the cigarettes in my back pocket, turned on my heels and went back past the reception desk; I don't think the security guard saw me that time either. I took the stairs, went along the hallway, opened the door to my room, clack, shut it, clack, dropped the cigarette pack on the floor, sat down. I didn't feel like looking at the old man's face, still frozen on the TV, so I turned him off. I didn't feel like looking at the Velázquez either, so I took it down, flipped it and propped it against the wall; it was the same size as the TV screen. The painting is the real birth and the TV screen its placenta, I said to myself. Then I thought that maybe the George Bush Sr. I'd seen being sick in the street was the placenta-George Bush Sr., and that his vomit had been placenta-vomit, and this was why I'd had such difficulty putting the x-ray puzzle together: it belonged to a different world. I wondered if all the objects before me in that moment belonged to my world or the placenta world. I ran my fingers over the pen to see if

I could find any evidence either way, the same with the blank sheets of the pad of paper, the towels and the faucets in the bathroom, the porcelain of the tub, and then, getting down on my knees, moving forward hand over hand, the floor as well. I inspected the remaining bar of soap, examined the cupcakes closely, including the cellophane wrappers with the expiration dates on them, before moving on to the new cigarette pack, which I compared against the empty one, nothing there to suggest it was part of the placenta world, I emptied the cigarettes onto the bed and, taking care not to tear them, disassembled the two packs with the aim of checking their interiors, but still found nothing, the details on each indistinguishable. But just as I was about to throw both packs away, I noticed something: the serial numbers were the same. I checked, and checked again, and checked one more time. In view of the fact that there can be no two serial numbers the same, here was proof that one of the Marlboro packs was a placenta-pack. I held one in either hand, they weighed the same. I sniffed them, no difference. Then, putting my tongue-braille skills into action, I licked one packet and then the other, and the paper tasted the same, slightly sweet, and the faintly embossed lettering for 'Marlboro' was identical, as were the faintly embossed horses rearing up on either side of the 'PM' of Philip Morris, and the faintly embossed crowns above it. Only when my tongue came to the legend beneath the horses and crown – 'Veni, Vidi, Vici' – did I notice anything different: on the packet I'd just bought it said 'Venio, Video, Vinco'. How had I not seen that? 'I come, I see, I conquer', present tense: so, this one was the placenta-pack, had to be. There was no doubt about it, 'I come, I see, I conquer' was the sign that the placenta world was there with me, that it had come to install itself, a slow, silent conquest, a gradual transposition of the people and objects from our world with others which were very faintly different, which, like tumours, would wind up occupying all available space. I sat on the bed, took a deep breath, only then noticing that I was bathed in sweat. I felt an urge to scream, or something along those lines, anyway, but before I could do so there was the sound of footsteps in the hallway, somebody approaching the room. I went to the door. The footsteps died away. Bringing my eye to the peephole, I looked out at a deserted hallway. I stepped back from the door. A few seconds passed, and once more I heard footsteps. This time the sound stopped right outside the room. A beat, nothing, and then knuckles rapping on the door, I wanted some way of stunning my muscles into inaction, but I couldn't, and though I hesitated, my hand reached out and grabbed hold of the door handle and turned it. I threw the door open, no clack this time, definitely no clack. I saw a man going away down the hall, KFC bag in hand. He turned to look at me: two identical faces, face to face, one a placenta-face. I passed out in the doorway.

9.

I opened my eyes, I was still on the floor, it was daylight. The night's events returned to me in detail as I splashed my face in the bathroom sink. I didn't know what to think, it seemed like a bad dream. I went to the window and stood looking out for a few minutes. The window to my apartment was open, the lamp on, nobody inside. Gathering the cupcakes, the bread, my drawings and the twenty cigarettes scattered across the bed, and putting it all in a bag, I left the room. In the lobby, I placed my key down on the reception counter. The concierge asked whether I was going to be back for breakfast, I said I didn't know. A platinum blonde woman was getting cigarettes out of the machine as I passed, the machine thanked her in a voice that seemed more human to me than ever. I crossed the street, the shadows were still long in the morning sun, 9.35 a.m. but already a slight give to the asphalt underfoot. There were more people out and about than usual, I guessed it was a Sunday. I let myself in the main gate, crossed the gardens, the only sound the pattering of water from one of the timed sprinklers. I slotted my key quietly into the lock and pushed, did not let the door go clack. Before I'd even shut it behind me, scanning the space, I couldn't believe my eyes: there were patches of vomit all over the carpet, easily a dozen in the living room alone. The same went for the kitchen, and the little hallway through to the bathroom and bedroom. It was immediately apparent they all contained some x-ray scraps. Only when I went into the room, picking my way between the mounds, and still struggling to credit what my eyes were showing me, did I see my two x-ray printouts on the door-table, both perfectly reassembled and complete. Dropping the bag of cupcakes, bread and cigarettes on the sofa, I went over. I think I was shaking. I shot a look over my shoulder, as though to surprise somebody creeping up on me, but there was only bare wall and the patchwork of vomit on the carpet. The KFC bag was nowhere to be seen. Worried a gust through the open window might scatter the two reassembled printouts, I shut it. On the sidewalk opposite, the elderly couple I'd seen kissing days before were sitting together on a bench, chatting with other elderly couples. Still standing, I started to read the first x-ray printout, small white letters on a blue background:

354

Son, it's me, your mother. I'm here, I'm here with you. I've been trying to get through: I never actually went away, though I am in heaven. Your father isn't interested in contacting you, his prostate's still giving him trouble. You shouldn't worry about us: everything's far easier here than it is down there – or, I ought to say, *up* there, because as it turns out heaven's *under* the earth, way, way down, under it all. You find this out as soon as you arrive. Heaven isn't heaven, it's the trashcan we feed with all the bodies that did good in life, bodies like mine and your father's that, luckily, could be recycled – which is to say, bodies that somebody's remembered. We are the stars that, though they've been dead for an awful long time, you can still see at night. The ones that got sent to hell – the ones you can't see at night – we hardly hear a peep out of them. But I don't want you to worry, son. Rest assured, we aren't in hell, hell is for the unremembered, the ones left to rot in trash cans exposed to the elements, the ones that weren't even good as feed for beggars or the birds, the ones whose ashes were scattered so far away and so carelessly that even here in heaven, try as we might, there's no way we can put them back together again. An absolute and definitive migration. Look at them, wandering lost for centuries on end, traipsing along freeways as grey as the dust on that moon of yours, barely even bodies, barely pets or stones or anything at all for that matter, these being the women and men who do not feature in the final reckoning, by which I mean God's account of the corporeal universe – if God exists, that is, because there's certainly been no sight of him down here in heaven. People are starting to wonder if God's actual place of residence is hell. And, son, something I have to tell you: you too are going to hell. You left your footprints on the moon, yes, but there was never any record of it, no photographs or film, no one even stopped to do a quick sketch of you, which means you as good as never travelled to that dead satellite. Sure, people know you were there with Armstrong et al. but, in the final computation, that isn't going to cut it. If there's no record of it, you won't be remembered. And that, son, means no heaven for you.

It ended there. I moved straight on to the second printout:

And this is why I'm here, to distract you for the duration of a story, before you set out on the last and final journey, a story to entertain you in this life and then, later on, when you find yourself in the endless winter of hell, for solace. Because hell is no inferno, son, but a place of endless cold, and actually that goes for heaven too. There isn't even the slightest hint of warmth here, another thing you comprehend the moment you show up; fire is a human invention, exclusively human, and heaven and hell, like the moon, are muted, gloomy places – Creation's cold cuts, as the people say. Certainly, it's people's first ever taste of pure, unmitigated silence, which you don't get anywhere on earth. Going to heaven means accessing a portion of Creation where, except for the occasional interference, finally it's silent. They let your father and me in because we at least left a mark on the earth, that mark being you, one of the truest and greatest morons humanity has ever known. That's what they said when we got to the gate, "You have created one of the truest and greatest morons humanity has ever known, and this means we're letting you in." On another note, your father wants me to tell you he isn't happy about you not holding onto the golf ball; what possessed you to go all the way to the moon just

356

to hit it into outer space? We sometimes see that golf ball
flying past, it's in orbit now, and it makes the most horrific
buzzing as it goes by. That's one thing that does occasionally disturb the peace here. We see it, it sparkles for a
second, and then it's gone. One day it's going to drop out
of its orbit, right onto the Iberian peninsula, and when it
lands it's going to leave a small hole in the ground, small
in circumference but deep, so incredibly deep that, gradually, unstoppably, it is going to turn those lands entirely
into desert. This has been proven: I had a dream about
it. The people here have got a point when they tell us we
created a monster. But I'm getting side-tracked: dear son,
you'll remember all those mornings you used to come to
me and ask – the first thing you did – what I'd dreamed
about. A person has to work, son, the good life involves
work, and my life's work was dreaming. A very useful job
given the fact that, unlike other people's dreams, which
are incoherent and have nothing to do with anything, my
dreams were clear and precise premonitions, they were
real – I don't know what it means for a dream to be real but
that's what mine were. And I've given it a lot of thought,
because what I find really troubling is the flipside, the
reverse: what did I *not* dream about? What *hasn't* come to
me in dreams, I who have dreamed everything there is to
dream? This is something I keep on turning over in my
mind – even here in heaven, it's been bothering me. And
then, just recently, it came to me: *you* are the only thing
I've never had a dream about. Your face hasn't featured
in a single one of my nocturnal premonitions. As though
your future is completely untold, or as though you simply
don't exist.

That was the end of the second x-ray printout. I looked
up. I think I was crying. I sat down. The ocean across

the street, some young surfers paddling out. I know that I stayed like this and didn't move for at least thirty minutes. I know that I spun the chair around several times, turning and looking across the field of vomit patches, which suddenly struck me as very similar to the minefields in Vietnam I myself created. I went over to the sofa, sat down, opened the bag. The twenty cigarettes were loose in amongst the cupcakes. I lit one. Taking the first drag, I exhaled quickly: the taste wasn't like tobacco, or for that matter anything I'd ever tasted before. I took another drag. It still tasted bad. I went on smoking, and at some point I passed out.

When I came round, I looked at the clock: half an hour had gone by. An alteration to the vomit field immediately caught my eye: next to one of the patches lay a complete x-ray printout, its hundred or more pieces seamlessly reassembled. Going straight over to it, I started to read:

I haven't gone anywhere, son, I'm still here. I always am, I'm always at your side. I want to tell you about the dream I didn't share with you, the one you asked about the day your father died. Remember a few minutes before your father's prostate played its final trick on him and he had his bidet collapse, when you came out onto the terrace and asked me what I'd dreamed about the previous night? And how I tried to put you off, but you wouldn't let it go, and I said, 'I dreamed something strange and terrible, something I can't fathom at all'? I want to tell you about this dream now, because I think I've worked out what it means. I want you to picture the following: the dream takes place in the appendage of the Old World that is the Iberian Peninsula. The country's entire population, more than fifty million souls, has long since been evacuated by airplane. This future Iberia has an unusual feature: a tongue of asphalt, 750 miles long and straight as an arrow, running the length of the country from east to west. They call it La Avenida. Apart from this, everything's turned to desert. La Avenida's construction was unusual too: when it became clear that the whole of the peninsula was on the way to turning into this dustbowl, the decision was taken to dismantle every single paved surface in the country, all motorways, all major and minor freeways, all city roads, every single stretch of asphalt, they ripped it all up and used it to create this great east-west drag – stitching it all together with the little remaining unused asphalt. This was the runway for the air-evacuations to come. Now, if there were anyone left to fly over the country in its current state, they would see in this runway a mishmash of spliced-together sections of road, a little bit like a plastic surgeon's preparatory drawings on a patient's skin. The moment came when thousands of planes took off in succession, carrying away the fifty million people that had comprised this country called Spain. But not everyone left. The few who stayed behind are scattered along the length of the 1250 kilometres of La Avenida. So scattered that if their paths ever happen to cross they know it will be months before they see one other again. These encounters, when they take place, tend to do so in one of the abandoned superstores, and a brief exchange will follow – never aggressive, never leading to conflict, because as you can imagine there's an abundance of leftover food, so nothing to fight over – and go on their way.

So ended the third printout. I didn't understand what was going on, but I tried lighting a second cigarette anyway. It tasted just as bad as the first. A few drags and I passed out again. When I came round, everything in the room was precisely as it had been before, except that another reassembled x-ray printout was there on the far side of the room, next to its corresponding patch of vomit. I went straight over and started to read:

I'm still here, son, I'm not going to leave you – there, I think you've got the point. One of the remaining inhabitants is José, and once a week José gets on his moped and drives six miles to one of the many abandoned superstores. He fills his backpack up with non-perishables and goes to the gardening section to water a yellow poppy bed there. In my dream I saw him pick one of these flowers, extracting it roots and all, and put it in a flowerpot to carry home in his backpack. Since the death of their son at the age of nine, his wife, Ana, has felt the constant need for a poppy to be growing on the windowsill at their home. Rows of houses run the whole length of La Avenida, rows upon rows of houses, in effect forming a sort of wall on either side. This was where the fifty million people lived for the ten years of the runway's construction. You can tell from a glance they were jerry-built – all the same style, colour, height, all using the same materials. That decade was spent with people doing little more than standing at their windows looking at the gleaming airplanes on La Avenida beyond their front gardens, watching the pilots who every now and then switched the jet engines on to keep them tuned. Some lent a hand preparing the huge amounts of food that would be needed for the meals on the flights nobody knew if they'd be coming back from. Once this principal runway was complete, there was the idea to build another Avenida, this one running north to south. With that in mind, and intending to make the two cross in the middle, works commenced simultaneously at the northern and southern ends of the peninsula, using

360

leftover asphalt from Avenida number one. But north and south never came together: the materials ran out and the construction workers lost their way in the fast-desertifying north and south. The country, one big sand dune by now, has bits of abandoned, broken-down machines all over the place, whole sections of freeway, work overalls, empty water bottles, lunch boxes – things that would be found were José or Ana or any of the remaining inhabitants to strike out into these wastelands, but they never do. There's such a large number of abandoned homes, shacks, factories, hospitals and offices, buildings of every kind, along the 750 miles of La Avenida, that as long as the population remains constant – as long as no couple engenders more than two offspring – they could survive for at least 250 years without having to produce any new foodstuffs or generate any more energy.

End of the fourth printout. I thought I'd got it now: with eighteen placenta-Marlboro cigarettes to go, I lit the third and waited patiently to pass out again. When I came to, another printout had been put back together on the carpet:

One day, having gathered all the supplies he needed, José zipped up the backpack, being careful not to damage the yellow poppy. Before starting off home, he looked up at the sky for a moment. He did up the golden buttons on his blue double-breasted bomber jacket, which had air commander stripes on the arms, and which he'd come across in the cockpit of one of the planes that didn't depart. Checking his jacket for the photo of his son, he puts his hands in his pockets and sets off walking down La Avenida, leaving the superstore behind. He came on foot today because the moped's kaput. He passes a makeshift air traffic control tower every mile, next to which stand waiting rooms with elevated airport walkways that now connect to nothing. Turning to look behind him, he gazes directly at the sun, which has shone anaemically for years, its reflection barely glimmering on the rooftops.

Ana is sitting in the ditch opposite the garden, working on the moped carburettor. She spots José approaching. "How's it going, Jose," she says – she always pronounces his name without the accent on the "e". "Jose". Unbuttoning his jacket, he says, "Fine, tired though," and gives her a kiss. He goes into their home, a hut they moved into after the evacuation with nothing more than a kick to the door. The whole place is seemingly built out of oak; they took to it. He drops his jacket on the sofa, takes the poppy out of the backpack. Ana puts the poppy next to a family photograph, the only memento of their family that José has kept. It's an old, black-and-white photo featuring a large group of men sitting in front of a stone wall, and in among them, smiling at the camera, one of his male forebears, a grandfather or great-grandfather, he isn't sure which.

Together they unpack the food and the bottles of water, piling it all up on the kitchen table – they'll put it all away later on. He collapses on the sofa. Ana washes her hands with mineral water, sits down on the carpet and considers the intense yellow of the poppy. José takes a bag of chips they left between the cushions the previous night. They sit sharing the chips in silence.

Cigarette #4

José and Ana's first kiss came at just sixteen, and in spite of present-day José's scraggly sideburns, his potbelly and his long, lank hair, Ana never needs an excuse to try and get him in the sack. That first kiss happened on her initiative, while the two of them were talking on the front step of his house one night, and for him the shock had been life changing. The next morning, upon her leaving to go back to her house 60 miles west along La Avenida, José said: 'When you kissed me last night, it was like I had a body for the first time, it was like being built again from scratch.' Ana, putting her panties on at that moment, said nothing. But then, taking a set of José's keys off the table and putting them in her bag, she said: 'I'll be back in a couple of weeks. Get the room ready, I'll be bringing all my stuff.'

Nine months later, their son was born.

One night, as the baby slept, Ana heard a noise outside. Jumping out of bed, she went into the garden and saw José on his haunches out in the road, using a blowtorch to gut an old TV set. 'Don't go,' he said. A half hour later, they had a small crucifix on their hands, assembled from the workings of the set: elements, condenser units, small light bulbs. The bulbs, positioned along the edges of the crucifix, winked on and off. Ana felt something both inexplicable and remote when, placing it in her hands, José whispered the word: 'Pioneers.'

These days, José and Ana don't think about any of that, and they aren't bitter at having been left behind. Not that this means Ana doesn't occasionally go back to the moment the plane took off, leaving them standing in the dust. She had watched as it took off with the final passengers inside. A beautiful Iberia Douglas, vanishing into the distance, into skies already pale. Tears in her eyes, she said in a low voice – as though not wanting the baby in her belly to hear: 'I wish you the worst luck in the world.'

363

Cigarette #5

The change comes when a man appears one day in the
doorway of the hut. He lives 150 miles west, he says, in
a place previously known as Kilometre Zero. He has a
moustache so long and droopy it seems about to drag on
the floor; José and Ana soon begin referring to him as
The Moustache. In exchange for food, he wanders La
Avenida offering antique objects to anyone he comes
across, things not sourced in the superstores, and dubbed
by him as 'relics'. He says he doesn't like getting his meals
from the superstores, 'it still feels like stealing to me', plus
he'd rather barter and do exchanges with real live people.
Facing José in the ditch, he shows him an ancient porcelain coffee set, at the same time eyeing the interior of the
hut, where Ana moves around unawares. José, more out of
a desire to get rid of the man than any interest in the cups
and saucers, goes inside and comes back out with some
canned pineapples to exchange. Ana, wanting to see what's
happening, goes to the window and, as she looks out, sees
a young boy, blond-haired and no older than seven, in the
backseat of The Moustache's car, about to get out. His feet
haven't so much as touched the ground before the man
whips off his belt and, holding it high, orders him to get
back in. It's then that Ana notices the gun tucked into the
left-hand side of The Moustache's belt. The boy, saying
nothing, disappears inside the car.

Cigarette #6

The Moustache is making his goodbyes when, well-versed
in the strategies of barter and exchange, he asks offhand
whether they've got a TV in the hut. José says he stripped

the last one to make a crucifix using the condenser units and light bulbs. The Moustache says, well, he's got a good little set he could let them have, it isn't very big but it's reliable, plus, for a few more cans of that fruit, he could throw in twenty VHS tapes. José looks at Ana, who nods. The Moustache opens the back door, pulls out a portable TV, the twenty tapes, and a video player which he says is 'on me'. Only once the exhaust fumes are out of sight does Ana say: 'That guy was packing.'

Cigarette #7

The Moustache would come by a couple more times in the following months. Without ever coming inside the hut, he presents José with more of the relics, asking for food in exchange, which José mostly says they don't have. But a day comes when José agrees to trade some food for some lead bullets that The Moustache claims to have extracted from the ceiling of a building at Kilometre Zero, a place he describes to them as having tall pillars and a pair of marble lions by the door. The bullets, the lead of which could be melted down, strike José as useful for fixing holes. 'The old people called lead "Saturn",' The Moustache says, looking to seal the deal. 'In fact, on the ceiling I plucked these out of, around where the bullets had entered, somebody had drawn these rings in chalk – like the rings of Saturn.'

Sometimes The Moustache has the young boy with him – looking paler and thinner every time – and sometimes he doesn't. He leaves him tied by the wrist to the gearshift with some roll string. The boy gazes out intensely at Ana, his face at the rear window, no attempt to escape, just looking at her with those blue, blue eyes. They remind her of her son's. And though it's about the last thing she wants to do, she goes back to the events surrounding the last time they saw him, the day he went on a walk to the gas station, wanting to surprise his father, who had gone to fill up on gasoline. It's beyond Ana how she let him go off on his own at such a tender age – just six. She kissed him at the door and saw him on his way, dressed in his little bomber jacket with his backpack on, and his lifebelt too, with its Bugs Bunny and Tweety Bird design, which the boy had found in an abandoned plane; he wore it constantly. Now she imagines him – though 'imagine' doesn't really cover it, it's as though he's actually right there with her: his small body, his gentle little frame. She sees him walking away flanked by the two rows of buildings, throwing stones, she imagines, at weather-vanes and windows, ducking under the belly of one of the planes left behind, still set on its blocks, chewing – with his milk teeth still – the sand-wich she'd made for him, seeing how long he could keep on staring into the sun. This is the scene – many are the scenes – in which she envisages him, until a point comes when a blackness appears, a zone comprising an unknown substance, because when the boy got to the gas station he didn't stop, just kept on going, as though having sudden-ly transformed into a real, adult walker. José never saw him, he was out back pumping gasoline. Ana has never come up with a reasonable explanation for why the boy carried straight on to the mall and didn't stop to see his father. Days later, following a search of thirteen hours-plus, ransacking the buildings, garages and airplanes, and having barely slept except to lie down for a few minutes on a mattress they happened upon, they were to find the boy's backpack at the superstore in the mall, there on the soil of the yellow poppy bed. It was Ana who spotted it, and when she did she stopped and sat down on a pile of compost

bags, couldn't go any further. José went on, shouting for
the boy at the top of his lungs, voice echoing off the ceiling
of the garden centre, now suddenly a dark and tangled
forest. He looked inside the backpack and, though it was
empty, looked and looked again: no clothes, no food, and
the lifebelt gone as well; no clue whatsoever as to what had
happened to the boy.

Cigarette #8

Since the disappearance, sex is the only thing they feel
they can believe in. It's the only way for them to confirm
their faith in one another. Only when having sex do they
feel they are formulating the right questions.

Cigarette #9

After dinner one night they set up the VHS player, picking out *The Birds* from the pile of tapes. They've never
seen it before. It's a home recording, the film having been
shown on TV at some point, so it includes ad breaks that
nobody bothered to erase – ad breaks always gave the
former inhabitants of La Avenida a sensation of life before, of real life. During one of the breaks, José gets up
to make popcorn. He sets the microwave going, three
minutes and the bowl looks like it's got a white, just-ex-
ploded brain in it. As they sit eating the popcorn, Ana
says: 'They say left-handed people are evil because they
come from the other side of the looking glass, a mirror
world, a place where everything's back-to-front.' 'Why do
you mention that? The Moustache's gun?' 'No, because,
haven't you noticed, the birds in this film always fly to

the left-hand-side of the screen?' The film ends, followed
by some Christmas toy commercials, followed by a programme with a group of women and men having a heated
discussion about the increasingly frequent phenomenon of
children going missing, children who disappear into thin
air, children who, apparently of their own accord, shut
the front door one day and walk away and are never seen
again. But José and Ana see none of this because, halfway
through the movie – even before the part where the birds
descend on the school en masse – they've fallen asleep on
the sofa.

Cigarette #10

They eat breakfast in silence. José clears the table, pours
mineral water into a pail, washes up. Ana hangs the laundry out on a line she's made by unspooling the tape from
all the videos they've watched and stringing it between
different poles. The tape has turned out to be unusually strong. One of these clothes lines is formed of the tape
from *The Birds*.

A few weeks later, three spurts of semen land on Ana's
face, running down to her mouth and then dropping onto
the carpet to form hieroglyphics. They look like tears,
thinks José, they look like tears. From then on, the sex
becomes a thing related to the darkness, a machine whose
instruction manual goes back to the beginnings of time, a
machine they don't know how to operate. Unable to sleep
one night, Ana gazes up as the small light bulbs on the
crucifix go out in sequence. It makes her think of the neon
sign for a show closing to the public forevermore.

Cigarette #11

José stands at the window, looking out as Ana works on
the moped in the porch – it's kaput again. He goes out,
runs a hand over her brow, while she, still working on
the carburettor, asks him to hand her a screw. He drops
it down the front of her shirt, which is hardly helpful:
she, annoyed, has to fumble for it in her pants. He pulls
up a foldable chair and sits down beside her. He holds
out the various parts for her in turn. They go on working, and at one point she asks if it isn't time for a trip to
the superstore. 'We're low on food and water,' she says,
'and that last poppy is on its way out.' He doesn't answer.
Then they decide that she'll go today, for the first time.
She goes through to the bedroom, fills her backpack with
several changes of clothes, a warm sleeping bag and some
energy bars. Going out back, she unclips the clothes-line
made from the tape of *The Birds* and rolls it up into a ball,
and this too goes into the backpack. She returns to the
porch, where José, sweating heavily, his forearms knotted with swollen veins, has taken over on the carburettor.
'Remember the best stuff is on the shelves just when you
come inside,' he says. 'It's all crap in the warehouses at the
back.' 'I know,' she says. He watches as she walks away,
and doesn't go back to the carburettor until she's out of
sight. It's a harder job this time as they've lost the two
rivets that are supposed to hold the ends of the carburettor. Then he remembers the four bullets he got from The
Moustache. He goes inside for them, and sets them in
the corresponding holes in the carburettor. The engine
starts now, and he takes the moped out for a short spin. It's
working nicely once more. After that he goes and washes, eats, and then sits out in the garden to wait. He doesn't
know yet that Ana won't be coming back.

Cigarette #12

In the following period, the sun gradually grew dark – so gradually that it was several months before José noticed it happening. But then one day another sun appeared, rising in the west. From then on, it would always be daylight.

Some time later, tired of searching for Ana, having checked every single house sixty miles in either direction, he comes to the mall, driving the moped right inside and stopping at the gardening section. The poppies aren't growing like they used to, and some have wilted completely. He decides to use what's left of his life to try to make this yellow poppy bed thrive again. He soon gives up the hut and makes the move to the mall; with Ana and the boy gone, there's nothing left tying him to that particular dwelling. He takes a few essentials, and one or two mementos: a couple of pieces of clothing that were his son's, a ring of Ana's, and the photo of the group including a grandfather or great-grandfather of his – a photo of a time when something called the Iberian Peninsula still existed.

Cigarette #13

A swallow starts coming and landing on the laces of one of his boots, before hopping along the instep to peck at a knob of butter José puts there for it. Finishing it, the bird looks up. Its animal eyes meet his human eyes, the same colour. It's possible this swallow has never been outside the mall.

Cigarette #14

Overhead, a flock of swallows is flying around in the
upper reaches of the mall. José lies down to watch the
shifting shapes against the plaster of the ceiling. Any time
he sets up his bed in the northern part of the mall, the
birds, seeking human warmth, migrate with him. When
he sets up his bed in the southern part, again they're quick
to join him. He can read the paths of their flights from the
droppings they leave on the mall floor: strange figures
of eight. If he gets bored, he has a race with the swallows;
him on the moped, them always coming first. He starts
leaving food out for them in the long rows of empty cash
registers: dry foods go in the coin compartments, water in
the bigger compartments meant for the bills. He watches as they descend in their hundreds to feed. Every time
thinking how trusting animals are, and how just a few
drops of poison would be enough to put an end to all of
them in one fell swoop.

Cigarette #15

It doesn't go well with the poppies. It started out with him
needing to sow fifty seeds for a single healthy plant to
grow. Now he's having to sow more than a hundred.

Cigarette #16

A banging on the glass doors at the main entrance wakes
him one day. Throwing some pants on, he hurries out
from the tent he's set up in the old outdoor equipment

371

store. When he gets to the entrance he sees the figure of a solitary boy, thin, very pale and not wearing a top. It's the first time in over a year he's seen another human.

'Can I come and try the playground?'

'Take a hike!'

The boy says something else, but José isn't listening. Before climbing back into the tent, he takes another look at the boy, who's still standing with his hands against the glass. José sees the knotted roll string around his wrists. His blue eyes remind him of his son's.

Cigarette #17

A while later, working on the bed one day, adding compost, watering and digging holes, he unearths the ball of video tape from *The Birds*. It's been lying buried in the soil. He holds his breath. He thinks he feels something, a strong emotion of some kind, though he doesn't know what's caused it.

Cigarette #18

There's a moment in the day when he's lying in bed and the clocks on display in the homeware section synchronize for a second – all the second hands align – and the entire mall shakes, as though the nervous system of the world were making its presence known. And there are moments when he and the birds are awoken by the sound of food cans expanding in the heat, bulging like footballs, or by the bicycles suddenly falling from their complex system of wall mounts, or a huge bang made by a box of snacks, all having rotted and fermented inside their bags and all passing their expiration date and exploding at once. A feeling comes over him as though he's the guardian of a kind of Noah's Ark, like this is a spiritual reservation, a museum for an extinct mode of being. Previously, he thinks, the frenetic consumption of products meant they had to re-fill the shelves constantly. Nobody ever got to see what would happen in a mall if you just left it to evolve with no human intervention, like a nervous system unto itself. This is a kind of destruction nobody was ever taught about.

Cigarette #19

Recently he's been taking the ball of *The Birds* videotape and turning it over in his hands. He never dares to unroll it, and far less to find an old cassette-carcass and try to re-mount the tape, which might mean he could work out what it was about it that mattered so much to Ana.

He's awoken by a noise one day, an array of noises in fact, a sudden, unannounced burst of noises. From a distance he sees hundreds of dead birds just inside the glass-fronted entrance. The glass is covered in cracks and vertical trickles of blood, like it's some kind of anatomy lesson. He has no idea how they all managed to fly straight into the glass given all the times they've skimmed not an inch above his head without hitting him. Going over, he finds a number of the swallows still alive. Kneeling down, he tries to revive the younger ones with taps to their breasts, where he judges the hearts to be. He puts their beaks inside his mouth and tries giving mouth-to-mouth, but that only makes it harder for them to draw breath. Few survive. I'm a Noah, he thinks dejectedly, who can't even look after his animals.

The magazines and books are the only products that seem impervious to the ravages of time. There's a '3 FOR 1' crate containing a big pile of both. José climbs in, clambering across and starting to sort through them. Picking one up, his eye's instantly drawn to a photo he recognizes: it's the same as the one he brought from the hut. A black and white group photo with one of his male forebears, a grandfather or great-grandfather (he isn't sure which), sitting in front of a stone wall, smiling at the camera. The photo bears the inscription: 'Prisoners gathered at the foot of the stairs, end of myrtle path.' Closing the volume, he looks at the title again: *Aillados*.

Cigarette #20

An impulse now comes to him that he doesn't know how to explain, and that, though remote, seems at the same time to come to him with no mediation whatsoever, from the very epicentre of his heart: he takes a can of tuna down from a sales stand, opens it and, using his fingers, and in a frenzy he's never experienced before, wolfs down the contents. He eats another can of tuna that same day, and more and more on the days that follow, until he's made his way through every single can of tuna in the superstore, hundreds or thousands of pounds of them. He then moves on to cans of ham and, when they're finished, begins in on the sardine and herring, and then, the frenzy, if anything, intensifying, the eel and rabbit meat. He'll make the change, this means, to a fully meat diet; it doesn't matter to him if it's meat from land or sea creatures. As long as it's protein, and the purer the better.

He is searching the aisles towards the back when something shiny beneath one of the shelves catches his eye.

Getting down on his haunches, he reaches under and pulls out a life belt covered in Bugs Bunny and Tweety Bird designs. Squeezing the life belt, he finds there's a small amount of air still left inside. He spends a number of hours wandering up and down the aisles with the life-belt in his hands, goes and sits at the old cafe, unstops the valve, hesitates, doesn't know if he has the courage, puts the valve in his mouth, and then proceeds to squeeze the lifebelt flat, taking into himself all the remaining air, until not a single drop of what was his son's breath remains.

BOOK III

Normandy (*Masters of the Night*)

1.

As if everything was fine and nothing could ever go wrong, one night, many years ago now, too many to count on the fingers of my two hands, I was laying the table and he was nearly done descaling the fish before we put it in the oven, the scales shooting up and spinning in the air like slivers of quartz, when he put the knife down on the counter and turned to me.

'Sweetheart,' he said, 'if I die, call me on the phone and leave a message.'

'What?' I said.

'Just that: call my phone and say everything you need to say to me, but never could have otherwise.'

In silence, I went to the kitchen, got the glasses and placed them on the tablecloth.

'Promise me that you will,' he insisted.

'I promise,' I said.

2.

The first thing I saw as the bus pulled in to the seaside town of Honfleur was a woman sitting on a cafe terrace stroking a small dog. This mania for the stroking of pets was something that always set my teeth on edge, even more so in that moment as it struck me that this dog could be a human being; in fact, there was no doubt that it was one. I've discovered something amazing, which is that in the beginning there were only humans; at the beginning of time, I mean, the only thing in existence were human beings. What then followed was a series of irreversible metamorphoses by which some of these humans became all the things we now see in the world: the flowers, the rivers, the stars, the lamp posts and the animals, the nations of the earth and the road vehicles, the books, et cetera. This makes us, women and men alike, not the perfect endpoint in an evolutionary chain, but its start, and everything around us not ancient remains but the very opposite: it is we who are the fossils. And this in turn makes the non-human world the culmination of a long and, in fact, faultless process: it's no coincidence that a mentally deranged animal is inconceivable, as is the idea of the planet ever malfunctioning. Any time we refer to a certain stone as beautiful or ugly, or see a bee buzzing around a flower and say it's working to make honey for our consumption, and even when we speak tenderly to a domestic pet, we're being completely ignorant, given that these flowers and rivers, these automobiles and bees, these books and animals have never needed us and never will; they have their own social structures, so infinitely separate from our own as to be forever invisible to us. Which means there's no way for us to converse with an ant or an automobile, a book or a nation, a river or a pet, and not because they don't understand us, but because we don't understand them. All of this I thought on arriving in Honfleur and seeing that woman petting her small dog. I wished he were with me to share this discovery. He, who was not a bee, or river, automobile, nation or pet, but a man – a male of the species, I mean.

I stepped off the bus and stretched, my back stiff after the five hour drive from Paris. The sun lay along the tiled roofs of Honfleur, the day unusually pleasant and bright for the Normandy coast. I supposed the emptiness of the streets was down to people being at lunch. Apart from the idling bus engine, the only sounds to be heard were the woman's voice and the dog whimpering – whether in pleasure or pain, I had no way of knowing. The windows of the houses, running parallel to the docks, were far smaller than I remembered them. The boats tilted on the swell, and their swaying masts, because of the ridiculous thing that analogy is, put me in mind of a metallic field of corn. A commercial aeroplane made a hypotenuse in the sky; I watched until it was lost from sight and remembered something he once said to me – four years earlier, to be precise, on a trip to this same Normandy coast – about times when aeroplanes crash in populated areas, and how the accident investigators find that the witnesses give an accurate account of events, all except for the chronology. They'll swear they were out watering the petunia bed when suddenly they caught sight of an aircraft up above, how they saw it bank hard left and enter a spiralling nose-dive, and within a moment or two burst into flames and come plummeting down, right into the roof of the next-door-neighbour's chalet. And what they tend to find is that events in fact unfolded in any order other than that. The investigators put it down to the shock induced by such a sight. But he, four years earlier, on our trip to this same Normandy coast, had another explanation: 'Reality is eminently disordered,' he said. 'We never perceive things in their correct order, which means that when we're talking or writing we don't keep to the correct temporal sequence either. Life is an nth degree plane crash, life is a great catastrophe, the definitive accident, and our attempts to recount it are shot through with that very same disorderedness.' Now, four years after hearing him speak those words, I went over to the pavement to get out of the sun, pulling my rucksack on its two small wheels behind me. Seeing me approach, the woman got up and, dog in arms, walked off. I found it funny the way she repeated everything she said to her dog three times: 'Oh, oh, oh', she said, and 'You hungry? You hungry? You hungry?' The dog meanwhile appeared to gaze into the distance, specifically towards the far horizon of the Channel and the coast of Great Britain. Resting against the front of a house, I tried to recall where the hotel had been – my silly refusal to consult maps, wanting to feel like a real explorer. I started along a street that, like the ones it led to, was empty of people. I heard a microwave alarm through the open window of a house. Another moment came back to me from the previous trip to this same place: him taking me to a field near the converted castle we were staying in, it was dawn and the summer's day already warm, but a layer of dew, dazzling white, still covered the grass. Taking two glass jars out of his rucksack and handing me a pipette, he asked me to help him collect drops of the dew one by one, 'Not that it's medicinal or anything like that,' he said, 'rather it's that our immediate future is concentrated in these drops, each and every one is something akin to the essence of the day to come.' And we gathered the dewdrops from the blades of at least a metre-square of grass, which as I found out for myself is a lot of dewdrops. I spent the rest of the day peering into my jar to see if I could discern something in the crystal-line dew, though in reality I didn't even know what I was looking at, whereas he, sitting down to breakfast at the hotel when we got back, took his and simply drank it in one, before closing his eyes and spending the duration of the morning as if asleep – 'as if' because, though he kept his eyes shut, he'd still answer when spoken to. That same day, in the afternoon, sitting together on a seafront bench in a nearby town, he said, in a tone somewhere between resignation and lament: 'Great Britain's over there, on the far side of the Channel; we should be able to see it from here, I don't know why we can't.' And we went on to see all manner of different beaches over the

382

following days, as we continued along the Normandy coast, convinced as we were that it's only from the peripheries of things, only from their farthest shores, that we have any chance of comprehending their true nature. And this is a universal principle for each and every one of us, such that we have to distance ourselves from our own lives if we want to get a view of its contours and its outline, to work out what kind of beast this life of ours really is, and then, only then, is it possible to call a life 'entire'.

I wandered on in search of the hotel. Everything was as I remembered it: everywhere the same smell of lavender and rotten seaweed, a smell that four years before had seemed inguinal to me, arousing, nigh hormonal. It was turning out to be a far more instructive trip than expected: the sensation of reproducing the legendary stand-off between agriculturalists and hunters, but in reverse: now it was me who was the hunter, and a woman who goes out hunting never comes back empty-handed, she isn't interested in epics of triumph or defeat: a woman always comes home having achieved something, something useful, not spouting morals and belles-lettres. I had gone to the north of France for precisely this, to do something of use: to delineate the final contour of a life that is a message left on a dead person's voicemail. And it had been two years since he'd disappeared, early in the autumn two years before he'd said he was going to an island in Galicia for a symposium on online networks and media, and then, just like that, he was gone: that was the last I ever heard of him. And still I had no explanation. Another plane flew overhead and, checking my watch, I realized I'd spent over half an hour immersed in these thoughts, the microwave alarms in the houses gently rocking me, and I was yet to find the Hotel Palais

Honfleur, small and very beautiful architectural remnant of that fortified seventeenth-century town.

At the reception, a semi-awake young man signed me in and gave me a key attached to an enormous fob that was heavier than my hand. I took my things up to the room and went straight back out to look for a place to have dinner. As I was going along, I stopped outside a small butcher's. The slabs of meat in the window display had plastic roses stuck in the fatty parts with wire. From a distance the roses gave the whole thing the air of one of those Monet lily ponds; in fact when I went over, having just turned a corner, I thought it was a gallery for local art, and in a way it was. There was another tray, set a little way back, with a mound of salted pig's ears on it, and these looked like a mass of butterfly wings. Next to that, calf's eyes had been stacked up in a pyramid; these, I later found out, were a local delicacy. They bake them in the oven. The eye at the top, the one the esotericists tell us only aliens have, seemed to be looking at me and me alone. I carried on along the cobbled streets. Honfleur is small, but so incredibly winding that barely going ten blocks is like covering the length of an entire avenue in one of the great cities of the world. I passed a house with a plaque stating that Erik Satie died there, and I had to assume this was the case. Nobody, myself included, has ever seen the people who put up these commemorative plaques, but I accept them like I accept the user warnings and terms of use that pop up on my screen all the time from different programmes. I wandered on; it wasn't so much having no fixed direction as being adrift, one footstep drifting into the next, and me thinking no farther ahead than where next to place my foot. I came out at the docks, a deep, quiet harbour with rows of near-identical stone houses on either side, and at the far end a moveable bridge. Just as I arrived, the two sides of the bridge started to rise up. A group of tourists stood frozen to the spot, terrified, I'd say, and as the bridge began to tip beneath their feet they got quickly back onto the pavement; having been following them (tourists always know where they're going), I hopped back too. Then, waiting for a boat to go through, I noticed a small esplanade over to one side with a merry-go-round and a Ferris wheel on it, both turning with nobody on them. I walked over thinking to have my first ever ride on a Ferris wheel. The man there – manning both the Start/ Stop button and the megaphone, over which he called in a tone so primordial it was as if he'd been there since the beginning of time – handed me the ticket, and as our eyes met I was instantly reminded of *his* gaze, a resemblance in the very depths of the pupils, one you could only appreciate looking into both eyes simultaneously; looking at him side-on didn't produce the same effect. The Ferris wheel kicked into life, and as I rose into the air the town grew small below, only, alarmingly, to return to normal size as I came down again. Reaching the top once more, I thought I saw in the far distance – sufficiently far away that several stretches of the coastline lay between Honfleur and it – a very wide beach. As the Ferris wheel continued around and around, I came to the conclusion that it was one of the D-Day landings beaches; at this, I felt I was going to be sick. I flapped my hands at the man as I passed him in my pod, and his gesticulations in return suggested that he couldn't stop it now, only in emergencies or in the case of something breaking; he had to let it run for a specific amount of time. Like a language, I said to myself, Latin, for example – once underway it can never be stopped by human hands, there's no such thing as a dead language, any such claim is like saying that the dead don't live on in us, when it's beyond doubt that the dead tend to be far more present in our day to day than any living person. The living pass by and you may never see them again, whereas a dead person remains, their presence sticks to your skin like the buttery smell does to everything on that stretch of French coastline. Feeling woozy, I closed my eyes so as not to be confronted with the sight of that distant beach, about which I'd already begun inventing things; I was in northern France in order expressly not to invent anything, all I wanted was to document, to delineate the farthest reaches of a life: the phone call to a dead person's voicemail, an outline for an ending. In northern France, as I say, you get the smell of rotten seaweed, lavender and butter, but there are other smells as well. The smell of stray bullets. All the bullets, I mean, that missed their marks. Has anyone ever stopped to consider where it is that projectiles fired into the air end up? Where they fall? And the inadvertent death toll? I'm reminded now of my first televisual memory: coming back from school one day, ten years before my first period, I was eating in front of the television, where in some place on the planet, which seemed to me to be Africa though it could have been anywhere, a group of men in civilian clothes were firing machine guns in the air, celebrating a war, whether the beginning or end of one I don't know, they might even have been celebrating a sporting event, shouting and laughing and making what to my young self were terrifying faces, and it then occurred to me that those bullets had to land somewhere, what went up had to come down. It wasn't until some years later that I learned they also had to fall at the same velocity at which the machine gun had discharged them, so that as it turns out my first televisual memory is the first frame leading to the future impact of a bullet, an image prefacing a death or a possible death, but at that age something stops you from guessing at the fatal final twist. The ingredients for the revelation of that death are all there, but you can't see it, I suppose that's what makes you a child and not a flower, a nation, a pet, or any other thing. I feel like this Ferris wheel is never going to stop, like I'm going to be stuck here until this guy decides he's had his fun, I bet he's hit that Start button at least three times by now, I said to myself as I thought, for the second time, that I was about to throw up, and at this I again became aware of the beach in the distance. And then the desire arose of wanting to go there, to walk across those rocks, feel the overwhelming sensations that must surely come when, as a woman, you set foot on a beach where vast numbers of men have died, creatures utterly different from us, I'd almost say another species: to set foot on sand containing tonnes of man-bones. Graveyards are full of women and men, and innumerable bones of both sexes lie beneath city concrete as well, I'd almost say they like being mixed up in that way, jumbled together in the mythological prestige of that which, though near at hand, though only a little way beneath the surface, is forever out of reach. But only on the D-Day landing beaches will you find thousands of bones belonging to males alone, male humans but also male dogs since at least five hundred sniffer dogs were sent along, and as I again reached the top of the Ferris wheel revolution the question came to me of what a woman ought to feel when walking across the resting place of such an all-male cast, what a woman ought to feel when treading on all those souls with phalluses surely still residing among the cockle shells, salt crystals and seaweed, and the sand, too, sand later to be used in the construction of houses, bridges and motorways, sand that by necessity will contain the dust of those bones, dust that in time will manifest inside the cement blocks of countless buildings. We see it almost every day: large stains appearing on bridge stanchions, smaller ones on the walls of houses, and, even in the concrete that goes to make up motorways and high streets, strange shapes, manifestations that, because they are of the dead, come on slowly yet intensely, similar to the way a song might begin to fade, only to come back in again louder and heavier than before. When he went away two years ago the two us were fading out as well, but I believe we deserved a better ending. It was so different to our Normandy trip two years before that, which was when our union, more than twenty-years deep by then, was at the most glorious section of its chorus: we were seeing things together that nobody had ever seen before, by which I mean visionary sharings, the kinds of things that any couple worthy of the name will sooner or later experience. Because sharing your life, which normally means inertia and repetition, suddenly, and without either of the two forsaking their individuality, can mean a couple merging, becoming a single entity, at which point they enter states that are unique, visionary. States, I would go so far as to say, in which the couple become a single mutant creature, a species apart and unto itself, one that is neither animal, mineral nor vegetable, nor all three at once, and the visions then generated by the couple are as unprecedented as they are formidable. So it was that, in such a state of total invincibility, we had covered that same stretch of Normandy coast four years earlier, moving forward inside the protective innocence of any who spend their time in the silliest of pursuits, like gathering drops of dew, or trying to spy the coast of Britain from a seafront bench. What power, what beautiful kind of trash was already contained in all of that, I ask myself.

3.

After stepping off the Ferris wheel, I wandered the streets a little more before going back to the harbour. Bars and small restaurants, terraces full of foreign faces that all looked the same to me; I found a table and sat down. I ordered battered fish with a side of vegetables and a glass of white wine. I could tell from the looks I drew from the tourists how unsettling the presence of a woman alone was to them, and more so because of my appearance, which, aside from the map poking out of my handbag, wasn't exactly that of a tourist. I travel in the same clothes and shoes I wear to work, in this case a cream, knee-length pencil skirt, a sleeveless blouse with a pattern of flowers and rural motifs and a frilly neckline for extra pizazz, and a pair of summer shoes with low heels because flat shoes make my feet ache. The waitress when she brought over my food reminded me of Frida Kahlo, not because she looked anything like the famous Mexican painter but because she had a badge in the buttonhole of her dress jacket which said, in her language, 'Down with Surrealism', an aesthetic current that Frida Kahlo is known to have hated, for all that the majority of art history books place her squarely within it. I took the waitress's badge as a reaction, one born out of boredom, against all the many surrealist writers and artists Normandy has historically produced. And, I must confess, this felt pleasing to me, seeing as I hadn't come to this coast for fantasies either, and far less in search of anything dreamlike, but to measure, to weigh, to verify, I said to myself, surveyor of all that he and I had experienced four years earlier. I finished up my meal, a man came up, begging for change, I fished in my handbag and my hand alighted on my mobile phone, it immediately came to me that I'd left my charger at home, Shit, I muttered several times, Shit, gave the man a couple of euros and turned the phone on, saw that the battery was fully charged, immediately turned it off. Drinking the last of my wine, I adjusted my bra with two cretins looking on from another table – the entire meal had been spent with the two of them openly eyeing my breasts – and set off for the hotel. The smell of fish and fennel drifted through the open windows of people's houses. Once more a symphony of microwave alarms accompanied my steps, I was surprised at the range of qualities it's possible for these alarms to encompass, covering the whole tonal scale, someone ought to use them in a song. Minutes later the receptionist was handing me my room key and looking me up and down in a manner so lacking in malice that I couldn't help but see him as a baby; an unborn baby, even. I got straight into bed, turned on the television, and with the lights off flicked through lots of channels, all of them talking about Great Britain and the imminent Brexit referendum, until I came to a channel showing the film *The Warriors*. It made me laugh to suddenly be reminded of the epic of these warring tribes in the night of late seventies New York City. The members of the gang known as the Warriors, in what becomes a kind of conquest of an urban planet, have to cross the territories of all their enemies in a single night, the twenty miles separating the Bronx from their own neighbourhood, Coney Island, on the southern tip of Brooklyn. They attempt it using the subway, but so primitive is their existence they don't actually know how to read a subway map, and have to undertake this great journey overland. On street after street the fights unfold, and the getup of each different gang, seemingly extracted directly and unfiltered from different sections of big department stores, responds mechanically to a theme; there are the Venice Beach-like roller skaters in their dungarees, there's the gang dressed like members of the San Francisco 49ers, baseball bats and all, the Hells Angels-types in their leather jackets, the gang in camouflage army gear like something out of the Vietnam war, another with bandanas like the Osaka Yakuza, one gang all in lumberjack shirts like Kansas or Minnesota field workers, another with silver bomber jackets like Apollo 11 astronauts, and so on, they all looked like they were in fancy dress, though no more so than the tourists I'd just seen down at the harbour, I said to myself, no more than the man I'd passed selling honey in the square, in his traditional regional outfit, no more than me, even, setting out on a trek through the countryside wearing city attire, all the way down to my shoes. In the glow of the TV set, my skirt and my bra hanging on the armchair back looked like the humped spine of a mythological animal. I closed my eyes. When he and I were first together I used to ask what he saw when he closed his to go to sleep, and he'd invariably talk about four dots floating behind his eyelids, 'Like astronauts drifting through space,' he'd laugh, 'like they're drifting off into interstellar space.' Over the years those dots gradually began to fade, and eventually they disappeared altogether. I sometimes wondered what those four astronauts saw from in there, from their place behind his eyelids. I heard the receptionist walking around downstairs, a sound that soon stopped, only for others to strike up – drums and musical instruments doubtless coming from the neighbouring streets, music that seemed tribal to me. I felt unsettled, I suppose on account of having watched *The Warriors*, but, like the waves on a sea shore, the noise swelled and faded without ever actually coming nearer, so that I felt it to somehow be rocking me to sleep. A short story by the Japanese writer Ryunosuke Akutagawa, 'The Wizard', which I'd read some months earlier, then came to mind: a country boy, no more than a teenager, goes to a job agency in Osaka and asks for work as a wizard, the man working there says that won't be possible, there aren't any jobs for wizards, the boy won't take no for an answer, pointing out the 'Job Agency' sign above the door and saying the job he wants is as a wizard, the man says he needs to look into it and tells him to come back the next day, the man then asks the advice of his doctor, a sage man, about how he can avoid disappointing the boy, the doctor shrugs but his wife, passing through the room, cuts in, laughing and saying that he should have the boy come back the next day, that she knows how to turn the boy into a magician, the doctor tells her to be quiet, says she shouldn't joke, but she insists, saying to leave it in her hands, and so the boy comes back the next day and the doctor's wife asks him if he's willing to do anything to become a magician, the boy says he is, and she says in that case he has to come and be a servant in the house for twenty years, and after that she'll show him all the magic tricks he wants, and the boy instantly accepts and a period begins in which he works in the gardens, carrying the coal, doing general maintenance jobs on the property, the roofs, all kinds of punishing jobs that nonetheless do nothing to dim either his hopes or his good spirits, and once the twenty years are over, the boy, every bit the man by this point though they still

392

call him 'boy', goes and demands the promised insights, and the doctor, who thought the boy had forgotten all about it, stutters, doesn't know how to respond, but his wife says yes, it's time promises were kept, but that he has to do precisely as she says, to the letter, which the boy says he will, very happily, and she begins giving him things to do, more and more absurd and difficult physical tests, all of which, to her surprise, he turns out to be equal to, and in the end she tells him to climb a very tall tree in the garden, which he also agrees to, and she says he has to go right to the very top, and when he does she tells him to get hold of the highest branch and hang from it, and the boy dangles high up in the air, and she orders him to take one hand away, which he does, and then, telling him not to be afraid, she says to take the other one away, and the doctor, looking on aghast, asks if she's lost her mind, saying the boy's sure to die, and as doctor and wife argue, the boy takes his other hand away, dropping a short way but then coming to a stop mid-air and, floating there, thanks them both for showing him how to be a real magician, before flying away into the clouds. This is the story they tell in Osaka. Nobody knows what happened with the doctor and his wife, or with the boy who wanted to be a magician, but the tree is still there, under the summer sun and winter snow of Osaka, and I then tried to get myself to sleep thinking about this tree, since, I realized, I was less interested in what the doctor or the woman saw, or even what the boy saw from up in the sky, than what the tree saw, what that great woody creature would have to say about it all, going on standing silently in the garden of a house in Osaka. It's like the tale of the Three Little Pigs: the interesting part of this, the thing that would really help us to understand the moral of the story, isn't what

393

the little pigs have to tell us, but what their houses would say, the two that were blown down and even the one belonging to the most responsible pig, which, though made of sturdy bricks and superbly designed, must be a ruin by now as well. The thought I finally fell asleep with was how little interest I had in what the D-Day landings survivors saw, compared to what the dead saw; this, the story of the dead, would be the True Story of the D-Day landings, information we have no access to and that must nonetheless be somewhere, hidden information, the unknown B-side to the fabric of our reality, so unknown that we spend our time creating substitutes for it: the story of the dead is substituted by the story we the living make up about them, and the unfolding of civilizations is that of an infinite chain of substitutions. Indeed, a painting of a landscape makes no attempt to know what might be hidden in that landscape, rather it seeks to substitute it, and a fire doesn't seek to know what is hidden in a forest fire, it just wants substitute it, and the lift has no interest in trying to understand what the hell these things we call stairs are, it just tries to substitute them, and saccharin doesn't try to find what's hidden in sugar, only to substitute it, and sugar in turn doesn't try to uncover whatever's hidden in other foodstuffs, it just substitutes their calorific potential with a single teaspoon, and, in turn, sugar was invented during the industrial revolution to get more out of the workers, the children who worked in mines especially, a dessert spoon of sugar was as good as two plates heaped full of beans and bacon, which means that the white of sugar is littered with the corpses of children. Yes, coal – not by coincidence black like coffee – and the industrial revolution it fired cannot be understood without its opposite, sugar so white. And in turn, the use of child miners never tried to understand what was hidden in their childhoods, but rather to substitute it for something else: its disappearance, its absolute disappearance. As for this last thought, I don't know if I had it that first night in Honfleur or the next day when, after a breakfast of toast with no butter but lashings of plum jam, the label on the jar of which declared that it was homemade though it wasn't, I left the town on foot.

4.

There was a moment when things changed between us. Not totally, I wouldn't quite say, but there was a definite departure in a direction unfamiliar to us both. We were at home together one night and he locked the front door before we went to bed. Never before had we taken any measures to stop intruders getting in at night. Looking back now, I don't know how I failed to see that, in fact, he was making an announcement to the opposite effect: neither of us were getting out, he was saying. Now, in my return to Normandy, it struck me that what I wanted to find was how to open that door, still locked from the inside. I've said that I was planning to return to the places he and I had been together four years earlier, but I don't believe I've said that I wanted to do it on foot, and so, that first day, I left the hotel to embark on my Normandy journey proper. Before I'd gone more than a couple of blocks in the direction of the Honfleur exit, arriving at one of the streets that fed onto the main road, I again started hearing the tribal drumbeat of the previous evening. Turning a corner, I found before me a crowd of people making a huge noise. Rather than farmers or local fisherman, they were dressed in sportswear, the kind urbanites refer to as 'athleisure', and they were banging drums and saucepans; this, from what their placards and banners said, was a solidarity march for the thousands of refugees arriving from Arab countries, Syria primarily, a march that had commenced weeks earlier in Paris and would soon terminate in the coastal city of Calais, just 275 kilometres from Honfleur but in the opposite direction from where I was going. Thousands of refugees had been held up in Calais attempting to cross the Channel to Great Britain. I remembered seeing it on the news not long before, there were more and more of these refugees every day, crossing Europe on foot or stowed away in trucks, arriving to the port of Calais and adding to the mass of children and adults crammed together there. The displaced families that had miraculously found their way to Calais, spilling from tents and jerry-built huts, spent their days in front of television sets, following the news about negotiations going on between the EU and Turkey, Turkey and the United States, the United States and Russia, Russia and Syria, Syria and the EU, and back round again, or glued to developments in the wars taking place in their home countries, as though they had been removed from those wars and yet still hoped for something from them: a truce being called in their own bodies, bodies they also sometimes saw televised on those same screens. And I, not unmoved by the tragedy but feeling I couldn't cut through to the other side of march, turned and found a different route out of town, coming onto the main road where it ran virtually along the shoreline. Nonetheless, I remembered having recently looked at a book called *A Short History of Migrations*, written by an Italian author whose name escapes me now, in which it said that during the Neolithic the spread of peoples across what is now Europe had advanced at a speed of two kilometres a year, almost the same speed at which today's refugees advanced, though the routes taken are different: if we could see an animated representation of the migratory flows in Europe during the twentieth and twenty-first centuries, we would be given a portrait of an apparently schizophrenic continent, one in which the fronts of human displacement are suddenly interrupted, only to advance at full tilt and then speed up even more, or go backwards or make illogical leaps. It's as simple as this: we wanted labour, and people arrived instead. And I pictured the continent from above with a fire raging over it that never goes out, everywhere tiny lively sparks that not even the most powerful satellite zoom would be able to detect. Communications satellites, like the water in the river described by Heraclitus, are constantly joining and separating the world from itself – which is the same as saying from us.

I passed field after green field, the hills rolling gently away under the gloomy light of the north – warm but never burning – and heard frogs croaking though there were no lakes in sight, the verges weren't particularly wide, but wide enough for my boots which I naturally put on for long walks instead of the low-heeled shoes, which were now in the small rucksack along with a few supplies and a sleeping bag, just in case. My hair was down, I imagined it practically blonde in the sun, I patted my jacket pocket, my mobile phone was still there, a phone I had bought expressly for the occasion, with a single number saved on it, his. I stopped and turned it on, checking it had enough battery to last the journey. I felt a resolve in my footsteps and in my flesh, a robustness to my muscles that made me feel very present inside my body, me the person and my body one and the same, me occupying the totality of my body. I went on, hoping none of the passing cars would stop to offer the single woman a lift, passing dense shrubby thickets every mile or two from inside which a chirping came, suggesting birds were nesting inside them, I remember thinking the tonal scales of these gave the microwave alarms in Honfleur a run for their money in originality. I came to a bridge over an estuary inlet, the aquatic antechamber to the ocean with its mix of fresh water and brine; I stopped to take in the meeting of these two currents. I was taken back to being in the city of Berne three years earlier with him, a bitterly cold winter, and standing by the railing of one of so many bridges we had seen in that city with a metal grille stretched between the pillars intended to stop people from committing suicide, a common pursuit in Switzerland according to an unlikely-seeming plaque on the railing. I remember taking his hands in mine and giving them a rub, they were frozen, like a dead person's hands, but fear was all it was – fear of war. We had often talked about it, the future seemed to us both a place of ubiquitous, invisible war – not country against country but, like in *The Warriors*, all against all, all-out conflict all across the planet, everyone for themselves. I let go of his hands, we went the rest of the way across the bridge, and there was the Einstein museum, our destination; now that did turn out to be a disappointment. There wasn't a single photograph, image or document of Einstein's that couldn't be found online by anyone clever enough to key in one or two search terms. The only thing of any interest were some documents belonging to his first wife, Mileva Marić, whom, it was suggested, in around 1902 had a decisive influence in the formation of Einstein's first theories, and who, by the time the German physicist became famous, wasn't part of his life any more. I must admit, that day in the Einstein Museum, I felt a little like Mileva. I made an extraordinary discovery which I then tried in vain to share with him. Specifically: some months before our trip to Berne, he had been to an exhibition on Karl Marx at the CGAC Museum in Santiago de Compostela, where they were showing a facsimile manuscript of *Das Kapital*, and he had spotted, among the many annotations in which Marx had talked about economics and the class struggle, a number the same as would be used years later in the early stages of quantum physics to describe the findings on the movements of particles and atoms, such that, involuntarily, in Marx's text certain expressions appeared that would make complete sense in the ambit of quantum physics as well. For example, when Marx made a note that in physics would signify the frequency of an electromagnetic wave divided by the speed of light.

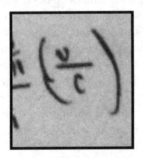

This is what he had seen months earlier at the CGAC, something which in and of itself he had found particularly unsettling seeing that it's easy to imagine the possibility of, for example, a reading of Planck's Blackbody Radiation Theory in terms of the class struggle, and vice versa, opening the door on an abyss that any person of even middling intelligence or simply inquisitiveness could not help but find perturbing. But in the Einstein Museum in Berne I noticed something else: Einstein's handwriting was very similar, not to say identical, to Marx's. I remember holding my breath for a few seconds before pointing this out to him, and him showing surprise and anger in equal measure since that was the kind of detail he would have liked to have picked up on himself. So annoyed was he that he couldn't help but begin to speculate as to whether, in reality, Einstein, born in 1879, and Marx, dead in 1883, had been one and the same person; he spent all of the rest of the day trying to find ways of substantiating the idea. It was some sight, him sitting glued to his mobile phone, spinning through web page after web page in search of any minor detail to back up his theory, and to top it off he found out that Marx had died on the same calendar day, 14 March, as Einstein had been born, a coincidence that, though the dates were in different years, was enough to convince him of the veracity of this crazy idea. And he often went off on tangents like this when I came up with an observation that was beyond his capabilities either in acuteness or intellectual boldness; he couldn't stand it. That night in Berne, very tired and with feet aching after all the streets we'd walked – and given his inability to have sex that was even faintly satisfactory since in reality he avoided sex just as much he did himself – I fell asleep, but woke in the middle of the night and, opening one eye, saw him sitting at the desk. He was writing, by hand, in something of a fury. When I asked what he was writing, he said it was a story that had just come to him, 'The story of the fourth astronaut,' he called it, and when I asked what that was, he told me that the four dots he saw when he was falling asleep had started to fade, it was as though they were drifting away from one another in interstellar space, and that before they disappeared altogether he wanted to get the story of one of those four points down. I left him working on his story of the fourth astronaut and went back to sleep. When I woke the next morning, he had a stack of paper, the pages filled with handwriting even more fiendish than that of Einstein or Marx. Remembering those moments in Berne, I crossed the rest of the estuary bridge in Normandy, I had been walking for some hours by now and rainclouds had moved in, my boots were doing a good job in spite of being new, the tide was out, it had left an assortment of different seaweeds, oyster and clam shells on display, as well as these objects that, after you throw them away, you don't know how or why they come back, bottle tops, for instance, bleached and slightly malformed, they seemed almost like pebbles, almost, I would say, no longer artificial. Why was it, I wondered, that nature caused things we call 'artificial' to bleach to such an extent, to the point that a bottle top becomes indistinguishable from a pebble, and at the same time creates things as colourful and clearly distinguished as flowers, insects and rocks; I couldn't come up with an answer, but I did suppose that it was because of this that houses periodically need repainting but cliffs and flowers don't.

5.
I spotted a town in the distance, the outline of which I recognized. I carried on, and at the shoreline, which had turned suddenly steep and blustery, small rocks started to appear that I straight away remembered, because of the red spatterings on them: a kind of miniature seaweed. He and I had seen them on our previous trip,

when I'd warned him not to be so vulgar as to liken them to spatterings of blood, and still less to dare make reference to blood spilt in the D-Day landings. He laughed at that, and started expounding on an idea about how the colour red is used little in cinema, but that when it is it's done in such a powerful way as to displace everything else, putting forward Kieślowski's *Red* as an example, a film we'd both always liked, especially the character of the retired judge who sits in his house and listens in on his neighbours' phone calls using a very rudimentary phone tap; neither of us could think of a better, more thrillingly mischievous way to spend one's old age. At one point in the film we see a billboard with a photograph of the female protagonist in a red jumper on a red background, blowing a bubble with some very red strawberry bubble gum. I said this was far too obvious an example, and countered with that of the teenage girl lying on her bed of flower petals in *American Beauty*, a film he'd always hated but I liked. And he then suggested *Spirited Away*, with the girl in the red kimono who stumbles on a new land on her way home, in which there's a profusion of colours red. This I countered with *2001: A Space Odyssey*, reminding him of the scene in which the astronaut, in a field of pure red, disconnects HAL's memory modules one at a time, these also being red, at which the computer begs for mercy, its voice fading but the colour staying as it is, growing more intense, even, as the life drains out of HAL. He put forward *In the Mood for Love*, the two protagonists of which, like one another's ghosts, move through a Hong Kong composed of red bedrooms and red hotel hallways, and I left it at that; I was tired of the game now, and it was cold and I wanted to get back in the car; before shutting the door and starting the engine he had crouched down to gather a few of the red-mottled stones, slipping them into his pocket. As I went on walking I thought that he and I had also always been each other's ghosts. My breath short, I repeated the words 'We were each other's ghosts, we were each other's ghosts,' and this thought, though I saw it clearly in my head, seemed strange, somewhat incomprehensible even, given that I didn't know then, and still don't, what it means to feel certain that you aren't the partner of the person you're living with but their ghost, the other's spectre after they die, and that this is what you'll be even while they're still alive. I didn't want to think about that any more and, pausing for a rest on a flattish rock beside the ditch, took a deep breath, captivated by the smell of Normandy chamomile, which until then I had only come across in soap and air fresheners. I put my rucksack down, got the water bottle out and sipped from it; a red Renault 4 drove by, going quite fast for such an old car; a man with black hair was driving, he waved at me – everybody in this part of the world waves at you, at every opportunity. There are other strange things they do at every opportunity, like closing their eyes and going to sleep whenever there's a hint of some down time, and not because they're tired, it's something I've seen people do in the western parts of India, central Africa and the Yucatán Peninsula, I've sometimes thought these people form a race unto themselves, a global race of sleepers. I drank some more water, a lizard came out from under a rock and approached my boot, it seemed unsure whether to climb across my laces or stay where it was, basking in the heat from my leather boots. We eyed each other. Since leaving Honfleur that morning I'd been seeing a constant succession of dead animals on the road, mainly hedgehogs and rabbits. As a little girl I'd noticed the way that animals dying of natural causes tend to do so at night and lying on their backs, looking up at the sky, as though both being blessed by the starry dome and in an attempt to be more than animals, as though in the final moment reneging on their animal nature, but none of the roadkill was looking up at the stars that day: without exception these dead creatures lay face-down. And whether it was because I'd come across the solidarity march those few hours before, I don't know, but I was reminded of the multitudes of photographs in the newspapers of men, women and children washing up dead all across Europe, principally in Italy and Greece, and all of them lying face-down. I felt a shudder when it came to me that the construction of the most significant state in history, the European Union, the postmodern state par excellence given that it was the first ever collective on such a scale created not through bloodshed but by persuasion and advertising campaigns, was now on its way out. We are the first generation to have grown up under the hegemony of advertising, I said to myself, and it's no secret that the only thing advertising cannot tolerate is death, which is a thing forever expelled from the paradise of consumerism. That's why, until now, we Europeans, the millions of us who didn't live through the Second World War, have had no idea of the posture death assumes when it arrives on our shores. I kicked some pebbles from my path, decided it was a good moment to take my bra off, I had no idea why I'd opted for a sports bra, which I never wear; so tight they seem designed to suffocate. Another car passed, a Renault Mégane, much faster than the Renault 4 of a few minutes earlier, and I didn't enjoy that at all, I've had a thing about high speeds ever since I was little: 1976, Germany, the forests of Eifel, the Formula 1 circuit of Nordschleife – the world's most difficult racetrack, not for nothing is it known as The Green Hell, sixteen miles long and taking in forty left-hand corners and fifty right-hand corners, set around the village and medieval castle of Nuremberg – and Niki Lauda's red and yellow car in flames, a car that on the primitive colour television in my house looked like one of those pre-constitutional Spanish flags that people burned in the Puerta del Sol hoping for the arrival of a transition to democracy that never came, and Niki Lauda's head a screaming match, a thousand degrees hot, and the picture cutting out for a moment, and my father getting up and whacking the set a few times, wiggling the antenna around and sitting down again, and then the ambulances, the firefighters spraying their foam, and Niki Lauda putting his hand to his ear and writhing about as though a snake was inside him, and no firefighters or safety protocols are capable of stopping that, and all the children at school the next day beside themselves with Niki Lauda the human torch, an awakening in all the boys of the virility and velocity that is secretly part of their make-up, all the girls horrified and sick to their stomachs, as though Niki Lauda's body were our own body and the accident hadn't occurred in the flesh and blood comic book that the television then was for us, and that night, and for months afterwards, I kept having dreams about Niki Lauda's ear, which they said on the news had been irrevocably incinerated, which they said was lost, non-existent, and how incomprehensible I found that mutilation, something being there and then suddenly not, as innocent as a digital yes/no signal, as sinister as turning a light switch on/off, and I remember waking up in tears, though whether out of fear or pity I don't know, but just hoping that somehow, against all hope, that ear would be returned to the side of Niki

Lauda's head, because at that age you could still make things either come into existence or cease to be just by wishing it so, and ever since then I've always hated high speeds. What is it about velocity that so excites men? As women, it takes great effort and a lot of overacting to feel any fondness for the 160km/h on offer by putting pedal to the floor, the same goes for 100m races, but there's no denying that birds fly, gravity acts on the flow of water, that there's such a thing as the speed of light, and the planets are in constant motion, so that, it's true, speed is a part of things and always will be, and this aversion of ours to speed, imparted to us through the culture, is an intrinsic disadvantage we women bear within ourselves, like a butcher with an irrational fear of knives, or a psychoanalyst of dreams, or a glass of the water inside it, and the Renault Mégane had just flown past my rucksack, and sitting in the ditch, I started to feel very anxious, and I wished that German racetrack had never existed, so large that it could be raining on one of the turns and yet the asphalt on others still be dry. I felt the warmth of the sun on my face and a brisk wind trickling down my back, the perfect combination for smoking a cigarette, a pleasure I nonetheless decided to postpone in case it sapped my energy for the rest of the walk. A terrible question occurred to me for the first time: when I got to my destination, what message was I going to be able to leave on your answerphone? It wasn't yet midday.

6.
I soon came to the town I'd seen earlier on in the distance, familiar for the reason that he and I had been there on our trip together. Its wide high street, featuring

a number of supermarkets with forgotten pretensions to being shopping malls, brought me out at the seafront road. I took a photo of a military jeep being obscenely flaunted on a roundabout, and another of a tank covered in graffiti of jumbled-together flowers, vestiges of war you see everywhere along that coast, cathartic repetitions, and on which I didn't feel like dwelling. I bought a hot dog and a bottle of water at a stand and sat down on one of the promenade benches, perhaps the same one on which he and I had sat trying to see the coast of Great Britain, but not so different in any case. 'Have you ever looked at the horizon and thought it's a dead horizon?' he'd said that day. Not wanting the memory to spoil my food, I squeezed the mustard sachet out over the hot dog, and tucked in since I'd worked up quite the appetite. When the two of us were sitting there, he'd also talked about a photo of a bridge over a pond, one he'd taken a few days before outside one of the converted castle-hotels. The image was a revelatory, cathartic vision, he said: 'It's a stone bridge,' he said, 'and the arch is reflected so perfectly in the pond below that they seem like two coasts separated by the sea; one, this Normandy coast, and the other, its mirror coast, its reflection, which is none other than the coast of Great Britain which, though we can't see it in this precise moment, is just over there, just across the Channel,' and he then turned his phone on and showed me the photo. The bridge was indeed so perfectly mirrored in the pond that it was possible to see them as two coasts with a body of water in between, one coast reflecting the other. I'd looked silently at the photo, before he added: 'This section of the Normandy coast so exactly mirrors the coast of Great Britain opposite that if Normandy were somehow to split off from France one day and drift north, the two would sooner

407

or later fit perfectly together,' and we both sat looking at the photo, as again he said: 'Yes, they'd fit together like a body and its reflection in a mirror,' at which he'd fallen quiet to take a sip from his can of Nestea. He always drank Nestea, went looking for it in supermarkets, bars and kiosks, I was pretty fed up with that drink by then, he wouldn't be happy with a plain ice tea in a cafe, it had to be Nestea in a can, though it is fair to say that it was thanks to Nestea that we'd found the chain of converted castles I've been referring to, where, for no more than you'd pay to stay at a small hotel, breakfast would also be included. It was a hotel chain made up of an association of aristocrats that, once agriculture and livestock had ceased turning a profit for them, wanted to make use of their assets in a more modern way; such was the mistrust of everything antique that the only way to book a room was through a web portal administered from somewhere outside France, though where precisely it didn't make clear. The counts, marquises or dukes would be there themselves to welcome you at the door, and they would make your breakfast the next morning, using meat from animals they'd raised themselves and plants and vegetables they'd grown. The photo of the bridge over the pond had been taken at one of those castles, a medieval fortification with huge, thick walls, which in the eighteenth century a military engineer, trying his hand as an architect, had tried to make easier on the eye by adding battlements and towers that looked like something out of Versailles; but the marriage had turned out so monstrously, and the execution had been so poor, that the sight of it was enough to stop you in your tracks: the whole thing was awful, from flagpole to foundations, with façades that didn't fit together properly, cracks wide enough to fit several human bodies in, and gaps in which PVC drainage pipes and electric cables were in plain view and exposed to the elements. Not by chance was it the most hypertrophied castle in France, a veritable Frankenstein big as a twelve-storey modern day building, and in which, for that reason, we'd chosen not to stay but only to visit, a visit during which he'd taken the photo. For whatever reason, the rest of the hotels in the chain were all lovely, and, most importantly for him, they all served Nestea, the brand happening to be a sponsor. I threw the hot dog wrapper in the bin, wiped the mustard from around my mouth and carried on, now deciding to take a bus since my feet were hurting and it was only a short ride to the castle – on the outskirts of town – that was my destination.

7.

The bus wasn't long in arriving. Though the road was winding, the driver kept a single hand on the steering wheel, using the other to take olives out of a bag and toss the stones out the window with a movement like he was rolling dice. He let me off at the bottom of a muddy track, it was only a twenty metre-walk to the doorstep of the main building. Nobody came to the door; I rang the doorbell several times. Over in an outbuilding, disused livestock trailers stood gathering dust next to a red Renault 4. A man with very dark hair came to the door, though, to judge by the lines on his face, he would have been over seventy. 'Ah!' he exclaimed. 'The Mallorca woman, I've been expecting you!' He was wearing a white polo shirt and white shorts, an outfit either for playing tennis in or for gardening on a Sunday. The polo shirt was covered in specks of fresh mud. He very cordially directed me to the living room, where, at the far end, mounted on a chimney breast so wide I think I could have fitted inside it, there was a plasma screen showing a game of tennis. He pointed me to a chair and, without further ado, and seeming quite excited, asked me who I liked more, Andy Murray or Rafa Nadal. 'Surely Nadal,' he said, 'seeing as he's a compatriot of yours. Nadal's my idol, look at this serve of his, look, see. When you rang the doorbell I was watching the match, that's why I didn't hear. See, your compatriot's winning.' He stopped talking, watched as Murray won the point, said '*merde*' quite loudly and stamped his foot with more force than Nadal himself hit the court with his racket – such force that the small oil portrait of a woman on the chimneybreast shook. 'That's my grandmother,' he said. Picking up my rucksack, he asked me to follow him, we went up an almost spiral staircase, and when we came to the third of the four floors he showed me my room, which was spacious but cosy at the same time, and, after demonstrating how to work the light switches, which were complicated because of some design fault, and after writing out by hand and with a show of secre- tiveness the Wi-Fi password – more or less pointless given, as I later found out, the thickness of the walls – he leaned against the doorframe and told me that he lived alone, not out of preference but because he was a widow- er and felt it was important to respect the absence of the body no longer there, so that, with his current girlfriend, their assignations always took place beyond those walls, either at her house or at one hotel or another. I quickly became aware that I found him attractive. Before going back downstairs he said he would make dinner for me but that, if the tennis match happened to go on, in con- travention of what it said on the web page of the hotel chain, he was sorry but he wouldn't be able to join me. I listened to him going down the stairs.

Seeing some salts by the sink gave me the idea of having a bath. The bath was next to a large window. Body submerged, I looked up at the moon, visible already though it wasn't completely dark, and, on the horizon, the invisible coast of Great Britain. I wondered if there might be a woman walking that stretch of the English coast as well, and if so, what that double of mine was doing at that moment – if lying in a bath as well, or if still years in the past, going on a trip with him, with her own partner – because isn't it true that mirrors always entail lapses in time, given the time it takes for light to travel any distance? And isn't it also true that when you move a hand, it's a few moments before the hand in the mirror reacts? And is it not equally true that if we're talking about mirrors the size of a coast, these delays will necessarily build up and you could even have a lapse lasting years? I felt a strong urge to masturbate, but then a multitude of laughable scenes filmed by men of women masturbating in baths came to mind, and the urge went away. From the ground floor there came the noise of things being kicked: Rafa Nadal had just lost another point, I could even have masturbated listening to the sound of those blows, which led the way to Nadal's sweaty, exquisite body, I decided I might as well wash my hair, which had been impregnated by the disgusting smell of butter. Before going down for dinner, and with a dressing gown wrapped around me, I sat in the armchair by the fireplace and flicked through the books on the table. One featured historical photos of the castle. A female nurse was tending to a soldier wounded in the war in 1915, a basin and some neatly folded cloths in her hand. The scene took place in the same room in which I found myself, and there was a reproduction of Velázquez's *Las Meninas* on the wall behind them; I glanced up at the wall, and where the reproduction *Las Meninas* had been there was now a black mark. The wounded soldier was lying face down on the same bed I was going to be sleeping in that night. Such things don't usually affect me, but I slammed the book shut and, as though hoping to erase what I'd just seen, opened another, this one on demographics. It had numerous graphics showing that the local male population had decreased by fifty per cent between 1910 and 1945. One showed that, nonetheless, there had been no decline in the overall population during that period. It offered no explanations, but I decided that the overall population wouldn't be affected no matter how many men had died, because of the fact you only needed one man to stay at home for many women to be inseminated. I immersed myself in that thought, in some way a deeply stirring thought, eventually coming back into the present at a series of whacks from downstairs; poor Nadal, I said to myself, closing the book and putting it back on the table. I got dressed and left the room.

I don't know how I found my way to the dining room at my first try. The table with a single place set, which I guessed was for me. A porcelain dome covering a food tray of the same material. Steak and vegetables, enough to feed at least six people. The man's voice burst from the adjoining room: 'Help yourself! The match is really hotting up. Your compatriot's in the lead again!' Startled, I said in answer: 'I thought he was losing.' 'He's making a comeback!' In a way I was pleased to be eating alone, the steak was excellent, I was worn out and it meant I could just concentrate on eating my fill. And that's what I did, rhythmic grunts and groans coming from the television, like a porn movie with the visuals turned off; several times I almost burst out laughing. It often happens to me, I always find it funny to shut my eyes and listen to the noises men make, but not with women – for me, the sounds women make during sex take on an added seriousness, sometimes even a frightening edge. I turned the plate over to see what kind of porcelain it was, porcelain is a fascination of mine, and this was an Ansbach, Swiss-German, very easy to find nowadays on eBay; I don't understand why people have begun selling it at such low prices. Looking up, I saw a series of copper pots and pans of all sizes hung on the wall ahead of me. Like an orchestra in its pit. I have a way of seeing such similarities. Once, on a tourist map of Bilbao I came across in a newspaper, I saw that the Guggenheim Museum is the same shape as a gun, a gun captured in the moment it fires a bullet, that is.

I didn't want to think about where that bullet would have ended up, or if it was even still in the air, yet to find its mark. I put down my knife and fork. I got up and went through into the living room. Sitting on the sofa with his back to me, he barely batted an eyelid, saying: 'Have a seat if you like, your compatriot's on the way to winning. If not, the billiards room and library are at the end

413

of this hall. Can I offer you a herbal tea, coffee, an aper-
itif? It's all homemade, all completely homemade.' 'No,
thank you,' I said, and went down the hall. The library
didn't have many literary works, but the ones it did have
seemed select to me; everything else was technical medical publications, principally on oncology. I picked up
a billiards cue and started hitting balls; I have no idea
of the rules of billiards, but there's something irresistible in the prospect of hitting things, especially round
things. In his tennis shoes, he padded in so quietly that
I didn't hear him come up behind me – I jumped when
he cried out: 'Nadal won!' Going over to the drinks cabinet, he took out a bottle of red wine, poured us both a
glass, and we said *santé* and drank. We sat down and he
asked me if I was interested in any of the books, and I
said lots of them; was he an oncologist, I asked? He nodded, but then added: 'Well, I was, now I spend my time
working the land around the castle.' He gestured to the
mud on his polo shirt, still drying. 'And you? Where's
your trip taking you?' 'I started in Honfleur and I'm
planning to walk to Juno, one of the D-Day landings
beaches, as I'm sure you know.' 'I see. And which way
are you planning on going?' 'The normal way,' I said,
'along the coast road.' Grimacing, he put his glass down
on the floor, got up and went over to a pile of magazines
on a shelf, extracting one and thumbing through it until
he found what he was looking for. 'Here,' he said, coming back over with it, 'it's an oncology journal, take a
look at this picture.'

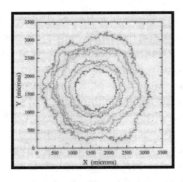

I looked at it for a few seconds, and when I looked up he explained: 'It's a representation of tumour growth, the technical details aren't the important thing here, just the lack of uniformity to the shapes tumours assume...' I had another look, as carefully as I could without having any idea what I was seeing, and he then turned a few pages and pointed me to another image.

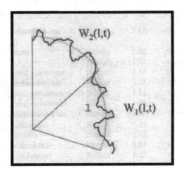

'This is the same outline of a tumour,' he went on, 'but magnified. See, the way tumours grow is fractal-like, tumours are fractals in motion, and that is my contribution to theoretical oncology. What do you think?' I said

415

nothing. Taking a seat again, he drank some of his wine and said: 'I first started thinking about tumours and fractals when, a long time ago now, I went on the same journey you're now undertaking. Knowing nothing, as I did then, I also went by foot, it was a photographic expedition, I wanted to take photographs of this coast, but I quickly realized that there was always a different way you could go, always another path down to the beaches and cliffs, always another photo to be taken, and with every footstep something tempting you to leave the road and explore every single metre of the coast, but inside every metre of the coast, and every one of its centimetres, there's another coast that, strictly speaking, is more of a coast, and inside this miniature coast, yet another coast, and so on in succession. And it then wasn't long before I remembered that Mandelbrot, the father of fractals, had first formulated these fantastical mathematical figures when thinking about what it would be like to walk along the coast of Britain, a line of thought he wrote about in his legendary article of 1967, "How Long Is the Coast of Britain?", published in the journal *Science*. The thing is, every centimetre of cliff bears within it another cliff that's infinitely large and identical in scale to its predecessor, and hence every coast is a fractal. This, as I say, is how Mandelbrot came up with fractals in 1967, a term he went on to coin in 1975, pretty shabby things by now given the abuse they've suffered at the hands of so many artists, who think they understand fractals but don't have the first clue, I can't stand artists who use fractals, I hope you're the same,' I nodded, for want of anything else to do, 'and then, while I was walking this coast, the idea came to me that tumours must also grow in a fractal-like way, it was a real eureka moment, pure thunderbolt from heaven, the kind of

416

idea that comes absolutely out of the blue, I went on taking photographs of the coast, metres at a time, zooming in on centimetres, millimetres, microns at a time, and every single photo looked exactly like the tumours I was so familiar with from studying samples under microscopes in the hospital, and then it came to me that I could try to come up with a mathematical model that would explain tumour growth in fractal terms, a model that has since been proved correct. Pretty amazing, don't you think? I've got the photos from that trip up in the attic, a hundred boxes or more, I had them printed out because I only trust things that decay, you know, paper, flesh, things like that, I can't put any faith in a bunch of pixels, bit of an oldie in that way, speaking of oldies, have you heard of the writer called W. G. Sebald?' Again I nodded, saying: 'Sebald wasn't old, though. He died quite young, in 2001, I think?' 'Well, yes, but in photos, with that big moustache and that serious look in his eye, there was something about him of bygone eras, but in any case, it doesn't matter... So, you will be familiar with one of his most famous books, *The Rings of Saturn*, in which he goes walking on his own along the coast of Suffolk, in Great Britain, a coastline that happens to be more or less straight across the water, on the other side of the Channel,' I nodded, and he went on, 'well, as you'll have read, then, Sebald goes on this walk, recounting the things he sees along the way, adding in bits of local history and the associations they produce in him, all accompanied with photos he takes as he goes, but none of it's as simple as it might seem: the story gets stuck, bogged down at different points, so it seems like he's never going to move on, though in the end he always does. Fine, the truth is I'd always considered this book of Sebald's a fractal in itself, which is to say that what the writer does is precisely to cover the same stretch of coast which Mandelbrot had already classed as the first ever fractal, but more than that, and what's truly significant about Sebald's book, the narration itself is fractal-like, I repeat, the narration itself is fractal-like. Sebald's style, the way he presents the facts and the history alike, is also a fractal, because he doesn't proceed in linear fashion like your usual itinerant storyteller, or like your usual writer either, stringing exceptional moments and more or less sentimental memories together, rather he approaches history and his own walking tour in a fractal-like fashion, folding it all together like a fractal, and this, as I say, was a thought I'd always had about that book, but it was on my walk along this part of the Normandy coastline when everything changed for me, when the stars aligned to such an extent that I can categorically state that my mathematical model on the fractal-like growth of tumours, which has now been proved correct in experiments in a multitude of laboratories across the world, was not Mandelbrot's work, but Sebald's, exactly that: it was Sebald who, with *The Rings of Saturn*, gave me that miraculous idea, and this is why I say to you, be very careful about the journey you're embarking on, because this coastline, like fractals, is infinite. Have you ever stopped to think of the infinity contained in every jeep and every abandoned tank you've surely seen along the coast, every deserted bunker, and in every one of these merry-go-rounds and Ferris wheels there're now so many of? Or the infinity contained in every rubbish bin on every promenade, every river stone, every Normandy sausage, every grain of sand and every pebble, every cow chewing cud in every one of the fields that run along the coast and every blade of grass in the ditches? Do you know? Do you know all this? Believe me, you may never reach your destination if you try it on foot, you may never reach that series of beaches renamed by the Allies: Juno, Utah, Omaha. In a car, or going by bus, that's different; you'd have no trouble getting there. But it's impossible on foot. If it's any consolation, and in spite of those beaches only being eighty kilometres from here, I've never managed to walk all the way. Do you understand what I'm trying to say? Do you? Not me, not anyone – no one's ever managed it. What's more, it's my view that the German defeat was because of exactly this: they were trying to hold a series of beaches which, technically, are infinitely big at the same time as being infinitely small. Do you see?'

By the time I'd nodded three or four times, he'd poured me another glass of wine, and got up, gone over to the bookshelves, put the journal back where he'd got it from, and come back over with a copy of *The Rings of Saturn*, which he opened to reveal pages heavily annotated with observations and maths formulae as well, all of it incomprehensible to me, while pointing to these pages and exclaiming: 'See, see, exactly what I was saying, all fractals, I've got it all written down here,' and he held the book in one hand, used the other to turn the pages, while, I'm not sure how, using yet another hand to drink with. There was so much formerly white space now covered in his jottings that it struck me his copy would be double the weight of my own, which was on one of the bookshelves at my home and barely thumbed given the fact, though I didn't dislike this UK-based German author, the fascination felt by so many had never knocked at my door. I asked if I could smoke, now it was his turn to nod, and, not taking his eyes off the book, he passed me an ashtray, waiting until I'd lit my cigarette before going on: 'I made an incredible discovery recently.' 'Oncological, you mean, to do with smoking?' 'No,' he said, 'a literary discovery.' 'Another one?' 'Yes, another one, and even more significant. I'll tell you it if you think you're ready?' 'Yes, yes, I'm ready.' 'Okay, here it comes: all the photos in Sebald's books are taken from inside a car.' 'What?' I said, genuinely taken aback. 'Just that, I don't know if Sebald travelled on foot or by car, I'm not commenting on that because it does actually seem to me that his writing was born out of journey on foot, that kind of thing comes through, the effort involved in a long walk affects the writing in some way, in the same way the effort someone puts in on the tennis court comes through in the way they strike the ball, but his photos are taken from a car, there's absolutely no doubt, you only need to look at the angle they've been taken from and triangulate it with the vanishing point to see that, if they'd been taken by someone standing up, that person would have to be a dwarf or a child, and Sebald was over six foot tall, plus there are some where you can make out squashed mosquitos on the car windscreen; there are even marks from windscreen wipers in some of the pictures.' 'I can't believe it,' I said, and I really couldn't. 'Well, believe it,' he said, 'I'm gathering a big body of evidence, but I don't and won't ever want to go public with it, there'd be all sorts of idiots wanting to use it to discredit Sebald, and nothing could be further from my intentions, for me it's a game, a way of keeping my mind active, the winters in Normandy are long and cold, I have to find something to distract myself. Plus none of what I'm saying actually does undermine Sebald as a writer, quite the opposite, in my eyes it makes him greater still, that's the greatness of all good literature, not only can it make us see things that don't exist, but things we'd be hard pressed to even dream up.'

I acted unaffected. To change the subject, I asked about Rafa Nadal's victory, and after half an hour in which he asked me what Nadal was like as a person, and what it had been like the first time I met the tennis player, and about the way Nadal used his right hand to shake yours, and if I had pretended to be left-handed in order to feel for myself the legendary power of his left hand, and such things about which he was so insistent I felt I had no option but to respond to them with absurd fabrications, seeing as I've never met the Mallorcan tennis player, I claimed I was tired and went up to my room. 'Take your drink, dear, take your drink,' he said. I left him playing billiards against himself, though from the force with which he struck the ball I should say he was playing against the rules of the game of billiards itself. I locked my door behind me and got straight into bed, though not before turning the mobile phone on and checking the battery. Between the sheets, the material of which was frankly abrasive, I thought that if the coastlines on either side of the Channel were mirrors of one another, then that made me the reflection of the walk which, across the sea, years before, Sebald had undertaken, I was his late reflection, his latter day self, a latter day W. G. Sebald, and in my attempt to dispel this thought, another came to mind, more troubling still: that of the dying soldier in the photograph from 1915, lying beneath the reproduction of *Las Meninas* in the bed I was now trying to get to sleep in, and, feeling afraid then, I got up and unlocked the door, and as I got back into bed I remembered a story a friend of mine once told me, a friend with a brother much older than her: she had come out of the cinema one day and run into a man she knew but hadn't seen in a long time, and, to her surprise, this

421

man had a son with him, a boy no older than six. She'd immediately been struck by the resemblance between the boy and her older brother, who, naturally enough, she had never seen when he was that age except for in photographs. To be standing in front of her brother as a small boy, to have him there in the flesh, gave her the feeling of penetrating another childhood, of making contact with a person completely unknown to her. For the few minutes they spoke in the cinema entrance, she felt – she told me – she had travelled to a moment in time previous to her own birth. It made her so dizzy she almost fell over on the pavement. Is this not then a projectile, I said to myself, before closing my eyes, a bullet that, fired into the air, comes down again years afterwards? There are such things that, paradoxically, arrive out of the past and impact us for all that we're yet to arrive in their future.

8.
The next morning, the hotelier had blue overalls on, patched at the elbows and knees, instead of his tennis whites. The breakfast, which had a large offering of fruits and salads but not much coffee, was otherwise unremarkable. Before I set out, having given me tips on restaurants, picnic areas by the sea and numerous shortcuts that might be of use, and asking me to pass on his best wishes to Nadal, he said good luck. With fewer inclines and bends than the previous day, it was immediately easier going on the road, with low grass on either side coated at that early hour with dew so white that it made you want to gather some in a bottle and drink it. You could see at least 100 kilometres out across the Channel, where the tankers going up and down the

shipping lane looked like fridge magnets. I kept seeing roadkill, a Citroën passed me with the windows down, 'Strangers in the Night' on the radio, sung by a voice in French whose 'r's' sounded like they were coming from the engine. The beaches here had fist-sized pebbles rather than sand, the tide was out half a mile, and I couldn't help but think about history, in the form of these pebbles, being shifted up and down the coast, to my eyes already tumour-like and yet very beautiful nonetheless. Aeroplanes flew overhead – their paths cross less populated areas, people say, so that if they crash fewer people will die – and their contrails lingered for hours, an indicator of the low temperatures at the altitudes they were flying at, while, down where I was, my body was a machine generating plenty of heat. My idea was to sleep the night in a castle he and I had stayed in, a 30 kilometre-walk away, which meant keeping up a decent pace. There was nothing obstructing the keen wind, but it whistled and whispered by, creating sounds that seemed like words; I kept on hearing the word 'marine', and started repeating it to myself. Maybe this was how language was born, I thought: with a restless wind which mouths then started to imitate. I know I came past people, but now when I close my eyes and remember that part of the walk, I see nobody. It wasn't the first time this had happened to me: there had been a period of quite a few months when, trying to remember the trip to Berne, I couldn't see any humans present except for us. Images of the Einstein Museum came back to me strongly, which, with all its staircases and mirrors, had seemed to me a genuine Piranesi labyrinth, but in my memory the streets of Berne itself were so empty that it was like we'd found ourselves in an inverse future where Switzerland was the only country that hadn't been neutral, and its population had been wiped out in germ warfare. I remember a set of footprints across a snow-covered athletics track, a single set of footsteps but, like everything in Switzerland, not in the slightest bit dramatic, and accompanied by the tyre tracks from a bicycle; it could legitimately have passed for a musical score. I can also recall the two of us going up the Piranesi stairs in the Einstein Museum, or perhaps I should say going down, and, in the first room we came to, stopping in front of a cluster of stones that looked like cooled magma, all told the size of a football, in a display cabinet. At the centre of those stones was a further cluster of half-broken porcelain vessels, which I could immediately see were of the highest quality. So embedded in the stone were they that it was as though they'd sprouted and grown from inside it.

We read in the museum hand-outs that these were rocks from Hiroshima that had been melted together when the atomic bomb hit, before the shock waves flung them in together with all manner of different domestic objects, with which they in turn melted. Another stand displayed drawings by child survivors at Hiroshima on a digital screen; this was overwhelmingly sad, while at

424

the same time you had to laugh at the curator's intentions. Everything in that country was so un-collateral, so merely substitutive of another thing; one thing is replaced by something else and the replacement is so perfect that nothing new is ever generated. Nonetheless, there was something else that caught my attention. I had been in China some years before, in the city of Jingdezhen, the cradle of porcelain; I was there studying its manufacture. Chinese porcelain is unusual for the way it uses calcined bone ash, which, mixed with china clay, gives whatever it's made into its characteristic colour, a white so pure that the pieces have a translucency when held up to the light but at the same time are marked with veins, blots and smears, as though someone had left tracks inside the snow of the material. 'That bone ash is the reason you see "bone china" on the undersides of some plates and cups in England,' I had said to him, over the scalding hot coffees with cream we'd had on leaving the Einstein Museum. 'It was the British who brought the technique from China to Europe, and they imported the bone itself from the Far East, believing as they did that the diets in different countries gave Chinese animal bones a better quality of calcium phosphate and its derivatives than the bones of British animals, which in turn made the porcelain not only whiter and more translucent but tougher as well, more break-resistant. This was one factor in the establishment of a vigorous porcelain market, buoyed by all the money washing around from coal mining and the sugar trade, and an emerging British middle class who went crazy for exotic Asian goods. To meet the demand, hundreds of boats started sailing the London to Shanghai route, and that was when you also saw the first ever factory boats, something which, as you know, is very common today in the fishing industry, where catches are packaged and deep-frozen on board the ship, and in textiles too, where you get clothes being prepared on board the boats that go back and forth constantly between China and Europe, so that when they arrive at our ports the sections of fabric have been stitched together but not yet made into finished garments, and thereby avoid import tariffs due on saleable products, but, as I say, these factory boats were already in operation by about 1860. I don't know how many conscript-workers from across the colonies would have shovelled Chinese animal bones into furnaces on board those boats as they sailed between Shanghai and London. And neither the boats nor the furnaces, once they'd left port, would have docked anywhere along the way, and if the wind was blowing from the east the smell of charred bones would announce their arrival in London several days in advance, and with that the artisans in Essex would start getting their moulds ready and firing up their kilns. And, whereas our civilization now prizes gold, grain and water above everything else, in those days it was coal, fire and bone. Another thing was that London society at the time was intrigued by the exploration of Africa, especially à la mode after the disappearance of Doctor Livingstone somewhere near Lake Tanganyika, a disappearance that soon became something of a cause célèbre, to the extent that in 1869 *The New York Herald* dispatched a journalist to track Livingstone down. The journalist in question was the incredibly tenacious Henry Stanley, whose reputation as a survivor preceded him: born as John Rowlands to an impoverished family in Wales, he was abandoned as a baby and spent his childhood in orphanages and workhouses, including the St. Asaph Union Workhouse, where, when he was between the ages of ten

426

and fifteen, his mother and brothers were also present without any of them ever realising. He was physically abused and forced to go down the coalmines, and lost most of his teeth before entering his teens because of all the sugar he was made to consume. He went on to have all manner of problems with his remaining teeth, to the point that, years afterwards, on receiving his first decent wage, and even before going out to buy the sort of clothes he had always envied, he invested in one of the first ever sets of false teeth in Great Britain. But long before that, at the age of eighteen, and with the aim of making his fortune, he boarded a boat in Liverpool bound for the USA. The moment New Orleans came into view, in his excitement, he jumped from the boat and swam the rest of the way to shore. It was in New Orleans where his renaissance really occurred, thanks to a cotton trader at the port he took employment with, on whose suggestion he changed his name to the one by which we now know him, Henry Stanley, as a way of making a definitive break with his past. He was then drawn into the American Civil War, travelled as a correspondent with British troops to Abyssinia and Alexandria, and was sent to Spain to cover the downfall of Isabel II, going on to become such a consummate Spanish speaker that he was later the leading correspondent for the English-speaking world on the Carlist wars. And it was while in Madrid that *The New York Herald* commissioned him to go in search of Doctor Livingstone in Central Africa. Stanley recounts in his memoir, *How I Found Livingstone*, that when the telegram came he was in the busy Calle de la Cruz, just next to the Puerta del Sol, where he was renting an apartment in a building on the ground floor of which there is now a bar called The Ear. Remember when we went there last year and had grilled pigs' ears?

The metre-high flames shooting up off the grill, and you saying the bar was going to go up in flames, me saying that all of Madrid was going to go up in flames, you that it would be the whole of Europe, and us laughing and eating; those pigs' ears really were delicious. And we got the bill, and when the waiter brought the receipt, the telegram Stanley had received in that very place came to mind, it was as though the waiter was handing it to me. "Act according to your own plans, and do what you think best," the editor of *The New York Herald* wrote, "but find Livingstone!" Stanley immediately set about the task, though his first port of call was London, where he went to retrieve two items he claimed were of the utmost importance. When asked what two items could warrant delaying his departure, he wouldn't answer. He made the trip back to the British capital, retrieved the two objects that only he knew about, stowed them in a chest, and then went back to Spain via Paris, and, with a considerable amount of money at his disposal and a team of some 120 men – some porters, some soldiers – crossed the Mediterranean and made the month-long journey overland to Lake Tanganyika, further proof of Stanley's toughness given that explorers like Burton, Speke and Livingstone himself had taken three times as long to cover the same distance. Many of the men died along the way, both in accidents and from a variety of ailments, the main one being a bacterial infection which starts out in the roots of the teeth, breaking them down before moving onto the gums, so that it becomes impossible to eat and you end up dying of starvation. Stanley managed to keep his false teeth which, I don't think I've told you, were made from porcelain, the strongest bone china in the United Kingdom; the locals give him the nickname Bula Matari, which literally translates as "he who breaks stones with his teeth". In November 1871, Dr Livingstone, who wasn't actually lost at all and wanted nothing from the continent he'd left behind, since he'd created a cult – to himself – among the locals and was being waited on hand and foot, was notified by two of his followers that a white man and a party carrying the United States flag were approaching. The rest is well known. As Stanley puts it in his memoirs, both men removed their hats, shook hands, and he came out with the line, "Dr Livingstone, I presume." "Yes," came the laconic reply. This is nonetheless clearly a fabrication, an attempt to narrate the meeting in accordance with Victorian archetypes, to present the story to British society as the triumph of British dignity however squalid, both materially and morally, the situation. In fact, the locals present had a different account: Stanley and Livingstone, they said, did indeed take their hats off and shake hands, but then, to the surprise of all present, and as if some strange baton were being passed from one to the other, Stanley said: "Give me the fire," to which, with their hands still clasped, Livingstone replied: "Take the fire", and less than an hour later flames were seen on the horizon. And Africa's on fire, and it's been on fire ever since. If you could look at a real-time map of Africa, you'd see a fire that goes on spreading all the time, the astronauts tell us so, and there's satellite imagery to confirm it. Geographers put it down to the natural combustion of a continent high in oxygen, very high in combustible materials and with propitious temperatures, but the history of Africa, the history as told by the people of the continent, has a very different explanation: this handshake was all it took – this closing of the colonial circle and this realization that, for the West, nowhere was off limits now – for a fire to start somewhere in

Africa that has been burning ever since. It also holds that this fire was referenced in centuries-old oral traditions, with prophecies of a man from the Cold World landing, becoming lost on their shores, and later being rescued by another man of the same colour skin, and that in the moment when the two men came into physical contact, a fire would be sparked somewhere nearby with the coming into contact of two blades of grass, the two blades exactly the same size and of the same species, two blades as commonplace as twins, you could say, which are obliterated on contact by a fire that will never go out. This is the real reason for the legendary hostility of African peoples to Westerners, not a fear of subjection and the consequent loss of culture, but the irruption of a fire which, they know, can never be extinguished. And African history also has something to say about us Westerners – we often forget that Africans also write, also observe, also have their own sociology, physics and anthropology, their own history of ideas and Big Bang and end of days, though they call them different names. In fact, they say that there's an equivalent in the West for this fire, and it is the money we use; better put, it is our markets and all the transactions that make them up which, just like the fires in Africa, will always be in existence, such that, while they simultaneously constitute it, slowly but surely they are laying waste to our Western society. So it goes, every time somebody buys or sells an object, every tim: there's an exchange of goods and every time you take money out of a bank and are charged a fee, in their view this is an onward transfer of the fire in which we Westerners are forever burning, our own particular "give me the fire, take the fire": greed. Cases such as the atomic bomb in Hiroshima are, in the view of African historians, paradigmatic of the fire in which we find ourselves; they see it as an exchange of money so brutal that there isn't any way for it *not* to create real fire, fire made real, a real transubstantiation of money into fire, and this is the moment in which we see an overlap between history according to Africans and history according to us; they become equivalent the moment in which our money turns to fire and their fire becomes our money. But African history also relates that following the greeting – "take the fire, give me the fire" – the two men withdrew to a cabin, since Livingstone wanted to drink a toast to his compatriot, and he then took out a bottle of spirits and some dust-covered glasses, at which Stanley said to him: "Dr Livingstone, put those glasses away. Before setting out on this expedition, I went to London specifically so that, when this moment came, we could use these," and he took two goblets of highest quality porcelain out of the little chest. Livingstone went over to the window, held them up to the light of the African sunset, turned them over, read the words "bone china" on the bases, and declared: "This porcelain also has a fire inside it," to which Stanley responded: "A fire small but eternal." Pouring a glass each, they drank a toast to the health of the Queen, and to all the bones ever to have turned to dust in the world. Anyway, I'm telling you all of this because I saw "bone china" on the bases of some of those porcelain pieces in the Hiroshima rocks at the museum, and there was a moment when I thought about the bone ash that porcelain must have inside it, and about all the bones of the people of Hiroshima which those rocks would have inside them in turn, the bones of animals, women and men which, indistinguishable now, make the exhibition actually worthwhile. It also means that Hiroshima itself, in being flattened by the bomb, thereby becomes the great porcelain artefact of the West, our definitive piece of porcelain, and,' I said, 'these were thoughts that genuinely horrified me.' And I don't know if it was the right thing to tell him all of this on coming away from the Einstein Museum, but from then on and for the duration of our stay in Berne, he started checking the undersides of every single porcelain plate, cup and jug that was placed before him to see if they had "bone china" written on them, a mania to add to his attempts, which I've already mentioned, to prove that Marx and Einstein were one and the same person. And so we stayed on in Berne for a couple more days, a place where, as I say, in my memory there's nobody but him and me, empty restaurants, empty museums, empty parks, empty streets and a lot of footprints in the snow, footprints that clearly weren't our own. We saw them every morning from the window of our aparthotel, and we wondered why the wind and snow in the night hadn't swept them away. We were quick to go out and have a closer look; we even took photos of them: all the footprints were the same, made by a pair of large boots so rectangular that the only way you could tell which direction their owner had been walking was by the position of the heel. I reached a point of wondering if they might all have been made by the same individual, a silly thought, one I recounted to him and instantly regretted since, just as instantly, it prompted in him the idea that not only Marx and Einstein but sometimes throughout a city, for determined periods at a time, all the people are one and the same person, 'Indeed,' he said, 'at this moment all the inhabitants of Berne are just one person, one single piece of flesh and one single set of bones, but we don't know who that person is,' and, years later, on my own in Normandy, wearing a pair of boots that were also rectangular, after leaving the Rafa Nadal fan's castle

432

and watching the waves lap at the shore and hearing the wind's ululation which to my ear sounded like the word 'marine', I also can't remember seeing a single soul, as though the world had reconfigured itself in order that, for the space of a few hours, I was the only person on planet Earth, and it was then that, for the second time, the thought occurred: 'When I get to the shore, what message am I going to leave on your answerphone?'

9.

I passed an intersection outside a town whose name did not make it sound inviting, it was midday but I didn't stop to eat. The trick to avoid getting tired is to keep your eyes on your feet, to look no further than the half-metre radius directly around you, to disregard the fact of any horizon; a point comes when you forget that it's you doing the walking and the road starts doing all the work: it slips by for you. Only in the inevitable occasional glance to either side of me did sparse houses appear, or farms rather, with islands of trees enclosing them, cork oaks and pines mainly, the product of reforestation efforts so successful that these trees could be said to be indigenous by now, and more loud birdsong, tones increasingly distinct from the sound of the microwaves in Honfleur. The birds fell quiet for moments at a time, and that was when I noticed a smell of silage and fertilizer, no doubt coming from silt traps and manure tanks I couldn't see. I caught sight of a barn in the distance that had a semi-cylindrical roof and the look of an aircraft hangar. A control tower soon came into view alongside it, a vestige of a network of small airports no bigger than bus stations created by the German army in 1942, and nowadays used for private local flights. The control tower had a black, concave radar which, as it rotated, went from looking like a half-moon to a sphere tapering at either end to a plain rectangle. I thought of a very black Earth, the planet burned to a crisp, and though it obviously meant losing some time I decided to go down the recently asphalted section of road that led to it, which gave off that smell of fossils brought back to life common in all petrol derivatives, always particularly strong at petrol stations – any time I stop to fill up, I pause and breathe it in, this being the yearning for fire we all of have inside ourselves: a match in my mouth at that moment and the whole place would have gone up in flames. Ushered along by neatly kept cypress trees on either side, I walked up to the airport doors, which opened automatically at my approach, and through them I went into a small lounge and ticket hall with the sun pouring in through a large glazed roof. There was nobody there. You could see the runway through windows at the far end. I went over to them, passing small car-hire stands all of which had their shutters down and 'Fermé' signs out. The ticket desks were also deserted. Reaching the floor-to-ceiling windows, I looked out at the runway, which was in perfect condition, no trace of any weeds and no cracks in the concrete either. Some cows were chewing away in an adjacent field. A strange sight the two of us had seen four years earlier came to mind: we were approaching Mont Saint-Michel, me checking the roadmaps, when I felt him put his foot on the brake; only when he gave an incredulous 'Look!' did I lift my eyes from the map, and there in front of us was a huge mass of cows silhouetted against the monastery hill beyond. We sat looking quietly out, I don't know how long for, before going on, neither of us ever mentioned the scene again, and now, the two cows in the field beside the runway

434

made me see the airport also as a monastery, and I felt sure that in centuries to come Japanese and Russian tourists would flock to see this passenger lounge, a place from which, I sensed, people would board planes bound for destinations from which they'd never return. I put my rucksack down, took a seat on a bench, the runway outside shone gold in the mid-afternoon sun like a strip of meat in the oven, I hiked my skirt up to get a bit of sun on my thighs. There was a newspaper on my right, presumably discarded by someone passing through the airport, with a headline about a column of at least five thousand Syrian refugees making their way north across Europe on foot, they had just passed the city of Berne which, one of the women in the group had told the journalist, they'd found 'completely deserted', adding further down that: 'Not even when they saw us approaching would the people of Berne have fled en masse.' I picked up the paper's Sunday supplement, and found, after the cosmetics section, the gossip columns and horoscopes, a short piece on the writer Stefan Zweig, whose dual suicide along with his second wife, Lotte Altmann, in Brazil in 1942 had caused dismay among the intellectuals of the day. It also talked about recent findings from one of his diaries which confirmed that he had been an exhibitionist, that he used to go out to parks at night in a trench coat and expose himself to young women. The compulsion was so strong that he also used to do it at parties with friends, none of whom suspected the compulsion of extending to a more public arena. The article also had a photograph of Zweig and his wife Altmann lying together in a bed. They were both fully clothed, lying face up with mouths slightly open and holding hands. I was struck by the gentle way their fingers were interlaced, suggestive of a very deep bond. I then saw that it was a police photograph of them on their deathbed. I put the supplement down. The only difference between a murder and a suicide, I said to myself, is that it's impossible to hide one's own body. The sun had barely moved, my thighs were beginning to resemble those of a fried chicken, the sky full of vapour trails, none coming in my direction. I drank some of my water and decided to set off again. A final look at the empty runway brought to mind another runway, also empty, and extremely famous: the one that comes at the end of *Casablanca*. I had a longstanding interest in the film's surprising and rarely commented on images which, right from the opening scenes, contain a simmering story of real violence. I mean the real footage of the Second World War that's included, filmed in no other place than the Normandy coast. Tanks rolling across Europe while entire families, mounded up on carts with luggage and bedding, flee. Indeed, when I think about the film now, it isn't the star-crossed lovers of Ingrid Bergman and Humphrey Bogart my thoughts are drawn to, but all of the real-life people, the ones fleeing. The archive images come back in at another point, this time with footage of Paris: we see a flashback of Bergman's and Bogart's romance in that place. The studio montage consists of the two of them, filmed on the Warner Brothers set, pretending to be sailing along the Seine, while real images play in the background of one of the bridges across that Paris river. And I, there in my Normandy airport, thought about how intriguing I found that Paris bridge. I recalled the tale of Frida Kahlo's trip to the French capital in 1939, where a retrospective of her work was supposed to be held, something she and André Breton had arranged. It became clear the moment she got there that Breton's promise had been quite empty. Neither did

that group of surrealists have a gallery in which to hold
the exhibition, nor had a hotel been organized, so that
she had to stay in Breton's home, where she would share
a room with his youngest daughter. It's beyond Frida
how the French can live in apartments so miniscule in
comparison with those in Mexico and the US. The tiny
tables in the cafes also stand out to her, and how the people crowd around them like they were crystal balls. It's
January, it's cold, Frida can't stand the cold, and her foot
and back hurt; her terrible health problems rear up once
more. At this point she makes it clear, in no uncertain
terms, that she is not a surrealist painter, an aesthetic
trend whose proponents she immediately declares good-
for-nothings, slackers, layabouts and cafe-residing
tittle-tattlers. In her words: 'These lunatic sons of bitches that are the surrealists'. She wanders Paris on her
own. In Notre Dame she lights candles for her husband
Diego Rivera, her sister Cristina, for Trotsky, for her
New York lover, Nick, and for herself because – she says
– fire may be extinguished but it never grows old. In the
Jardin du Luxembourg she feels the lack of the three
children she miscarried; she often sits there for hours.
These visits lead her to write the lines: 'Painting has
filled my days. I have lost three children and many other
things that might have done the same in this terrible life.
Painting has been the substitute for all of it. I think there
is no better thing than to work.' With nothing to occupy
her in Paris, she comes up with the idea of making a corset to ease her back problems. She doesn't want to ask a
Parisian orthopaedist to make it: she doesn't trust them;
she can do it herself. Shutting herself in Breton's daughter's room, she says she doesn't want to be disturbed.
The daughter has to sleep on the sofa for several nights.
Taking inspiration from the girl's children's books, she

decides the corset ought to have joints similar to the ribs of certain extinct reptiles, and that it ought to go from the neck all the way down to the groin, where it will attach to the legs by leather straps. It isn't long before she's created a prototype using hemp string and splints fashioned from the blinds, which she simply tears down from the bedroom window – when Breton sees this, he flies into a rage and says from now on it's her who's going to be sleeping on the sofa. Frida couldn't care less, the only thing that matters now is the corset. She goes for a walk to try it out, strapping the contraption tight across her hips and chest. It does help, but comes apart when she's gone no more than half a mile. In her annoyance, standing on the bank of the Seine, she throws the thing in a public bin. The corset will go up in flames a number of days later when a lightning bolt hits the metal bin – a storm that the Breton family and Frida watch together from the apartment window, and which marks a turning point in her relationship with old, domesticated Europe: 'The natural world can be savage here as well.' Not until the following day does she learn that the corset has been burned: deciding she wants to put it back together again, she goes down to get it, and finds the remains still smouldering. She later goes on to say that those embers prompted a powerful vision in her of the propagation of flesh from one body to another, a vision she returns to at different points throughout the rest of her life. And I, in the deserted Normandy airport, with its runway also empty and its four cows having turned and started to wander away, remembered Frida Kahlo and the scene in *Casablanca* with Bogart and Bergman on their boat and the archive images of a bridge over the Seine behind them. Some-one is walking across the bridge. It's Frida Kahlo. Her silhouette exits the shot to the left, on its way, we can suppose, to the bin containing the still-smouldering corset. And I was then drawn to the idea of those two women, the fictional one and the real-life one, the one who, on a runway in the city of Casablanca, won't permit herself to fully unleash her enthusiasm for a social convention, and the one who, facing down an entire army of surrealists, makes a corset with which to heal herself. I thought about the moment when, on the screens of their lives, they passed one another but didn't recognize who the other was. If one had passed the baton to the other, perhaps nothing would have been the same again. For now they remain indissolubly fused but at the same time know nothing about each other. Somewhat similar, I said to myself, to those pieces of bone china indissolubly fused with the rocks from Hiroshima, a contact that nonetheless does nothing to break down the two things' natures, which remain utterly at odds. I walked towards the exit. Up above, the vapour trails had proliferated; if it carried on like that there would be more vapour trails than sky. As I passed one of the car-hire stands, a telephone started to ring, a landline by the sound and volume of it. I cast around, expecting somebody to suddenly appear. I went over and put my hand on the receiver; I was going to pick up but at the last moment thought better of it, and hurried on to the door, which slid open just as precisely and courteously as it had when I came in. As I started down the asphalt path the telephone was still ringing.

10.

I got back on the main road again, which gradually turned a washed out grey. The ditches also took on a different aspect, roads and ditches being two natural features that must always correlate. A group of seagulls in a field pecked at something on the ground, though I couldn't see what, and they didn't so much as flinch when I passed by. A flock of the same birds turned raucous circles over the sea, there must have been a shoal in the water. In the kilometres that followed, the sea horizon turned so murky that I was sure nobody would be able to see the coast of Great Britain from my coast, after that the walking turned monotonous and I wished I at least had the stones from before with their red flecks of seaweed to look at. A little while earlier, other, more commonplace layers of geology had started to emerge: granite mainly, seamed with quartz, which would have made life hard for the German sappers tasked with creating bunkers like the ones I soon started to see. These had the air of half-finished Easter Island effigies. The buildings in our cities are supported by a skeleton of pillars, vectors plunging vertically into the ground, reaching towards the centre of the earth, while bunkers are a compact, unitary mass, like a loaf of concrete bread baked just once and in a single mould and, more significant than that, they go in no particular direction, and are apparently unaffected by the earth's movements, if an earthquake hit they'd simply roll over on themselves until they came into a new stability, a new equilibrium: they could soon be re-inhabited again. Bunkers are more like a cork bobbing around on water than something actually built on the ground. And I hopped down at one point and tried to get inside one of these bunkers, but there was a heavy steel door with padlocks blocking my way – the padlocks covered in marker-pen declarations of love. The concrete had turned so black – due to the proximity to the sea, and the sea winds – that it had come to resemble rock. An absurd piece of graffiti on

440

one of the bunker sides gave me the idea that in places where there's been a lot of death, it often means the triggering of even more absurd mechanisms of forgetting. And, the thing is, the only things to have been inside these bunkers since the war were rats, worms and flies. Nobody had ever bothered to drag the dead Germans out of the bunkers, and that had led to some unique mutations taking place in the animals and insects also inhabiting them, which had, decades later, led to some very insightful studies on the part of entomologists in a frenzy of erudition. How far must a war spread before it can be termed a 'world' war, I asked myself as I stood in front of the bunker door. Maybe, I thought, it's when the war begins to have an effect on places entirely removed from the causes of the conflict. The existence of the internet, and the worldwide reach of telecommunications, has meant that all wars, however domestic, have, ipso facto, become 'world' wars. War, however, can spread unexpectedly not only in the continuum of space but in time as well: just then, a fly appeared from under the bunker door, not very large but of a shimmering green I'd never in my life seen before; the war had been brought to me, now, in the current moment, by this fly, which was doubtless an inheritor of the rotten flesh of the people who died there in 1944. I nudged it with the tip of my boot and it flew up until it came level with my eyes, then dropped back down under its own weight, before, with a movement that reminded me of that young would-be magician in Osaka, suddenly flying up and out of sight. Around the bunker, low vegetation covered the many shell craters – you could see these from various dips and concavities in the covering of grass and scrub. To me it seemed undeniably true that all this before me was holding back any possibility of a full and autonomous life, an existence above and beyond us humans, and I thought how unnecessary we are to flies, rats, scrub and stones, and to the dead as well – none of these things need us, we simply invent connections to them, like or dislike, where no connections in fact exist. I had seen a few months earlier that 2016 was the year of Aristotle, since it was the 2,400th anniversary of his birth, but is it really possible to talk about the anniversary of a birth that happened so archaeologically long ago? How can the exact year of Aristotle's birth be known? It can't. We make it up. That birth happened so long ago that it now exists outside of time. We're forever anthropologizing. It's a little like the quotations attributed to famous people on the internet: ninety-eight per cent of these are incorrect, and it makes as much sense to attribute them to those women and men as it does to the corpses populating these bunkers or the flies that come buzzing off them and land next to our feet, made-up quotations that only succeed in creating a somewhat coherent representation of the past, which is the same as saying they project a convincing hologram of the future; we look for certainty, we die in fear, that's all there is. It then seemed very clear to me that war filters through everything, not just through geological layers but botanical, biological and even informational layers; a veritable network of war is spread out below the ground on which we stand. Deciding I ought to get a move on, I turned and walked away from that concrete casket, with its surfeit of flies and worms, which is the same, paradoxically, as saying a surfeit of life. My feet were sore, I was thirsty but my water had run out, I wished it was still early in the day so I could rip up a clump of grass and lick the dew to quench my thirst. I still hadn't seen a single car go by. Down in one of the bays, in a square half-mile uncovered by the outgoing tide, a few men, little more than silhouettes, were busy with what I guessed were oyster nurseries. I hadn't until then noticed these, in a sense, mollusc factories beneath the surface, a grid of metal compartments that can only be accessed twice a day when the moon drags the water down and away from the land. At that moment tractors and heavy machinery were being used, they were going around selecting and gathering up molluscs, the men carried hoes, rakes and various tools specifically for the task, the whole thing looked like a boat was being disembarked, or rather a practice-run for a boat being disembarked. The grey of the wet sand was surprisingly similar to that of the bunkers I'd just seen, as though there was a cement platform reaching all the way from Great Britain, underneath the sea and up. I kept going – I've learned from experience that if your feet start hurting, it's best not to stop, not to let the blisters settle, you've got to punish those blisters for them to let you go on walking. I patted my jacket pocket, checking the mobile phone was still there, before turning it on: 100 per cent battery. And possibly because of the bunker I'd been looking at, another bunker came to mind, another one full of a surfeit of life, namely Noah's Ark in the picture I'd seen in an encyclopaedia we had in the house when I was small, in which a grounded boat teetered at the peak of a mountain that appeared completely cut off: the Ark a reservoir of species saved in the Bible, the Normandy bunker a reservoir of mutated species, and both entirely adrift from the course of natural history. The caption for the picture in that Espasa Calpe encyclopaedia read: 'Noah's Ark on Mt. Ararat'. Below, it said that the picture was a detail from a map made in 1422 by one Leonardo Dati, part of his popular book *The Sphere*, which was written in ottava rima and comprised accounts of journeys around the world as Dati knew it. Mount Ararat, the highest peak in Turkey, lies near the borders with Iran and Armenia, and is a dormant volcano whose perpetually snow-capped peaks stand more than 5,000 metres above sea level. It is the symbol of the Armenian people. As Wikipedia puts it: 'It is claimed that a large "anomalous" shape at the summit could be Noah's Ark, according to research carried out by Porcher Taylor on satellite images taken in 1955. The "anomaly" (a structural abnormality not common to a mountain) shown in these images is 309 metres long, which would tally with the 300 x 50 cubits the Ark is described as measuring in the Book of Genesis.' Astronauts also claim to have seen these shapes. This kind of thing may be satellites' and astronauts' best-kept secrets, and by this I mean not what they see when they are up in space and look into outer space – the contents of which has no importance except for in novels, films and comics – but what they see when they look down at Earth, at our home, the only thing that actually has any impact on us. The day they feel compelled to say what the Earth is truly like from so far away, we won't even be able to believe it, we'll go higher and higher but only in order to look back down, down into the centre of ourselves. And I suddenly thought: a picture of anything terrestrial, by the mere fact of representing something on Earth, in that same moment becomes very real, akin to a photograph. Whereas any photograph of outer space, by the mere fact of showing something that is not the Earth, instantly becomes a drawing, and a drawing always remains fiction. And after that I focused on the rectangular shape of my boots and the shore, where the tide was coming in, meaning the moon was getting closer.

444

11.

I arrived in a town I hadn't been in before, and which to all appearances seemed uninhabited; it would have been early evening. A plain, unadorned square broke off into four streets lined with houses, the cement frontages of which, in charming contrast with the stone, were painted lime green. A banner between two street corners marked the finish line for a cycle race. I passed a mechanics, closed, and a field with a pair of work horses that appeared to be sleeping standing up, and then a church with a granite relief depicting a kind of mythological animal, also seemingly asleep, the horizontal stretch of its body providing an elegant strut between two small rooftops. I heard voices playing on a radio or television echoing from inside a building with a sign saying 'Bar' above the door, and went over to it. Behind the bar, a very overweight woman was eating mussels while watching a game of tennis; she squeezed lemon directly into the shells before knocking them back. With no break in this operation, she asked what I wanted. Why the question took me by surprise, I don't know; 'Nestea,' I said. I sat down, she brought me the can more or less straightaway, it was ice cold, and she went back to her mussels, which she continued to prise open without taking her eyes off the television. Novak Djokovic was winning against Rafa Nadal. I got comfortable in the chair and, though I don't really like Nestea, took a long swig while looking over a wall calendar with nitrates propaganda on it and advice for rearing livestock. The bar lady went on watching the tennis ball go back and forth and saying things to herself that I didn't understand. 'Do you want Djokovic or Nadal win?' I asked. 'Nadal, always Nadal; we're great fans of him around here,' she said, and, still not turning to look at me, added:

'Have you met him?' 'No, no,' I hastened to answer. 'I have,' she said, 'he visited on the anniversary of D-Day. He went to Juno and did his big whack.' 'His what?' 'He brought his best tennis racket with him and a special ball, one he'd had made especially, and went down to the beach and whacked the ball as far as he could out to sea. It went miles. The ball had a message inside it, one he'd written, something to do with peace, that kind of thing. He whacked it so hard that it took, oh, minutes for the ball to float back up to the surface.' I finished my Nestea, then commented how quiet the town was, to which she said that everyone was asleep, that the people in this town, when they had nothing to do, all slept, though in reality they weren't sleeping, she explained, really they just shut their eyes for a while. Apropos of that, I pointed out that the mythological animal joining the two church roofs also seemed to be asleep; she didn't respond –x I don't think she understood me. I asked if there was any-where nearby to stay the night. 'The nearest place is more than two hours' walk,' she said, 'but I can give you a bed upstairs for a few euros. I go home at night – I'm just next door – so you'd have it to yourself.' Looking at the clock over the bar, I said I'd take her up on her offer. Rain had just stopped play in the tennis match, so she led me up a wooden staircase with imitation-wood lino on the steps. On the other side of a bevelled glass door stood a queen-sized bed in a room that was both exceptionally small and cold. It had a couple of shelves with sou-venirs of everywhere from Berlin to Bermuda, and on the bedside table a religious card of the Virgin Mary, and a gold ring; trying unsuccessfully to conceal what she was doing, she picked up the ring and slipped it in-side her skirt, while with the other hand pointing out the bathroom back along the hall. We went back downstairs, the heat from the wood-burning stove was a relief. She made a soup of chicken and green beans, and I ordered one of the homemade ciders they served. While I ate she went back to her silent consumption of the steamed mussels and to watching the television, which was now showing a repeat of *The Warriors*. One of the characters, little more than a boy, sometimes gets called Rembrandt or Velázquez by the other gang members, because of the brightly coloured graffiti he sprays on every wall, tree and even cemetery they pass, proof that the gang has been there. Once they reach Manhattan they go south through Central Park with what looked to me like falcons shadowing them overhead throughout. The closing scene comes, with the sun rising over New York and the gangs that have stayed alive coming together on the beach, and then the silhouette of the ocean, a silhouette into which the world appears to be crumbling, communicates some obscure thing to them – whatever it is, it prompts the gang members to go their separate ways, they all drift peacefully away. The city returns to its natural order during the final credits, like a great nation state that has just been established without any bloodshed. It was in these final credits that I read the words: 'The Warriors, Masters of The Night'. I was about to say to the woman that though I'd seen the film hundreds of times I'd never been aware of the 'Masters of The Night' subtitle, but she, putting the mussels to one side, had already gone off to the back of the bar to feed the woodburner with various planks. It would have gone 10.30 p.m. when she gave me the keys and went out, shutting the door behind her.

I had never until then been aware of the silence of bottles in a bar when nobody's there clinking them together, or what a desolate place a bar is without any customers or the owner present, or of the absurd futility of a hundred stacked glasses, one on top of the other. I went and sat in an armchair the woman had put there for herself; at my feet, a tub full of empty mussel shells, which had the overall colour of blue skies, a bruised, purplish blue; I flicked through some out-of-date newspapers. I thought I'd make some coffee, but couldn't see how to work the coffeemaker, and I soon felt tired. I turned out the lights and went up to the bedroom, even colder now than before, so cold that my only ablutions were to brush my teeth. I got into bed. Outside, neither the wind nor the noises you'd usually expect in the countryside at night. With the lights still on, I spent a long while looking at the souvenirs on the shelves, which were extraordinarily various and at the same time identical. Isn't it true, I said to myself, that the longer you stare at a souvenir the more it seems like there's a human inside it making fun of you? Then I noticed one whose provenance was a mystery: it was a pair of life-size wooden hands which looked like they'd been sawn off some religious figure; the right hand, closed in a fist, was holding rosary beads. I shut my eyes and, somewhat absurdly trying to imagine a scene in which Rafa Nadal struck his tennis ball out over the ocean and these saint's hands then caught it, I started to fall asleep. It's been the case with me ever since I was small: I can't get to sleep without some kind of stimulating idea going round inside my head. If not, it feels like I'm empty, like I'm nothing more than a dead body, a pointless slab of flesh. And when this happens, I feel like I'm never going to wake up again.

A sudden burst of voices woke me. After several seconds' confusion, I realized they were coming from the television. I got out of bed and, putting my jacket on, went downstairs. The television was deafeningly loud; I

448

instinctively grabbed the remote control and pressed the Off button. A dog started barking outside, setting others off in a chain, creating a barking network. Within seconds my head also created a network of reasons why the television had suddenly come on. Going over to the electrics box, I found the general control switch and turned it down, and when I turned it back up, the television came on again. Clearly there had been a power cut in the town, and when the supply had been restored all the devices in standby mode had been turned on – had been, in a manner of speaking, woken up. Unsettled by such a ridiculous incident, I pulled my jacket close. The clock on the wall read 3 a.m. The woodburner had long since died down. I took some planks out of a basket – remnants of a boat of some kind – and placed them on the thin layer of embers still going inside the woodburner. I opened a bottle of water, drinking compulsively from it while also compulsively changing channel, stopping on one of these newscasts that go out on a loop in the early hours of the morning. After an update on the Brexit referendum, which was due to take place imminently, a live football match came on, one being played on the other side of the planet. The ball went from one end of the pitch to the other and I thought what a terrifying and at the same time irremediably magical thing it is for 300 million people to be turning their heads to the left in unison; this perhaps is the last truly communal action left on the face of the Earth. There came a rapping of knuckles on the door, making me jump. I raised the blind, and it took me a good few moments to make out the face of the landlady. 'I thought it would be disrespectful to use my key,' she said when I opened the door. She had a big coat on which reminded me of one of her souvenirs, specifically the Turkish clay amphora. 'I

heard some loud noises,' she said, 'was it the TV again?'
I told her what had happened and she said she'd suspected as much, she'd only come to tell me not to worry; it
happened all the time. 'The electricity in the whole town
goes sometimes, not even the regional electricity company know why, they think there could be come general
switch somewhere in the county that's so old nobody
knows where it is any more, possibly it dates back to the
end of the nineteenth century when the porcelain factory-
boats went between Asia and Great Britain and used to
stop at the ports along this coast, infrastructure which
meant electricity was needed here for the first time. One
of those boats was shipwrecked off the coast, it quickly
became legend not because of what it was transporting,
which in the end was just ground-up bones, bone-dust
that's sunk to the bottom of the estuaries around here
and nobody's ever going to get out, but because people
said the boat was made from these Asian trees inside
which diamonds grow; bizarre as it sounds, you get diamonds spontaneously appearing inside one in ten
thousand of that kind of tree; it's generated by an imper-
fection in the carbon inside the trunk itself, a little bit
like the way pearls are generated inside oysters. People
around here have burned every single plank or scrap of
wood that's washed up on the shores ever since, hoping
to come up with one of those diamonds.' At this, she
looked over at the planks mounded up next to the woodburner, which indeed, from the colour, looked like the
kind used in boats. 'Since we're both up, I can make us
some herbal tea.' She filled a kettle from a see-through
bottle and placed it on the metal of the woodburner, then
pulled over a chair. As we sat facing the flames, I said I
guessed she travelled a lot, to judge by the souvenirs, but
she said not at all, and that most of them she'd bought at

a flea market that ran the first Sunday of every month in Caen, which was the nearest city, and the inhabitants of which are almost all addicted to mementos from abroad, because of the fact the Allies liberated the city – not before it was first flattened in the bombing raids. In the days immediately after the liberation, the soldiers had filled the devastated streets of Caen with stereotypical American things – miniature Brooklyn bridges, wooden sculptures of cows from Kansas, small-scale Statues of Liberty and, of course, renderings of the Stars and Stripes. The Australians, British and Canadians also left souvenirs of their countries around the place, but the quantity of objects brought by the Americans, as well as their allure, was incomparable: far beyond anything the Canadians, with their little pine trees carved from pine wood, could manage, or the British gentlemen with their tin effigies of the Queen for that matter, or the Australians, who were the most unsophisticated of all, with their miniatures of an animal that looked like a deformed rabbit with a very long tail. It was her mother who had recounted all of this to her; right until her death the year before, she had apparently talked about the glorious American arrival in the city, the soldiers standing astride the tanks as they advanced along the city's main avenue, playing a crude kind of jazz, which was a kind of music that very few of the French had ever managed to pick up on the radio, and throwing bras designed by an aeronautical engineer out to the women in the crowds, as well as a sweet pastry called a doughnut for the children, also a novelty in the area. 'To chew on those doughnuts,' her mother had often told her, 'which were soft as sea sponges and covered in sugar that glittered like dew drops, was the greatest gift of my childhood. It still brings a tear to my eye, thinking about all of that.' We soon finished our herbal teas, and I got up and poured us another round. She said that, in her view, people in the area closed their eyes and appeared to sleep at any given opportunity because of the fact that they used dew drops to make their herbal tea, and this made people drowsy without actually slowing the mind; I was just finishing my second cup, but felt nothing. Looking at my chest, she asked me why I didn't wear a bra, to which I said I found them uncomfortable for walking in. 'Women should always wear bras,' she said, 'regardless of what cup size they are. Bras are our victory, they're highly political: if the Nazis had won we'd have been made to go around without bras to support us, even the saggiest of udders like yours. That's precisely how the Nazis liked their women, natural, like something sprung from the very fields.' With that, she fell quiet and closed her eyes. Her hair, slightly greasy and held back with clips on the sides, shone like a doughnut, and I said to her: 'Those wooden hands you've got upstairs, they don't look like souvenirs. Where are they from?' 'I bought them at the flea market as well, the people who sold them to me said they came from a statue of Saint Roch that had been on a Spanish boat that ran aground hundreds of years ago. I always want to burn them and see what's inside, but I can never bring myself to do it.' Sipping my tea, I said: 'I have travelled quite a lot; I think I've been to most of the places your souvenirs come from.' I listed some of the ones I meant; she put some more boat planks into the woodburner, before, without a word, getting up and going upstairs, coming back down with various objects in her hands, which she lined up on top of the woodburner; I thought they might melt. 'Aren't they nice?' she murmured. An ebony carving from Senegal, a skull from Mexico, the Saint Roch hands, a flying fish from

452

Shanghai, and that's all I remember. We gazed at them, I'm not sure exactly how long for, I think the herbal tea was starting to take effect. I focused my sight on the flying fish from Shanghai and was reminded of the one time I'd been to that Chinese city, for a work trip in my twenties, when I was a location scout for television. On that occasion I was working for a producer in Barcelona who was planning to make a series of documentaries about a little-known chapter in our recent history, namely the emigration of Spanish workers to Shanghai in the 1970s, where they'd been contracted to build the dam that to this day waters the city and the great river that bisects it. It turned out to be a far easier job than I'd expected: I quickly found a well-established Spanish community in the city, which left me with plenty of time to wander the streets and read up on the history of Shanghai. I found out about the internment camps created there by the Japanese during the Second World War, when they were still in control of that part of China, and how large numbers of British still in the area from the nineteenth-century colonies were placed in these camps. I had the chance to visit Lunghua internment camp one afternoon, which had been operational between 1943 and 1945 and where the death toll had been particularly high, and which was now a tourist attraction, with recreations of the cells, waxwork prisoners lying in the cots and waxwork children playing football in the yard, where their football, paused between the feet of the tussling children, looked to me like an exact replica of the moon or of some other satellite. I was struck by the innocent name they had given it – Lunghua Civilian Assembly Centre – which I think is why I've been suspicious of anything containing the words 'centre', 'assembly' or 'civilian' ever since. I took the bus back at

nightfall, getting off several stops before my hotel, wanting to stretch my legs, as people say, have a bit of fresh
air. Sitting on a bench by the river, I'd seen a cargo ship
go past, bound for a European port, I supposed, carrying fake fashion accessories and movies, plates made of
imitation porcelain, and other pirated objects, and I
wondered what the millions of people working in clan-
destine workshops, basements and caves would think,
those who work for us and whom we nonetheless look
down on. People talk about the damage these illegal
economies do to our own, but never about the fact the
millions of people involved in them also have their own
economy, and their own accompanying culture and history therefore; money never exists without generating
its own non-transferable form of religion and way of life.
They produce counterfeits, yes, but wasn't the film that I
was, in a manner of speaking, participating in, concerning now-departed Spanish immigrants in Shanghai,
also a counterfeit? Might not my work have been yet another counterfeit in history, one of all the great many
not-entirely factual documentaries that there are? Might
not human beings themselves be the result of an inces-
sant counterfeiting, genes upon genes, all of which are
nothing but very slightly altered copies? I'd go further:
might humankind not possibly be an idea that could disappear at any moment, something that could suddenly
cease being human and become something else entirely,
either purely animal or post-human? The cargo boat
went by, the lights along the side giving it the look of a
birthday cake with more candles than any person could
ever hope to blow out. I started back towards the hotel.

I lost my way several more times but always managed
to find the main road again. I came to a KFC that was
open 24/7. A van with TV antennas coming out of it.

It seemed that a programme was being made about the fast food chain. I came to a stop. There was a man inside dressed up as Colonel Sanders, doing mimes for groups of adults as they sat eating. The TV crew was following the old man-mascot's every move as he went from table to table; a couple laughed when he pulled out a large fan with a chicken-wing decoration on it, and I remember wondering what the man would be wearing under the Colonel Sanders costume, and, for that matter, what all the mascots in the world wore under their costumes, the Mickey Mouse making tourists laugh at Disneyland Paris, for example, or the Ronald McDonald in the restaurant chain to which he gave his name, what brand of underpants might they go for, what colour and what size, what kind of fabric might their vests have been made from, and whether they too needed to keep warm, and whether those underclothes were part of the costume, and if so, when they got home and took the costume off and went into the kitchen in just a T-shirt and pants and chopped some potatoes and fried them up with an egg, whether they still remained the mascots of the world, and whether the dreams they had at night were mascot dreams, and, if so, what the contents of those dreams might have been, and where the endpoint lay in their role as the mascots of the world, and I went on watching the Colonel Sanders going through his repertoire for the people at the tables, with his chicken-wing- design fans and his magic tricks, and I wondered how far beneath the skin the mascots of the world ceased to be what we all are, which is mascots of ourselves, at the second or third subcutaneous layer, perhaps, or much farther down, in the internal organs, say? The spleen? The intestines? The lungs, perhaps? And I wondered if these internal organs were also the organs of a mascot of the world, and if so, whether those organs were the organs of the real world, and if that was so, what they did, what functions the internal organs of a mascot of the world might perform, what they pumped, what filtered, what excreted, how they were created in the first place and how, after death, they would be broken down by time; perhaps they would be broken down in the same way that a tumour or any other illness breaks down the internal organs of a person who isn't a mascot of the world, I said to myself, and the next thing I wondered was what the tumour belonging to a mascot of the world might be like, a tumour that surely wouldn't be the normal kind, but whose growth inside their body must also create a map of the world, with national territories and all the geographical accidents corresponding to those of the countries in which the respective corporations had installed themselves, and what could be said of the dream life of the mascots of the world, which, fittingly, were the world's dreams, because while they slept they were still the mascots of the world, what plasticity, what texture those dreams took on, unimaginable for those of us who aren't the mascots of anything, except, I repeat, of ourselves, and I wondered if those dreams might be sexual in nature, and if so, if a mascot of the world could be said to have sexuality, and how a mascot of the world penetrated or was penetrated, what fluids they secreted, what monsters stalked the mascots of the world in their dreams, perhaps it would be monsters related to the company they represented, or, on the contrary, monsters originating in their childhoods, like normal people's monsters, the ones generated in childhood that never go away, and, ultimately, I wondered whether these women and men who transform themselves into the mascots of the world are a maquette of the world, a life-size representation of it, the world's Great Archive, which would be the same as saying the gods of the world, or, in this case, semi-divine figures, but if they were semi-divine was it then possible to establish relationships with them, to talk to them, to observe their movements as though they were our own, could we touch their garments and hold their hands without feeling ourselves confronted by an organism far greater than us, far greater even than the corporate entities which the mascots of the world are the mascots for? Old Colonel Sanders then went over to some people eating at a table and, bending down, held out one of the red boxes of chicken and chips to a little girl, that week's meal deal, and the scene, as it seemed to me – the interior in light and shadow, the arrangement of the people relative to another, the dog on the floor next to the feet of another little girl and, of course, the old man to the scene's left holding out the aforementioned red box with its heap of fried food items – was identical in composition to Velázquez's *Las Meninas*. I was still processing this thought when the TV crew stopped filming; I heard them say that something had unaccountably gone wrong with the take; the foreground, with the old man in it, had frozen, he was stuck there. Millions of people in China, and all across the world, were watching this: old Colonel Sanders's face frozen on their screens. The director kept shouting at the camera people, and to my surprise one of them, a man, started crying, and that made the Infanta Margarita start crying too, and that instantly set off her ladies in waiting. All were in tears – all except Mari Bárbola, the macrocephalous dwarf, who set her jaw. What a girl, I thought, what grit. I started off again towards the hotel and, I remember, before I turned the corner, looked back and was sure I saw Colonel Sanders sitting on a stool, utterly oblivious to the crying girls, a cup of coffee in one hand and the ash grey wig swaying from the other. He appeared to be a young man.

I went for something to eat at that same KFC branch the next day. The mascot was there, but not dressed up this time; I recognized him from his shoes. He was eating alone. I went and sat next to him, he wasn't Chinese but Caucasian, and, as I'd intuited the previous day, he was also closer to my age than Colonel Sanders's. I said something to him in English, and he picked up on my Spanish accent. We struck up a conversation quite easily, and it turned out that his parents had been among those employed in the dam and river works, and that he'd taken this job as a mascot simply as a way to stay on in Shanghai; though he planned to eventually settle in Spain, there was something about the sky above Shanghai he wanted to work out first, something that troubled him. I warmed to him immediately. I confessed to having spied on him the previous night, and went so far as to say how ridiculous I'd found his act; I used that very word, ridiculous. It didn't however seem to bother him, and after a moment's pause he said: 'It's a mistake to take the things we've seen as a given.' We both laughed, almost in unison. From that moment on, until his disappearance two years ago, we spent all our time together; two peas in a pod, as people say.

I found out that day he was living in a room he rented from a Spaniard, a chef, to be precise, a man who rarely showed his face, having moved in with a Thai woman twelve months earlier. It was getting dark when we left the KFC, and he pointed at the sky and said: 'See, doesn't it look bluer than normal to you?' And it was true, from one end to the other the starry vault was a purplish blue. 'It's the universe,' he said, 'it's coming back in.' I didn't

458

know what he meant by this, so he explained that the universe wasn't expanding but, having reached the full extent of its expansion, was now contracting, coming back in towards us, returning again, and that this explained the almost purple blue we were seeing. 'Exactly as the Doppler effect predicts,' he said. 'Do you know about the Doppler effect?' 'I think so,' I said, 'it's like when bullets are fired in the air and the way, as they go up, they produce one sound, but then on the way back down a different one, even though the trajectory's the same.' 'In effect, it is something like that, but instead of sound, light: when the universe was expanding, it tended towards redness, and now that it's contracting, it's tending towards this purplish blue. That's just how it is.'

In the days that followed, he showed me parts of the city I'd never have seen otherwise, and when he wasn't working as a mascot he took me to the old English neighbourhoods, and the old French neighbourhood too, and pointed out the enormous items of underwear on the washing lines outside the Shanghai buildings, something that was a mystery to him given that people in Shanghai are mostly quite slim. All these gigantic pieces of underwear he called satellites: he said they were veritable satellites no longer in orbit with their bodies because nobody ever wore them, they just wash them and hang them out, and went on doing so endlessly. Across the way from his bedroom, there was a dovecote with homing pigeons being lovingly looked after by an old woman. They sometimes flew up and started squawking and flapping around in the air, turning and tumbling at such a rate that they came to form a very dense cloud of feathers. But then, once they calmed down again, they wouldn't go back to the same niches as before, but settled instead wherever they happened to land. This constant swapping around irritated the old lady, who would come out with her walking stick and start banging on the walls of the dovecote, wanting the birds, once they'd flown up and done their flapping and squawking in the middle of the dovecote again, to go back to their correct niches, though it rarely happened that way. I was witness to this spectacle one day and he told me it was down to the universe contracting as well: 'The birds aren't confused, it's that instinctively they always try to go back to places they've been before, such that these homing pigeons could now be called something like "messengers from the past". Believe me: things go in reverse, things get mixed up. It doesn't always work like this though, fate sometimes steps in and the reverse direction of travel generates a new and surprising order among things, things that didn't previously exist.' Picking up on what he'd said, I suggested that this same quality of fate inverted was responsible for our meeting at that KFC, such an unlikely thing to have happened under normal conditions. It's true that I enjoyed this kind of talk. The day after the spectacle of the homing pigeons, he said to me: 'Imagine you got your hands on the keys for every house in this neighbourhood, mixed them all up and then gave them out to the residents. A simple and basically silly act like this would be all it took to create such confusion in the neighbourhood that it would take centuries to undo, and this is what's going to end up happening in the universe as a whole. You and me for instance, we're already hopelessly mixed together.'

On some of the evenings when he was doing his mascot job at the KFC, I went and looked in from the window without him knowing, as I had that first time. He always performed the same tricks and moves for the customers; I ended up treating it like a game, seeing whether he'd ever vary his act, which he never did. More than something happening live, it felt like I was watching a film. But then, because the company refused to pay to have his costume washed, the whole neighbourhood got to see his red apron when we hung it out to dry; on the washing line, it took on the same pointed-tear shape as Africa, a continent that looks like it's draining into the South Pole. And his striped shirt hung on the line too, and his ash-coloured wig, which he had to wash with good shampoo once a week seeing as it was made from real hair. I think our neighbours also thought those clothes satellite-like, though in this case ones that had been dismantled. In Shanghai people bring their caged canaries and goldfinches out at midday, the whole city fills with the deafening sound of these birds singing at the tops of their avian lungs, even going up a notch when a plane flies overhead, which happens every five minutes. I wondered whether the canaries and goldfinches thought the planes were metallic ancestors of theirs that were now being brought back to earth because of the contraction of the universe. He took me to the main local cemetery one day, a place, as is well known, inhabited by colonies of the socially marginalized: children and adults eating, procreating and sleeping in niches and tombs, which had all as a consequence been plundered. This included the tomb of his grandfather, the family's original immigrant to China, who had died a few years earlier. I was surprised that the epitaph was in Chinese. I asked him to translate: '"Separation is the younger sister of death",' he said. 'It's a line by a Russian writer called Osip Mandelstam; my grandfather liked him a lot.'

It was a few days later that it happened: we were in one night and, having been talking about our permanent return to Spain – I was in favour, given that, after an initial period of wishful thinking, I was finding I actually understood nothing about Eastern culture – I was setting the table, he was nearly done descaling the fish before we put it in the oven, the scales shooting up and spinning in the air like slivers of quartz, and he put the knife down on the counter, looked at me and said: 'If I die, call me on the phone and leave a message.' 'What?' I said. 'Just that: if I die, call my phone and say everything you need to say to me, but never could have otherwise. Promise you will?' In silence, I went to the kitchen, got the glasses and placed them on the tablecloth. 'I promise,' I whispered.

Some days later, we were passing the Church of Saint Ignatius, one of the few Catholic Churches in the city where you can hear Mass said in Chinese, when he told me about the Belgian priest, physicist and astronomer Georges Lemaître, who, after serving in the First World War, had come up with one of the most significant propositions in the history of science, doing so in solitude and while maintaining almost no contact with the scientific community at large. He posited a 'homogeneous universe of constant mass and growing radius accounting for the radial velocity of extragalactic nebulae', and made the first clear case for the Big Bang as the origin of the world and cause of the expansion of the universe, which had been taboo until then, since, among many other thinkers, Einstein was opposed to the idea of a universe in motion. Lemaître's discreet nature, his lack of ambition and all-round rejection of what we might call the politics of science meant it took some time for his discovery to circulate. For the same reasons, the idea of an expanding universe was for many years wrongly attributed to the well-known astronomer Hubble. It's easy to imagine how Lemaître must have suffered to see his research ignored in this way, but he never appeared bitter, quite the opposite, his enthusiasm was unfailing, and, in Shanghai, while we watched the television together, or after sex – always a let-down – or when we went on expeditions to the different flea markets in the city, he spoke to me of Lemaître, of his titanic fight and of his unwavering faith in his theory, which nonetheless never shook his religious faith. He began by mentioning a few random details, but then, I suppose because I showed an interest, he talked nonstop about Lemaître's epic intellect, and it was then that I saw what was really going on: he actually saw himself as another Lemaître. Indeed, one had discovered the expansion of the universe, and the other its contraction, and to him there was no getting around the parallels between their lives. He told me of a little-known episode in Lemaître's younger life when, shortly after the First World War, he had felt a kind of spiritual calling to cycle from Brussels to the north coast of France, a place he considered to be the endpoint of the European landmass, and where he intended to spread God's word. He there became a very young hermit who, not yet troubled by the weight problems that were to dog him in later years, ate what little he was given by the people of Normandy, and would sleep in churches or shelter under any rock he happened to find. In all the towns and villages he came to, he went from house to house handing out a pamphlet of religious maxims he'd been inspired to write while in the trenches, entitled 'Religious Constants of The Universe and Others of The Soul's Invariables'. Such conversions had been quite commonplace during the First World War; you only need to think of Wittgenstein, who wrote his *Tractatus Logico-Philosophicus*, one of the most spiritual books of the twentieth century, while manning Austro-Hungarian artillery; less common was for such converts to go on to be ordained. One of the maxims in the pamphlet disseminated by Lemaître in Normandy was: 'The world is the progressive diminution of light', an idea evidently containing the seed for all his later scientific work, given that if the light in the universe is diminishing it's because its expansion means the stars are growing further and further apart, the endpoint of which is a time when we won't be able to see them any more, and thus no more light. It was a phrase that appealed to me because, while on the one hand it seemed real, the existence of such a phrase also seemed impossible; a phrase, I mean, so melancholy and implacable, so staggering and at the same time so absolutely real. 'The world is the progressive diminution of light.' I then felt, for the first time, convinced that scientists are all deranged. They've got us fooled, the truth is that they live in a state of constant hallucination, and this makes them something akin to the hidden underground among thinkers. He talked about Lemaître a lot more, but above all insisted that we one day visited the coast of Normandy and retrace the priest-scientist's footsteps, and I laughed and went along with it all, though I don't really know what was funny. My knowledge of Normandy went no further than *Asterix and the Normans*, which I'd read countless times as a girl, and which presents the Normans as suffering from an endemic illness: they don't know what fear is. Sometimes he seemed like a Norman who had just been plucked from the pages of that comic; I never saw him frightened at anything. But just as strange to me, if not more, was the fact his friend the chef-landlord was never around. I only ever saw him once, two months after the first KFC encounter. He came into the apartment one day around lunchtime without knocking, and caught the two of us in bed; I was on top, trying, with little success, to coax a sufficiently stable erection out of him. The position of the bed in relation to the door meant the chef was only afforded a view of my bare back, but the shock was enough to make me scream, which woke the canaries and goldfinches in the building from their siestas, and started them singing in unison, in spite of the lack of airplanes flying overhead at that moment.

I remember the two of us going to the cemetery together. Since 2008, when the global population of people in cities first surpassed that of people in rural areas, the dead contained in urban cemeteries have also outnumbered those alive in cities, and this is the case in Shanghai particularly, given that at the moment of its founding, it instantly had over 100,000 inhabitants – all of whom had fled en masse from the Mongols in the fifth century – which means the dead in Shanghai cemeteries outnumber by five to one the city's 24 million living inhabitants. It wasn't until our second visit to the cemetery, standing in front of the grandfather's tomb and reading the epitaph again – 'Separation is the younger sister of death' – that I turned my mind to these demographic statistics. After that, holding hands for the first time, we walked the paths between the niches, which it struck me could qualify in themselves as real housing estates; pairs of feet, apparently belonging to sleeping people, could be seen sticking out of every single hole. We zigzagged our way past the graves, which numbered in the thousands of thousands. We found women in some of the clearings between, down on their haunches cooking meat and vegetables on camping stoves, the blue flames of which looked like foxfires. Bourgeois rats and lizards sunbathed on the horizontal gravestones, slotting themselves into the clefts of the inscriptions, which, being in Mandarin, were particularly wide. The women's children made little mounds in the sand nearby, these doubtless containing the ash of ground-up bones. Men played cards on broken slabs of marble, others stood hanging clothes out in clearings that seem to have taken on the functions of public parks, we saw at least twelve sets of people having sex in broad daylight, and mausoleums repurposed as farm buildings, and stalls selling alcohol and cigarettes, and old shrines that had been turned into little kitchen gardens or bars, and nobody said anything to us, nobody looked at us: it was as though we didn't exist, as though we were the ghosts, and the strange idea came to me that all these cemetery inhabitants were agents of a purification, a superficial layer of humus and photosynthesis, as it were: the always troubled, never fully understood, fundamentally impure link between the world of the living and the world of the dead inside a city, and so a point came where you didn't know whether you were walking over the bones of chickens, pigs or humans, or whether the pebbles underfoot were made of stone or the broken off bits of skulls, and I now wonder at what point in the human chain this border between the human and the nonhuman dissolves, that's if such a border ever existed, at what point the placenta that once nourished us falls away, taking on a life so autonomous it's beyond us to imagine. We walked a little further on and, coming to the exit onto the street, he said: 'It's the truest cemetery on earth.' I can recall with complete clarity the way he squeezed my hand as he said this, and me saying to myself: 'As if everything was fine and nothing could ever go wrong', words I repeated, whispering them to myself, sitting by the woodburner in the Normandy bar, and at that the Shanghai memory faded, and I knew that the

466

effect of the herbal tea had run its course.

I looked away from the flying fish, half-melted now on top of the woodburner; semi-liquefied, you could have been forgiven for thinking it a souvenir of the European Union. I looked at the woman on my left, eyes closed, legs crossed, still in exactly the same position as before, and I think fully asleep now. The clock said 5.30 a.m. Going over to the window, I parted the blind and looked out; it was starting to grow light on the horizon. A tractor drove past, behind it a trailer overflowing with watermelons; they made me think of a big mound of skulls. The small front wheels spun around like fireworks, while the ones at the back went around with a sort of ox-like ponderousness; what a strange vehicle, I thought. As the woman snored away in her chair, I took the flight of steps up to my room. I fell asleep thinking about those two tractor wheels, the one slow and the one quick, which, nonetheless, like the living and the dead, proceed together in the same universe.

12.

When, after eleven that morning, I woke up, I immediately wanted to get out of that building as fast as I could. I threw my clothes on, put my things in my rucksack. I went down the stairs, tiptoeing for some reason. The bar was closed. The landlady, not there. I opened the woodburner door, and there inside were the Saint Roch hands, all turned to ash except for the fingertips. One by one, I gathered up those fingertips. Before wrapping them in some tinfoil and putting them in my rucksack I paused to consider the fingerprints; I didn't know if what I was looking at was the natural grain of the wood or actual fingerprints.

It was sunny when I stepped outside, a different feel to the town entirely – even the mythological animal on the church seemed to smile when I went past. The sun on the back of my neck drove me on, its warm impulse carrying me through the town and past its outskirts. I was planning to make it to the D-Day beaches of Juno, Sword, Gold, Omaha and Utah that night, and specifically a converted castle-hotel in the nearby village of Banville; I'd booked it a month before and from the photos on the website it seemed like there could be no better place to rest at the end of such a journey. I checked the mobile phone battery, which had gone down; someone else was making calls for me, I joked to myself. The land was flat for several miles; where it hadn't been divided up into grids and turned into farmland, there was something of the *altiplano* or steppe to it, and that made me feel at ease given how little I like forests, their natural opposition to light, their endemic damp, the mud everywhere and all the foliage too, good only for movies about werewolves, zombies, serial killers and that kind of thing, and I was thinking about such a forest when, as I came to a crossroads, the flatness of the land meant I had a clear view of a mustard-coloured limousine approaching on the road perpendicular to the one I was on. It slowed down as we were about to converge at the crossroads, and then stopped. Someone wound down the rear window. A woman with blonde, back-combed hair stuck her head out. She didn't look at me, but started immediately to vomit profusely onto the asphalt. I recognized her straightaway: Marine Le Pen. A hand emerged from behind her, grabbed her by the back of her jacket lapel and yanked her back inside. Only then did our eyes meet: I think Marine Le Pen was crying. The limousine accelerated away. For several moments her gaze, of a primitive depth not yet quite archaeological, remained fixed in my sight. At first, I simply stood rooted to the spot, the sun directly overhead by now; I remember some sheep in a nearby field eating grass, and a gentle, whistling breeze in which I tried to discern that word – 'marine' – but couldn't. I approached the crossroads, stopping when I reached the mustard-coloured pile of vomit, hot as molten lava, a knee-height column of steam rising from it. Among scraps of what had surely once been a breakfast of coffee and croissants – the buttery smell a giveaway – there was a combination of foods from across this strip of land that gave birth to the world we nowadays call civilized, stretching from the Greek Mediterranean to Armenia: couscous, scraps of lamb and some vegetables I was unable to identify. I'd heard the tales of politicians who, in the vortex of the campaign trail, force themselves to vomit, but thought it a myth, the kind generated when musicians go on the road, an attempt like any other to create an epic around the candidate for office. Far more quickly than I'd have thought possible, the liquid element of the vomit was absorbed by the porous tarmac. I know I ought to have taken some photographs of that multicultural vomit, made a record of it, but the incident had so unsettled me I simply set off walking again, as though in a bid to forget it or put it into the same compartment as things dreamed. And as I walked on, crushing ditch weeds underfoot or kicking stones knocked from the road, I kept thinking about Hercule Poirot, the detective-protagonist in Agatha Christie's books, which I'd enjoyed reading as a girl, who said the crimes he was dealing with hadn't only been committed already, but had always been solved ahead of the fact as well. A good detective had only to be attentive to their surroundings and it would all, ipso facto, present itself, both motive and guilty party, in turn making the crime no more than a simple detail knocked into the path of the everyday, like a stone your toe meets as you walk along a ditch, a pile of vomit, a weed or a flower effortlessly blossoming and then withering before your eyes without you being able to intervene in any way. I carried on, my head full of these thoughts, and over the course of that day I saw another butcher's with flowers stuck in the meat in the window display and a pyramid of calf eyes next to it, and I saw a cathedral that had been bombed but then restored, and a bumper car ride, the cars in which were stationary but contained people seemingly picnicking – passing baskets of snails and wine bottles between the cars where they sat – and some men there told me it was the county fair, and that in the place where I was heading I could expect open-air dancing and fireworks throughout the night, and I saw an old Allied tank covered in election posters with Marine Le Pen's face on them, and then I remembered her vomit, and that reminded me that I hadn't had breakfast, which meant she and I both had empty stomachs, and then I felt like I desperately needed to eat something but I couldn't see anywhere selling food, it was like everything edible along the coast had been jettisoned, and then I saw a bay with a mound of empty oyster shells taller than the heads of the people walking past, and I saw another bunker pitted from bullets and mortar shells and wondered if its concrete walls would take less time than natural stone to crumble, and if that in turn would mean all the cities on the planet were condemned to crumble sooner or later like the clocks of sand and cement that they are, and I saw fragments from letters sent home by soldiers on the front projected onto the side of a building: 'Food's awful but I'm fine, I pray for all of you every day', was the most frequent; on one there was a list of the nineteen names of the members of the soldier's family, and next to each an 'x' by way of a kiss, and I found Lemaître's 'Religious Constants of The Universe and Others of The Soul's Invariables' in a souvenir shop, and it was as astonishingly brief as it was cheap, five euros, cheaper than the bundle of postcards next to it, and as well as that maxim, 'The world is the progressive diminution of light', it noted the amusing fact that the subjects most written about in applied-science journals at the end of the nineteenth century had been the possibility of colour in photography and the possibility of building a tunnel under the Channel. After that I saw a sky full of dark clouds that seemed somehow unthreatening, then a lighthouse out to sea supported on neither an islet nor a craggy rock, and later a poster at the roadside announcing fair rides and fireworks that night, and through the bars of a chicken coop a large number of local cider bottles, I don't know how many, the cloudiness of which made me think they'd bottled up mud, and in a grocery window a collection of Coca-Cola bottles with the same name – Benjamin – printed on the label in place of the brand name, after which I spent a long time unable to think of anything but that other Benjamin, Walter, and in the entrance to the town hall a painting featuring a group of French women, men and children from the eighteenth century walking towards a boat destined to take them to the colonies in what is today known as California, and then I saw a workshop with a young man chiselling names, dates and epitaphs onto gravestones, and a dog at his side which, tied up with a chain so long it would have been heavier than the creature itself, barked at me from the moment I came into sight until I was all the way past, and I saw a second-hand shop selling Quimicefa games and some immaculate porcelain dishes which I inspected one by one but found none to be bone china, and I saw a cyclist who'd just had a collision with a hedgehog – sitting crying in the ambulance with a gash to his head, while a policeman used a stick to flick the animal into the ditch – and I don't know how many restaurants I saw that, each cheaper than the last, had signs for incredible mixed seafood grills, and on the wall of a bar an oil portrait of Guy Debord, surely painted by an amateur since the philosopher was pictured roaring with laughter, which, as is well known, he never did, and I saw a swimming pool with a mosaic at the bottom of two intertwined dolphins, and a cat looking down at them from a windowsill, and in a park a marble bust of Leonardo da Vinci dressed as a spice merchant from the nineteenth century, hat and all, which I didn't understand, and I became lost in a clump of trees, the branches of which resembled roots and, vice versa, the roots of which were like branches, and that I didn't understand either, and I saw antler horns on the back shelf of someone's car, and a group of teenagers passing a bottle around, gearing up for the night's festivities, and a bridal gown shop making no attempt to hide the fact the mannequins were both male and female avatars, and a man on a cafe terrace who'd had a tracheotomy and was using a gold cannula, his words echoing out from his neck as though extracted from a South African gold mine, and in the small lens of a video door-phone I saw my face reflected and didn't at first know who it was, and I saw a painting of Joan of Arc, head tilted skywards in raptures, and what looked like vomit at her feet, the steam rising from which then morphed into an angel, and I saw a cemetery for the Allied troops full of flowers and visitors, and, further on, a German cemetery that was completely empty, and on the door of a small cinema a poster for a showing of Cronenberg's *The Fly*, and I would have liked to have gone in, and doubtless I would have had the place to myself, because people who gather together in towns and villages are very concerned by flies but not at all by man-flies, and I saw more churches than I can remember now and it came to me that all churches on the planet smelled the same, and what they really did was to create an olfactory trail, the secret virus that ensures the propagation of the communal religious sense, and that, I thought, meant that all churches are the same just as medical science claims all livers, lungs and hearts are the same, though they aren't, and I then thought that this trail of endemic odour also exists in big supermarket chains: isn't it true that every commercial chain has its own particular smell, whether you find yourself in Lima or Shanghai? And I saw a lot of women and men with dirty hair, an inherent dirt, very deeply ingrained in the scalp itself, and it didn't seem to do them any harm, and I also saw a lot of people sleeping and I then thought that since no two people leave the same legacy, it isn't death but sleep that makes us all equal, and I then thought there isn't any difference therefore between a sleeping Pericles and a sleeping Hitler, or between a sleeping John Lennon and his killer Mark David Chapman when asleep, and as I walked past a supermarket I realized that all evil and conflict in literature has to do with either food or madness, and that makes the intestines and the brain the two poles of everything that's been written, and both these poles are inside you, and in the reception area at a golf club I saw a young girl with a vacant look on her face, clearly not in her right mind – she was looking out at the golfers moving over the course – and I said to myself that this girl

473

would be thinking about all the golf balls that are struck into the air and never come back down, and in a shop for electrical appliances I saw a wall comprising dozens of TV screens that had been tuned to the same channel – Rafa Nadal and Roger Federer had met in the final, and Nadal was winning – and another television in the shop was showing the news, with images of the march I'd seen in Honfleur in support of refugees, and at the bottom of the screen an information bar said that if neither the weather nor the police stopped them these people marching would reach Calais that same night, where thousands of refugees awaited their arrival, and I continued walking and in a port saw a small fishing boat with *K2* as its name, or at least that was what it said on the side, and I remembered reading about a Spanish boat in the past called *K2*, before the famous mountain in the Himalayas had been given that name or even made an appearance on any maps, and that this boat transported large quantities of rape, the brassica that would go on to be sown across the Iberian Peninsula in the following century, and I saw a distant forest fire, possibly the result of stubble being burned and that fire then getting out of control, and the fire must have been serious because shortly afterwards I saw it spread to a country house, or what looked like one from where I was; the roof was on fire, a fire engine drove by, and I was pleased I didn't own a house in Normandy as it meant avoiding the worry of the house in flames being my own; it meant feeling utterly disconnected from events, and I wondered if this is not perhaps what defines travelling: moving through places as animals and children do, with no memory of the painful moment, and further on I saw a group of food vans with signs for traditional British food, and in anticipation of not being able to find food later on I

bought some fish and chips, which they gave to me
wrapped in a copy of the *Guardian*, and W. G. Sebald
then unavoidably came to mind, followed, just as unavoidably, by a thought about all the fish and chips
wrapped in newspaper he would have eaten in his life,
and I thought about his death, which happened in 2001
on a road in Norfolk: it was raining, his car swerved
across the road and collided with an oncoming lorry,
and his daughter, who was in the car too, miraculously
survived; it was an accident I had often thought about,
and my thoughts had been sluggish in the days since the
man in tennis whites had told me he believed that the
landscape shots in Sebald's books are all taken from inside a car, an idea that now, with my fish and chips before
me, took on a dimension strangely anticipatory of the
writer's road accident, and with my appetite then evapo-
rating I put the newspaper wrap of fish and chips in my
rucksack and looked up to see another fire engine pass
me by, so close to the kerb that its wing mirror nearly
caught me on the head, and the fire on the horizon had
leapt up enormously, so I could see the column of smoke
rising from a farm building and from the country house
and the woods bordering it, and I began to hurry since it
was getting late and all I wanted was to get to my converted castle and have a bath and eat my fish and chips
and go to bed and find something to occupy my mind, a
good subject to reflect on before closing my eyes and
sleeping till break of day, and it was that fire, as it spread
on the horizon, that reminded me of the African fire;
Africa's burning, I said to myself, it could be said that
Africa's always burning, a thought I found unsettling in
the extreme, and in the woodburners in the bars and the
fireplaces in the houses, visible through windows, I
could see that there was nothing but people burning

planks, tonnes of planks which, from the colour of them, could only have come from boats, and the more I walked the more boat planks the people burned; yes, I saw all this and much more, but what I couldn't see no matter how hard I strained to look across the Channel was the coast of Great Britain, and the thought came to me again that I was W. G. Sebald's late reflection, years late, and of the walk I was on as the late reflection of the one he'd undertaken on the coast of Great Britain, and I thought that, as in the nineteenth century when two blades of identical grass in the vicinity of Lake Tanganyika, as it were twin blades, had touched, striking the African spark never thereafter to go out, so W. G. Sebald and I were twins, in our own way two blades of grass, and that all it would take would be for our paths to cross or for us somehow otherwise to come into contact and a fire of unimaginable proportions would start on the European continent, a fire that could never be put out, and I say I thought about these things because, as I drew closer to the forest and the burning house, with more and more firefighters, police and volunteers arriving all the time, the idea grew stronger in me that the burning building and woods were in fact my destination, an idea that, to my horror, was then shortly confirmed; on the verge that turned into the drive to the house a number of French policemen had set up a barrier. I saw the main part of the converted hotel ablaze with the woods burning beyond it and on either side. The intense red inside the dozens of windows put you in mind of a sunrise, of a sun coming up inside the building. The fire streamed upwards through holes in the roof, and around the tips of the flames you could see a ring of purplish-blue; it was as though the sky itself was on fire. The fire hadn't started in the adjacent woods but inside the converted castle,

476

the French police officers informed me, when the owner and his family had placed a large section of a very old boat onto one of the fireplaces, the boat having that day washed up on Juno Beach. They then suggested I retrace my steps and look for somewhere to stay in the town, that I should try near the beach, which was a little over a mile away in a straight line; yes, they said, the festivities would mean all the rooms were taken, but the general drunkenness would also mean most people who had booked rooms wouldn't get back until long after midnight, 'So someone's bound to let you have a room until then at least.' I turned and walked briskly back. It was beginning to get dark. I could feel the heat of the blaze pounding my back, but from the coast ahead it was no better: the reverberations of French bangers and the bass echoes of drums came thudding into my sternum.

Minutes later I was making my way along the seafront, slaloming between people of all different ages. Marquees with families sitting at long rows of tables eating seafood, teenagers on the sea wall passing cigarettes and bottles, an elephant perched on a tank, rearing up on its hind legs to applause from the people gathered around; I heard two teenagers, as they overtook me, grumbling over the bitter news that Great Britain had just voted in favour of Brexit. And not a single hotel or hostel in sight. I carried on to where the docks ended, the din of the festivities gradually grew quiet behind me while I, as it were, dove once more into the night. Listening to the sea, I tried to pick out familiar sounds, words, even, but there were neither, and, having decided to spend the night in my sleeping bag, I walked on a further half mile or so and came to the last of the groynes; some steps brought me down to Juno Beach, the sand of which gave way meekly, spongily underfoot, which made it hard going, particularly in my boots and with the rucksack on my back; all I'm missing are the helmet and the rifle, I thought. I remembered what I'd read those hours before in Lemaître's breviary, and I said to myself that it made sense about applied science journals at the end of the nineteenth century being full of articles on the possibility of colour in photographs and the possibility of building a tunnel under the Channel, since you only needed to think a little to see that the two subjects concerned the same thing: how to see in the open air and how to see underground; how to see above and how to see below. Because looking is the great subject; looking is and has always been our primary concern: to look out from the top of a Ferris wheel at a beach replete with millions of ground-up man-bones and then to travel to that place, to feel an urge to walk across a multitude of bones totally unlike your own. I can say this for certain, because I found it to be true as I walked on Juno Beach. Then I stopped. I took out my sleeping bag, laid it on the ground and, so as not to profane this cemetery any more, sat down on the sleeping bag, took out my bottle of water and the fish and chips, the newspaper now covered in grease. With such a diet, it was a mystery to me how Great Britain could ever have been an imperial power. The seashore was so dark that, except for the murmur of the waves, it was like it didn't exist. Despite not having eaten all day, I took my time over the food, chewing more than usual. I patted my jacket to check for the mobile phone – with so many pockets inside and out, it took a few moments to locate it; the battery was now beginning to drain. Then I heard a noise down in the water. At first, I thought it must be a large fish splashing about. Less than a minute later I saw people, what were undoubtedly people, emerging from the sea. At first only their upper halves, then bodies entire, walking up the beach, coming directly towards me; I was dumb-struck. There must have been at least a dozen of them, and they were staggering, struggling to put one foot in front of the other. Reaching the sand, they collapsed, all except two who continued coming closer – I got up and took backward steps – I can't remember what I said to those men, but I can remember them asking for my help, in English with an Arabic-sounding accent. One took me by the arm and led me to where the others were. Women, men and two children a little younger than teenagers, all of them coughing and spluttering; they'd swallowed a lot of sea water. We managed to drag them up to where I'd left my rucksack, I offered them what food I still had left, which wasn't very much at all. They'd come from Calais, they said, having tried to cross the Channel from there in an old wooden ship they'd bought from a man, but the boat was so old and in such bad con-dition that it had sprung leaks and sunk several miles out. The figurehead had swung around towards this part of the coast, and the current did the rest. They thought the rest of the ship had probably washed up on rocks nearby. I suggested I go into the town with them, buy whatever they needed. The man who spoke for them said the police would be sure to arrest them the moment they set foot on the first zebra crossing, but that I could go and get them some water and something to eat, and after that they wouldn't bother me any more, they'd go, they'd find an old bunker somewhere to spend the night. With the two children wrapped inside my sleeping bag, I set off in the direction of the town; when I'd gone fifty yards, I turned and looked back, but it was too dark to see them. A few minutes' walk brought me back to the fair, I bought some grilled meat and chips at a food van, and more fish and chips at another. I found a supermarket that was open, filled a trolley with bottles of water, biscuits, chocolate bars, dried fruit and any other energy snacks I could find that didn't require cooking. There was too much for me to carry, so I asked the man if I could take the trolley and bring it back later. But the man didn't hear me, deep in concentration as he was listening to a radio on the counter, voices discussing the fire at the converted castle, which had revived, and the fact there was still a chance the town would have to be evacuated. I had to repeat the question, and now he said that if I wanted to take it I'd have to pay for it, which I did, pushing it ahead of me out of the shop and through the people – doubtless they thought I was homeless – down to the seafront. The bumper cars careened around, slamming into one another; the elephant was picking up logs with its trunk now. Coming to the last of the groynes, I stopped for a moment and looked inland: the light from the blazing castle was now plain to see; the people on the radio had doubtless been right, and in fact the flames were now producing a secondary light, the very outer edges of which illuminated the beach. This I suppose was why I could instantly pick out the silhouettes of the shipwrecked refugees; they would have been able to do the same with me and the trolley. A few came straight over and took the food back to the others. They fell on the meat, bottles of water and biscuits like they were suckling at their mother's breast for the first time. Casting my mind back now, I find it impossible to conjure their faces, not only because their features blended together in the semi-dark but because of how little contact I usually had with people from their part of the world – to me, they all looked somewhat alike. Whether out of tact, or because I felt there was little more I could do, I moved off a little way. So the minutes passed, half an hour perhaps. The spokesman came over to me. They'd decided to go in search of some kind of shelter, again he mentioned the possibility of finding a bunker to spend the night in, or even a few days, in, and thanked me on the group's behalf. He, however, was going to stay on the beach: one of their companions hadn't made it to the coast, and whether this person was to wash up dead or alive, he planned to wait for him until the sun came up. Some of the people in the group called him over. After a long conversation, he came back and asked me one last favour: could they borrow my mobile phone? They'd have need of it in the coming days, which were bound to involve evading the authorities and unlikely to be easy, and a phone would mean they could call their people in Calais, or their families at home, to let them know they were alright. I took it out of my pocket, deleted the pin for unlocking it, and gave it to him. I also handed over my rucksack, they could put its contents to better use than I could, even the Lemaître book and the tinfoil with the saint's fingertips inside, the perfect fingerprints on which – the absurd thought came to me – they could use to create fake identities. The group hadn't gone fifty yards when I got up, shouted to them to stop, and went over. I asked them to let me have the phone a moment, searched through the contacts for his number, pressed the compose message button and, after a moment's hesitation, typed in: 'It's a mistake to take the things we've seen as a given.' And hit send. I was about to hand the phone back when the screen lit up red and the icon appeared to indicate he'd received the message. I stared at this icon: the most precious tick sign of my life. I handed the phone over again. Masters of the night, away they went. Their footprints in the sand, like tracks in the snow. Returning to the beach, I sat down next to the man and we waited – him for his friend, who might have been dead or alive, and me, I don't know what for, in reality I wasn't waiting for anything. We sat like that, neither of us saying a word, for a long time. The wind blew in off the sea, I felt a chill, though we then started to feel the heat of the spreading fire on our backs, which grew closer all the time. There was a loud bang, a great thundering boom that made me jump. Seconds later the sky lit up with fireworks from the town, explosions of all different shapes and colours. One, stretching from east to west, was in the shape of what appeared to be a pregnant dog. 'Have you ever been in a war?' the man said. 'No,' I said, still looking up. 'Well,' he said, pointing at the sky, 'it's more or less like this.'

Acknowledgements

The Things We've Seen was begun in 2013 on San Simón Island, developed in many different places, and was completed on the island of Mallorca in 2017.

The Things We've Seen would not have been possible without the copy of *Aillados* given to me by Manuel de Saa in 1995, or the insights on United States culture Luis Macías shared with me, or the complex culture of porcelain-making – as precise as alchemy – to which Aina Llorente Solivellas introduced me.

The photographs from *Aillados* were taken by Dámaso Carrasco Duaso (1907–1987), who was imprisoned on the island between 1937 and 1939. My small homage to him and everyone else who endured the torments of that place.

The translator would like to thank Ana Sánchez Resalt, Becca Hall and Margaret Jull Costa for their help in preparing this text.

This work has been published with a subsidy from the
Ministry of Culture and Sport of Spain

GOBIERNO
DE ESPAÑA

MINISTERIO
DE CULTURA
Y DEPORTE

DIRECCIÓN GENERAL
DEL LIBRO
Y FOMENTO DE LA LECTURA

This book has been selected to receive financial assistance from English PEN's 'PEN Translates' programme, supported by Arts Council England. English PEN exists to promote literature and our understanding of it, to uphold writers' freedoms around the world, to campaign against the persecution and imprisonment of writers for stating their views, and to promote the friendly co-operation of writers and the free exchange of ideas.

www.englishpen.org

Supported using public funding by
**ARTS COUNCIL
ENGLAND**

Fitzcarraldo Editions
8-12 Creekside
London, SE8 3DX
Great Britain

ISBN 978-1-913097-30-1

Design by Ray O'Meara
Typeset in Fitzcarraldo
Printed and bound by TJ Books

fitzcarraldoeditions.com

Fitzcarraldo Editions